THE SAVAGE HEIR

A DARK ROMANIAN MAFIA ROMANCE

MONIQUE MOREAU

Cover design by Steamy Designs
https://steamydesigns.net

MEET MONIQUE!

Join Monique's Newsletter (and receive goodies and release information) https://bit.ly/SteamyReadNewsletter

Join Monique's FB reader's group
Possessive Alpha Reads

Like her Facebook Page
https://bit.ly/MoniqueMoreaufb

Follow her on TikTok:
https://bit.ly/MoniqueTikTok

Follow her on Book Bub
http://bit.ly/MoniqueBookBub

Learn all about Monique's books
MoniqueMoreau.com

AUTHOR'S NOTE

A quick note about the Romanian mafia, or *mafie*. After doing quite a bit of research on the subject, I can honestly say that there isn't a plethora of information. I've let my imagination run wild and taken liberties by inventing rules and societal norms I have not found any proof of in the real world, in either Romanian culture or Romanian *mafie* culture. For example, Romanians do not have clans, they have families, but I have created them for the purposes of this *mafie* world.

I've also given certain Romanian words special meaning within this unique world. I've introduced the Lupu clan, the main Romanian *mafie* family, whose center of power is in "Little Bucharest," a name I've coined for the Romanian community in Sunnyside, Queens, New York City.

The surname Lupu does in fact mean "the wolf" in Romanian, but I created the Lupu tat, a wolf baring its teeth, that is required of all members of the Lupu *mafie* clan.

And with that, I'll leave you to enjoy Nicu and Jewel's story!

Monique

1

JEWEL

I clutched the velvet curtain separating the VIP section of The Lounge nightclub and swept it aside when Cat made a little squeaking sound. Taking a step back down the staircase, she tugged at my elbow.

"Jewel, I can't go in there," she whimpered.

Glancing over my shoulder, I caught her by the arm before she got a chance to turn around and slip out of my grasp.

"Catalina Popescu, don't you dare. It's too damn late to chicken out now. You're going in there if I have to drag you by the hair, and after the hours I spent fixing it, you better believe that's not going to happen. Now get up here," I hissed.

I'd dressed Cat up, and we were in search of Luca at his family's club. And when I said family, that was a euphemism for *family*. As in the criminal, mafioso kind. But that was neither here nor there. This was Cat's world, after all. Not mine.

The plan was for Cat to seduce her fiancé's brother, who also happened to be the man she was in love with. And if I knew anything, I knew he loved her back. Besides the fact that I was a sucker for a Romeo and Juliette romance, all they needed was a little nudge in the right direction, families be damned. She might come from a fucked-up, patriarchal world, but I wasn't about to let my best friend lose every shred of agency she had. Until a ring was slipped on her finger in front of a priest, she still had a chance to go after what she wanted. And what she wanted was Luca.

If all went according to plan, she'd lose her virginity to him, and they would become tied for life through the concept of the blood bond. In the archaic, backward society she came from, that was as good as married. I shuddered at the thought and thanked my lucky stars that I hadn't been born into the bosom of her family, no matter how lovely they were to me. Only Cat could find a way to be authentic and still remain loyal to her folks.

Grabbing a strong hold of her, I secured her arm in mine and shoved the curtain aside. With a bright smile plastered to my face, I stared up at the ginormous bodyguard guarding the entrance to the VIP lounge. Luck was on our side because Vladimir recognized Cat instantly and let us pass. So, in we went...

I was taken aback by the gorgeously appointed room, where the motif had clearly been reduced to red, black, leather, and velvet. Black crystal chandeliers illuminated the black leather couches and scarlet-red velvet chairs scattered around dark wood coffee tables. The black and scarlet theme continued in the floral velour wallpaper, giving the whole place the vibe of a...Rococo boudoir? I'd call it intimate and sexy, but it definitely crossed the line into *extra*.

Scanning the crowded room, I stumbled when I got hooked by a pair of iridescent, light-colored eyes. Reeling, I stoutly ignored the rugged beauty of the man showcasing that glittering glacial stare. Why? Because I was on a mission, dammit.

I was about to charge forward when Cat clutched my arm and murmured, "There they are."

"Where?" I asked as my gaze followed her index finger to the very booth where those wicked eyes were stationed.

I swallowed hard.

A man who shared similar features to the hot, smoldering one straightened up, his face flashing a mixture of emotions. Anger. Worry. Anger again. It didn't escape my notice that the blue-eyed devil whose stare shook me to my core was sitting beside him.

"Wh-which one is L-Luca?" I stammered out. *Please, not him. God, please, not him.*

"There," she whispered. "The hot one with the gray eyes."

Relief whooshed out of me in a long breath.

Rallying, I ordered, "Let's go," before I lost my nerve. "Be strong. Take what you want," I repeated, as I had at least a dozen times on the way over to the club.

Skidding to a halt, we stood before them awkwardly. I stabbed Cat in the side with my elbow and she squeaked out, "Hey, Nicu." Her gaze turned and locked in on his brother. "Luca."

"Hey, Cat," replied Nicu.

There was distinct tension in the air. From the way Luca was checking Cat out, I could tell he was simultaneously turned on and pissed off. Sounded like the perfect combination for instigating a blood bond to me.

"Who's your friend?" asked Nicu. His eyes had never left me, I noted. Which was downright rude, considering his fiancée was standing beside me. My face flamed with shame at the way he'd completely dismissed Cat. Thankfully, she was too jittery and focused on Luca to notice. But Luca noticed, and I heard the low growl beneath his breath. At least the way his eyes burned for Cat relieved me. He was clearly enthralled by her. As any man should be.

But not her own fiancé, Nicu. *God, what a dick.* A sexy dick, but definitely a dick. What else was new? He was engaged to a gorgeous, sweet, loyal woman, and yet—he cared nothing for her. In fact, he seemed to ignore her on purpose. While I prayed it turned out well for Luca and Cat, that didn't take away from the ruthlessness of Nicu's behavior.

"Nicu, this is Jewel. Jewel, Nicu," she introduced, slipping into the seat beside Luca. I knew she'd only done that because her knees were about to give out.

"What the hell are you doing here, Cat?" Luca snapped.

Cat's eyelashes fluttered like she was close to crying. I was about to intercede on her behalf when he pushed her out of the booth and onto her feet. Coming out after her, he turned to Nicu and said to me, "Why don't you sit down, order a *non*alcoholic drink, and get to know Nicu?"

That was an order and a warning patronizingly wrapped up into one. I would've done anything to tell him to go to hell, but for the fact that this was what Cat and I wanted to happen.

He took my friend's arm, said, "I have something to discuss with Cat. We'll be right back," and then they were gone.

I blinked down at Nicu, whose lips twisted up seductively, promptly disarming my moral compass. The curl of his mouth, coupled with the ice-cold fire of his eyes, spoke of a blazing furnace inside what was surely the darkest of souls. But as cold and calculating as he seemed, there was an untamed energy to him. It blew off him like the harsh wind off the Siberian tundra.

Savage, brutal, and uninhabitable.

I wanted to take a step away, and another, until I backed myself right out of the VIP area. Then I'd hightail it out of this place, because I distinctly felt like bait thrown into a predator's lair.

But I couldn't. As part of our plan, I was to hold down the fort and distract Nicu while Cat attempted to seduce Luca. So I did the one thing I knew was bound to give me the most trouble. I sat down.

At least I had the wherewithal to sit across from him, keeping as much distance as possible between us.

Settling against the high back of the banquette, I raked my eyes over him. Starting at the top of his perfectly tousled hair, I slowly meandered down to the large, masculine hand wrapped around the glass of liquor he was nursing.

So this was Nicu.

I could say, without an iota of exaggeration, that he was a deadly specimen of a man. Powerful, with the familiar arrogance that came from men who were naturally intense. It wasn't his icy-blue eyes—deadly but piercing, framed by black eyelashes—that unsettled me. Nor was it his tawny skin with a five o'clock shadow that I instinctively *knew* would leave delicious scrapes on my inner thighs. It was his beautifully sculpted, cruel mouth that did me in. Especially when one side curled up in a devastating half smile.

With the full bast of his attention on me for so long, I shivered in the black crepe Dolce and Gabbana dress that barely covered my full ass. Grasping the wineglass in front of me, I took a couple of deep swallows.

"Cold?" he asked.

Startled out of my reverie, I jerked slightly and went with a casual response. "Not too much."

"Here," he replied as he stood up and began stripping off his jacket.

Eyes bulging, I swung my gaze left to right. "What are you doing?"

He handed it to me over the table of the booth.

I stared up his long arm and then back down his hand to long, elegant fingers that tapered into perfectly groomed half-moon nails.

He pushed the jacket closer.

"Go on, put the men out of their misery. There's only so much they can take, and I'm not in the mood to fight tonight."

I glared at him.

"What does that even mean?" I asked suspiciously. Figuring I'd have to distract the bouncers at the door to sneak Cat and myself into this club with our awful fake IDs, I'd worn a low-cut dress that did little to hide my assets. Although Nicu's attention was not on my chest like the other men in the club, I assumed he was referring to my outfit. My gaze scoured the tables around ours.

"I don't see anyone staring at me," I replied, indignant.

"Then you're blind," he replied blandly. He pushed the jacket closer and hardened his tone with a command. "Take it."

Giving him an annoyed grunt, I snatched the jacket and put it on. His ravenous gaze watched every moment of me struggling with it. Finally, I managed to wrap it around me and sat back down with a huff. Dear God. His scent surrounded me, earthy, with clean and bright hints of citrus. Like my favorite tea, Earl Grey. Damn him for being so sexy that even his smell was perfect.

As if that wasn't bad enough, the jacket was warm from his residual body heat. I hadn't realized how chilled I was, now that I was no longer dancing, as I had downstairs to work up Cat's courage before we made our way upstairs.

"Better," he muttered.

"What did you say?"

One side of his mouth ticked up again. "I said, 'better.' I'd much prefer to sit down with you and relax than fight a man for ogling you."

"You're delusional. No one was ogling me."

"Oh, believe me, pretty doll." He nodded sagely. "They were ogling, for sure."

"A woman's allowed to wear what she wants," I countered.

He draped an arm over the back of the booth. An eerie pattern of a red wolf head baring its teeth was worked into the black leather and shimmered under the light of the black chandelier above us.

The Lupu wolf.

Talk about advertising who you were.

"Certainly. Especially in a place like this. We want everyone who comes here to dress up. Dance. Drink. Party. But when a woman sits in a booth reserved for me and my brothers, then men need to keep their eyes to themselves. At that point, it's no longer only about you."

"If not me, then who could it be about?" I asked somewhat snottily. I had a more-than-strong inkling, but I wanted to see how he would put it into words for me, an outsider.

"It's about respecting the Lupu name."

Clever answer. Succinct, while remaining vague. His response did assume that I knew a fair amount about his world, but I wasn't about to let him off the hook so easily.

"I'm not property," I snapped.

He gave me a slow look-over. "Everyone's property, pretty one. You included." He paused. "Especially you."

A jolt of electricity zipped through my body at the corrupting ownership dripping from his tone. I opened my mouth to ask him what the hell he meant by that when Luca and Cat emerged from wherever they'd snuck off to.

Cat tugged my hand, begging me with her eyes to follow her to the bathroom. Grateful for the chance at escape, I stood up when Luca addressed Nicu, "Cat doesn't feel well. I'm taking her home. Watch over her friend and drive her to her place when she's ready to leave."

He did not just order his younger brother, in no uncertain terms, to take me home, did he? Nicu's cold eyes turned on me, hungry. Oh, fuck, he did. Cat mumbled something, and I let her drag me away. We turned the corner into a quiet hallway and stared at each other.

"What happened?" I almost screeched.

She hopped up and down, squealing with joy. "Oh my God, didn't you hear him say he's taking me home? He's going to claim me. I mean, we're going to go all the way." She grabbed both my hands and squeezed them tightly. "I'm a little scared and a lot nervous."

I squeezed her back. "Woman, you've got this. Remember, you're strong and you have the right to choose your mate."

"But I'm a virgin, and it's going to hurt."

I brought her close to me and locked eyes with her. "Listen carefully, Cat. Yes, you're a virgin, but Luca knows that. He will do everything in his power to make this good for you. First off, that's the kind of guy he is, and secondly, it's obvious he cares for you. So stop worrying."

She nodded vigorously. "You're right. You're right."

"Come on. You're ready for this, Cat. You've been ready," I said encouragingly, hauling her back into the main room.

Luca caught sight of Cat and met us before we made it back to the booth. He'd stripped off his jacket and promptly draped it over Cat's shoulders. An instant later, they were gone. Staring after their receding figures like a deer in headlights, I was desperate to follow. I swung my gaze back to Nicu and found him already halfway out of his seat, his face hard and resolute as if prepared to run me down. With one final glance at the entrance, I dejectedly made my way back to the seductive monster.

Nicu's low, growly chuckle greeted me as I dropped into the booth. The sound coasted over my skin like a gust of decadent, sultry, charred smoke. He slid across the banquette until he was by my side.

My head whipped in his direction, my eyes narrowing on him. "I don't know what you find so amusing. Nothing about this is funny."

"Oh, I'm laughing because you and I both know the truth," he spoke with a smugness that made me want to smack it right off his face. A frisson of fear ran down my spine. Wait a minute... Was he talking about Luca and Cat?

Keeping my breathing even, I leaned back and crossed my arms over my chest. The fine wool of his jacket rubbed against my bare skin, the slight roughness almost erotic. I'd never realized how sexy it felt to wear a man's jacket while barely clothed.

"Oh, and what truth is that?" I asked nonchalantly, praying he didn't know.

"That you'll be writhing under me, screaming my name, by the end of the night," he boasted.

A mixture of relief and fury tangled in my chest.

Conceited. Fucking. Bastard.

"I highly doubt it," I sneered. Swiping the glass in front of him, I knocked it back. The taste of an unfamiliar liquor burned a path down my throat to my belly, causing me to cough. What the hell was this? Nasty motor fluid or the awful Romanian brandy Cat's mom had me taste once?

Another sinful chuckle triggered a spray of goosebumps coasting down my arms.

"Easy there, tiger. That liquor's not for little girls."

My head went up in flames. Was it only pure anger? Or a mixture with lust? Most likely both.

"L-little girl?" I sputtered. "I'm no one's *little* girl."

He gave another evil chortle. One that said I was lying. But that's where he was wrong. If anyone knew the most basic facts about me, they'd know I was no longer *anyone's* little girl. Having your father incarcerated at the age of twelve obliterated any fantasies of a childhood. If not for my mother, regardless of her many faults, I'd be a ward of the state.

"That remains to be seen," he murmured as he gestured the cocktail waitress over. She was there in under a second, batting her fake lashes at Nicu in a way that made my hands curl into fists. My spine hit the back of the booth, shock reverberating through my frame. Since when did I get a whiff of jealousy, much less the desire to rip another woman to shreds?

Never, that's when.

Until now.

I stuffed down my fury at her blatant flirting and at myself for getting triggered by said flirting. As if she, and everyone in their insular world, didn't know he was engaged to *my best friend*.

Ugh.

When flirty slutty cocktail waitress sashayed her way to

the other end of the VIP section, Nicu's eyes found mine and crinkled at the corners. God, it was his first full smile. And it was stunning. My breath caught in my throat. Everything he did drew me in.

His hand found mine over the table. His touch scorched me.

I quickly withdrew my hand. "Don't touch me. I'm Cat's best friend," I hissed. "So whatever sick thoughts you have bouncing around in that head of yours, get rid of them instantly."

His mesmerizing cold eyes drilled into mine. "What thoughts are those, baby girl?"

"Don't call me that," I gritted out, fisting my hands.

He leaned over until he was so close that his breath skimmed over my lips, as light as a feather. I licked mine. His eyes flicked down to my mouth before he opened his own and said, "You don't know me, so I won't take offense to your tone of voice. This time. But let me make one thing clear. I do what the fuck I want, when the fuck I want."

The sweet scent of his breath had me biting down on my bottom lip to suppress a moan.

He leaned back. "I'll call you what I damn well please, princess."

"I'm not a princess," I scoffed with a harsh laugh. "Cat's the princess."

"That's where you're wrong." His eyes coasted over my face and down to my chest in a proprietary way that had me breaking out in a sweat. "Every inch of you screams princess, baby doll. I should know. I'm royalty."

Maybe it was the fact that Cat had gone off with Luca, that there was no mistaking the fixation on Luca's face when he looked at her and knew he was never letting her go, that made me weaken toward Nicu. Maybe it was the liquor on an empty stomach or that Nicu was the sexiest, most dangerous man I'd ever met. Whatever it was, he was eroding my defenses.

Enough so that I allowed him to guide me out of the club. Slipping his hand into the jacket, he laid it on my lower back, exposed from my low-cut dress, searing my skin. I regretted my choice of wardrobe, liking his touch way too much as he maneuvered me toward a sleek black Ducati bike. According to Cat, both Luca and Nicu were obsessed with Italian vehicles.

Handing me his helmet, he arched his brow in challenge.

"Nice bike," I mused as I circled it.

"You know bikes?" he asked, surprise lacing his question.

I rolled my eyes. "My father liked anything fast. Bikes. Cars. He was like a kid that way." I exhaled a resigned sigh. It was what made his current stationary situation, trapped in an eight-by-eight cell, so very tragic.

"Don't you need this more than I do?" I questioned, swaying the heavy helmet from my finger in his face. "Considering you're driving."

"Is that concern I detect in your tone?" he teased. "I'm touched. But there's no need to worry about me." Patting the engine, he added, "She's my girl. I could ride her in my sleep. Nothing will happen to me." His eyes turned sharp and accusatory as if I'd insulted him by questioning his skills. "Or you. Although unnecessary, if one of us should wear it, it should be you."

With that, he took the helmet and placed it on my head with a gentleness I hadn't expected and adjusted it to fit me. He swung onto the bike and turned to me expectantly. I shifted from foot to foot. Not only was my dress backless, but it was short as hell. Even though it was midsummer and humid in the city, I wasn't about to return Nicu's jacket just yet. Even with its coverage, there was no getting on that bike without flashing everyone within a block radius. Especially the crowd milling in front of the club not too far from us.

"Problem?" he queried with another arching of his brow.

"There's no way I can get on this monster without exposing myself."

He snorted. "Thank fuck you're not Romanian *mafie*. I don't have to worry about your modesty."

Hurt slashed through my chest like the serrated edge of a steel knife.

"Excuse me?" I shrilled.

He gave me another one of those awful, decadent laughs that made my knees weak. I bit my lip. *Damn the man.*

"Baby doll, that's far from an insult. It's one of the things I like about you."

Something about the way he said it made it sound like a high compliment. But if he wasn't insulting me, that meant he was insulting Cat. I couldn't let that pass. Until they weren't engaged anymore, if that even happened, I wasn't about to let him get away with dissing my friend.

"*Cat* is a Romanian *mafie* princess. My best friend and your fiancée."

The bright blue of his eyes shuttered like a wall of ice, cutting me off from the hot burn behind his gaze. I felt it in my gut, like I'd been thrust into a meatpacking cooler with the door slammed behind me.

"How could I forget?" he drawled, a bitter edge to his tone. "Hopefully, Luca will do what's right and break the shackles he's single-handedly cuffed around my ankles with his tenacious stupidity."

My bottom jaw unhinged and dropped open. I gaped at

him. He *knew*. He knew what was happening between Luca and Cat. In that moment, I strongly suspected he knew more than Cat and I combined. There were dynamics between these brothers, probably within the entire Lupu family, that we were likely clueless about.

"Hop on. I don't have all night," he ordered curtly.

Casting my gaze around my surroundings, I shimmied my dress up to the tops of my thighs. Gritting my teeth, I swung my leg over and plastered myself to Nicu's back, hoping against hope that I'd covered everything important. I glanced at him and found his eyes glued to my long leg, bare from the crease of my thigh down. I let out an embarrassed groan and covered my eyes.

His hand moved to my outer thigh and gripped it, causing me to gasp against his ear. I squeezed my eyes tighter.

"I like the sounds you make when I touch you. You're so sensitive. Responsive. I'll get you making sounds you've never made before, sounds just for me," he promised darkly.

I blew out a breath, half exasperation, half unbridled lust. Yup, that comment confirmed he knew the effect he had on me. It was infuriating, but I barely restrained myself from panting.

"If you were a gentleman, you would've kept that to yourself," I suggested.

He gave another chuckle.

"Lesson number one, little girl. You've got the wrong brother if you're looking for a gentleman."

Images flashed in my mind of the ungentlemanly things I wished he'd do to me.

Shut it down!, I screamed to myself as he twisted the throttle and his bike shot off from the curb. My fingers tightened around his taut waist, and I let out a little scream. His callous laugh flew past me as he increased his speed and ran a red light on the near-empty street.

If I faltered, there was one redeeming factor in this train wreck I was on. I was neither Romanian, nor *mafie*, nor a virgin. I could never be lassoed into his fucked-up, male-controlled world, because I knew a future heartbreak when I saw one, and the moment I laid eyes on him, I knew he'd be nothing but trouble.

2

NICU

I slapped my hand on the flimsy door beside Jewel's head. The clap shook the wood in its frame, the sound reverberating in her dorm room, catching a few strands of her long, dark hair between my fingers. That wasn't the only thing that'd be shaking by the time I was done with her. It was late. Real late, but her roommate was nowhere to be found. Good. I could already feel my control slipping. Fortunately, she was neither *mafie* nor a virgin, because the things I wanted to do to this woman would be considered illegal in some countries. It was time to warn her before the point of no return.

"I don't fuck gentle, and I have no intention of starting now. I'm going to fuck you till you're screaming my name like it's God's."

The light streaming in through her window from the streetlamp outside bathed her in a dusky glow. The hazel irises of her eyes stood out like a riot of meadow wildflowers, interspersed with flecks of gold. The humidity from the hot city night seeping in through the window exhaled a sultry breath. The noise of cars driving along Broadway intermingled with the rhythm of her erratic breathing. A deep, heavy beat throbbed between us.

Big, gorgeous eyes, framed by dark lashes, glared to me. My heart rate ticked up. I loved provoking her. She was a vision when angry, setting my body on fire. I was nothing if not an adrenaline junkie, and she was my new thrill ride.

"Is that supposed to scare me, Nicu?" she taunted. "Because I'm not one of your little *mafie* virgins. I know how to fuck."

My shoulders tensed as I bent over her and a whiff of rose petals drifted up to me, leaving me aching. I clenched my jaws to stop myself from grabbing her hourglass hips and crushing her to me. Barking out a laugh, I warned, "Wait till you meet my demon cock, little girl. You may *think* you've been fucked right, but you haven't been fucked by the likes of me."

Stepping closer, she eliminated the couple of inches between us and bared her teeth. "You arrogant prick. Bring it, then. Because from what I've seen, the men who brag the most, fuck the worst."

"What do you know about *men*?" I scoffed before fisting her hair in my grip. I yanked it back hard, banging her head against the door. My mouth smashed down on hers, devouring her red lips like I'd been aching to do from the instant I saw them as she stepped into my club alongside my fiancée. Not that that fact had stopped the roar of lust that surged through me at the sight of her.

She pressed them together tightly, denying me access.

That was a no-go.

She wanted to test me. *Fucking go for it.* I wasn't about to back down. Not a motherfucking inch. Gripping her jaw, I pried it open for my invasion. This was why I never wanted a virgin or a staid *mafie* wife. Because I fucked dirty, and I fucked angry. The moment I spotted her wicked curves in my club, I knew that sexy body could handle anything I threw its way. And when she tossed her head and shot me a look of challenge, I knew *she* could handle anything I threw her way.

Her nice rack and thick ass may have piqued my interest, but her haughty look is what had sealed her fate.

"Make sure you're ready for whatever I dish out," I warned against her lips, "because we may be in a building full of women, but I'm not subbing you out."

Jewel pulled against my tight clasp on her long tresses.

"Talking is just that. Talk. You need to prove you know what to do with that precious dick of yours," she taunted just before flicking my lips with her tongue.

Her comment almost made me laugh. Almost. But the time for words was over. She wanted proof? I'd give it to her the only way I knew how. I'd give it to her hard. Time to domesticate this wildcat.

Without wasting another second, I attacked her mouth. Teeth clashed, catching skin. The tang of iron flooded our mouths, but neither of us stopped. She gave as good as she got. Her nails came out, raking down the side of my neck, eliciting a growl from deep within me. Little kitty had come out to play. Who knew what else was buried in that devastating body? She tangled her fingers in the longer strands at my nape and dragged me closer, crushing her mouth to mine. I loved the way her soft curves melded against the hard angles of my body.

My hand raked up her bare thigh, dragging her dress up, up, up, until I roughly cupped her pussy.

Fuck, that's wet silk.

Mother of God, she was ripe for me. I couldn't wait till I got my fingers between those sticky, plump lips of hers.

Griping the gusset of her panties, I ripped them down and thrust two fingers past the knuckles.

Tight and wet, just the way I liked it.

She jerked in my hold, taking in a sharp breath. Her lips were swollen and bruised from my ministrations. Seeing my mark pleased me, but it wasn't enough to satisfy the beast raging within. Not by a long shot.

If I were a good, honest man, I would've paused. I would've slowed down. But the thought held no power over me. Her supple, moist flesh clamped around my digits, and she started riding the heel of my hand. Mother*fucker*—she was as filthy as I was. A perfect fucking match. Her nails scraped down the buttons of my shirt, ripping at them until the shirt was half torn open. Then she fumbled with my buckle.

Tearing my mouth from hers, I threw a glance over my shoulder.

Bed.

Batting her hands out of the way, I caught the back of her thighs and lifted her up.

Stalking to her bed, I threw her down.

She bounced a few times before catching herself.

With a scathing look and a growl, she got to her knees. "I'm not a fucking doll," she snapped.

Knees spread open, chest heaving, eyes flashing, she was glorious. She wasn't a doll. She was a fucking treasure. A jewel, just like her namesake, and best of all...she didn't want to be treated like one in bed. I scented the naughtiness off her from across the VIP section of my club.

"No, you're right," I acquiesced, pausing as I stripped off my tie. Eyeing her narrow single mattress, I found nothing to tie her to. Returning my attention to her, I declared, "You're not a doll. You're my new fuck toy. My dirty little whore. Are you going to be a well-behaved slut for me, Jewel?"

Her eyes flared wide with desire. It was like a lit match to the kerosene that was my blood. *Poof*, it caught on fire. My control was slipping. Keeping back this wall of energy about to overtake me was hard, but I had to do it until I got her consent.

I took a step closer.

Then another.

Clutching the back of her neck, I pressed her face into my chest as I leaned down to whisper in her ear, "Or am I going to have to tie you up to keep you still while I suck on your clit? It's your choice. Remember, I'll always give you a choice, 'cause I'm generous like that."

I felt the muscles of her throat shift as she swallowed hard. My fingers wanted to coast around to the front, grip the slim column, slam her down, and trap her on her bed with that hold alone. A shiver coursed through me, and my erection vibrated with need. *Reel it in.*

Pulling back to watch her, I got lost in her expressive eyes. "Baby girl, you have to trust me to know what you need. I'm rough, but my endgame will always be your pleasure. Either by my hand, my tongue, or my cock, but you *will* come."

When she tipped her head back, I saw a bit of the lust fading from her eyes, reality streaming back in. Thoughts had entered her mind, taking her away from me. Damn, did I regret that. I liked this girl wild for me.

There was one way to get her back. I thumbed her plump bottom lip, opening it slightly, and slipped two fingers into her mouth. After pumping in and out roughly, I pulled them out and gripped her chin with my wet fingers.

"What is it?" I demanded with a little shake of her head.

Remaining silent, she averted her eyes.

"Use your words, Jewel."

"We shouldn't be doing this..." she trailed off. "Cat would be hurt."

My fingers slid down her throat and cradled it in the palm of my hand. I could feel her pulse going fast. Tilting her head up, I waited until her eyes met mine. There was guilt. There was desperation, as well. She wanted this. There was no doubt about that. We wouldn't have ended up here otherwise. She knew I was her best friend's fiancé from the moment she met me, and yet, here we were.

"If everything goes to plan, Luca will be feeding Cat his dick right about now."

"Ugh, you're so crass," she griped, smacking my arm.

I chuckled. "Yeah, I am, but don't pretend you don't like my nasty mouth. You'll like it even better when I'm eating you out." I bent down closer, so close that I felt the gasp of breath escape her open mouth. "Stop overthinking it. As of now, you turn your will over to me. I'll decide what we do, when, and how we do it. Understand?"

Her eyes searched mine.

I held my breath, waiting. My fingers instinctually tightened around her throat the longer she remained silent.

I pushed the strap of her dress off her shoulder with a shaky hand, exposing the beautiful slope of her full breast. My palm caressed it. Cupped it. Weighed it. I tweaked her nipple, causing her lush body to jolt. Damn, but she was responsive. That was enough of an answer for me. Guilt was making her hesitate, but we both knew I was in control. To prove my point, I gave the tip of her tit a sharp smack.

She gasped harshly, her mouth gaping. Her breaths came out in pants, the rough and needy sounds setting my loins on fire.

"What'll it be, Jewel? I don't have all fucking night to wait before I push my cock into your tight paradise. Whether now or at another time, I *will* be inside you. Have no doubt of that."

Canting my head to the side, I continued, "What if I share my plans for you? Will that help make up your mind? Alright, then. First, I'm going to lick your pussy from end to end. Play with your little pearl between my lips. Slurp down the juices you smear on my face when you lose control and ride my mouth. I'm going to consume you so many times, you'll plead for me to stop as you collapse on the bed, limp."

I gripped the thin material of her dress and *rippp* slashed through the air as I tore it down to her navel. A through the air. Damn, it felt good to let loose. "And if you beg me to fuck you, which you will, do you know what my response will be?" Gripping the remnants of her torn dress, she shook her head as she stared up at me. "You'll have to earn my cock with orgasms before I allow you to take a single inch of it. You think you can do that for me, pretty doll?"

Chest heaving, she stared down as her dress slunk down the sides of her body and pooled at her hips.

Her eyes snapped to me, blazing a kaleidoscope of colors.

Then she did something so goddamn beautiful, I almost faltered in my resolve to make her wait.

She threw her shoulders back, pushed her chest out, and intoned the one and only word I ever wanted to hear come out of her mouth. "Yes."

And there it was.

The consent I was looking for.

3

NICU

Standing in the empty hallway of Jewel's dorm, my back slumped against her door, I flicked my wrist to check the time. It was past three in the morning. After coming four times, she saw the writing on the wall: I planned to fuck her till the break of dawn.

So she kicked me out. It was okay because fucking her had brought my blood back down to a simmer. For now. My brain chemistry had changed, like taking a hit of fentanyl for the first time. I was no psychic, but even I could tell chances were, I'd need her again.

I shook my head. *What is it about this girl?*

Sure, she'd caught my eye the moment she waltzed into my club. Alongside my fiancée, no less. But then my fiancée left with my brother, and I was only happy to see the back of them. Cat and Luca were meant to be together. They left to sort out their shit, and I was given the chance to chill with Jewel. Later, I took her back to her dorm room, making her come with my mouth and on my cock before taking my own pleasure.

I heard her shift behind the door. I had no desire to

move from my spot guarding her, but the communal bathrooms were down the hall, and there was a chance she'd step out to use them before going to bed. I didn't want her to find me there.

Throwing one last glance over my shoulder, I forced myself off her door with an irritated huff.

We had a hell of a time hooking up, so I should be good, no?

It was the first time I'd been told to leave moments after pulling out of a woman. That should have pissed me off. Instead, my anger had burned away, quickly followed by amusement. The woman had a little brat inside, waiting to bust out, and I'd be there to put her back in line when it did.

But not quite yet. It was too soon to show her the full spectrum of my dominance.

I wanted more from her. So much so, that she'd be scared off if she knew the extent of my intentions.

Moving to the stairwell, I took the flight of stairs down to the lobby.

Jewel might be young, but the pain in her eyes spoke of something else. She'd been through things. While she lived almost as shielded a life as the flocks of *mafie* girls her age, she wasn't gazy-eyed. I sensed that if I revealed to her the crazy shit I've done in my short life, she wouldn't blink an eye. Instead, her amber irises would deepen in color, a beguiling mixture of brown and green, like they did when she was processing something.

What I liked about her was that she wasn't breakable. Smart as a whip. Incisive. Sassy. Oh, and sexy as fuck. For an overprotected young woman, whether American or Romanian, she was a rare gem, indeed. She was the full package, and if she thought I was going to step away after one night, she had another think coming.

Although my oldest brother had married an outsider,

chances were that wasn't in the cards for us. I might be the youngest in line, but I was still a Lupu prince. I had to marry for the family, and my future wife had to be both Romanian *mafie* and a virgin. Jewel was none of those things, and for the first time, I was tempted to defy their expectations.

Which was a scary thought.

Luca was the black sheep, the contrarian who went against everything demanded of him. If I didn't love the bastard, I would've strangled him to death long ago. I might be a savage, I might struggle with my impulses, but I didn't disregard familial obligations. That was his role, and he took it to the extreme, pushing our eldest brother and head, or *șef,* of our family, Alex, into apoplectic fits.

Slipping out into the lobby, I carefully eyed the night guard at the counter. A man in his mid-thirties, he shook the Daily News newspaper in his hands.

"Anything interesting?" I asked casually, lifting my chin to his paper.

Spotting his New York Yankees cap, I struck a conversation about their stats this season. Not that I gave a shit about baseball, but you couldn't be male without knowing the state of sports in this city. By the end of the conversation, I let it be known that my girl lived on the first floor and that I wanted him to keep a special eye on her. I exchanged numbers with him, slipped him five immaculate hundred-dollar bills with a promise that if any of his buddies wanted to help me out, they would get the same treatment.

His eyebrows lifted to his forehead, but good man that he was, he slipped the Benjamins into his wallet and said, "Sure thing, bro."

That was the good thing about New York City. People were quick on the uptake. Between the thread count of my suit and the crispness of those bills, he knew I was not someone to fuck with. I made sure to have eyes and ears on Jewel before I even stepped out of her building.

I made my way down the quiet stone-paved path to the crenellated black iron gate of her college, crossed the street, and stopped at the corner, across from her building. Feet frozen, I looked up with a sneaking suspicion that I would become well acquainted with this corner. Her figure passed back and forth across the sheer white curtains of her windows. My jaw tightened when I saw the motions of her undressing behind the gossamer material that left almost nothing to the imagination. The chick was fucking insane. Six years in some boarding school up in rural Massachusetts and she'd forgotten what it was like to live in the city. There were Peeping Toms everywhere, and I wasn't even counting myself.

It was a given I'd be watching her.

My cell phone vibrated.

I pulled it out and swiped the video chat open with a grin. "Hey, little sis. Is your boy keeping you up at night?"

"Eight minutes. You have eight extra minutes of life on me, and you still lord it over me by calling me 'little' sis," my twin, Tasa, grumbled.

"Hey, you had your chance to come out first, and your complaints would've been moot, but you snooze, you lose," I teased.

"Oh? And how was I going to manage that, sharing such a tight space with your bossy ass?" she quipped, one eyebrow raised high.

"Tasa, it's almost four in the morning. Is everything okay?"

The image on the screen shifted, and my nephew came into view, asleep with his little baby mouth open. Her voice came through the phone. "He woke up, and I couldn't stand to let him cry. Whistle told me to let him ride it out, but I can't do it. I'm wide awake, and since you're a night owl, I thought to try you."

Whistle, a former-Bratva-prince-turned-biker and her man, was right for once. I didn't like to see the shadows under my sister's eyes. He was a stubborn fuck, but conveniently turned to putty in her hands, so I knew he'd be worthless when it came to changing her mind. *Eh, he does what he can with what little power he has.*

Leaning against the brick wall of the building, I glanced up at Jewel's window to find it dark. Good, she needed her rest after the workout I'd put her through. Turning away, I walked to my car.

"He's right, you know," I stated. "I don't like to see you tired."

Her face came back on screen. She waved my concern away. "Ah, it's alright. I'm glad to be here for Mason."

"How's the other little devil doing?"

"Roman's good. *He* sleeps like a baby. Not like this one," she replied, tapping my nephew's button nose.

Her inquisitive eyes returned to me. "So how are you doing? You're out late. Coming from the club?"

"Nah, came from a woman," I replied. Now that she was grown, and a mother of two, I no longer hid that aspect of my life from her.

"Anyone I know?" she asked coyly.

I grabbed the back of my neck, feeling reticent about telling her the truth. Not that I felt an iota of guilt about fucking Jewel. I wanted Luca to claim Cat already and get this stifling noose of an engagement off my neck. But Tasa had driven down from upstate where she lived to attend my farce of an engagement party, and she'd taken a liking to Cat.

"Who is it?" Her tone turned sharp at my noticeable pause. "I've never seen you hesitate before, so you probably did something you shouldn't have done. Is she married?"

"Come on," I retorted. "I'm not that bad."

With the scrapes I'd gotten into growing up, nothing was off the table. While I'd learned to control myself since then, my reputation preceded me wherever I went. In elementary school, I'd been suspended for TP-ing the bathroom. In middle school, for wrapping Ms. Doyle's classroom in tin foil. High school was too easy; I got expelled for fighting. I made it through college, just barely. There's a strong possibility I have attention deficit disorder, a learning disability, or both, because school of any kind was always a struggle. Even Alex saw me backsliding from the stress and backed off about graduate school. Considering a PhD was a requirement in my family, that was saying something.

Her tone softened, "Nicu, since when have I ever judged you?"

Straddling my bike, I checked to make sure the street was empty before answering. "Since now," I replied as I turned the ignition on. The conversation switched over to the car speakers.

"That bad?" resounded Tasa's voice through the enclosed interior.

"It sounds bad when I say it out loud, but it's not as bad as that," I hedged.

"Uh-oh. I'm used to you getting into trouble, but you never get into girl drama."

She was right. I might fuck women, but I didn't fuck with women. One experience with what had turned out to be Cristo's girl taught me a lesson early on...and created a toxic competition between him and me that's lived on to this day. Anyway, until recently, my brothers and I were too busy for relationships. We got our needs met and went back to business. Our business was our clan. The Lupu clan. Family was our priority.

Granted, things had changed now that Alex married Tasa's best friend, our next-door neighbor, Nina. Luca was recently toppled off his high horse, where he lived the solitary life of a sanctimonious prick, and had fallen in love with Cat, my fiancée. If he had one brain cell left in that twisted head of his, he would see he was meant to marry her. It was disgusting to watch them eye-fuck each other in public. Under the rules, which he constantly ignored, he should've been engaged to her instead of me.

"This isn't girl drama," I muttered.

"Tell me already. The suspense is killing me," she demanded.

"You swear not to let it slip to anyone, Tasa."

"Yeah, yeah. I'm not even in the city anymore. No one up here cares about what happens in Queens. And since when do I spill secrets, Nicu?"

Point taken.

When it mattered, Tasa always had my back. A wave of guilt hit me that I hadn't watched over her carefully enough and spared her the heartache she went through with Alex. I may dote on my mother, respect my eldest brother, love-hate my other brother, but the one and only person I loved unconditionally was my twin sister.

"It's Cat's best friend. Her name is Jewel," I blurted out, and then cringed. I shouldn't have said anything, but there I went again. My impulsivity got the best of me. It was a constant battle between my savage impulses and my stringent suppression of them. I worked hard to restrain myself, only letting go when fighting, killing, or racing. Yet, despite compartmentalizing, I slipped. Like now.

"What?!" she practically shouted.

"Relax, it's not as bad as it sounds—"

"How in the world do you not see this as bad?" she asked, her eyes wide with dismay.

"Because Cat's in love with Luca. I'd bet my life that she's in his bed as we speak." Tasa gasped and slapped a hand over her chest. "Don't act so surprised. I never cared for her, and it's mutual. Luca was assigned to guard her for a summer class she was taking up at Barnard College. They've spent a hell of a lot of time together, and earlier tonight, she came to the club with her best friend to force Luca's hand. Cat left with Luca, and if everything goes as planned, they should be blood bonded by now," I explained.

She looked at me with horror. "You planned this?"

"Don't look at me like that. It's more like I got out of the way and let nature take its course. You should see them. It's downright embarrassing, the way they moon over each other. And they think they're being sly about it, but I know Luca inside out. He wants her, and Luca gets what he wants," I elaborated.

"Blood bonded, huh?"

"Yup, perfect for this little Romeo-Juliet situation that's unfolded. He takes her virginity, and she ends up with the guy she's supposed to be with. Which, for the record, is not me."

"Well, damn, I'm missing the soap opera of a lifetime," she grumbled.

"No, you're just living your life. As it should be. You're preparing for a wedding to the man you love. You have two beautiful boys and a life to live. It was just a fuck, Tasa. Nothing more," I lied.

"Bullshit," she shot back. "How many times have you spoken the name of a girl you've had sex with? Never, that's how often. Jewel, Jewel, Jewel," she recited, letting that beautiful name roll off her tongue as if she were savoring a fine wine.

"For fuck's sake, what are you repeating her name like that for?"

"Because this girl means something to you," she rejoined.

The back of my neck burned up. She knew me better than anyone and was digging too deep. Regretting my truthful outburst, I tried to put a stop to this.

I snorted. "She does not. I don't do relationships. You know this."

"Whatever, Nicu. Go ahead and lie to yourself all you want. I've been where you are. I've avoided love, and take it from me, you're only opening yourself up to heartache if you do that."

"I'm not lying to myself," I snapped.

I wasn't. I was lying to *her*. I rarely remembered a woman's name while fucking, much less afterward. I was committed to leaving them satisfied, but nothing beyond that. My reputation preceded me. Tag on my addiction to speed and no one thought I'd live long enough to procreate.

My life revolved around risk and family. I took the biggest risks of anyone in my clan. It began with the bloody revenge that followed my father's death. I'd begged Alex to bring me along and ended the night with my first kill at thirteen. By the end of that summer, when blood ran through the gutters of Queens, I had been forged into a vicious weapon and was inducted into my clan.

Risk and family had kept me sane over the years, but my bullshit engagement with Cat revealed cracks in my shield. It had triggered a bone-shattering sensation of being set adrift, like when my father died. In that moment, Jewel popped into my life like a rare orchid. An orchid that needed cosseting.

The fact that she was my fiancée's best friend might have stopped a better man, but to me, it only spoke to my predilection for thrill and risk. But first, I had to get Tasa off my tail. I didn't need to see my sister's expression of worry. *Oh, no, here he goes again.* I could practically hear her internal dialogue. Plus, in a big family like mine, nothing stayed secret for long and nothing was sacred.

"I likely won't see her again," I continued, attempting to deflect my sister's attention.

"She's Cat's best friend. Regardless of what happens with your engagement, you'll see her again," Tasa said knowingly.

I was saved from answering by my nephew, who'd woken up. Thank Christ. His eyes blinked up at his mother as she turned the screen toward him so I could see from my phone propped up in the dashboard mount. I was pretty sure the same dazed look of adoration was mirrored on my own face when thinking back to Jewel's face as she was coming. A whole new world had opened for me, and I was ready to grab it with both hands. Unluckily for me, her guilt likely meant she'd blow me off. But I wasn't about to let Jewel's caginess get in my way.

"He's hungry. I have to go and get him his bottle." Tasa swung the phone back to herself. "I'll talk to you later." She paused. "And try not to get into any *more* trouble, yeah?"

I gave her a wide grin. "Sure thing, little sis."

With a last groan, she clicked off. I turned on my bike and rolled down an empty side street onto Broadway and headed downtown to my apartment.

I always broke what I played with as a kid, while Luca preserved his toys with a preciousness that made me gag. I thought he was priggish. He thought I was a brute. He wasn't wrong. I got obsessed and played with the same toy until it broke from overuse. That tendency lived in me, and I feared I might break Jewel. Unfortunately for her, that fear had never stopped me before.

4

JEWEL

I ce-blue eyes stared down at me.

I jolted up in bed, waking up with my hand clutching my chest.

My gaze swiped right, left, right. The room was awash with sunlight coming from the sheer curtains because both my roommate and I loved it that way. Sofia's bed and desk, clean and tidy, mimicked my own side of the room. Drinking in the view of everything in order, blazing in sunlight, relieved me, and I flopped back into bed.

A prickle of awareness tickled down my spine. My eyes darted across the compact dorm room. I had to reaffirm that no one was there. What was this guy doing to me? Nicu was long gone, although his scent still lingered in my bed. There were the unmistakable hints of bergamot from his cologne mixed with his seed, which he'd shot over me and my bed. A moan slipped out as I took a long whiff. I already loved that scent.

I might be alone, but there was no doubt that those were Nicu's eyes, hovering over me. Damn him for infiltrating my sleep. His eyes weren't the color of the brilliantly warm sea off the Greek island where I went on vacation with my parents, either. No, this was a shivery cold tint of blue. I imagined they mimicked the color of an icy sea, like the North Sea. A stunning blue, indeed, but with a distinct chill in it. Better yet, his eyes resembled the Black Sea, which was more fitting since that body of water wrapped around the coast of Romania, where his family hailed from.

I stared at the poster of bell hooks's words of wisdom on the wall beside me. *The moment we choose to love, we begin to move toward freedom* hovered above me. Those words usually gave me solace. But not today. Guilt slammed into me. Today was the first time I woke up haunted by the eyes of a guy I'd just hooked up with. And Nicu wasn't just any guy, either.

He was Cat's fiancé. Cat, my best friend of six years. Cat, my other half. Cat, my savior. I'd been flirting with suicidal thoughts when Mother dumped me at school in the middle of nowhere after the catastrophic year when Dad was arrested and we lost everything. Family, home, life as I knew it. All of it was gone.

Gone.

I clutched the gold medallion hanging from my chain, reminding me that my visit to prison was coming up. Dad had gotten it for my tenth birthday. Inscribed in the center of the medallion was "The Perfect 10," because I was obsessed with gymnastics at the time. I'd gone pro by then, even taking a trip to Texas to the Karolyi Ranch for training. So I was familiar with Romanians even before meeting Cat. After my father's fall from grace, I stopped practicing. I stopped everything. If it hadn't been for Cat...

I slapped my hands over my eyes and groaned. *God, I'm an awful person.* The worst. While I knew my bestie didn't care a fig about Nicu, it was still disloyal. I, better than anyone, knew what it felt like to be betrayed by someone you loved and trusted. It didn't have to be on purpose or targeted for it to have a lasting impact. The only silver lining of this whole mess was that I'd never be foolish enough to go for a guy like Nicu and break my father's cardinal rule: never fall for a criminal. And there was no doubt about Nicu's criminality. Besides being a prince in one of the most notorious crime families in the city, the man oozed savagery.

I rolled over to my side on my narrow twin bed to check my cell for a text from Cat, my head splitting from the movement. I wasn't a big drinker, what with being underage and all. Besides going to bed after three in the morning, the fact that I'd tossed and turned for a long while before falling asleep didn't help matters any.

As I scrolled through my social media for any sign of life from Cat, I shifted my legs and felt a twinge, reminding me of last night. Of how big he was. All over. Of how well he'd taken care of me. Thank God I'd had the presence of mind to kick him out before I got addicted to his mouth and cock. I squeezed my eyes shut. *Shit, who am I kidding?* I was already halfway there.

While poking my phone, a text from Cat came through.

MISSION ACCOMPLISHED, B-YACH.

I let out a sigh of relief and quickly shot off a reply. She'd go on to marry Luca, even if I fucked her cheating-ass fiancé. Guilt doused me like a bucket of freezing-cold water. I had to be the worst friend ever. Normally, I'd text that I'd had someone in my bed as well, and we'd go back and forth, but I couldn't. It was the first time I had to hold something back, and it felt awful. Just awful.

I'd really messed up, but from now on, I would do better. Glancing down at the sheets, I knew I had to get rid of Nicu's scent, a combination of his cologne, his natural fragrance,

and his come, which I'd shamefully but greedily inhaled. I'd
rolled out of bed and grabbed my pillow when the tip of my
big toe butted against something stiff yet silky. I wiggled my
toes and grasped the item beneath my bed. I leaned back
and got a look at the mystery item, already guessing what
it was.

His tie. It was a saturated Egyptian blue that enhanced
the sky-blue topaz color of his eyes. I squeezed my own eyes
shut, trying in vain to block out the image of his as he drove
his cock into me, stretching my tight flesh because I hadn't
had sex in a long time. I remembered the thick slabs of his
pecs moving in sync with his driving hips as he held himself
above me. Or before that, when his head was nestled
between my legs. His grip kept my thighs spread for him to
feast on me, an expression of bliss permeated his face. He
was clearly enjoying himself.

A moan escaped. I bit down on my bottom lip and
grabbed a folder from my desk and began fanning myself
forcefully. It's like he'd put a hex on me the moment he cast
his hauntingly arctic gaze my way. the sexy blue-eyed devil.
When we'd gotten back to my room, he was so damn cocky
that I taunted him to prove himself. And he had. By God,
did he ever. With his tongue and his cock. In fact, I can't
think of a single time a man's cock had pleasured me so well.
He had skills, there was no doubt about that.

And the wanton slut I'd turned into... I distinctly
remember screaming at him to fuck me harder as I
slammed my heels down on his ass to spur him on. I mean,
who was that? I had a normal teenager's appetite, but it had
never been so savage before. I hadn't experienced it yet, but
the kink was there, right under the surface. I saw the way
he'd looked at my bed, his tie hanging from his hand as his
head tilted to the side as if trying to figure out how to tie me

to it. There was no doubt in my mind that, next time, he'd swat my ass. Maybe even with a belt.

Next time. What the hell was I doing? Reminiscing about last night and pining for a "next time." Those thoughts hit me with another wave of guilt. Not only for Cat, but because of my father. Nicu was a criminal. *I repeat, he's a criminal.* I needed to bitch-slap myself back to reality.

The guy had never held down a real job in his life. Not that I was one to talk. Many of the men in the refined society I came from didn't necessarily work. They could if they wanted to, but they didn't have to. And if they did, they usually worked in their family's business. Much like Nicu. *No, not like Nicu!* They directed a hedge fund or managed real estate. They didn't sell weapons to dictators or whatever it was the Romanian *mafie* clans did. And I'd already seen what criminal activities did to families. It destroyed them, that's what it did. I could say, without a shred of doubt, that it had destroyed mine.

A one-time fuck was one thing, but anything else was out of the question. One would think that because my father was currently incarcerated, I might be more understanding, even forgiving, about a man who'd committed crimes as a way of life. The opposite was true. My father lost everything. He lost my mother and his social standing. His partners and closest friends turned against him, going so far as to testify against him during his criminal trial. His life was a cautionary tale. Much like the original Brothers Grimm tales, not the sanitized Disney cartoon version. The real fairy tales were sinister and, at times, gory but with a hard lesson behind them.

With that thought firmly at the forefront of my mind, I dove for the tie. Crushing it in my hands, I tossed it into the small wastebasket underneath my desk. Staring at the offending piece of clothing cradled in a nest of crumpled paper, I felt a sudden sense of glumness. I stood there, moodily contemplating this new feeling as the sounds of the traffic on Broadway drifted in from the windows I'd left open during the night.

I grabbed my robe hanging over the chair at my desk, draped it on, and tied the belt. I'd lost my virginity, but I tended to give relationships a wide berth. That was my MO, so I didn't want to fall for a guy. It must be the incredible sex talking. Maybe it had caused some alterations in my brain chemistry, because I normally flew from intimacy like a bat out of hell.

Anyway, Nicu had to marry a *mafie* princess. Despite the fact that he was pissed when I kicked him out last night, I was deluding myself that he would even approach me for seconds. Unconsciously, my hand dipped into the wastebasket. My fingers clenched around the crushed silk, and I dragged the tie up. Clutching it to my chest, I decided to keep this memento precisely because nothing would ever happen between us again.

That's right. I'd likely never see Nicu again.

I glanced at my bed.

I was still stripping the sheets, though. I wasn't *that* much of a masochist.

5

NICU

My brothers, Tatum (our *consiliere*), and Sebastian (our half brother from a decades-long, illicit affair my father had had with another woman), convened at my penthouse apartment in the Time Warner Center. My father, in his infinite wisdom, had locked down the top floors of both towers when the edifice was being constructed, and split each floor into two apartments. Luca and I shared one floor. Alex and Nina lived in one apartment in the other tower, with Tatum in the penthouse next door.

We used to meet at Alex's place before he and Nina hooked up. This was after years of pining after each other while we all pretended we didn't see anything. Nina was Tasa's best friend and our next-door neighbor in Sunnyside, Queens, so we'd known her most of our lives. She may not have been Romanian *mafie*, but she was practically family.

Once Nina was ensconced in his apartment, Alex got absurdly territorial, so we moved our operations to Luca's apartment. Now that he and Cat had been official for a few short weeks, we'd been kicked out of there as well. His exact words were something to the effect of, "I don't want my fiancée to be inconvenienced by the likes of any of you."

When I asked how the fuck we'd be an inconvenience, his ludicrous answer had been, "She'd have to get dressed, wouldn't she? I like her best naked."

Considering the lengths I'd gone to bring them together, I wasn't about to push back. From the get-go, I'd seen how he reacted to Cat at our engagement party. He bit my head off simply because I didn't agree with him that she was gorgeous and that I was a lucky bastard to have her as my future wife.

After that, I watched carefully. At one point during the weekend, I caught her slipping away to the lower level of his country home, where we'd hosted the engagement party. Luca was working out downstairs in the gym. She'd disappeared for a while and came back upstairs with flushed cheeks, confirming that something was going on between them. Afterward, I went out of my way to ignore her while pushing them together every chance I got.

If Luca was now acting like a possessive dog over a bone, so be it. It was a hundred times better than when I was engaged to her. My penthouse was my comfort zone, so it was a sacrifice to have my brothers trampling around in my space, but it was a price worth paying if it kept Luca and Cat happy and preoccupied.

Preoccupied being the pertinent word here. With eyes on each other, they weren't paying attention to either me or Jewel, thereby giving me space to pursue her. Because our first night together would not be our last, that much I vowed to myself. She'd blown off my texts and calls, so I'd decided to back off and give her time to get over the guilt of fucking me. But I was starting to jones for her like a drug. So I was plotting. Cat and Luca's engagement party was coming up, and she wouldn't be able to get away from me there.

Alex, Luca, and Sebastian had arrived and settled in by the time Tatum showed up. Sinking into one of several leather couches positioned around a coffee table in the sunken area of my living room, he came straight to the point, "We have a problem on our hands."

"What? Another virgin fell for you?" I quipped with a cock of my brow. I'd recently opened an account for him on Insta as a joke, and he took to it like a fish to water, which was surprising because Tatum was notoriously private. But every *mafie* and mafia girl under the sun now followed him. He was fucking perfect, the closest to a hero an impressionable girl in our world could have, dominated as it was by criminality. Add his pristine Anglo looks to the mix, and anytime he posted a selfie, he was inundated with heart and kiss emojis. Pity the guy shied away from being touched.

"Haha. Not funny," he replied. "This is serious, *frate*. Cristo has been 'drunk-grieving' Simu's death. Acting out is not unexpected. Problem is, he's been threatening to retaliate by gutting you."

Taking a sip of my Turkish coffee, I waved away his concern. Tatum focused on the risk in any situation, which was why he was so good at what he did, but I wasn't a daredevil for nothing. I wasn't about to be cowed by Cristo's drunken ravings.

"The rules of engagement are clear, and Simu's death was as clean a kill as they come," I reminded him. "He attacked Luca because his plans to marry Cat and utilize her to become the Popescu *şef* were ruined. He had to be eliminated. End of story. Hell, it's not like Luca didn't put a cleaver in Simu's back right before I shot him between the eyes."

"As true as that may be, Simu was the Popescu *consilier* and Cristo's closest confidant. I'm sure Cristo wants to carve Luca into pieces, but he's off-limits now that he's Cat's fiancé. The man is a prick, but he'd never hurt his sister. Which means his focus has turned entirely on you," elaborated Tatum.

Tatum was rarely wrong. He wasn't wrong this time either, but I just couldn't be bothered every time Cristo had a fit about something. Our rivalry went back years, from the time I'd fucked his girl, Una. Rightly so, he lost his shit. Technically, it wasn't my fault. They'd been on and off for years. Who could keep track? If she wanted to fuck me, I only assumed they were off.

But the shame rose anyway because I'd fucked her during one of my episodes. I was still learning to manage my energy, and during the occasional setback, someone either got fucked or killed. I shrugged. Guess it was lucky she lived, since she was now Stegan's woman. Unfortunately, fucking his girl, inadvertently or not, had solidified Cristo's rage toward me.

"Cristo might talk trash, but he knows better than to touch a hair on my head," I replied.

I got it. Tatum was only doing his job, but I didn't need anyone watching my back. *I* was the protector and enforcer of our family. *I* took care of them, not the other way around. At least, not for years, and I didn't want to go back to those days when they took turns watching me.

Alex spoke. "Nicu, you better not antagonize him unnecessarily. At least, not until the worst of his grief blows over. I know you two constantly needle each other, but that man is in a sensitive place right now. He lost his sister to a man he hates, and he lost his closest friend to his biggest rival. This isn't about beating up a bunch of low-level Popescu soldiers for the sake of riling him up. Simu wasn't just anyone. He was their *consilier*."

I bowed my head in deference to my oldest brother and *șef*.

"Don't get down on Nicu, Alex," piped up Luca in my defense. "That little fucker needs to be taught how to shut his mouth. He can't go around disrespecting a Lupu."

Both my brows lifted. This was a new development. Until recently, the status quo between Luca and me was to fight. Alex had his own problems with Luca, and Tatum stayed out of it as much as he could, only taking Luca's side when Alex and I ganged up on him. I always thought it was to play peacekeeper, but it turned out Tatum had known Luca's secret.

It was a bombshell of a secret. It turned out Luca wasn't our parents' biological son. My mother took Luca in after her beloved sister died giving birth to him. True to form, Mamă loved Luca like her own. My father, though? Not so much. The man I looked up to as a god had tortured my brother, taking out his insecurity about his infertility on his adopted son. None of this made any difference to Alex or me. Mamă made him our brother, and that was enough for us. It had also killed any squabbling between us.

Sebastian asked, "How real is Cristo as a threat if he knows he can't kill Nicu?"

Alex, who had been the first to suggest bringing our half brother into the family business, liked that Sebastian asked questions. It demonstrated his eagerness to learn about the dynamics within our world. Growing up with an American mother and an intermittent Romanian father, he wasn't raised to learn the subtleties of our world.

"If Cristo keeps running his mouth, at some point, we will no longer be able to ignore the disrespect. However, I don't want to have to bring it up with Nelu. He's only going to defend his son, as the future leader of the Popescu clan. With Luca and Cat's wedding coming up, we've finally settled into a productive working relationship. Despite Simu's death, tensions are at their lowest point ever. If I approach him about this, it will only come off as an insult."

My gaze wandered over my apartment, occasionally pausing on different wall hangings and paintings hung throughout the large open space. Although modern, the decoration was the most Romanian-inspired of all my siblings. Looking around, I wondered what Jewel would think. I fully intended to bring her here at some point. The sooner, the better. I wanted to watch her curious eyes alight on different elements in my apartment. Her face had been like an open book the few times she relaxed around me.

I wasn't worried about Cristo. Scratch that. There was one area he could best me in. He could try to seduce Jewel. He couldn't win in a physical fight or a shoot-out, but the man was attractive and could turn on that fake-ass charm of his when he needed to. I never understood it, but then again, I wasn't a woman. And with me accidentally fucking Una, it would be the first thing on his mind.

Alex turned to me with a warning. "Which is why I want you to stay as far away from Cristo as possible. The less you see of each other, the less of a chance you'll provoke each other."

"Bro, Luca's wedding preparations are in full force. Simu shows up at every event along with the rest of his family." I reminded him.

"Then you'll have to work extra hard to avoid him, won't you? If he can't catch you, he can't start a fight, now, can he?"

"Running away?" I grimaced. "That's not my style."

"Your style is confrontation. I'm well aware, thank you.

Let me make myself clear. This isn't a request. It's an order," Alex declared.

"Yes, *şef*," I replied immediately.

What else could I do? It went against my nature, but Alex was right. Avoidance was the best method of handling Cristo, which is why I rarely used it. My MO was usually to encourage him.

"Up until now, you've never given me trouble, Nicu," he continued. It was a point of pride for me, considering what Luca and Tasa had put him through over the years. "Don't start now."

I gave him a firm nod of acknowledgment. I wouldn't let him down.

Alex then turned to Luca. "Moving on... How is the Hagi situation in Cali going?"

"Not great," he grumbled.

We'd recently expanded our operations to Los Angeles. Luca was spearheading the California expansion, but there was a wrinkle in our plans. A previously unremarkable small clan, the Hagi family, took issue with our presence. In their eyes, we were stepping into their territory. We saw ourselves more like the pioneers of old, forging westward. Right or wrong, it wasn't in our interest to recognize anyone's claim on land.

"As you know, last time I was out there, I had meetings with several other *şefs*. They were leaning toward supporting us, but I've had to back off since my focus is on Cat. Peace treaty or not, I don't trust the Popescus. I refuse to leave Cat alone, but I don't think it's safe enough to bring her along with me either. Without face-to-face meetings, the other clans are backsliding to their former position on the Hagi family, which is effectively to allow themselves to be bullied by them. I can't maintain the gains I've made from afar. I need someone out there to regain what's been lost," Luca concluded.

Our eyes naturally turned to Tatum. I wasn't exactly known for my finesse or negotiating skills, and Sebastian was too green to be able to handle such a monumental task alone. Alex was *șef*, so he wouldn't show up until every other option had been exhausted. Having Tatum out of the city would work to my advantage. He didn't know about me and Jewel, but the guy was too smart not to pick up on it soon. This gave me time to pursue her unhindered.

Noticing our stares, he groaned. Tatum was a creature of habit. He didn't seek out different experiences. The idea of traveling to California to wine and dine a series of clan bosses, with a sprinkle of violence mixed in, was most definitely out of his comfort zone. He preferred working behind the scenes, not being the Lupu poster boy.

"Come on, you're good at this kind of shit," I prompted.

"Being good at something and liking it are two entirely different things, and not mutually exclusive," griped Tatum. Being perfect was a hard burden to carry, especially for a purist like him. When I got obsessed with something, I was only interested in excelling at that one thing, while Tatum strove to be the best at everything he did. It was no wonder he was exhausted from the pressure he placed on himself.

"I'll come along," Sebastian suggested, taking a sip of his Turkish coffee. For a man who hadn't grown up in a Romanian household, he certainly took to our traditions with gusto.

I tossed out my hand toward Tatum and said, "There you go."

Tatum looked at Sebastian askance, and I knew exactly what was going through his head. Sebastian wasn't Romanian, and he wasn't *mafie*. Alex had researched Sebastian and our half sister, Emma, extensively before vouching for them. He said he was trusting his gut on this one, which was quite an endorsement. But Tatum was a suspicious man. It went hand in hand with his compulsive perfectionism.

"Yeees," he mused to himself as he eyed Sebastian up and down, calculating his chances of survival by allowing him to tag along.

Leaning back casually into the soft leather cushion, Sebastian was doing surprisingly well under the intense scrutiny. Man-spreading, he looped his arm over the back of the couch, exuding the kind of confidence that came naturally with being an American male. Romanians were confident, but it was a different brand. Toned down and more controlled.

After a few long moments, Sebastian held Tatum's eyes. "So are we good?"

Despite his relaxed tone and posture, there was a challenge in his look and his words.

A tense moment passed between them. Tatum broke the staring contest by turning toward Alex and replied, "Yeah, we're good."

It was a pointed, if silent, statement: *I'll accept you, but ultimately, it's because of my șef. You still need to prove yourself.*

And for Sebastian's sake, I hope he did.

I liked the guy, I did. Besides being sociable, he was quick-witted, even-keeled, and seemed to be loyal. The last had never been tested, so one could only assume, and a made man never made assumptions, especially about something as vital as loyalty. It was one thing to trust a blood relative or a man you've been around your entire life, with families who've known one another since the old country. Sebastian was a half-breed, with one foot in our world and one foot out. But he could be useful for that very reason.

"So it's settled," I concluded with a slap of my knee, grateful I'd gotten out of this chore. "Sebastian goes with Tatum."

Alex pointed his index finger at me. "And you stay away from Cristo."

Not a problem, I thought to myself. I'd put him on the back burner for now. I couldn't pursue Jewel if I was busy fighting Cristo, and there was no doubt the three of us would be present at Luca's engagement party.

6

JEWEL

Fuckity fuck, he's here. Until today, I'd managed to avoid Nicu since that insane all-night fuckfest over a month ago.

He'd texted. I'd ignored him.

He'd called. I'd blocked him.

Cat invited me to places where I suspected Nicu would be, I bowed out, even though it was excruciating. Not only did I already miss her, but Cat was my other half. My better half. For six years, we'd spent every day together, and almost every holiday, since she'd drag me to her family's home like the orphan I was. On my end, I made sure to devote at least part of every summer in the city with Cat, even though I was supposed to spend it wherever Mother was.

I knew our lives would change once we graduated, and I was so happy for her and Luca, but it wasn't easy. Even though we attended the same college, there was no denying that things were different. She lived with Luca. It was doubly, no, triply hard to skip out on spending time with her because I already lost out on not having her around. With the level of shame I felt, it was a sacrifice I had to make. Still worse, I didn't trust myself in Nicu's presence. The man did something to me that was indescribable. I never lost control like I had with him.

Despite my strategy of dodging him for all eternity, there was no way I was missing my best friend's engagement party.

And now, here he was, sauntering into Alex and Nina's brand-new house in the Hamptons for Cat and Luca's engagement party. Time stopped. Everyone around me continued to talk and gesture and sip their champagne, but they receded to the background. They were an array of black, white, and gray, while Nicu glowed from head to toe like he was capped in a halo of gold.

Hot damn, did he look good! My gaze traveled from his dark hair, not one strand out of place, over the crisp, starched white shirt to the classic, three-piece gray suit that fit him like a glove. The diamonds on his cuff links winked at me from across the living room of the beach house, or rather, beach mansion.

It was his eyes that brought the sound of crashing ocean waves to my eardrums. Those crystalline ice-blue eyes pierced right through me, even from a distance. They followed my every move. And the smile that followed...was devastating. *De-va-stat-ing.* God, but he was a deadly threat. His lip twitched as if he was holding back a smile while a woman approached him and lifted onto her toes to skim a kiss over his cheek. His eyes swept over me for a hot moment, that sexy half smile fixed on his mouth. My knees went weak.

His gaze shifted over to the man at my right, Cristo, who I'd totally forgotten was there. Nicu's eyes narrowed on Cristo's hand on my arm. His sexy, enigmatic smile abruptly dropped off. His eyes darkened to a stormy blue, like the sky seconds before a thunderclap that had you diving under the covers. Ah hell, Cat told me about the rivalry between the Popescu and Lupu men.

Cristo had always treated me kindly, although I had a bone to pick with him over his recent treatment of Cat. The Popescus were in financial trouble, and he had convinced Cat to go behind Luca's back to pilfer information that would help them out. It was a sneaky, cruel move that had almost torn the couple apart. But Cat, being Cat, forgave her brother once she and Luca had reunited. I wouldn't be so quick to forgive, but I tended to follow her lead when it came to her world. After what I had done with Nicu, I wasn't exactly one to cast stones.

Whipping around, I strove to ignore Nicu and made it my mission to track down a waiter with a tray of champagne when I heard Cat calling my name. Cringing, I slowly turned my head in her direction. One hand on Nicu's arm, she was all smiles as she motioned for me to join her.

Nicu's eyes burned with unholy glee. Oh, he was going to enjoy this. Sadist.

I scooped up a glass of champagne, holding the flute so tightly that I feared the glass would shatter as I dragged myself in their direction.

"Jewel, come here. You remember Nicu, don't you? He drove you home from the club that one night," my bestie said.

"Yes, of course," I gritted out between the fakest smile I could force onto my face.

Having clearly recovered his poise, he took my hand in his, very gallant-like, and murmured, "Lovely Jewel. How could anyone forget? Of course, I remember you."

Grrr!

His falseness made me want to wrap my hands around

his throat and throttle him. He was mocking me with over-the-top courteousness. He may have tried to contact me, but I knew it was nothing more than a booty call. After our tempestuous night together, I'd subtly questioned Cat about her soon-to-be brothers-in-law and learned Nicu was a notorious player. He didn't do relationships. It was either a one-night stand or an engagement to a *mafie* girl. Nothing in between.

As much as my body hankered to rub against him like a cat in heat, I wouldn't betray my friend again. Especially for a guy who had no interest in me beyond casual sex. With my bestie getting married to the love of her life, I was surprisingly, and for the first time in my life, eyeing men for more than a romp in the sack. Either way, Nicu was off-limits. And it would behoove me to remember that I was off-limits to him as well. We may fuck like energizer bunnies, but I wasn't a *mafie* princess, and a *mafie* princess was what he'd have to marry.

He gave me a quick wink as Cat's mother touched her shoulder, distracting her attention from us with a question.

First chance I had, I was going to kill him.

Turning back toward us, Cat suggested, "Nicu is going to be Luca's best man, and you're the maid of honor, so you guys should get to know each other."

My face paled.

"Oh, that's great," I forced out. *God, please no.* "That's so... I'm so glad for the chance to get to know you better," I purred insincerely. *Like hell, I am.*

"Yes," Cat said with a sage nod of her head. "You guys will be thrown together a lot. I mean, we know my mother is in charge, but the bachelor and bachelorette party will be yours. There will be speeches at the rehearsal dinner and toasts at the wedding," she ended with a clap of her hands.

"Can't wait," murmured Nicu. His smile had returned, although this one was more like a cat licking cream off his chops.

Another woman came up to Cat with a squeal. Nicu shifted his body to grab an hors d'oeuvre from the table behind me and whispered in a low voice, "Meet me outside. The stairwell by the kitchen."

He straightened in time to get the full force of my glare. *Not happening*, I silently communicated with my lips.

Cat was too busy listening to her friend to overhear his murmured threat. "Do it or I tell Cat."

"Fine," I snarled at him and stomped away before I was tempted to crack my hand across his cheek.

I made him wait a good quarter of an hour to teach his bossy ass a lesson before I inched toward the exit, inspecting the crowded room to determine that no one had noticed me, and ducked out into the hallway. I hurried down the empty corridor, doing my best to not *click-clack* my heels too loudly against the marble mosaic flooring.

I pushed the door at the end of the hall open and found myself outside, greedily inhaling the salty sea air through my nostrils. I followed the length of the house to the kitchen entrance. He was already there, waiting, his broad back to me. He whirled around at the sound of my steps, and I forgot to breathe for a moment. He was tall, so much taller than me, with shoulders that seemed to go on for miles and block out the setting sun behind him. I took a deep inhalation and instantly regretted it when I was assaulted by his delicious scent.

Shaking the fog of lust threatening to drown me, I skipped the pleasantries and hissed out, "Blackmail doesn't suit you."

"It does if I get what I want," he replied smugly.

God, I wanted to hurt him. Smack. Hit. Punch. Any one of those would do to wipe the arrogant smirk off his gorgeous face. My gaze dropped to his sculpted lips, one side quirked up sardonically, as usual. The top one was plumper than the bottom by a smidge, and I recalled how pillowy soft they felt on mine and all the ways he used them, along with his talented tongue, to make me come.

"Thinking about anything in particular?"

His words snapped me out of my reverie. My eyes lifted to his, where he watched me with an all-too-knowing look I deeply resented.

"Shut up," I snapped.

Not my best comeback, not by a mile. His diabolical smile only broadened.

"Now that you got me here, what do you want? I have an engagement party to get back to."

His hand snaked up my arm, leaving goose bumps in its wake, and yanked me up the flight of stairs going to a balcony above the kitchen. Pushing open a set of French doors, he pulled me into a large, well-appointed library.

"You didn't respond to my texts. Or my calls. No one ignores me, Jewel," he warned.

"You already had me once," I rushed out. "I asked Cat about you, and I know about your reputation. I'm not about to be your side whore."

I tried to shake him off, but his hold only tightened. Frowning down at his grip, I went on, "Even if you wanted more, I can't violate Cat's trust again. It wasn't right the first time, and nothing's changed that."

I kept the fact that he was a bad guy to myself. I wasn't about to divulge my family history to him.

His fingers coasted farther up along my shoulder and curled around my nape. My eyes briefly fluttered closed.

Fuck, his touch felt good. Strong, demanding, controlled, yet with an inexplicable undercurrent of wildness. Everything about it made my heart sing and my body melt. He gripped me by the shoulders and tugged me close until his lips were a hair's breadth away from mine. Small puffs of air feathered over my skin, bringing back a cascade of memories from our night together.

"Normally, one time is just right. With you, it seems once is not nearly enough. As for Cat, everything has changed. She's no longer engaged to the wrong man. Instead, she's going to marry the right one. We're their best man and maid of honor, for fuck's sake."

A shudder racked my body. He felt it and wrapped his arms around me, drawing me deeper into his embrace. His lips pressed against mine. Firm. Not demanding. Not yet. Too bad, because I melted when he got controlling and took what he wanted. I felt the slight tremble as he held still, grappling with his self-restraint. Considering I'd already been ravished by him, I admired the story his self-control told me. He was trying to respect me by giving me a choice.

I slid my palms up his chest. God, what a chest. My breathing picked up. What was I doing? I should be stepping away from him. Fleeing the scene as if a murder had been committed. Instead, my hands followed the chiseled outline of his pecs.

No, no, no. Cat, remember Cat. I still felt fiercely loyal to her and guilty for what I had done, but she was the happiest I'd seen her in her life, so that wasn't working quite as well as before. *Criminal, remember, he's a criminal.* Yes, that was more like it. It was like a splash of cold water in the face.

I shoved down the desire to explore and pressed hard, demanding space from him.

With a belabored sigh and a flick of his tongue that had

me cursing my choice, he put a minuscule amount of distance between us. His palm slid up my spine and took hold of my nape. His fingers threaded into my hair, tangling in the long strands. Pulling my head back, he stared into my eyes, delving deep. So deep I feared there wasn't a corner of my soul left unexposed for his perusal.

"You're scared," he declared, followed by a tsking sound as if he wanted to comfort me.

I clenched my jaw. "Of course, I'm scared. Cat's my best friend, and while she may now be marrying Luca—"

"The love of her life," he added.

"—she was engaged to you when you...when we...when you and I—" I cut myself off, snapping my mouth shut, refusing to let the words tumble out.

"Fucked?" he offered succinctly.

I ground down on my back teeth, a bonfire of fury simmering in my belly. "Yes, that. I messed up once, but I can*not* do it again. Out of the question."

"I admire your tenacity and your loyalty. Loyalty is necessary in our world."

"I'm not in your world," I huffed, ignoring the frustrating shrug of his shoulders that said, "You say tomato, I say tomahto." "And don't mock me by calling me that. I *betrayed* her."

He tugged my head back hard, eliciting a gasp from me.

"Hey," he snapped. "We were engaged in name only. We never spent time together. I never touched her. She and Luca were in love from the instant they met each other. She and I meant *nothing*."

"You think saying that makes what we did okay? Also, I saw the way you treated her—more like *ignored* her—and it didn't endear you to me. Which brings up another thing... You're not even my type. For one thing, you're *mafie*. I hate your world and its backward traditions, like the blood bond. I should be with a nice guy. I *deserve* to be with a nice guy, a safe guy, and that will never be you."

"Baby doll, I may not be a nice guy, but have no doubt, I'm *exactly* your type. You fucking *melt* under my touch. Don't try to deny it, or I'll slip my hand down your panties right this instant and prove you wrong."

Oh, God. He knew. He absolutely knew that our little spat made me wet. I'd never met a man so wrong for me, yet who turned me on so badly. Even worse, I knew he was a man who did bad things, but the truth was that everything he did—his touch, his nickname for me, even the dirty words that slipped out of his cruel mouth—made me turn to liquid. He'd snuffed out my anger like a tiny flame between his long, slim fingers, reducing me to a pile of mush.

But the way we'd hooked up had been wrong, and there was no moving on from that awful mistake.

I had to deflect his charm and try to save myself. I had to fight the good fight, so I lied, "Ugh, that nickname. Why do you call me baby doll? It's godawful. I'm a grown woman. It's terrible, just terrible."

His voice dropped. "Oh, believe me, I'm well aware that you're grown." His hand slid down to cup my ass. *Oh, shit.* "I call you baby doll because that's what you are to me. When Luca and I were kids, we'd get the same toys, even though we were five years apart. No idea why, other than that Mamă always thought we should be treated equally."

His eyes darkened to that scary "thunder in the sky" color as he stared off into the distance. "Maybe because our father treated him differently."

He shook his head and was back with me. "Anyway...he would treasure his. He'd take care of his toy, play with it gently, and return it to its original packaging afterward, to preserve it. Meanwhile, I would wreck mine within the hour, using and abusing it as if it were made of steel." One side of his mouth quirked up at the memory.

"But you, you're the most beautiful thing I've seen," he confided in a low, gravelly tone. His eyes glided down my body, leaving it tingly as if he'd touched me with a gentle caress. "For the first time, I want to treasure something as precious as you. You are a jewel, and just for once, I don't want to break it. I want to keep it near and coddle it."

My core melted. He touched me in places that my soul hadn't been touched since Dad was taken away from Mother and me.

He touched my cheek, letting his fingers ripple along my jawline and down my throat. Collaring me, he continued, his voice turning rough, "And fuck you like you're my toy. A toy I want to treat oh so right." His fingers slid down to cup my breast, his thumb rubbing my nipple. "I want to—no, need to—hear you scream my name again while you come on my cock. It's non-fucking-negotiable, Jewel. I *need* it. I need you."

He walked me back into the wall, letting me feel his hard cock against my belly. "The mask you show the world is of a strong woman, but with me, you can be a pampered little doll." His hands fell to my waist. "Let me take care of you. Pull down your panties, lift you up, and settle you on my cock. Bounce you up and down like the precious little fuck-doll you are, while you claw my back with your tiny nails and bite my neck until you scream out your release."

By now, my chest was heaving up and down, rubbing against him with every elevation and descent.

"You'd like that, wouldn't you?" he mused.

I was a red-blooded woman, wasn't I? I'd had his cock. I

was well aware of what it could do. They were things no man had done to me before.

His lips were on my battering pulse at the base of my throat, and moans were coming out of my mouth as I rubbed against him frantically. Fuck, I wanted him. Fuck, fuck, FUCK! He knew I was weak when it came to him.

I couldn't. I couldn't do this again. It was one thing to mess up once. I was barely over it, but to do it twice was really bad. Plus, the irrevocable fact that he would always be a mob guy. It wasn't only in his family; it was in his blood. His lips had turned to teeth, and he was sucking my flesh into his mouth, probably leaving a mark on purpose, the fucker.

"Stop," I threw out. My hands came up and clutched at his shirt. I was weak, so weak, but I had to be strong.

"Stop," I begged again, my voice husky.

He gave a last nip before pulling away and slapping a hand against the wall beside my head. Frustration wafted off him. His eyes were wild. God, I loved seeing him undone. His biceps bulged against the fabric of his jacket as he raked his fingers through his perfectly coiffed hair, leaving it looking just fucked. This was how I liked him best. With his iron-clad restraint slipping.

If I was his doll, then he was my beast. Wild, untamed, and savage. I liked it too much, which meant I could fall for this guy. He was right when he said he was my type of guy. I *should* want a nice guy, a guy that didn't come from a complicated family and an even more complicated world. But he was the guy that made my skin crackle, that made me feel alive.

Which meant I had only one choice.

To shut it down.

7

NICU

I admired Jewel's fighting spirit. It spoke to her integrity and, most importantly, her loyalty. She said it didn't matter because she wasn't in my world. I didn't bother correcting her that she wasn't of my world *yet*.

But it was too soon to say such a thing, even if it was the truth. Fucking Jewel the night I met her had created an unnecessary complication, triggering her guilt over betraying Cat. Most people didn't fuck with them. Normally, I was one of those people, but I was learning that some complications were worth it.

Because of those complications and her staunch rejection of my texts and calls, there'd been the slim chance that I might let her go. Granted, "letting go" was not my strong suit, but the possibility had been there. That had vanished, *poof*, the moment I laid eyes on her again. Because seeing her had brought a tsunami of need to the forefront. Need I'd thought I had successfully battled down. Apparently not.

I was like a drug fiend. I couldn't go back to being satisfied with spying on her from the street corner, the rooftop across from her building, or from a few glimpses of her crossing Broadway to attend her classes. I couldn't exactly melt in with the students, especially at Barnard, which was a women's college.

When my gaze fell on her glossy chocolate-brown tresses, the ones she'd flung over her shoulder, when my eyes locked on her multi-colored ones, my insides twisted up. Right then and there, something shifted in my chest and clicked into place. Like the final missing piece of a puzzle jiggled into place, I was now complete.

Jewel was the missing piece.

I knew it in my gut.

She stared up at me as if I were the devil incarnate. Her mouth spewed nonsense about how we could never repeat what happened a month ago. Her eyes flitted around nervously, avoiding my gaze. Meanwhile, her nails dug deeper into my shirt, little half moons pressing into my skin, signaling her inner conflict. She didn't want to want me, but she did. I'd take mercy on her this time, but there was no way I was letting her go long term. Her fate was sealed.

I've never wanted a woman before. Now that I wanted one, I was going to have her. No matter what. Arranged marriage, be damned. That last thought shook me. Outside of racing or other daredevil activities, I was a stringent enforcer of the rules of our culture. I was a conundrum: an enforcer addicted to the adrenaline high. What people didn't see was that both were flip sides of the same coin: control. What I loved best was the challenge of controlling the uncontrollable. It never got old. It was the same with Jewel; she was a sassy whirlwind who'd constantly keep me on my toes.

Like watching her flirt with Cristo in front of me. I'd struggled with my temper and retaliated by bumping shoulders with Cristo as I passed him on my way out of the party.

He'd followed me out, slamming me against the wall of the hallway and hissing, "If you think I'll let you have whatever you want when I've lost everyone to your clan, Una, Simu, my sister to that brother of yours, you've got another think coming."

I shoved him off me, got in his face, and threatened, "Try me, motherfucker. I'm ready for you. Any time. Any day." I stalked off before we got into a fight at my brother's party and because I wasn't about to miss my rendezvous with Jewel over that worthless idiot. That interaction was a good reminder that Cristo would always be a thorn in my side. Not a threat. A threat was going too far, but always a thorn, which brought me to something that needed to be addressed with Jewel immediately.

Gazing down at her nails digging into me, I demanded, "What's going on between you and Cristo?"

Her nose crinkled in distaste. "Nothing. I've known him for years. We flirt casually, but nothing's going on. He's a player and he's *mafie*. Nothing would ever happen between us."

"Better keep it that way," I warned, my body vibrating with tension.

Her palm slapped against my chest. I huffed out a laugh, her slap having knocked the anger out of me. Fuck, I liked it too much when she defied me. My dominant nature rose to the challenge.

"Dude, you have no say in who I hang out with or who I bang."

I swiped her hand off me and twirled her around, pushing her front up against the wall.

Pressing my forearms on either side of her, I caged her in and growled, "Listen and listen good, Jewel, because I'm not fucking around. Cristo and I have had beef since I can remember. I killed their *consilier*. Cristo always despised me, but his hatred has increased tenfold since Simu's death."

I dug my hard cock into the small of her back and murmured in her ear, "I saw the way he looked at you, flirted with you. He wants you, and if he gets a whiff of anything between us, he'll work twice as hard to take you from me. Let me make this point crystal-fucking-clear: he can't have you. You're mine. Got that?"

She pushed her luscious ass back into me, making me groan.

"Ugh, you're such a bossy asshole. I don't want any part of your stupid *mafie* world, much less to get in the middle of a pissing contest between you two idiots. He can't have me, but not because of *you*. I'd never mess around with Cat's brother. It's bad enough that I had sex with you, but it won't happen again. I already told you I hate everything about your life. You guys are insane."

Her head whipped around, her gaze drilling into mine.

"How can you stand it?" she asked.

She squirmed against my cock until I eased up on her. With the little amount of space I gave her, she turned around and faced me, a little furrow hovering between her brows. Damn, she looked cute with that confused expression on her face.

She shook her head. "I don't understand. What good is there in any of it?"

I huffed out a soft laugh. "There's never been an easier question to answer. One word, Jewel. Family. Sure, I like the thrill of what you call 'insane,' but at the end of the day, it's about my family. My clan. These are my people, and I will do anything, *anything*, to protect them, to see them prosper and grow."

"Family," she repeated bitterly, her lovely eyes cast downward.

The sounds of crashing waves from the shore of the beach came through the open French windows.

I cupped her cheek. "Doll, not every family is like yours. My family is the best. My mother is a saint. She's done things for us you couldn't begin to imagine. *Bunică*, my grandmother, is a strong woman, more intelligent than any man I know and with a wicked sense of humor to boot. And Tasa...well, besides being my twin, she's a talented dancer, a doting mother and wife, and my other half."

I placed my hand between her bouncy breasts, moving it slightly to the left until I felt the strong beating of her heart. "Then there are my brothers and Tatum. Alex sacrificed his life for me, my siblings, and our clan. I would never leave him to bear the burden of leading us alone, especially after what he's had to forfeit to raise us right. Luca is the biggest pain in the ass, but he's also taken hits for this family like no one else. Tatum is everyone's best friend, and hell, Sebastian and Emma are the only ones to keep us sane because they're only half Romanian. I haven't begun to mention the rest of our clan. Each one of us would do anything for the another. We are one another's rock."

And you will be part of this family one day.

The last part I kept to myself. The pain and vulnerability in her eyes made me want to punch a hole in a wall. What kind of fucked-up head trip had her parents done to her that she was so wary, so suspicious of family.

Family was everything.

And now Jewel was part of my everything.

"When you talk like that, you almost turn me into a believer," she murmured.

"Damn straight," I replied, brushing my lips against her

soft ones. She made a disgruntled noise and made to turn away, but I gripped her throat and warned, "Stop. Just stop fighting me for a minute."

Her constant pulling away was beginning to irritate me. I knew she felt guilty, but my patience snapped, and I slipped my hand between her thighs. Scorching heat greeted my questing fingers.

She groaned but, this time, didn't retreat or push me away. That was all the incentive I needed. We were alone, everyone too busy downstairs at the party to interrupt us or even miss us yet. Not about to waste a perfect opportunity, I slid my hand past the silk gusset of her panties and speared her cunt, spreading her slippery lips wide with my invasion. Her breathing accelerated. She arched her back in a silent plea, writhing against my hand and pushing my fingers deeper. Her inner muscles squeezed around my digits. Goddamn, I loved the way Jewel reacted to me.

"How long has your pussy been wet for me, baby doll?" I demanded, letting my other hand wrap around the garter at her thigh.

I snapped it, and she jerked against me. My blood was running hot. "You're my dirty little fuckdoll, aren't you?"

She moaned, but that wasn't what I was looking for.

I tightened my grip. "Aren't you?"

"Yes," she rasped out in a husky tone.

"I want to hear those exact words come out of your pretty mouth. *Say it*," I commanded. I was laying my dominance on thick, but I didn't care. This is what she needed. What I needed. Fuck, did I need it. In our time apart, my energy was getting scattered, my ADD worse. Unless I was stalking her, because then, all my focus was on Jewel. Only Jewel.

"I'm your dirty little fuckdoll," she husked out. Her eyes flashed. "Satisfied?"

"Fuck yeah, I am," I lied. I wasn't close to satisfied, but it would do for now. I'd be marginally satisfied when I had my tongue licking her sweet cunt and her lips screaming my name.

"If you're really my filthy little girl, prove it," I tested her.

Ravenous, I watched every distinct emotion flitter across her face. Lust battled fear as her eyes flicked to the closed door before returning to me. I kept my expression stony, demanding. She licked her full lips nervously, leaving them glossy and bright.

"How?" she breathed out.

I released her thigh and captured a stiff nipple, rubbing it between my broad fingertips over the slippery fabric of her dress, all the while keeping my fingers pumping in and out of her pussy. She bucked against me, reminding me that my girl liked a bite of pain with her fucking. My jaw went tight. It turned her the fuck on when I got demanding, urging me to let my roughness loose on her.

"Turn around," I gritted out, sadly retracting my fingers from paradise, eager to watch her follow my command.

With one last quick glance at the door, she slowly turned for me, dropping her head forward in compliance. Christ, this girl's submission had my strangled cock fighting my boxer briefs.

"That's my good girl," I breathed into the curve of her ear.

My fingers traced the edge where her dress met her silky skin a few times before latching onto the zipper and ever so slowly dragging it down the length of her back. It parted and dipped to the sides, exposing her delicate shoulder blades and the bumps of her spine. She wasn't wearing a bra. Dirty girl.

Pushing the straps off her shoulders, her dress slunk to the ground, leaving her in only a black silk thong. She arched her back for me, spreading her ass cheeks enough to show me the string nestled between two gorgeous globes of jiggling flesh.

Holy Christ, have mercy on me.

I dropped to my knees and took a bite out of one ass cheek before making it better with a long lave of my tongue. Her rosewater taste lingered on my taste buds. I couldn't wait till I had my entire mouth on her, sucking her essence down. Yanking off my jacket, I flung it off and loosened my tie. Once comfortable, I was determined to take my time and relish this. I gently hooked my fingers into the sides of her panties and dragged them down her thighs. I lifted one foot, then the other, whisking the panties away. There she was, standing tall in all her naked glory in front of me.

Gripping her hips, I placed her exactly how I wanted her, like the baby doll she was. Bent over, forearms planted on the wall, with her pussy spread out for me like an Easter feast after a midnight mass marathon. This moment felt every bit as sacred.

I began teasing her lips with my fingers, praising her, "Look at this pretty pink pussy you have spread out for me. You ready for me to feast on it, little one?"

A full-body shudder racked her lithe frame.

"Yes, please," she scratchy voice pleaded.

"So polite," I chided. "Since you're being so good, ask me properly to feast on this pussy."

"Please, Nicu," she whined.

I hardened my tone. "Do it."

"Please, please, *please* feast on my pussy," she begged,

winding her luscious hips in my face. Her pleading words, following my demand to a T, clicked everything in place. My energy streamlined like a fast-running river, crystal-clear and smooth.

Her ass cheeks bounced, and I slapped one hard. She yelped, biting her lip to stifle the curse she was about to let drop.

"Don't try to tempt me, siren, or I'll walk out of here and leave this pussy weeping. *I'm* in charge," I mock-snapped, giving the front of her pussy a sharp tap from between her spread thighs. "That's a lesson you need to learn immediately."

She let out a desperate mewl, but I ignored her. "*Înțelegi?* Understand?"

"Yes," she gasped, her head popping back to look at me. Her face was flushed, eyes alight with a mixture of rage and lust run rampant.

I gave her a brisk nod. "Since you've asked so nicely and this pussy is such a needy little thing..." I leaned in and gave it a long lick, from end to end. Her head fell back, long dark tresses tickling my forehead, and she let out a long, desperate moan.

"Fuck, that feels good."

The door to the kitchen below us smacked against the brick wall as it opened. It was a reminder that we weren't far from a party in full swing.

Making a shushing noise to remind her to stay quiet, I gave her another lick and murmured quietly, "What about this?"

Parting her lips for better access, I knifed my tongue inside. Her inner muscles spasmed around the thick muscle buried deep. Then I leaned into my task, tongue-fucking her with relish.

While I mostly went down on women to prep them for my cock, like last time I'd tasted Jewel, this one was pure selfishness. Her scent and taste intoxicated me, a honeyed mixture of sugar and roses, like *cozonac*, the sweet bread baked with bits of Turkish delight, or *rahat*, that we ate at Christmas and Eastertime.

I found my rhythm, grinding my face in her pussy, licking her in and out, nipping and sucking, only pulling away as she was about to climax.

After backing off a third time, 'cause my girl was quick to come, I decided to heed her when she complained. "Dammit, Nicu. Enough already."

What could I say? *I love tonguing your sweet-tasting pussy so much I don't want you to come.*

I shoved a couple of fingers into her, thrusting fast. As she was about to come again, I stood quickly, gripped her chin, and pushed my glistening fingers in her mouth.

Her eyes flared wide.

"You take what I give you without complaint. The only words out of your mouth should be *thank you, Nicu.* You'll come when I say," I declared.

It might seem harsh, but she had to learn who was the boss. I didn't know what kind of American pussies she'd been with, but I was Romanian and a *mafie* prince, at that. She had to learn that unless I was punishing her for insubordination, my principal goal was always her pleasure.

My grip remained firm on her chin as I pulled my fingers from her throat.

Her eyes flashed as she taunted, "If you can't finish me off, I can always go to Cristo."

Flashing lights and blaring sirens exploded in my head. I saw red. *This brat.* She thought she could kick up my jealousy to make me do what she wanted. Problem was, she was right. "Try it over my dead fucking body."

Picking her up, I stalked across the library and dropped her on the chaise-lounge. I dropped to my knees and sunk my teeth into the soft flesh of her inner thigh as a reprimand for provoking me. She let out a yelp, and I planted my face in her spun-sugar pussy, attacking her with my tongue and teeth. I could've fucked her by now. There was no doubt she'd let me, but I chose to hold back. After throwing Cristo in my face, I'd make sure she came so hard she'd get wet anytime she thought of me.

With my hands full of her juicy ass, I buried my face so that there was nothing between her and my thrusting tongue and suctioning lips. She rubbed against my mouth, nose, and chin, taking what she needed. Shoving my hard cock against the cushion below me, I humped the chaise-lounge as she kept grinding and working for her orgasm. As I'd commanded, my name dropped from her lips, each time a little louder, until it was one, long screeching chant as she peaked.

"Oh my God, N-Nicu, Nicu, *Nicu!*"

I shushed her, checking the partially open French doors, but there was no denying that my chest exploded with pride as this beautiful doll of mine flooded my tongue. The brute in me clamored to tear its way out and rut her into the ground, but I locked my shit down and licked and suckled until she slowly came down from her high.

Panting above me, her hand jerkily flung out to the side. Her chest rose and fell like bellows. I placed a chaste kiss on top of her mound in reverence. Her muscles tensed slightly, and I knew reality would soon set in. Jewel would snap her eyes open to find herself naked at her best friend's engagement party with her bestie's ex-fiancé between her creamy thighs. She'd freak out, run away, and avoid me for the rest of the party.

My baby doll was predictable like that. I'd allow her to *believe* she'd escaped me. With a hundred guests downstairs and a multitude of people to hide behind, I'd let her throw up the distance she sought to erect between us.

I could be magnanimous and give her the space she was so desperate for, considering she'd just creamed on my mouth, and I had every intention of being back in her life soon enough.

8

JEWEL

I opened my eyes, only to be blinded by the bright, morning light gushing through the window beside my bed. Throwing my pillow over my face, I let out a groan.

Today was visitation day.

Moments later, my roommate's alarm blared out a maniacal bleating sound that made me want to smash it to pieces with my biology book. Apparently Sofia felt the same way because her hand snaked out from under her covers and smacked the top as she attempted to put it out of its misery. One inadvertent swipe of her arm, and the clock was swept off her night table, smacking hard against the wooden floor and finally stopping its incessant racket.

"Thank God," she muttered, turning over and snuggling back under the covers.

Rubbing my eyes, I sat up in bed. I'd give her another fifteen minutes before I attempted to wake her up again. I swear the alarm was more for me than her. She banked on the fact that I would most definitely be awake and give her a few extra minutes before prodding her to get up. Sofia was not a morning person. I had lucked out, having her as my roommate. She had roomed with me in the summer, when we both stayed on campus to take classes, and now again for the academic year.

Super smart and hardworking, Sofia was a native New Yorker like me, although she grew up in a predominantly Dominican neighborhood in East Harlem. Unlike the girls I grew up with, she and Cat didn't judge me for having a father in jail. Like Cat, who'd had relatives in prison, Sofia had a first cousin in Rikers Island. Now, that was a real hellhole.

I tiptoed around quietly, gathering what I needed to take a shower, and softly closed the door behind me. Once I was back from the bathroom and dressed, I woke her up.

Stretching, she picked up her cell phone to shoot a text to her little sister, whom Sofia followed carefully. Once done, she tossed her phone on her night table, wrapped her arms around her bent knees, and asked, "Today's the day, right?"

"Yup," I mumbled out.

Today was the day I went to visit my father upstate at Otisville Prison Camp, a minimum-security prison for nonviolent, mostly white-collar criminals.

"Want me to come along?" she asked.

My brows rose at that one. Cat had once asked me the same thing, which was more proof that Sofia was a good egg.

And I replied to her the same way I did to Cat all those years ago. "No, I'd rather go alone. I appreciate the offer, though."

I didn't want to mention I might not even see Dad today. On more than one occasion, I'd made the trek up there and been told that visitation had been rescinded due to behavioral problems. It was wrong and irrational, but I hated him a little bit on those days. Not only had he broken our family and landed in jail, but then he couldn't keep it together to make sure that I saw him?

It was tough, the seesaw emotions of having an incarcerated parent, because I knew it wasn't easy for him in there. My father was a proud man. He was independent-minded and used to being in control of his life, the two things that were automatically taken away when you became part of the prison system. The movies that showed inmates living a life of leisure were depicting a thing of the past, if it had ever existed. My father had dropped twenty pounds in the first month because the quality of the food was so awful, and it wasn't only because he was used to eating like a king. He never did gain them back, either.

And I couldn't even complain when he was guilty of the crimes he was accused of, ruining the lives of thousands of people. His situation was considered a luxury compared to most other prisons, like where Sofia's cousin was doing time.

"Alright," she said. "But if you change your mind, I'm ready to go."

"Thanks." I smiled and gave her a quick hug.

We both had early morning classes. Afterward, she would leave campus to spend the weekend with her family, coming back on Sunday after church.

"Text me when you're done with your visit, you hear me, *chica*?" she commanded as her dark eyebrows lowered into a serious expression. "If you're feeling down or whatever, I'll come and hang out with you tonight. I know Cat's busy, and I don't want you to be alone if you're bummed out."

"I've been through it enough times to know the drill. I'll be okay, Sofia," I promised.

I pulled the door open and stepped out as Sofia called out after me, "Text me or I'll hunt you down!"

With a last wave goodbye, I closed the door behind me.

I PASSED a court of middle-aged men playing handball, dressed in white shirts and khaki pants, and walked up to a dreary beige-colored building that housed the inmates. Like every other Friday afternoon when I came to visit my father, I drove eighty miles north of the city and turned into the now-familiar two-mile road up to the parking lot. The first and only time I came here with Mother, I'd been frightened as our car swerved around the sharp curves of the thick forested road. Now, I could appreciate the scenery, with its pop of color in the autumn leaves.

Going through security was always a hassle, but at least Dad hadn't misbehaved, because they let me through. I let out an involuntary breath of relief, remembering the many times I'd reached the end of the line only to be turned away because his visitation had been pulled. The fact that it crushed a teenager coming to visit her only father was a nonfactor. Family unity wasn't high on the list of priorities for the U.S. Bureau of Prisons, I thought angrily.

After so many years, it was still a shock whenever I entered the visitors' room. Everything, and I meant everything, was painted a variation of the color gray. It was as if they'd brought in a decorator to create the most depressing room possible for the reunification of families. The floor and walls were a light gray while the doors, tiny window frames, and bolted-down tables and stools were a darker gray. I watched the other partners, spouses, and children greet their loved ones as I waited in the drab room.

My father stepped inside, wearing the requisite forest-green outfit, shirt buttoned up and tucked inside his pants, fastened with a cheap belt. His head was neatly shaved, as per regulation. Even though this was a minimum-security facility, my father never completely let down his guard, although his hazel eyes warmed upon spotting me.

He gave me a brief hug, all that was allowed, before sliding onto a metal stool across from me.

"Hey, sweet pea. How are you doing?" he asked, using the nickname he'd had for me since I was a little kid. My throat clenched tight. I never had the adolescent acting-out phase that usually stamped out the usage of such childhood nicknames between child and parent. Once he was gone, Mother dumped me at boarding school, and I had to grow up fast.

I swallowed hard and gave him a bright smile. "School started a few weeks ago. I like my classes. My roommate is cool. She's the same one I had during the summer. Oh, and Cat started as well. She got wait-listed, so she didn't learn until just before school started that she was accepted, but we're together again," I finished in a rush.

It was sometimes awkward to recap my life to my dad in a few sentences. One would think I should've been used to it, but Otisville was an artificial setting, and nothing could change the harsh reality of that fact. He had access to call me collect, but he rarely used it, preferring to wait for me to visit to talk. It was frustrating that he should be stubborn about communication, but I reminded myself that he must have his reasons. Perhaps our calls were recorded. Either way, it was one of the many reasons why I never missed a visit.

"See the guy to your left, two tables away?" my father said suddenly.

I angled my head slightly and spotted the table he indicated.

"Wide receiver for the Giants."

"No," I said in a low hush.

"Yes, and the guy two tables to the left is a rapper. Nicest guy you'll ever meet. More importantly, move up one table toward us, and check out the man with the graying crew cut."

I turned my head slightly and squinted just enough to see a middle-aged man with graying short hair gesticulating wildly with his hands.

"Yes?"

"One of my old associates. Total dick. The US Attorney finally nabbed him for insider trading. God knows he'd been getting away with it for decades. Like I've told you in the past, you always get what's coming to you. Thought I'd at least get away from the assholes so far away from everything." He shook his head sadly. "No such luck."

My heart fluttered with fear. Not sure what to say, I remained silent.

"The guy plagues me, talking on and on. I know life is dead boring on the inside, but he's making my life hell."

He slitted his eyes in the man's direction, as if plotting his death.

"Don't," I said. My father's crimes were financial, but there'd been some witness tampering and threatening that had led to a hung jury at his first trial, so I knew there was more than meets the eye. And seeing this side of him, the possibility of what he was capable of, frightened me.

"What?" he replied innocently.

As if.

My dad may be many things. He may be charming, wickedly intelligent, and still handsome, but he would never be innocent. I didn't think he'd take a hit out on the guy or anything that drastic, but he could still do underhanded, conniving stuff.

"Whatever it is you're thinking of doing, don't do it. Tell him to leave you alone. Be up-front and honest about your needs and leave it at that," I advised. "Because if you get caught, like you said, you'll pay the price." *And so will I.* His incarceration was a price I was continuing to pay as well. Absent father. Absent mother. Broken family. A bitterness coated my throat, and I swallowed it down, as I always did. Who was there to show it to? My father was in jail, and Mother erratically flittered in and out of my life like a butterfly with damaged wings.

His eyes slanted away from me to the man for a long moment, as if weighing the options of how to get rid of him. Finally, they returned to me, and he resumed our prior conversation, "I'm glad to hear you and Cat are together, at least. It must be a relief to have your best friend with you. I'm surprised she isn't your roommate. Is she living in the same dorm as you?" he asked.

"No, she's actually engaged and living with her fiancé off campus," I replied.

"I thought you said her engagement fell through," he said.

Talking to my father about a subject that was marginally related to Nicu made me nervous. Of course, he didn't know what had gone down, but he'd be adamantly against Nicu. He didn't know about Cat's family. Not only was it not my business to tell him, but I tried to keep our conversations light and not burden him with any stressors.

While he wasn't in a horrible max-security facility, I knew it wasn't easy for him. He didn't sleep well in the bunk bed in the barracks he shared with over a hundred other men. The guards were none too quiet when making their rounds throughout the night. He might have sounded cavalier about it, but I saw his jaw muscle tick as he ground down on his teeth.

"It did, but she's now engaged to his brother, which is for the best. They truly love each other, and Luca is good to her," I replied.

"Love..." my father said with a slight edge.

I grabbed his hand and shook my head. "Not everyone is like Mother." Meaning, not everyone dumped you the second things got difficult.

Remaining silent, he gave a curt nod. Mother had been the love of his life. I believed she returned his feelings, to the point she was capable of. They'd been a golden couple. It had been easy to be with my father. He'd been a charismatic and handsome man and came from the kind of wealthy family that was integral to my mother's lifestyle. But when things went to hell, she'd shed him like an old fur coat at the end of the winter season.

"And what happened to her first fiancé, being the brother?" he asked curiously.

"Everything was fine. Nicu was happy for them," I blurted out.

I shifted in my seat, and my father's eyes sharpened and narrowed slightly, a sign he had caught the scent of something he wanted to learn more about. The man was incisive and extremely perceptive. His curiosity was a dangerous thing to have turned on you.

"Nicu, is it?" he asked casually.

"Yes, Nicu and Luca," I replied, praying he wouldn't delve any deeper into the subject, since I couldn't tell him the truth.

"Interesting name," he observed.

"He's Romanian. They're all Romanian. Traditional families and all that," I mumbled.

My heart pounded against my breastbone. I'd never spoken about men with my father. It was unspoken between us that I would focus on school, on graduating college, and creating a "normal" life for myself. One free of drama and tragedy and, it went without saying, crime.

A life free of crime was paramount. More than betraying Cat, this was the reason it would never work out between Nicu and me. I wasn't about to fail my father on this point.

His fingertips rapped on the surface of the metal table. The sounds of other conversations drifted over us.

"I hope he's a good man," he mused.

He loves his family, so I'd say he's a better man than you, I thought harshly, but instantly stifled it.

"It doesn't matter what kind of man he is because I'm focused on college," I responded. That, at least, was the truth. I was doing everything in my power to stay away from him. Since Cat's engagement party, I'd gotten a text from him. I didn't reply. He'd called me. I'd blocked his number so I wouldn't be tempted to pick up.

"Glad to hear that. It's important to surround yourself with the right people," he said in a stern tone. "You only have to look at me as a cautionary tale. I'm the poster boy of a life gone wrong."

I gripped his hand in mine. "Don't say that."

His eyes softened on me. "It's the truth, sweet pea. If there's one thing that came out of what I put us through, it was learning the hard lesson that when you do wrong, you'll inevitably face the consequences. No matter how rich or powerful you are, no matter how clever you think you are, your closest friends, hell even your spouse, will turn on you in a heartbeat. And you will have to face your sins alone, having been abandoned by everyone."

"I didn't abandon you," I cut in, my throat tight and my voice raspy. My heart was bleeding. *Bleeding* for him.

"You're the one exception, the only proof that blood is thicker than water. Only blood will stay strong, Jewel. To depend on anything else leads to tragedy. You would be remiss to believe otherwise," he finished.

"Visitation time over!" came a booming voice from the guard at the entrance.

The sound level in the room rose exponentially as families sped up to finish their conversations. Women and children began crying at the imminent separation. It was like this every time, and every time, the reactions of others echoed my own emotions.

I had to stuff them deep down and put on a brave face. If my dad knew how much it killed me each time I walked out of Otisville and left him behind, he'd forbid me to visit him. So I kept it inside until I got into the rental car and bawled my eyes out.

We stared at each other. I caught the look of anguish on his face before he masked it, smoothing over his features.

"Thanks for visiting me, sweet pea, but you don't have to come every month. You're a grown woman with your own life. You're too busy to trek up here that often."

Ignoring his comment, I patted his hand. "Thank you, but you know what you can do for me. They didn't rescind visiting hours and actually let me in, so I'm guessing you've been on your best behavior."

His mouth broke into a boyish grin. "Always. For you, always."

That was a lie. I'd come and been turned away, having to wait another month to try again, but I appreciated that he was trying to be good so that my trips upstate weren't in vain. It wasn't a stretch to say that following rules didn't come naturally to him. He thought it was a hardship for me to see him, but the irony was that I saw him more often than I did Mother, and she wasn't incarcerated. Resentment suffused my chest, but I reminded myself that it was pointless to be mad at her. Angry outbursts never changed her behavior. Her narcissism ran too deep for that.

"Next month will be Halloween—"

Before he could finish his sentence giving me an out from visiting him, I interrupted, "It'll be perfect. I can come here and visit my favorite goblin. Then I'll be back in the city in time to hit a Halloween party at school."

The guard called out a last warning. I gave my father a hug and walked out with my "chin up and no looking back," as he had taught me.

Back outside, I joined the rest of the family members who had been able to hold it together in front of their inmate for a good cry, each of us in our individual cars.

9

NICU

Jewel wore her thick hair back, in a high ponytail, which swung from side to side when she strutted past me, begging me to grab it and wrap it around my fist. She wore a white button-down dress shirt and short plaid skirt that showcased her lithe thighs. That outfit was filthy; at least it was to me. It begged for me to drag her by that cock-tease ponytail of hers off to some dark corner and role-play before fucking her raw. Instead, I stifled the urges raging through me and stuffed my hands into the pockets of my tailored Stuart Hughes slacks to keep them to myself.

If it weren't for my mother's commitment to traditions, this outing to "taste" the food at the reception hall that was catering Cat and Luca's wedding would be patently ridiculous. But no one had the heart to break it to her, or the Popescus, that Luca and Cat were already married. One day, we got a call from Luca to meet him the following morning at City Hall, tipping us off about what was about to go down. They couldn't wait until the day of their big Romanian Orthodox wedding and even bigger reception to get married. Whatever. The more committed they were to each other, the easier it was for me to go after Jewel.

Her pointed silence when she passed me in the foyer of the reception hall broadcasted her plan to ignore me during this get-together. That was fine by me. I'd raced obsessively this past week to get my urges under control because I knew there'd be little chance for us to slip away, even for a quick fuck. Miracle of miracles, it worked, and while being around Jewel always hit me like a punch to the gut, I was managing my energy remarkably well.

My lips spread into a broad grin.

Her little attempt at distance was...cute.

"This is going to be fun," I confided to Tatum, who was standing beside me.

"In whose world?" he grumbled, poking at the detailed calendar on his phone. He'd come back from California for the tasting. "I'm inundated with a to-do list a mile long, and I shouldn't have left Cali for this."

Tatum went on, complaining about the barriers he was facing as he tried to sort shit out with the Hagi family. I tuned him out, relieved that I didn't need to suppress my intentions for Jewel.

"There's one particular thorn that keeps coming up, time and again. Anytime I make headway with one of the smaller families, *she* butts her way into my business, sabotaging me right and left," Tatum griped.

Only half listening to his complaints, I leaned in, nodded toward Jewel, and divulged, "Her pussy is magic."

His eyes jolted up to my face, quickly following my line of vision.

Not blinking an eye, he grunted out, "No one woman's pussy is magic. No *one* woman is special, period."

He didn't even bother to chide me for having sex with

Jewel, which confirmed in my mind that her guilt for fucking me was all in her head.

I snorted at his ignorance, even if I'd felt the same way not so long ago. He and I had taken to hanging out more, now that both my brothers were married. Alex had been in love with Nina since forever, so his surrender was no surprise.

Luca's fall, however, had been spectacular. As the next in line to marry after Alex, he was supposed to have Cat in an arranged marriage with the Popescus, but in pure Luca fashion, he'd rejected her from the outset. Stubborn bastard. The responsibility had then fallen on me.

In the end, I didn't regret my brief engagement, because I came across Jewel. It was an unforgettable night. Sure, I loved that she wasn't a *mafie* girl and that I could fuck her dirty. But it had morphed into so much more. She was spirited, which is what had first caught my attention. She was loyal, as shown by her unrelenting devotion to Cat. And she was stubborn, like the way she chose to ignore me just now. It inflamed me, bolstering my determination to break her down and *make* her love me. Being with her reminded me of the first time I drove my bike. I was hooked. It was like a missing piece filled a gaping hole that I couldn't plug up, no matter what I did. Just like racing, I didn't want anything else. Dare I say, I was obsessed?

I never cared for marriage. Marriage to a *mafie* girl was about two things, which were really the same thing: family and clan. It was never about the woman. After watching Alex choose Nina, and the trials and tribulations they had to surpass, I wanted what they had. What Luca and Cat had. I'd dodged a bullet with Cat, and I had a small window of opportunity to go after what I wanted. Go after *whom* I wanted. And go after Jewel, I would. Ruthlessly.

I already felt like I owned her, but I didn't want to simply *feel* it. I wanted to possess every part of her, and—I wanted everyone else to know. Regardless of my feelings on the subject of marriage, if I chose a woman, marriage was the nonnegotiable conclusion to our relationship. I was taking a huge step by violating the tradition of an arranged marriage.

Can I do it?

She passed me again, this time to talk to Cat's mother, who was standing near me, about the menu. My gaze took her in greedily.

Hell yeah, I can. Every inch of her is worth it.

Right now, she came around me on purpose. My heated blood kicked up a few degrees. I had no doubt that she was highly aware of my presence. My eyes zeroed in on her body language. Her hands were fluttering around a little too fast, her laugh was a little too high, and her eyes blinked a little too rapidly. She was quite aware of me. As it should be, since I was more than highly attuned to every move she made, in and out of my presence.

Things weren't going as planned after licking her pretty cunt at Luca's engagement party in the Hamptons a couple of weeks ago. She continued with her campaign of ghosting me, refusing to answer my texts or calls. I found out she'd blocked me, so I got a man I knew to unblock my number and put a tracker on her for good measure. She blocked me again. I unblocked myself again. I think she figured out I had some hold on her cell, and let it be. Unfortunately, I didn't have the power to get her to text me back.

I had an obstinate brat on my hands.

And I loved it.

Her nervous behavior told me I'd gotten into her head, regardless. By blatantly ignoring me, she was making me more voracious to have her and more willing to do anything to get her.

Cristo sidled up behind Jewel, placing his hand possessively on her lower back before she turned slightly. My eyes drilled into them as she replied to his greeting, and they kissed each other on the cheek.

He cast a brief glance my way with a dirty smirk on his face.

I clenched my jaw. Fuck, he'd clocked that I was into her and was making a move. He was begging for an ass-beating, taking advantage of the fact that I wouldn't attack him at Luca and Cat's shindig. Payback for killing Simu.

From the corner of my eye, I recognized the proprietor of the venue hurrying to the foyer on his short stubby legs. He greeted us before sweeping his hand in front of himself to show us around the place. After a brief tour, while Cristo hugged Jewel's side, we were ushered into a reception room set up with platters of food laid out on two large tables. Cristo knew how to get on my last nerve, but luckily for him, he was forced to leave Jewel's side and join Cat at the main table.

I strategically placed myself near Jewel just in time to pull her chair out as she chose a seat. Realizing she was cornered, she gave me a long-suffering sigh and plopped down in the chair, which I smoothly slid into place before taking a seat beside her.

"Seriously, Nicu, you couldn't find anywhere else to sit?" she spoke in a low voice.

"Now, why would I do that when I fully intended to sit beside you despite Cristo clinging to you like a second skin?" I queried.

With a snap of her teeth, she hissed, "He was *not* clinging to me."

She blew a soft raspberry between her pouty lips that almost had me adjusting my burgeoning cock.

I fixed my sleeves and cuff links, placed my forearms on the table, and gave her a droll look. "Don't pretend you don't want me. It's beneath you."

"I'm not pretending. I don't want you," she snarled.

"I dare you to make me prove you wrong. What do you think I'll find if I slip my hand up that short skirt of yours, hmm? You knew I'd be here, and yet you chose to dress like a slutty little schoolgirl, begging me to bend you over my lap and tap that sweet ass with a ruler."

Tatum was close enough to hear me and choked on his sip of water.

Eyes darting to him, Jewel's face went up in flames.

"Oh, shut up," she snapped. "This may come as a shock to you, I know, but the world doesn't revolve around you."

"The world may not, but what you wear most definitely does," I replied smoothly, eyeing a small beauty mark near one corner of her mouth that I wanted to suck between my teeth.

"Stop staring at my mouth," she chided harshly under her breath. "It's rude, and everyone can see."

"Baby doll, my staring is the least of your worries," I quipped.

"And get out of my phone. I know you've been messing with it, because each time I block your number, it miraculously unblocks itself," she accused.

I gave her my most innocent expression, batting my eyes like I had no clue what she was referring to.

"I haven't the slightest idea what you're talking about," I lied blandly, pulling my eyes away from her for an instant to nod thank you to the waiter who deposited a plate of food in front of me.

I heard a shushing from behind me, a sound any good son recognized immediately as a public chiding from his mother. The proprietor, a wizened old Romanian whom my mother knew from the old country had been going on about the dish I was supposed to sample.

I snapped my mouth shut and straightened up. From my side-eye, I caught Jewel suppressing a small chuckle.

"What a mama's boy," she crooned softly.

Eyeing my mother discretely over my shoulder, I responded quietly, "You have no idea." I paused before continuing in a low, gruff tone, "But being the perfect son won't stop me from riding you until your nails draw blood from my back."

"You're incorrigible," she wheezed out, but once she'd recuperated from my outrageous statement, a smile lingered on her lips.

She was softening to me, even knowing full well that I'd fucked with her phone. It was a small miracle. Little things, from the way she'd dressed to the way she purposely ignored me, told me she was thinking of me. Each of them caught my attention and stirred the predator inside.

What I needed was the chance to be around her. If she spent time with me, I'd wear down her resistance. She knew it, which was why she refused to give me a chance. I may not be known for my charm, but I wasn't a dolt either.

My lack of access to her had me going down a darker path than I had anticipated. I was no longer satisfied with watching her from afar. With the help of my guard friend at her dorm, I got access to her room while both she and her roommate were in class. I'd lain down on her bed, her rose-sugar scent invading my nostrils, tempting me beyond belief to pull out my cock and give myself a hand job.

It was a close thing, but I refrained and jumped off the

bed to rummage through her stuff. There was a framed photo of her and her parents from when she was a child, smiling happily with the Mediterranean in the background. There was another of her and Cat in their graduation gowns.

I stalked over to her chest of drawers, spending way too much time playing with her panties. For a nineteen-year-old, she had quite a collection. That, along with her pink vibrator, left me salivating. I snagged the black silk thong from the day at the Hamptons as a memento and used it to fuck myself later that night, fantasizing that I'd sneaked into her room while she was sleeping and fisted my cock over her prone, nude body. That's how she slept when her roomie wasn't around. I'd spray my seed all over her high tits and soft belly, marking her as mine.

And mine, she would be, I promised myself.

I turned toward her, my lids dropping to half-mast, and let the lust pour out. Her eyes widened in surprise, but she didn't retreat. And retreating was as good as a green light with Jewel, at least until she got over her guilt about Cat.

Soon, Jewel, soon, I promised her silently. *But first, I have a little lesson for you.*

I TRIED FOCUSING on what the wizened old man with the thick Romanian accent was saying about the plate of food in front of me, but instead, I was ruminating on how I must be sick in the head because I liked Nicu's stalking. He wasn't exactly subtle about it. With his fine Italian suits and polished leather shoes, he stuck out like a sore thumb on a campus where students wore pajama bottoms to class. I saw him repeatedly gazing up at my dorm room windows from the street corner. I'd caught him on the street when I crossed from one side of campus to another or outside the various coffee shops where I studied.

Summer was long done, and my first semester of college had begun without having seen my mother since my high school graduation. It was a shock that she'd shown up to that, and I suspected her primary motivation had been that several mothers in her circle had kids at my boarding school. Her absence would've been noted and commented on. Mother had never been maternal, but she'd resorted to pure narcissism once Dad was out of the picture. Not that he wasn't the cause of it all. God, it was hard to balance my lingering anger at him with my love and continual worry over him.

With many years left before Dad was eligible for parole and Mother never around, my sense of neglect was legit. On top of that, I was in a bit of a self-pitying, grieving slump over the new distance between me and Cat, ever since we graduated from boarding school and she moved in with Luca. So how could I not feel taken care of by Nicu's constant presence? How could I not fall at seeing that he was always there, even on the outskirts of my life? I admired that he didn't barge into my life. He demonstrated he could respect the boundaries I erected between us. For now, at least, because the hunger in his eyes spoke of a man who was actively managing his baser instincts.

Unfortunately, in his presence, my resolution melted. As much as I rationally knew he was a bad man who lived a violent life, my brain shut down when I was around him for even a minimal amount of time.

Finally, the man finished his soliloquy, and it was time to taste the food. My stomach grumbled because I'd had to skip lunch to finish my work before I met Cat to help her dress for this tasting. Lifting my fork, I took a bite of the cabbage-wrapped, rice-and-meat dish I recognized from Christmas dinners with Cat's family and almost inhaled the entire plate. My thoughts weren't as easily distracted as my stomach, though.

I wasn't shy, but I was an introvert, and as an only child, I was used to being alone. I *needed* my alone time to function in the world, but sometimes, being alone could get a little... lonely. The sixth sense of being watched and followed was like being wrapped in the cocoon of a warm blanket, lounging by a fire while a blizzard raged outside.

Then there was the little performer nestled inside me who liked being watched. I found myself doing things just to tease him. Standing in front of the large window near my bed and stretching my arms over my head, letting my crop top drift up high enough to expose the bottom swells of my tits for him. I could feel his eyes searing through me from the distance. Or sensing his presence, I'd taunt him by chatting up guys in coffee shops or in the library, knowing he wouldn't break the distance.

Earlier, I let Cristo touch me, stand a little too close to me, walk with me during the brief tour of the premises. I shouldn't have done any of that, knowing the tension between the two of them. Cristo was touchier than usual, so I'm guessing he was using me to get to Nicu as much as I was using him, but I let him get away with it. I'd caught the unholy spark in Nicu's eyes, like a man possessed. I was playing with fire, but I couldn't help but torture him, guaranteeing he was rabid by the time he caught me.

And rabid was how I liked him best.

Instead of doing what was expected, which was to get me alone and use me to pound out his aggression, he chose this moment to give me a taste of my own medicine. Nicu switched seats with Tatum and began flirting with the gorgeous young woman sitting next to him.

My eyes turned to slits as I observed him lift his fork, piled with a perfect sample of the dish, and bring it to the woman's mouth. Her perfectly applied red-lipsticked lips popped open. Eyes widening with surprise, she savored the bite of food with an unseemly moan that had me clenching my own utensils with a death grip.

He gave the woman a brilliant smile, and I might've bent the handle of my fork.

Two could play at this game.

Turning to Tatum with a smile so bright the muscles of my cheek hurt, I asked, "How's the food?"

Flicking a quick look at the young woman before returning his attention to me, he replied, "I'd like whatever she's having."

"Oh, she thinks she's having Nicu," I grumbled out.

His eyebrows lifted slightly, laughter dancing in his eyes.

"Don't laugh at me," I warned.

"I would never," he said somberly, although I distinctly saw a twitch of his lips.

I pointed my knife at him. "There," I accused. "I saw that."

He threw his head back and laughed.

"Busted. Sorry, I'm usually much better at restraining myself," he admitted.

He leaned toward me slightly, and I got a whiff of his alluring cologne, but it wasn't nearly as enticing as Nicu's. There was probably more to pheromones than I knew because Tatum was beyond gorgeous and he smelled good, but he simply didn't have that brooding-brutish-pirate look Nicu had. His eyes were warmer than Nicu's glacial baby blues, but it was Nicu's cold inferno that froze me in place whenever her turned his gaze on me.

"You want to make him jealous?" Tatum asked casually.

I waved my hand. "I do that all the time." His eyebrows hit his forehead this time. "He's trying to give me a little taste of what I do to him. I suppose I'm not as good at taking it as I am at dishing it out."

"So this has been going on for some time," he mused. "Even if you have, trust me, there's no winning when a Lupu puts their mind to something. And Nicu is the most ruthless of them all."

"*Frate*," I heard the growl-like word coming from Nicu.

My eyes shot to him, and the smoldering look in his eyes caused a shiver to run down my spine.

Tatum turned toward him in a leisurely fashion. "What's up?"

Nicu leaned into him, and I heard him speak in Romanian. Whatever he said was clear enough for the young woman beside him to let out a gasp.

Tatum smirked, while nodding in agreement. "Point made," he replied with a grin. "We're just conversing."

Nicu gave a rapid-fire response in Romanian.

Tatum chuckled as the waiters whisked our dishes away and placed new ones in front of us all. I liked how nonplussed Tatum was. It was almost as if he regarded Nicu like a younger brother. Watching their dynamic was fascinating.

The proprietor was explaining that this was the vegetarian option. Tilting my head, I cast a look at my perfectly grilled salmon. *Is this what typically passed for vegetarian to Romanians?*

I grabbed my wineglass and downed half of it. While I wasn't yet of legal drinking age, the rules were different here. Not only did they apparently consider fish to be a vegetarian option, but whenever I had dinner at Cat's house, wine and *țuică*, a Romanian liquor that went down like gasoline on fire, was poured into the glasses of every person present, regardless of age.

Nicu's eyes snapped up to me.

He pointed a finger at me and warned, "And you, watch how fast you drink."

"Yes, Daddy," I retorted.

His face contorted, giving me a glimpse of the raging sexy beast inside. He snuffed it quickly and muttered, "Brat, you're lucky we're in public right now."

The girl beside him made a shocked, gurgling noise.

I gave him my best, satisfied smirk.

Gotcha.

I'd gotten his complete attention, despite his attempt at making me jealous, and he'd just claimed me in front of everyone.

Irritated, he crossed his arms over his wide chest, which bunched the fabric of his suit around his biceps in a way that made me want to strip and lick every delicious inch of him.

"You've won this round," he conceded.

"That's where you're wrong, Nicu. I win every round," I replied with a seductive drawl. I didn't know what it was about him that drove me to prod and taunt him. I was normally polite and conversational, but something about him tore up my insides, leaving me achy and needy. Worst of all, it made me want to push him over the edge and get a reaction out of him.

He was a maddening blend of conflicting traits. There was a wild, untamed quality to him, and yet he clearly prided himself on his self-restraint, on quelling his animal-like tendencies. From what Cat told me, he seemed to only give in to them in a few prescribed areas, such as racing and other crazy activities, like snowboarding and bungee jumping. From my own limited experience, he clearly let loose when he had sex. But outside of those areas, he was as controlled and disciplined as his eyes were glacial.

"That remains to be seen," he retorted. "There've been only a few skirmishes between us as of yet." He leaned over, holding my gaze with a stern one of his own, and said, "I've *allowed* you to win these minor scuffles, but I intend to win the war."

The way he husked out the word *allowed* sent heat pooling between my legs. Dammit, it was unnerving how easily he got to me.

"Ha, easy thing to say when I got you, right here, right now," I refuted his claim, pressing my index finger into the table for emphasis.

"Mediocre wins, at best. Trust me, when it counts, you *will* yield to me."

Hands trembling from the desire to choke him—or kiss him, I wasn't sure which—I sputtered at his conceit, "Y-you, your arrogance is staggering."

Everything around me had fallen away; nothing existed outside of Nicu, me, and our showdown. Yet, even with my complete attention on him, I noticed from my side, Tatum's head swinging back and forth, following our tit for tat, unsure whether to intervene or not. The girl who'd been flirting with Nicu, had all but shrunk in her seat like a wilted flower.

Good, I thought viciously, she was a nonfactor.

"It's only arrogance if it isn't true, and we both know you can't help but give in to me. In fact, I'd go as far as state that you *ache* to do so."

The insinuation was beyond blatant and was close to goading me to physical violence. Images of his dark head moving between my thighs rose to the forefront of my mind. Suddenly hot and bothered, I shifted in my seat. Besides turning me on, his comment angered me because it suggested we'd been intimate. I didn't care what people thought of me, but this was Cat's world, and I didn't want anyone gossiping about us. He was her former fiancé, after all.

"Don't suggest things that never actually happened between us," I boldly lied, hinting for him to back down when my gaze moved to Cat at the next table over.

If nothing else, the man was quick on the uptick. He pulled back as if I'd offended him, but at least he covered my lie. "There you go, letting your imagination run wild again. Is it because, underneath that prickly personality, you can't help but want me, I wonder." He checked his nails nonchalantly. "No worries, I'm used to that kind of attention. Nothing to be embarrassed about.'

I snorted. "As if."

His eyes lifted to mine.

"Nothing could be further from the truth," I retorted. "Again, you're letting your conceit cloud your perception of reality."

"Mm-hmm," he mocked lightly.

I clenched my fork and knife. Fantasies of stabbing him danced in my head. "You're impossible."

I refocused my attention on my plate, which I belatedly realized had been changed to another dish without my noticing. He was impossible, I thought as I viciously stabbed my fork into a sausage of minced meat and spices. *Keep that in mind, Jewel. He's impossible. They're impossible.*

He leaned in and threw me a bone. "It's going to be a

long dinner. Why don't we pick it up at a later point in time...when we're alone?"

Of course, I'd want that, but I cast a look over my shoulder at Cat in worry. Having caught me, she gave me a bright smile and a wave.

I returned her smile and waved back, inwardly groaning. No, I couldn't do that. I couldn't allow a repeat of what had happened at her engagement party. If I'd at least confessed to her that we'd hooked up, then maybe the guilt wouldn't be so all-consuming.

Turning back around, my gaze slammed into Nicu's blazing one. He knew what I was thinking.

Have mercy on me. Let me go.

With a purse of his exquisite lips, he shook his head in disappointment. My belly dropped. I didn't enjoy rejecting him. If we'd met under different circumstances, I would've made different choices, but Cat aside, he was a criminal bad boy. The worst kind of man for me. I couldn't fall for him, not when I could so easily conjure up the image of my father in that awful, gray-colored Otisville vising room.

He gave me a searing look of fury, switched seats with Tatum and struck up a conversation with him. I shivered at the sudden loss of his heated looks and the sparks that flew at our sparring. He was sparing me; he was even tossing another bone my way by not returning to patently flirting with the girl beside him again. Unfortunately, it didn't feel like he was doing me a favor. Irrational as it was, it felt like he was freezing me out. Truth be told, fighting my attraction to him was feeling worse and worse.

With a sigh, I returned to my plate and picked at my food. Despite the wonderful savory fragrance wafting off the seasoned dish, I'd lost my appetite.

10

JEWEL

My father's parole had been denied. His attorney, an old family friend, called me to patiently explain how, yet again, it was impossible for Dad to get parole. When James Weston's name came up to the parole board, influential victims came out of the woodwork to rehash their suffering. I couldn't blame them, considering my father was guilty of ten counts of various levels of fraud. I listened while Jack rattled off the various types—mail fraud, wire fraud, investor advisor fraud, securities fraud—until I couldn't take it anymore and cut him off. Being reminded of his guilt didn't make it any easier to swallow. And there was no doubt of his guilt. He wasn't only guilty of ruining the lives of his victims; he'd ruined mine and Mother's as well. We were the unintended victims, and I continued to suffer from his absence, from his imprisonment.

Dad even called me.

He was resigned to the idea that he was destined to remain under lock and key, whereas I'd always held out hope. It was dashed every time, and still, I didn't seem to learn my lesson.

I was getting off the phone with my father when Suzie, one of the girls who lived in my residence hall, waltzed in, sashaying back and forth in a revealing outfit. I lived in a double room with Sofia, but all first years lived together in various halls in what was called the Quad.

Flipping her blonde hair over her shoulder, she cocked her hip and asked, "What do you think? Too much?"

Suzie had recently been accepted into a sorority at Columbia University. Not only was she all about Greek life, but she wanted to share it with the rest of us living on her floor.

"There's a party tonight at Delta Sigor DSig, and you must, must, *must* come!" she insisted. "I'm not taking no for an answer. And to get you in the partying mood, I brought a little something."

From behind her, she pulled out a bottle of frozen Tequila. Her other hand jiggled a saltshaker that looked suspiciously like the ones in the food hall.

Plopping them both on my desk, she fluffed up her perfectly coiffed hair.

Uninvited, she took a seat, licked her hand, sprinkled salt on it, gulped down a shot of tequila, and lapped at the salt. After a slight shudder of her narrow shoulders, she handed me the bottle and saltshaker with a grin. "Come on, Jewel, live a little. It's Saturday night!"

The door swung open wider, and in stalked her roommate, Jenny. Swiping the bottle from her friend's grip, she shook it and said in an exasperated tone, "Jesus, Suzie. This isn't even yours!"

"Oh, come on, Jenny. I know you're an only child and a little princess, but you gotta learn to share."

"I can share if you'd only ask instead of grabbing things out of my fridge," she huffed.

These two were snarky and a little ditzy, but they weren't snobby or cliquey, like some sorority girls could be. They lived to party, and if they weren't at a Greek party, they were at another party on campus or hitting a club downtown.

With a nod in my direction, Suzie said, "Jewel's coming with us tonight."

Jenny halted mid swing of the bottle to her mouth and shrieked, "Yay!" with the little happy dance she did when she was excited. "A few other girls will be coming as well. This will be fun! Brooks Hall is gonna represent, yo!"

The news about my father's parole hung around me like bad mojo, and I was grateful for the distraction they offered. If it wasn't for them, I would've moped around all weekend, what with Sofia visiting her family and Cat being away in the Hamptons with Luca.

In the past, I counted on Cat, but that was when we lived together at school. Now, I didn't feel comfortable interrupting her time with Luca to ask her to spend it with me. During the week, Cat and Luca were at their penthouse in the city, but come the weekend, they either escaped to his mansion in Westchester or the Hamptons. After the drama they'd been through recently, I couldn't blame them for wanting to bask in each other's company and recharge. I couldn't complain since Cat and I managed to meet up every day she was on campus. I was still adjusting to not having her around, and at times like these, I missed her the most.

Suzie walked to the door and shouted in the hallway, calling a few other girls in my room for an impromptu preparty party.

Jenny handed me the bottle of tequila. I hadn't eaten much at the food hall because I was nervously anticipating

Jack's call, so the first shot went straight to my head. I grabbed an energy bar and tore off a bite, hoping it would soak up the alcohol. I didn't drink heavily, but if there was a night to do it, it was tonight. Uneasiness tickled the back of my neck as if I was doing something wrong, and I instantly knew where the feeling came from.

Nicu.

I sensed his disapproval even in his absence. With his possessive Neanderthal nature, I strongly suspected he wouldn't approve of me getting drunk and going to a frat party with these girls, no matter how nice they were. That feeling of being taken care of swooped in again, making my belly flip-flop. Even though I was an adult, I hadn't had someone looking after me in a long time.

Suzie shot to her feet and pointed at me. "I have the best outfit for you tonight." She rushed out and came back holding a black satin dress with red piping down the front and cutouts above the hips.

"Oh, no, I'm not wearing that," I immediately replied.

She shook the dress and fluttered her fingers at me. "Why not? It's *hawt*, girl, and you'll look incredible in it."

"Ugh, no, thank you," I muttered.

Her brows gathered in confusion. Propping a hand on her hip, she demanded, "Give me one reason why not."

"It's too revealing. You can pull it off because you're skinny, but I have hips," I replied with a slap at said body part.

"It doesn't fit me right, because I *don't* have hips. I look like I'm wearing a smock, but with that hourglass shape you have going on, you'll look like a sex kitten. It will fit you *purr*fectly."

I squirmed in my seat on the bed. "I don't know…"

I wasn't ashamed of my body, and I didn't have issues

with nudity, but this dress was provocative. It told a story I wasn't sure I was comfortable with, and it would garner attention I wasn't sure I wanted. I might flaunt my body around Nicu to taunt him, but I was still an introvert. I admired women who could grab the notice of every man in their vicinity but having guys I didn't know gawking at me wasn't my thing.

"Listen up, you need to represent me and Jenny here, and this dress is the best way of getting that done," she insisted. "Am I right, Jenny?"

Jenny piped up, "That dress is savage, Jewel. Don't you dare wear anything else. Try it on, for God's sake!"

With a defeated sigh, I dragged myself up. It was this or wallowing in self-pity over my dad all night, and I'd done that enough times to know it was worth it to fight my own introverted tendencies and go out there to get my mind off my troubles. Jenny gave me the bottle for another gulp of liquid courage. I pulled off my shirt and dropped my pajama shorts to the ground, snatching the dress from Suzie with a little growl that she answered with a pleased giggle.

Stepping into the dress, I shimmied it up and over my thighs and hips, struggling with the thin straps of the bodice. I wrangled my arms through them and tucked my breasts inside, although there was still a fair chance they'd spill out.

"Are you sure this is a size eight?" I asked suspiciously. "Because I can tell you these are definitely not C cups."

"Yes, yes, it's an eight. Sheesh, you're so difficult," Suzie trilled, with a waving motion of her hands that said *keep going.*

I adjusted the dress this way and that until it fit comfortably. Smoothing my hands down the front, I shimmied a little bit.

"It does feel nice," I admitted begrudgingly. I didn't often wear such tight-fitting clothes, but I had to admit that it fit like a glove.

Clapping her hands with glee, Suzie said, "You look fantastic!" She handed me the bottle for another chug. "Go look at yourself in the mirror in the bathroom if you don't believe me."

Returning the bottle after another taste, I went into the hallway. My RA whistled as she passed me in the corridor, singsonging, "Hot mama."

Shaking my head at her, I stepped into the bathroom, turned toward the mirror, and paused. My mouth parted slightly.

Jenny came in right behind me, lifting my hair, and said, "Wait till I get my curling iron on this and put some smoky-eye makeup on you."

I tilted my head to the side, checking myself out critically. *Hmm...not bad, if I say so myself.* What looked godawful hanging from Suzie's hand, looked pretty good on. She was right; it was a perfect fit. The cutouts, which I had always thought looked cheesy on dresses, served to accentuate my curves by showing a little skin. They weren't hugely large, and with the sweetheart cut and the hem ending just above my knees, I looked sexy, but...classy.

"I could live with this for one night," I conceded.

"Michael Kors can do no wrong when it comes to knowing how to design dresses for women, I tell you," Jenny replied. "You're going to shine tonight, and why shouldn't you every once in a while, Jewel?"

I supposed she had a point. When I went out with them, which admittedly wasn't often, I tended to dress like a supporting actress to a headliner. It was easy since they reveled in the limelight. But they were good eggs, and they wanted me to be the shiny, glittery one for once. They wanted to support me. It would be rude not to get behind that.

"Alright, for tonight, I'll take center stage," I agreed.

"Good. Stay right there. I'll be back with my makeup case and hair stuff."

"Okay, let me put some panties on, and I'll meet you back here."

She placed a hand on my forearm. "Oh, no, bitch. No panties tonight. First, you don't want to ruin the dress with panty lines. Second, you have no idea how freeing it is not to wear undies. It gives you a touch of naughtiness that can't be faked."

My eyes widened. Whether it was the alcohol making its way through my system, the revealing dress, or that I wasn't wearing panties, I did feel unbelievably sexy tonight. I needed this right now, I reminded myself. Now, if I could only shed the niggling sense of Nicu's disapproval, I might manage to let loose and forget about that wretched denied parole for a night.

11

NICU

J ewel was drunk.

My hands curled into fists.

At a frat party, of all places. I knew this because I was outside, watching as she'd left her dorm with a group of girls. I followed them as they made their way to a frat house on 113th Street, where giddy girls and rowdy bros mingled outside and streamed in and out of a brownstone.

After following her for days, I'd learned my little doll's habits. For one, she liked to coffee shop hop, although she had one particular favorite, The Hungarian Pastry Shop, on Amsterdam Avenue. It was situated across the street from the Cathedral Church of Saint John the Divine, whose gardens she often wandered around in afterward.

One day, after she left, I went inside and grabbed a coffee to feel closer to her by simulating her experience. I almost spit the sludge out. Sure, I was a coffee snob, having practically grown up in a café. Tasa went through a phase in high school when she worked in our family shop daily, modernizing it and adding newfangled drinks, like the flat white. What in the fuck that was, I still didn't know.

I could tell Jewel had been drinking before leaving her dorm, but instead of slowing down, she continued to drink from the moment she arrived at the party. My instincts pricked up. Something must've happened in the past twenty-four hours to unsettle my little doll, and I didn't like it. As I milled around the front of the frat house, I peered in the front room of the brownstone. Beside me, two frat boys exchanged their thoughts about Jewel. She was slumped back on the couch, drunk, and some fucker had his hands all over her, his lips on the side of her throat and—my control snapped.

Roaring out loud, I elbowed my way through the thick crowd of college students. Storming into the brownstone, I stomped through another throng of kids to get to her. I reached the couch and yanked her out of the groping hands of the little prick. He glared up at me, sober as fuck. Way too sober to be touching a woman in her position. Dragging her off the ratty couch, I placed her on her feet. Giggling, her head lolled to the side. She was too drunk to be angry at me, her usual reaction.

"Nicu," she hummed. Normally, her humming my name would've gotten me going, but I was fuming at the situation she'd gotten herself into. Where were her friends? I scanned the crowded room and recognized no one.

The little piss-fuck tried to protest, rising to his feet and putting a hand on my forearm to stop me.

Oh, fuck no, he didn't.

Jewel swayed toward me, and I wrenched my arm away, cradling her to my side so he'd have zero chance of touching her again.

"It would be my pleasure to cut off your balls and feed them to you," I growled in his face. Then, I flicked my jacket open wide enough for him to see my piece.

The coward stumbled back and ran off so fast I almost burst out laughing. *Please, motherfucker, I only gave you an inkling of who I am.*

"W-what are you doing here?" Jewel asked, blinking up at me as my hands tightened around her waist.

She leaned into me, rubbed her nose into the lapel of my jacket and inhaled deeply. "Hmm, you always smell so good. It's the bergamot in your cologne, isn't it? What's the name of it?" she chattered.

Her own sweet rose scent seeped into my pores, wrapping my head in a fog, getting me drunk on her.

Focus, Nicu.

"I'm taking care of you," I grunted out. "Since you're clearly not in a state to take care of yourself."

She frowned, giving me a little pout. "I always take care of myself. Only me. It's always only been *me*."

"Not tonight, it isn't," I replied between clenched teeth. If I allowed myself the freedom to speak my mind, I would've replied that her night was a date rape waiting to happen. "Not tonight, and not from now on. It's my job to take care of you. Your job is to stay in your lane."

"H-how did you know where I was?" she asked, a little crease between her brows as she swept the room to see where I'd come from.

I ignored her question with a grunt and prodded her to walk. She stumbled in her first step, and I caught her before she face-planted into the sticky floor of the frat house. It wasn't a hardship to keep a tight hold on her so she wouldn't slide down to the ground as I got us out of there and to my Bugatti, which I'd conveniently left double-parked a little way down the street. When I saw her and her dorm mates weaving their way through the streets on their way to the party, I sensed I wouldn't last long waiting and got my car to follow them.

Gently, I helped her inside my car, putting my hand on the crown of her head to guide her inside so she didn't bump her head. Heat suffused my chest when she sank into the leather seat and let out a sigh of relief. As if she was where she was supposed to be—in my care. She wiggled her shoulders and butt, settling in deeper before dropping her head back and closing her eyes.

I rounded the hood of the car, started up my baby, and jetted down the street, taking a sharp turn onto Amsterdam Avenue in the direction of my penthouse apartment.

Flapping a hand behind us, she slurred slightly, "I live thataway."

"You're not going home," I gritted out, eyes focused straight ahead, fists clenched around the steering wheel.

"What do you mean? W-where are you taking me?"

"To my place," I replied succinctly. My patience having snapped long ago, there was no way I was about to take any shit from her. If I had to kidnap her, so be it. She wasn't going back to her dorm room where she could get into trouble again. And when she was sober, we were going to have a serious discussion about her behavior tonight. I was done with this bullshit. She didn't overhear the frat boys outside whispering about their intentions, like I had. She'd put herself in a precarious position. For the first and last time.

From a side-glance, I saw her brows furrow.

Her fingertips reached out and caressed the muscle jumping in my jaw.

"Why are you mad?" she asked.

My eyes flashed to her, searing her with waves of anger and possessiveness. "Are you for real?"

She didn't realize, I reminded myself as I felt the adrenaline rush through my veins. She didn't realize how feral I could get or how I'd lost control in a way I hadn't in forever. She didn't realize, but I wasn't about to divulge any of it to her. The shame crawled up from my gut, but I stabbed it down, like I always did.

She pressed her lips together and replied, a bit more defensively, "Yeah."

"Because you could've gotten fucking raped," I bit out, barely leashing my fury from spilling over and smearing everything.

Her hand dropped away, and I cursed myself for instantly missing her touch.

A laugh tinkled out of her. "Of course, I wouldn't have. I was with my friends."

I let out a low growl of frustration. My gaze scorched over her face. "Yeah? Where were your friends when I waltzed out of there with you in my arms? Nowhere. I heard two little pussies outside, plotting on how to get you in a room alone. What do you think would've happened then? Hmmm?"

Her mouth dropped open.

"No," she replied, shaking her head in denial.

My palm slammed against the steering wheel, a curl bounced against my forehead from the abruptness of my movement.

"Fuck, yes," I roared. This girl was going to be the death of me. "Answer me, Jewel. What the fuck would you've done if I hadn't interfered?"

Eyes wide with fear, she shrank into the seat.

"Fuck," I muttered again. I raised my hand to her face. She flinched slightly. Braking at a red light, I turned toward her, my eyes stark with regret. "I'm sorry, baby doll. Didn't mean to scare you. I was so fucking pissed off when I saw you lying on the couch, drunk off your ass and helpless. Then, when I overheard those little pricks, I was done," I finished with a shake of my head. "Done."

"Uhhh..." was her only reply, eyes blinking.

Yeah, I've got your back, baby doll.

I bet she wasn't used to anyone really looking out for her. Although she'd erroneously assumed her friends would be there for her, they were the worst kind of irresponsible. I would've trusted Cat to take care of her, but she left campus at the end of the day to be with Luca.

The way she was blinking at me, her dark lashes casting long shadows on her cheeks in the dim light, made my heart stutter. There was astonishment mixed with a vulnerability that had me swallowing audibly. It reaffirmed my decision that it was time to push this thing between us because she needed my love and care as much as I needed hers.

Luca's anger sliced through my brain fog, jolting me back to reality. I was almost fully aware now. The world had been spinning when I was at the frat party. I rarely drank to excess, but today was one of those days when I just wanted to forget. Of course, in the process, I would've opened myself up to a whole world of pain if Nicu hadn't shown up like some avenging god and hauled me out of there.

I inhaled, his scent filling up my lungs in the small cab of his Bugatti Chiron. Instead of the alcohol, it was his delicious spicy citrus fragrance that made me dizzy. This time, with lust.

I might not have been drunk anymore, but I was still a little tipsy. That, on top of the thoughts of my narrow escape, shed my inhibitions, allowing my lust to came roaring to the forefront. Like an insistent drumbeat, it was hammering at me to *take, take, take*. I'd been good for so long, pulling back like I did at Cat's tasting for the wedding. The reserve of my self-control and my reserve of good intentions were swept aside in an instant.

He turned into the underground parking of a tall building I recognized from visiting Cat. We were at the Time Warner Center, where Nicu shared a floor with Luca, and now Cat, who'd moved in with his brother.

I gulped. "Is...is this where you live?"

Placing an arm on the back of my leather seat, he glanced backward as he pulled into the parking space. "Don't worry, Cat and Luca are away this weekend."

I exhaled audibly. That's right, I remembered now.

My tense muscles visibly relaxed. I was done fighting whatever was between us, at least for tonight. I was doing this. *We* were doing this. Unlike my almost disastrous outing, this had nothing to do with throwing myself into another distraction. This was all Nicu.

He was out and moving around the hood of the car to open the door for me. I gripped his strong, warm hand and let him help me out. It took a moment to stabilize myself on the heels I was wearing, and then he was leading me toward the elevator. Once inside the gold and mirrored box, he tapped a fob on his key chain and activated the penthouse floor.

The elevator shuddered slightly as it ascended, and I was done waiting. Grabbing his tie, I yanked to bring him closer. At first he resisted, as immovable as a boulder, but when I tugged more gently a few times, he came to me with an impatient sigh.

He slowly backed me into a mirrored wall and caged me

with his body, his forearms resting on either side of my head. He could pretend he was giving in to me, but I didn't miss the tent in his pants. How could I? I was attuned to everything about this man. He might be infuriated with me, but that didn't impact his desire for me. The feeling was mutual, because no matter how much I worked to maintain distance between us, my body was constantly clamoring for his.

With only a couple of inches between us, he stared down at me with an exasperated expression, although there was that distinct slight curve of one side of his mouth.

"What do you want?" he asked gruffly.

Lifting my gaze from the blue and gray pattern of his tie, I twisted it in my hand and yanked down while lifting on my tippy toes. "The same thing you want."

I pressed my lips to his, pushing into his mouth with my tongue. He opened just enough for me to have a taste, and, God, did I take it. I moaned at the delectable flavor. It had been over a week since I'd seen him. He tried to stay stiff and distant, but I pushed his jacket open, wrapped my arms around his neck, and plastered myself to him, rubbing my erect nipples against his chest.

His hands landed on my hips, keeping me in place, neither bringing me closer nor pushing me away. His fingers swiped across my exposed skin, but other than that...nothing. Why was he being so reticent? Usually, he mauled me. Which was how I liked it. Had I pushed him too far? I whined against his mouth when he didn't make a move between us. Nicu didn't care that we were in an elevator. If he wanted me, it wouldn't matter where we were.

Pulling back, I inspected him. "What is it?"

"You're drunk," he answered simply.

"It's sweet of you to be concerned about that, but no, I'm not."

"You're not entirely sober," he pointed out.

"Well, not *entirely* sober, no. But I'm not drunk. I've got my wits about me."

"That doesn't work for me," he replied.

Okaaay, not what I expected. My brows slammed down. "What does that mean?"

"It means I won't have you regretting that we fucked because you were drunk. It means I'm not going to let anything happen between us so that you can use it against us tomorrow."

"What? No, I wouldn't do that. I'm not drunk; I'm *tipsy*, and I want to be with you tonight. God, do I," I emphasized.

"You say that now, when your judgment is impaired. Tomorrow, you'll run out of here, more guilt and shame piled on what you're already carrying. I had a hard enough time getting you here. Not going to fuck it up now."

Of course, considering how I'd behaved in the past, I could see where he was coming from. I did throw him out and run away because of guilt, but for once, I wasn't feeling guilty. He'd saved me from danger, and I was done fighting this thing between us. Not only that, but I ached for him. I wanted him, and I didn't want to wait.

"That's not true," I insisted, frustration building inside me. Here I was, throwing myself at him, and he'd chosen this moment to go hero on me. *Grrr*, just when I was ready to give myself to him, he had to choose this moment to start acting decently. It was beyond the pale, dammit. My fingers clawed up and down his shirt, grabbing onto the tips of his collar and twisting them.

Frowning down at me, he shook his head. "Let it go, Jewel. It's not happening. Not tonight."

Ping. The elevator door took that moment to open. I was about to scream in frustration when he grabbed my hand and pulled me down a corridor to a door and flung it open. Cat had told me the brothers and Tatum, who shared the penthouse floor with Alex in the other tower of the building, didn't lock their doors since they had exclusive access to these floors.

He prompted me to enter with a sweep of his hand, and I sauntered in only to stop dead in my tracks. Now, I wasn't a stranger to opulent luxury. When I wasn't at school, I lived with my mother in an apartment that took over most of one floor of a luxury building on Park Avenue. They were family apartments she had grown up in, but while spacious, they were cold and dreary. This place, on the other hand, was breathtaking.

From my position in the foyer, I faced two walls of glass that gave way to an expanded view down 59th Street, Central Park West Avenue, and a swath of Central Park itself. The black and white tiles below my feet morphed into a set of stairs that led down to a wide-open space rivaling the size of a loft. There was a living room area sunk down from the rest of the room, filled with a variety of oxblood and black leather couches around a low coffee table. While everything was sleek and elegant, there was a lived-in quality I was already in love with.

While the decor was modern, there were red and white accents in several rugs, wall hangings, paintings, and a few pillows scattered among the couches that were inspired by traditional Romanian decorative embroidery.

"Your place is incredible," I said as I stepped down from the foyer and crossed the expanse of the apartment, passing the living room area on my left and the dining room area on my right, straight to the view. I could see the outline of trees outside, on the wraparound terrace.

He was behind me, standing close. I leaned into him.

"The mother of one of my soldiers helped decorate it. She has a real eye for making it modern while retaining the sense of it being Romanian. Know what I mean?"

"I do," I replied, nodding. I liked how his culture was close to his heart.

"Glad you approve."

I wasn't sure if he was being facetious, but when I glanced at him over my shoulder, his expression was somber.

"That means a lot," he added.

"How could it? We barely know each other."

He gave a light shrug of one shoulder, a gesture I've seen him do often. Without answering, his hands lifted and rubbed my arms. "I'll get you a couple of glasses of water, and then we should turn in."

I circled around in his arms and eyed him carefully. "Oh, yeah? And what will we be doing when we 'turn in'?"

"Sleeping," he replied, grimly. "Only sleeping."

We'll see about that.

12

NICU

"I want to come!" Jewel shouted as she slapped her hand on the blue bedspread like a spoiled child. I loved to see her greedy and losing it from wanting me so badly. It was a welcome distraction from my near aneurism back at the frat house. God, I ached to spoil her with my fingers, my tongue, and my cock. At the same time, I also itched to crack my hand across her ass cheeks until they were a nice shade of pink. Teach my girl a lesson. For being in my bed, the way I'd imagined for so long, and not being able to take her roughly, the way I wanted.

My eyes almost bugged out of my head when I discovered she wasn't wearing panties. Sure, I was all for my girl being naughty, but I was acutely aware that it hadn't been for my benefit. I was equal parts turned on and equal parts pissed off, which did nothing to buttress my eroding self-control.

Consent, consent, consent, I echoed to myself. The first time we fucked was one thing because, even though she'd been drinking a little bit, she'd been under my surveillance. She'd been in my club; I'd monitored how much she had to drink and how much time had passed before I'd laid my hands on her. She'd been a little tipsy, at most, by the time we started fucking around.

Tonight was an altogether different situation. Even now, her eyes were still a bit glazed over. Enough that I wasn't going to go there, no matter how much she begged for it. And make no bones about it, I loved to listen to this woman beg. It filled a hole inside my black heart I didn't know existed until she slid into my life, head held high like a goddamn goddess. But that didn't mean I couldn't worship her pussy.

"I'm not fucking you, and that's the end of the matter," I warned. "But...I'll give you my mouth."

Her eyes lit up.

Not exactly a hardship on my part since I wanted to taste her as much as I wanted my next breath.

Nodding vigorously, she clapped her hands together in a pleading gesture, repeating, "Yes, yes, yes."

"But I'm warning you, Jewel. That's all you get. Don't demand more than I'm willing to give." My hand slid down to cup her tight, juicy pussy. "Greedy thing, isn't it?"

Her eyes fluttered closed, and she let out the sexiest, neediest little sound. Hell, it had me by the balls. "So responsive. Such a hot little pussy you have for me."

She squirmed under my touch, shoving the hem of her dress up to expose her bare cunt. I traced the seam, pushing the tip of my finger between her outer lips. The heat coming off her practically scorched it.

Wiggling her hips, she spread her luscious thighs for me, and when I pulled my finger away, it was slick with her honey.

I growled under my breath. Fuck, I couldn't wait to take

her again. But since that wasn't going to happen until the morning, I needed the taste of her on my tongue. Now.

Yanking at my tie, I tore it off and left it twisting at my feet. My shoes and jacket were already abandoned somewhere in the living room. I returned to sit on the edge of my huge bed, and she was on me in a second, tugging my shirt off and then my pants. She tried to yank at my boxer briefs, but I gave her a stern warning, so she switched tactics and sat on my lap instead. *Such a bad girlie.*

Fuck me, I loved every minute of being with her.

Snuggling into me, she wiggled her bouncy ass against my stiff cock.

"Stop it, Jewel," I snapped, stifling a moan.

"I can take care of that for you," she cooed.

Thank fuck I still had the wherewithal to keep my boxer briefs on, or there'd be no way I could've stopped myself from sliding right into her inviting, tight hole.

"I'm not fucking you tonight," I reiterated, more to myself than her.

Her head whipped over her shoulder.

"I'm not drunk," she snipped, her regal chin held high.

Then she pressed her lips against mine. A little giggle slipped out. "Unless you count being drunk on your wicked mouth."

The little chit thought she could tease me, unaware that I was, yet again, skating on the edge of my control. Groaning, I moved her head away before I lost hold of my fraying self-restraint.

"I'm not like one of the pretty boys you've fucked with in the past. I'm a fucking man, and a bad one at that. No little girl is going to seduce me into doing something I don't want to do. If you keep pushing me, you'll only end up with a red ass. Then I'll bring you to the edge with my mouth and leave you hanging. Is that how you want this day to end?"

Even if she was sober enough to fuck at this point, I had to prove I was the boss. If this woman had an inkling of how much I was wrapped around her pinky finger, my life would be fucked. She'd take advantage of me, right, left, and center.

I knew two things as clear as day. One, she was addicted to my brand of fucking. And two, she wasn't in love with me. Not yet, at least. At this early point in our relationship, if I let her, she'd jerk my chain like I was a whipped puppy, and the prospect did not bode well for me.

She huffed out her frustration, but instead of taking heed of my warning by letting me lick her pretty pussy or going to sleep like a good girl, she slid down to the ground between my knees and gazed up at me with wide eyes.

"Let me take care of you, Nicu."

Hands smoothing up and down my thighs, she batted her eyelashes over her big, whiskey-and-moss-colored eyes, and I was putty in her hands. Her proposal took me off guard. Women didn't usually opt for giving a blow job right after a man declared his intention to go down on them. Whatever her reasons, she'd busted through my wall of control in the way only Jewel could.

I gave her a short nod of acquiescence.

She was watching me so intently that she was quick to react to my consent. My hand skated up her neck to cup her throat as she helped me disrobe completely. My cock slapped hard against my abs and bobbed in front of her as if he, too, was anticipating her mouth.

Writhing her wet pussy on the floor, she took my shaft in both her hands and licked from the root to the tip. Jesus *fuck*, I almost came from the vision alone: her long tresses unraveled down her back, her cheeks were flushed red, and her luminous eyes were on me. Her backside flared out near the floor, hips winding round and round in search of the right amount of pressure on her clit, no doubt. She was a sight to die for, or to come for, as the case may be.

I took a fistful of her hair as she licked a path up and down my shaft before taking me into the warm cavern of her mouth. I watched, riveted, as her lips spread wide over my girth. She pushed down, down, down until the tip hit the back of her throat. My brain short-circuited. The animal I had caged up inside was loosening its bonds. My hips flexed against my will as she swallowed and clenched her throat in a way that had me spurting, embarrassing myself.

Fuck, I wasn't going to last long.

I bared my teeth, conjuring sounds I didn't recognize. Goddamn, but this girl knew how to suck a man off. She didn't have much of a gag reflex, and she'd also clearly had practice. The latter part didn't faze me, because from now on, I'd be the only man she practiced on.

I tugged her hair to let her know she could come up. She popped off, leaving my cock wet from her mouth. Before I had a chance to catch my breath, she was back on me. Bobbing up and down, she suctioned my cock and used every dirty trick to make me come, fast and hard.

Another bratty move on her part, but she was grinding so hard on the rug, looking up at me with such pride that I wouldn't have stopped her, even if I could.

But what I could do was take over.

So, I did.

Her eyes brightened in excitement. Instead of wrestling me for dominance like she sometimes did, she hunkered down and relaxed her throat even further. Her hand continued to stroke me, but I was taking what I wanted now, using her mouth and throat to get myself off.

"That's right, baby doll. Relax and give me what I want. Your mouth and throat are mine for the taking, aren't they?"

She nodded once, just enough to answer. I got a little rough with her to test her boundaries, but she stayed with me. I was concentrating so hard on every flicker of her lashes, every twitch of her facial muscles, that I wasn't paying attention to my own body. Before I knew it, it grabbed me by the throat and threw me into a twister of an orgasm. The sound of rushing water flooded my eardrums. My flesh was torn apart like a bomb had exploded inside my guts. Eyes clouding over in pleasure, I shuddered in place as my cock jerked and spurted. She began to swallow my seed, but I wanted to paint her in my come. With a shaking hand, I forced myself to pull out and sprayed her chest, marking her as mine.

It seemed I couldn't get enough of doing that.

Although not fully recovered, I slammed down to my knees and took her mouth. Raking my tongue over hers, I gave her a brutal, manic kiss. Moaning shamelessly, she wrapped her legs around my waist and rocked against me, grinding her mound against my softening shaft. My hand found her supple backside as we attacked each other. I kneaded her ass cheek with one hand while the other sought out her hard little clit, ripe for my touch. Circling and pinching that nub, a sense of accomplishment filled my chest. I slid a long finger inside, savoring the clench of her inner muscles at even that minor invasion. *Fuck, imagine my cock in there.*

"You haven't been with anyone since me," I declared.

She was quick to agree, panting out, "No one but you."

I swirled my tongue in the shell of her ear and nabbed

the lobe in between my teeth for a sharp bite that left her breathless.

"Such a good, proper fuckdoll you are, aren't you?" I whispered. "Riding my hand. Taking what you need. Only I can give it to you right." My tone went hard and commanding. "Only me."

Loving my dirty talk, she let out a low, keening sound, half whimper, half cry. I added another finger. Her hips shifted back and forth to get more traction as she fucked my fingers, grinding against my palm. My fingers were thrusting inside her, but my filthy words would tip her over.

"Wait till I feed you my cock in the morning," I promised darkly. "I'm gonna fuck you raw until you beg me to stop. But I won't. I won't stop until I've flooded your tight pussy with my come."

"Oh, God, Nicu," she cried out.

"That's right. Call your god. Call my name," I demanded, adding a third finger, while picking up my pace. I took hold of her breast, alternating between pinching and pulling the beaded nipple while I put greater pressure on her clit. Her climax hit her fast and furious. Her cunt locked down on my fingers. I wiggled them, but I couldn't pull out if I tried.

I chased the emotions running across her face, hungry to watch her lose control. Her face twisted as an explosive climax washed over her. I held on to her jerking frame so she didn't collapse against the floor. Body trembling out tiny aftershocks, she clung to me like a spider monkey.

I couldn't get enough of her clutching to me.

Lifting her gently in my arms, I placed her on the bed, coming in right beside her. My head hit the pillow, and she snuggled into me like a small animal seeking comfort from a protector. I wrapped my arm around her waist and pulled her in tight.

Within seconds, she was out. She was exhausted from whatever had triggered her to drink and go to the frat party. Then the orgasm had tipped her over. Her chest moved rhythmically against mine as her breathing evened out.

Recalling my loss of control, I clenched my teeth tight. I'd fucked up, and I didn't fuck up like this anymore. This wasn't like putting black-and-red inked-up slime on the seat of Mr. Cartinelli, who only wore white pants. This was fucking serious. If the frat guy hadn't backed off, I wouldn't have given two fucks. I'd have thrust the muzzle of my gun in his jugular and blown a hole through his head for touching my woman, fuck the consequences. And consequences there would've been. No one shoots up a frat house at Columbia University without some serious blowback. Blowback for my family. My clan. *This isn't a fucking joke, Nicu. Get your shit straightened out.*

I let out a long, rough sigh. It was hard to stay upset when she looked so pretty, nestled in my arms. Her very presence calmed my frayed nerves. I'd never wanted a woman permanently in my bed. Not once. Now that I knew what she felt like in here, with the tension leaking from my body just from her curves settling more comfortably against me, I knew I was in a whole heap of trouble. There was no way I was letting go of a treasure like her. Eyeing my crotch, I cursed softly to myself. I was hard again, and her hip scraped against my dick as she shifted in her sleep.

Tomorrow. First thing tomorrow morning, I was going to punish her for what she put me through tonight. Then I was going to give her the fuck of her life.

13

JEWEL

I woke up to a cool breeze on my back and a heated furnace on my front. I snuggled into the bed, seeking more of the heat. Rubbing my eyes, my knuckles grazed warm skin on their way up.

My heart stopped.

My eyes popped open.

Shit, I was in his bed. How could I have forgotten I was at Nicu's?

Head pounding with a hangover, my eyes shied away from the thin rays of diabolical light piercing through the Venetian blinds. Memories flooded my slow-waking brain: drinking too fast, narrowly escaping a potential sexual assault, returning home with Nicu, sucking him off with relish, coming on his fingers, and then falling into a sleep fit for the dead.

I was presently cuddled into his chest, with him bowed over me, sheltering me from the world. My gaze shifted to the face slightly above mine. God, he was gorgeous. His tar-black hair curled up on the sides now that whatever hair product he used to tame it had faded away. A little notch marred the otherwise smooth olive skin between his prominent brows, as if he was thinking and scheming, even in his sleep. With the bold slash of his nose and his sculptured lips, he resembled a decadent god, maybe Dionysus. His mouth was parted slightly, and his breathing made adorable little snoring sounds.

Too much.

God, he was too much.

And this was before he opened his pale-blue eyes. I recalled how they deepened in anger or lust, like when they smoldered at me. I'd seen him around plenty of women, but I'd only seen that happen when he looked at *me*. A warm gooey feeling spread through my chest. I shouldn't like it as much as I did, but the core of my femininity reveled in it. At that thought, I bit my lips, and a tiny giggle slipped out.

Instantly, his thick arms tightened around me, bringing me in closer.

A smile tugged at one side of his mouth.

He was awake.

Without opening his eyes, he made a low humming sound that sent blood pooling between my legs, igniting a cauldron of heat. He pressed his impressive cock, which had not escaped my notice from the instant I woke up, into my soft belly.

"I could get used to waking up like this," he murmured, his voice a raspy growl that almost had me squirming against him.

I was about to retort that he'd better not get used to it, but I didn't have the energy to let the snarky comment fly. We were too cozy. The moment was too intimate. My knee-jerk reaction to throw up a wall between us had vanished somewhere along the line last night. Something had shifted inside me. Was it that I still felt vulnerable about my father's now-useless parole hearing? Or that Nicu had swooped in and saved me from a dicey situation of my own making? Perhaps it was that, time and again, he was there for me, no matter how hard I pushed him away.

Whether he was a bad-boy criminal or not, the fight was gone. I was an empty vessel, open for him to fill as he wished.

All I wanted to do was snuggle into him and let him take care of me. A decidedly *un*feminist thought, but one I could no longer deny. I'd been taking care of myself for years, and for once, I was willing to lay down the sword and let someone else take over. The man had certainly shown that he wasn't going anywhere, and there was no doubt of his capability to get the job done. He even seemed to take pleasure in being my protector. And after being my own protector for so long, it was a relief to turn the burden over to him for a little bit.

His hand clapped my buttock lightly.

"You were a bad, bad girl yesterday," he said in that husky voice, eyes still shut.

I wiggled against his thick cock.

Licking my lips, I cooed, "I was, wasn't I."

His eyes slid open slowly, his lids lifting and revealing more and more of the brittle blue until I had two ice-cold eyes blazing into me.

"Don't sound so proud of yourself," he replied.

"You like me bad," I teased.

His expression became stern. "I like you bad when you're with me. When I have control of the situation. You're free to do whatever you like when I'm around. But let me be crystal clear; I most certainly do not like you misbehaving when I'm not there to keep watch and protect you. That is unacceptable, and I won't stand for it."

I understood what he was saying. Even through the alcohol clouding my brain, there was no mistaking how upset he was at the prospect of anything happening to me. And I had been reckless. I had walked into a situation with strangers and hadn't taken the necessary steps to make sure I remained safe. I could blame the girls, but it wasn't their job to look after a drunk me. The fault was mine and mine alone.

Humbled, I lowered my eyes. "I understand."

"Do you?" he asked dubiously with a cocked brow.

"Yes. You don't want anything bad to happen to me, and something awful could've gone down yesterday."

Pulling back to inspect me, he reflected, "While you're saying the right things, I don't think words will suffice. There's a better way to guarantee that my point has penetrated your thick head."

His inscrutable comment put me on the alert. I hung back a little to get a better view of his face, but he returned my perusal with a blank look, absent of any clues.

My muscles tensed. "What do you mean by words won't suffice?"

"Afterward, I plan to fuck you within an inch of your life, the way I would've fucked you yesterday if you hadn't gotten wasted."

Alarm lifted the hairs on the back of my neck. "What do you mean by 'afterward'?" My voice had risen a few octaves by the time I'd finished my question.

His fingers gripped my butt tightly. His gaze bored into me, a determined expression notched on his face that made him achingly gorgeous.

He arched a cocky brow at me. "What do you think I mean?"

I wiggled my butt to dislodge his hold without success. A sinking feeling snuck up on me.

Panicking a little, I shrilled out, "What do you mean?"

He gave me a long look, full of meaning that I was too anxious to decipher.

"You know exactly what I mean," he stated resolutely.

"Just spit it out, will you?" I snapped.

"I'm going to make absolutely sure you understand what I mean. I will not allow you to put yourself in danger again, and there is only one way to ensure that you remember this lesson...by *feeling* it."

He swatted my butt lightly. *Smack.* "Right." *Smack.* "Here." *Smack.*

"Nooo," I breathed out.

"Oh, I'll be fucking you, too. Have no fear about that," he promised darkly.

My hands flew up, palms slamming against his bare chest.

"No!" I cried out.

"Yes," he growled low.

In a flash, he had me on my belly, legs spread out. This guy had some serious ninja moves because I did *not* see that coming. He landed on top; his groin nestled between my ass cheeks. He'd fallen asleep naked, as well, because I felt the smooth skin of his hot, thick shaft on my butt.

I turned my head, cheek on the smooth sheet, and spat out, "I don't want this!"

"This isn't about what you want. This is a lesson. If I know you at all, it will be one of many to come. Which makes the first one particularly important because it sets the stage for the future. I can assure you, Jewel, that today is the beginning of the rest of your life. Nothing will be like what came before. Your parents allowed you to do whatever the fuck you wanted. Because of Cat, I allowed the same thing. That was my first mistake. Then I mistakenly trusted your sense of self-preservation, but you obviously have none, which means I'm taking over from here on out."

"That's not fair," I cried out, struggling against him. I wasn't entirely opposed to him smacking my butt, but I wasn't about to make it easy on him either. *Where's the fun in that?* And his domineering, take-control attitude was definitely making me wet.

"Oh, it's more than fair. You're so strong and independent that I assumed it would override any truly dangerous impulses on your part. I was wrong, but I don't make the same error twice. Ever. If I hadn't been there last night, you'd be in a doctor's office right now, legs spread open to get samples for a rape kit."

I gasped as I shifted underneath him to test if I had any wiggle room. I didn't. "That's going too far."

"No, no it's not," he countered. "Don't do that. Don't minimize what happened because it didn't turn into a fucking nightmare. The fact remains that shit is going to change, starting today. You're in my care now." The way he said the last part sent a tingle down my spine with an awareness that I'd barely scratched the surface of who Nicu was.

"Conveniently, you were made for me because, from now on," he continued, "we're joined at the hip."

"What about your family?" I gritted out.

"What about them?" he rejoined. "I don't care who knows about us."

"I don't belong," I argued.

"You'll have to learn how to belong. As for them, they'll have to learn to accept you. That's all there is to it."

"What the hell are you talking about?" I smacked him hard on the flank. "What? Am I going to be your *girl*friend?"

I spat out. "For how long? Sooner or later, you'll have to marry a virginal *mafie* girl like the one you were sitting next to at Cat and Luca's tasting."

"Fuck that, I'm keeping you," he snarled, popping me hard on a butt cheek.

I let out a little scream. Talking sense to him was like trying to take a bone away from a starving, wild jackal.

"And don't you dare hit me," he warned. "If I smack your ass, it's for one of two reasons. To give you pleasure or to teach you something. I'd never raise a hand to a woman, and I expect the same level of respect in return."

"I can't spank you, so I don't see how this is fair," I griped.

A guttural chortle came from above me. "Oh, baby doll, you can spank my ass anytime, and definitely when I'm inside you. As for a lesson, you won't need to give me one because I'm not impulsive. Not anymore. I don't make bad choices based on runaway emotions. A made *mafie* man can't survive otherwise. And now, as a *mafie* girl, you'll have to take your safety seriously. I won't always be around and—"

"Mafie *girl*?" I sputtered out. "Have you lost your mind?"

Panic was rising fast in my chest. My breathing accelerated exponentially. He couldn't be serious. Fucking him was one thing, but I wasn't about to become part of his criminal society.

Cat was a *mafie* princess, and she'd explained how things worked in their world. They had a twisted arranged-marriage tradition for high-ranking families. A marriage was, first and foremost, about the consolidation of power between families. Alex had married his little sister's best friend, but he was a mob boss, so he could do whatever the hell he wanted. He'd also known her practically his entire life. She was a trusted person who had grown up on the periphery of their world. I was neither of those things, so chances were, Nicu was just talking.

As if reading my mind, he answered, "I'm dead fucking serious. I don't have girlfriends. I fuck or I have a wife. Those are my two options, and I've made up my mind as to which one you'll be."

I craned my head so he could see the horror on my face from above me. "You can't be serious... I don't even want to know what's going on in your mind." Shaking my head, I decided to switch tactics and jested, "This is not a conversation I'm having with you. You're sitting on me, for God's sake."

I refused to listen to his ramblings. They cracked something open in my heart that I didn't even know was there, something about belonging. Belonging to his family. Belonging to him. I couldn't afford to develop any kind of deep feelings toward him, the kind that spoke of a future between us. My chest felt tight. Honestly, it was cruel of him to even bring it up. We both knew anything permanent between us was impossible. Him, because I was an outsider. Me, because he was a criminal.

Luckily, he didn't press any further. Instead, he responded to my joke with a chuckle. The tension between us broke.

"Total overexaggeration," he said. "I am not *sitting on you*. You can breathe perfectly fine. I'm simply making sure I have your full attention and that you're in the correct position for what I plan to do next. You didn't think I'd give you an inch, now did you? Especially, considering you're about to get your fine ass tanned."

With a dramatic sigh, he went on, "If you take your

punishment well, I have a surprise for you...but only if you're good."

"I am not a child," I sneered at him. "Stop treating me like one with your condescending comment about giving me a reward if I play nice and let you smack me! Ugh, you're such a brute."

"For a grown woman, you sure as hell act like a child. You're my baby doll, and I fully intend to treat you like one *after* I make certain you learn to take your safety seriously. As for being a brute, you betcha I am, and don't pretend like you don't love it."

Without thinking, I let my hand fly out and smacked his flank.

He pressed deeper into me as he warned, "I told you not to do that. See, that's your way of telling me you need my immediate attention. And don't you worry, you've got it."

It didn't help that I was already buck naked, having fallen asleep in the nude right after he gave me an orgasm. His cock hadn't flagged during our argument, either. If anything, he'd gotten harder. It was cradled between my spread butt cheeks, taunting me with the thought, *what if he actually uses it? Penetrates me?* I had never done anal. Had no real interest in it and had never anticipated changing my mind. But with him rubbing against me as he moved or when I tried to wiggle out from under him, I was getting seriously aroused, and the notion was suddenly intriguing.

As if he'd discovered my enjoyment, he lifted off me. I quickly tried to flip over or roll away, but he caught me effortlessly. Pinning me down, he looped his legs over mine and placed a firm hand on my lower back.

"I will hate you forever if you do this," I threatened.

His hand palmed my bottom, completely unmoved by my warning.

"Mm-hmm. This is going to be good," he mused to himself.

"Fuck you," I growled.

Barely an instant passed between my curse and his hand connecting with my backside.

Smack.

A hiss escaped between my clenched teeth. "Ow!"

It didn't hurt that badly, but more was coming and, knowing what I knew of Nicu, he wasn't going to hold back on his so-called *lesson*. I tried wiggling around but found myself effectively trapped. Realizing that I was good and truly fucked, I stopped struggling, and with a searing look that would've crippled a lesser man, I gave up with an irritated huff.

"Better," he hummed.

"Shut up," I barked out, nipping him for good measure. For some reason, everything that came out of his mouth felt patronizing. Rationally speaking, it probably wasn't true, but I felt helpless. I didn't do helpless. Thankfully, the man was smart, and after one last chuckle, he refrained from saying anything more.

He began to give me the spanking he'd promised. My buttocks bounced from the impact of his hand each time it made contact. Flushed red with a mixture of embarrassment and arousal, I focused on the Persian rug beneath the bed, following the various lines of blue in the pattern as it wound around this way and that.

Every so often, after a hard smack that had me gasping and my skin flaming with pinpricks of pain, he'd smooth it over with his rough palm, stimulating an unexpected response. I shouldn't have been enjoying any part of this. While it was useless to fight him, I should've at the very least snubbed him. I should've made a show of my ire by hissing and spitting curses at him.

But I didn't. I lay there, absorbing every ounce of comfort he gave me. There was another underlying reason why I wasn't fighting him with my every breath. It was a reason I didn't want to probe into too deeply, but I wasn't willing to turn away from it completely either. Yet again, he was making me feel cared for. I knew what neglect was, and this was most definitely not it.

He'd been genuinely horrified yesterday, and he was taking the time and effort to correct me. A man like Nicu wouldn't take the time to do that unless he cared. It was twisted, for sure, but a part of me simply couldn't garner the requisite amount of fury. It certainly didn't compare to the impotent rage I felt when Mother had dumped me at a boarding school for the sole reason that she didn't want to be bothered with raising me.

After a particularly strong swat, he made a comforting sound in the back of his throat that instantly took the sting away. The heat of his palm rested on my abused flesh, soothing away the undeniable bite from his spanking.

His hand stilled; his fingers spread over my two cheeks in a possessive gesture. When he stared down at his palm planted over my behind, I had the eerie sensation that I belonged to him. His hand slid down, splaying my thighs open to his scrutiny.

Even though we'd had sex, I'd never felt this vulnerable and exposed before. He stroked my inner thigh, reaching the apex and tickling my clit before petting the other thigh. Again and again, he caressed me in the same rhythm until my hips twitched impatiently for more.

He swatted my pussy a few times before returning to my clit.

"You're mine, and you'll learn to take care of what's mine," he whispered gruffly, although I was only half listening, what with my insane state of arousal.

His hand clapped down on my buttock, a reminder of his ability to punish me as he saw fit. At this point, I was so needy that the pain didn't really register as such. It blended in with my overall craving, only acting to accentuate it. Knowing that I was under his watchful eyes, I gyrated my hips with increasing desperation.

"I need more," I moaned. "More."

"Insatiable little pussy you have, hmm?" he purred.

Humping the bed and still unable to get the needed pressure, a plea broke out of me, "Please." I begged, "Nicu, please."

"Fuck," he cursed. Grasping one of my thighs, he widened my legs and settled behind me.

"Up," he commanded as he grabbed my hips and brought me to my knees.

I whimpered, feeling the cool air waft over my fevered, wet flesh. But thank God, a moment later, he was pressing into me, pushing deep and spearing my heated, pulsing pussy until he was buried to the hilt. His hand landed on the back of my neck to brace and hold me steady. For some reason, I loved that rough hand of his.

Adjusting my position on my forearms, I let out a sigh of relief. My eyes practically rolled back in my head as I moved forward and back against his bare shaft, fucking it without restraint. It was like an inferno between us, and Nicu wasn't about to be left behind. He began to thrust, each one hard and thorough, his heavy balls smacking against me. He was determined to prove his supremacy with a commanding and exhaustive pounding, and I relished it.

"Who does this pussy belong to?"

I clamped down on him, letting him know how much I got off on his show of dominance. Such a good girl I was.

"Who owns this pussy?" he demanded again, speeding up, his hips slapping against my tender ass.

I clenched hard again, spewing out a desperate moan.

"Who? Tell me, dammit," he grated out, his impatient grasp tightening around my tresses. His touch might have been impatient, but he abruptly slowed his pistoning hips to an irritatingly measured pace. To torment me, I was sure.

"You do," I whined.

"You fucking love when I remind you who this pussy belongs to. You bear down on me each time," he warned, his tone now smug. "Such a good little doll. My dirty whore. Just for me."

A shiver rippled through my body at the way he twisted those filthy words into an endearment. Nicu had the capability of looking straight into my soul and ascertaining my darkest fantasies, fantasies I hadn't known existed until he unearthed them. And my fantasy now was that I wanted to play the good little slut for him. Spread my legs wide and fondle my pussy right in front of him. Show him how wet and desperate I was for him. Beg him with my body to fill me up. Ravish me. Defile me. Treat me like the dirty little secret that I was. I wasn't a virgin or *mafie*. He didn't have to be careful with me. Quite the opposite, in fact. I wanted him to take me, to use me. I wanted him to lose the control he held on to so tightly and pounce on me like a rampaging beast.

I've never wanted to feel owned like I did with Nicu. He was the only man to elicit this feeling, and I gloried in it. A niggling reminder prompted the thought that it was dangerous to be owned by the wrong man. *Could he be the right man?* With my history of abandonment, there wasn't supposed to be such a thing, making the possibility terrifying...and deeply alluring.

I heard slapping sounds as he fucked me with leisure, as if he had all the time in the world. He was purposely going slow, the bastard, to teach me who was boss. Frantic lust shot through my veins like balls of fire. I clenched my inner walls to retaliate...and to incite him to go faster, but nothing doing.

I slapped the mattress in frustration. "Fuck me already," I cried.

"What was that?" he queried smoothly, pretending he didn't know what he was doing to me.

The man was diabolical.

Swiveling my head to the side swiftly, I clamped my teeth down on the bulging muscle of his upper arm. I may have been pinned beneath him, but I took him by surprise. He chortled deeply, as if the mouthful of flesh I'd taken between my teeth was a pesky mosquito bite, but he did pick up his pace. Eyes to the ceiling, I gave a quick prayer of thanks.

His thrusts got faster and more forceful. I felt it on my sore butt again, but I didn't care, because I was consumed by the feel of his bare cock splitting me open the way I craved it. Only Nicu knew how to give it to me just right. I arched my back, inviting him to go deeper.

I was getting close, skating the edge of an orgasm, when he abruptly pulled out.

Shaking and furious, I screeched in frustration. Then I begged. "Please, Nicu...please, oh God, you can't leave me like this."

"One last time: *Who owns this pussy?*"

This last show of power and authority seared into my brain the truth of the matter.

"You," I said in a raw voice.

"That's right, and don't you ever forget it, Jewel," he intoned. "I own every fucking inch of you, and I'm going to flood this pussy with my come."

His hand slid down to cradle the back of my neck, and then he proceeded to fuck me for all he was worth. He slammed back inside so hard that my head would've hit the headboard if his firm hold hadn't kept me in place. His cock pummeled me, spreading my pussy for him. He pulled out entirely and then plunged back in, making sure to brand me with his thick staff, using brutal strokes so I would never forget.

Normally, I couldn't come from penetration alone, but the combination of his words, his strength, and his demanding power overwhelmed me. My senses overly taxed, the pleasure barreled down on me, and I came with a scream. With Nicu, I always seemed to end up coming while screaming his name. Silence wasn't an option. He stripped me of control. His iron will wrenched everything from me and rewarded my submission with unstoppable orgasms. Just when I thought I was coming down, he shifted and bore down again. One climax rolled right into another.

A few thrusts later, he joined me, grunting and gnashing his teeth as he coated my womb with his come. The thought caused a barrage of shivers to run through my body. I shuddered out a silent thanks that I was on birth control because he fucked me like he meant to breed me.

14

JEWEL

The contrast of fucking me to oblivion and then treating me with such tenderness could give a girl whiplash. After manhandling me like I was his personal toy, Nicu was unbelievably tender. But I'd be lying if I said his assiduous care wasn't exactly what I needed. Normally, I was a morning person, but apparently a good spanking followed by incredible sex and a full-body massage could reduce me to a puddle of goo, even at this early hour.

His fingers gently tested the heated skin of my buttocks as I lay splayed across his bed, limp from the inundation of pleasure. It was another example of the juxtaposition I was beginning to get used to experiencing with this complicated man. The hard and the soft, he had them both in spades. Anyone who took Nicu at face value, as a single-minded made man who only cared about following directions and enforcing rules, woefully missed an entire part of who he was.

Caressing my behind with feather-like touches, he spoke

softly, "You took your spanking so well. Now I will reward you."

My breath stuttered in my lungs, goose bumps breaking out on my skin at the raspy, guttural tone and the implication of those words. Who knew a spanking could be so cathartic? I felt as if all my problems had melted away. Even my father's denied parole, the cause of so much angst for me, seemed far away, as if I were reading a novel about someone else's experience.

I shifted beneath his touch to shake away my visceral reaction and covered it up by joking, "Besides fucking me to oblivion and then massaging my butt, you mean?"

"Well, I plan to feed you," he revealed.

"What, feed me your cock for breakfast?" I quipped. "You can't possibly know how to cook, being a traditional *mafie* guy?"

His grip tightened on my butt cheek. "Careful with that mouth of yours...could get you into trouble," he cautioned. Returning to rubbing the red imprint of his fingers on my flesh, he made a scoffing sound. "My *bunică* and my mother brought me up right. Of course, I can cook."

"I'll believe it when I taste it," I retorted.

He gave me a light pop on my flank that made me yelp.

"Ye of little faith, I'll show you," he replied. "I have plans for you today. After I make sure your appetite has been satisfied, I'm going to wash you down in the shower. Once you're nice and clean, I'll introduce you to your real reward."

"Oh, the plot thickens," I observed languidly.

Getting a home-cooked meal—if he could really cook—and showering together, seemed like reward enough to me. I didn't need him to give me a gift. Typically, guys with money liked giving gifts of jewelry, but it wasn't particularly interesting to me, considering I grew up with all my material needs met. My emotional needs were the real challenge. If he thought I'd go gaga over a pretty ring or watch, he was about to be sorely disappointed. Yet I caught the gleam in his eyes, and because he was taking care of me oh-so-well, and because I didn't want to rain on his parade, I decided to play nice. Considering he'd elicited the most intense orgasm I'd experienced to date, he'd proven himself worthy of cooperation.

Pulling me to my feet, he wrapped me in an emerald-green jacquard robe, which was permeated with his distinctive woodsy, masculine essence. He tied the belt around me firmly, his brows pinched in concentration. It was adorable, the way he took care of me so seriously. The silk of the robe rubbed against my peaked nipples. Yes, I was the little slut he'd labeled me earlier because, apparently, all the man had to do was wrap me in an item of his clothing, and I was squirming with the desire to be filled by him, yet again.

After donning a pair of pajamas, he took my hand and led me out into the living room. The sunlight flooding in through the wall of windows attacked my eyeballs. With a groan, I slapped my free hand over my eyes.

With a deep chortle that slid down my spine, he suggested, "Let's get something for that hangover, shall we?"

Placing his palm on my lower back, he steadied me as he guided me into the kitchen. The room fit the modern edge of the rest of the apartment, accented with rural-looking painted utensils and art naïf decorative plates on the wall. He sat me down at a rustic kitchen table, where I laid my forehead face down on my arms to escape the ruthlessly cheerful sunlight.

I listened to gently opened drawers and other noises he made as he puttered about the kitchen. Moments later, I heard a soft *plunk* near my head. I peeked out from between the fingers covering my eyes. There was a tall glass of water and what I assumed were ibuprofen pills beside me. I swallowed the pills and greedily drained the water.

"Sheesh, I guess I was thirsty after a night of debauchery," I noted.

"I've had a few of those myself," he shared as he carefully placed a well-loved, chipped red-enamel pot with a long handle, which I knew from visiting Cat was called an *ibric*, on the stove and set about making Turkish coffee. I hadn't expected to see him using such a worn pot, considering he lived in the lap of luxury.

"You?" I looked at him doubtfully. "You always seem so in control."

Stirring the pot filled with water and coffee grounds, he gave me what I now recognized as a little self-deprecating shrug. "Now, I am. It took me a few years to learn how best to harness my excessive...energy."

Funny, I couldn't picture him getting trashed despite the untamed quality so evident beneath his cool exterior. "Oh, and how did you manage it?"

He gave me a devilish, unrepentant look.

"You've seen how I fuck," he replied simply.

A spray of water spewed out of my mouth. I grabbed the dish towel he handed me, wiped my mouth, and dabbed at the water soaking his silk robe. He laughed deeply, the rumbling sound emanating from his chest. My toes curled. Nicu chuckled often enough, but it was a rare privilege to hear his deep, throaty laugh. I could get addicted to this man, and not only because of the way he took care of me in bed. Far from it. I was learning that Nicu was complex.

His phone on the counter beeped. Picking it up, he read through his text and rumbled, "Fucking Tatum. Texting me this early in the morning. It's even earlier there."

"Where is *there*?"

"Cali. He's in a rage, and that never happens. Let me reply, baby," he mumbled, texting back and forth as he watched over the brewing coffee. I was riveted by the adorable expression of concentration on his face as he focused on his phone.

"Sorry about that. Things aren't going well for him over there, and he needs moral support."

"You're always there for them, aren't you? Your family?"

He turned serious eyes on me and replied, "Always. Just like you are for your father."

"Touché," I murmured, touched that he realized the lengths I went to for my father. By linking the two, he was showing how similar we were in our loyalty.

Nicu broke the serious moment by returning to our original conversation with a ridiculous confession. "I'm a bit of a speed junkie. I like my cars fast, like my women."

I rolled my eyes. "As much as I'd love to own the label, I'm not that fast."

"You're the perfect speed for me."

"Oh my God, was that supposed to be a compliment?"

He lifted the *ibric* off the flame for a few seconds, letting the foam settle before returning it to the stove.

"Baby doll, I've given you more than a compliment. I've given you a nickname," he said with a meaningful look.

That, he had. A warmth spread through my chest. Dammit, how did he manage to make me feel so weak around him?

Needing to break the intimate mood, I asked, "Do you like all your women fast? I can only imagine how many have traipsed through here."

Jealousy shot through me at the thought that he'd made

other women coffee the morning after, just as he was doing for me.

He poured the hot liquid into two small porcelain demitasse cups, the handles and lips dipped in gold paint. His cup had a tiny chip on the delicate gold of the handle.

Placing a cup and saucer near my hand on the table, he warned, "Don't do that."

A little frown creased my forehead.

"Do what?" I asked, feigning ignorance as I lifted the coffee cup to my lips. Tasting the dark, earthy flavor with hints of honey, I moaned.

"This is so good," I gushed. I was already feeling better after downing an entire glass of water and taking the medication, but the first hit of this coffee was ambrosia.

"Glad you like it. I made it with a hint of sugar to balance out the bite in your personality," he teased.

I shot him a caustic look, but pointedly ignored his cutting little comment. He might complain, but we both knew he liked my prickly side as much as I liked to turn it up for him.

"It's divine," I murmured gratefully as I took another delicious sip.

Sitting down beside me, he took a leisurely sip as well and returned to the topic at hand. "You mentioned other women to throw up a wall between us," he chided softly. "I may have had my fair share of women, but I'm far from a manwhore. Romanians aren't prudish. We're not ashamed to enjoy sex. I've never claimed to be a saint, but I've never brought a woman home before, and I certainly don't make a habit of preparing coffee for them, of cooking for them, or of taking care of them." His voice lowered an octave. "Not in the ways I take care of you."

My cheeks flushed hot. His little speech had softened

me. I shifted in my seat a little, the tenderness of my behind a reminder of exactly the type of "care" he was referring to. Since yesterday, he was no longer letting me get away with anything, and I liked it.

"Really? That surprises me. You seemed to know your way around a woman's backside."

"I may have experimented a bit, but yesterday was about you."

Again, a gooey warmth splashed across my chest. If he was trying to woo me and make me feel special, he was definitely on the right track. While I didn't know exactly what he meant by experimentation, I truthfully didn't want to delve deeper into Nicu's past with other women. He'd called my bullshit when he accused me of bringing it up to throw up some distance between us.

It had also triggered the same weird Nicu-specific jealousy that occurred the night I met him, when the cocktail waitress flirted with him. I was aware of how ridiculous it was for me to be possessive of him, considering there was no chance it could last between us. I'd never felt this way about any of my other partners, but then again, why should I be surprised? Anything having to do with Nicu was different. He was like no other man I'd met before.

I finished my coffee and stood up to replenish my cup when he placed a hand on my forearm. Getting up, he brought the *ibric* from the stove and refilled my cup.

"I don't have any *ciorba de burtă* to help you get over your hangover, but I can make you eggs with tomatoes and peppers. How does that sound?"

"Sure, that's perfect. Uh, what's a chiorba di burbba, whaa?"

"*Ciorba de burtă* is tripe soup. It's an old Romanian hangover cure."

I made a gagging noise.

He smirked at me. "What? You don't think a serving of cow stomach like in the old country would do you some good?"

I made a face and muttered, "Hard pass."

He laughed again, the sound setting my belly to fluttering in the best of ways.

"Alcohol plays a big part in Romanian culture. We like to drink, thus we need a cure that really works. But you're a neophyte, both in drinking and hangover cures, so I'll spare you. This time. But when I bring you home to my mother and grandmother, I assure you that you will lick the plate of any dish they set down in front of you."

The image he'd conjured up in my head, tripe soup aside, sounded wonderful. The self-assurance and pride in his mother and grandmother touched me. One thing undeniable about Nicu was his love of family. I saw the way he picked up the phone whenever his twin called, no matter the time of day or night. He picked up, even if it was only to say he'd speak to her later. No one did that nowadays. Hell, people barely talked on the phone, period.

Nicu got up and pulled out veggies and eggs from the fridge. After peeling off the skin of the tomatoes and dicing them, along with a green pepper, he tossed them into a pan to simmer. Then he did something I'd never seen before. One by one, he cracked the eggs directly into the tomato-pepper concoction. With a wooden spatula, he rapidly beat them in as he asked me to cut slices from a country-style bread inside a breadbox.

"If either of them gives it to me, then maybe I'll try it. You, I don't trust that much," I said with a sniff.

He gave me a third laugh, and another swarm of butterflies exploded in my abdomen.

Three in a row.

Wow, just wow. I needed to get drunk and stay over more often. Normally, I'd pull away from such a thought, but in this cozy kitchen, drinking tasty coffee made by a gorgeous guy cooking me breakfast without his shirt on, I was ready to relive this scenario time and time again.

"*Bunică* made some yesterday. It's made with polenta as well as flour. Romanians are big into using polenta in their cooking and baking. You'll love it," he declared confidently.

For some reason, I didn't doubt it. The man hadn't been joking when he said he knew how to cook.

It was official; I was impressed.

I had grown up eating meals prepared by private chefs. We ate bread bought from French bakeries on Madison Avenue, near the apartment where I lived before my father was caught. But outside of visiting Cat, I had never eaten homemade food prepared by a family member. Mother would've been appalled by the very notion of ruining her manicure to knead pasty flour dough to bake bread. The very idea was preposterous. Perhaps because it reminded me of visiting Cat's home in Queens, I loved the smells wafting through the kitchen as he prepared our meal.

My stomach grumbled.

"Hungry, I see," he remarked.

Touched by the intimacy of having this strong, virile man whipping up a meal for me, I decided he'd earned the chance for me to open up and share with him.

"This reminds me of vacations from school when Cat would bring me to her home, and we would be greeted by the scent of cooking and baking when we walked into her house. Mother didn't do holidays in cold, wintery New York, but I had to stay and visit my father up in Otisville, so I spent most winter holidays with Cat and her family."

"Cat's is a very traditional Romanian household, for sure," was his only comment.

"Her grandmother always made that Romanian sweet-bread with walnuts for our homecoming. What is it called? Kazanac?"

"*Cozonac*," he said as he indicated for me to put the slices of bread in a toaster oven.

"Yes, that's it. *Co-zo-nac*," I repeated carefully.

He shot me a brilliant grin that made my knees go weak.

"Nice accent," he complimented. "I'll make a Romanian out of you yet. So you've been around the Popescus quite a bit, then?"

His tone was deceptively calm, but I knew better. He wouldn't blatantly probe into my life, but I could feel his curiosity like it was a living, breathing thing. I didn't think I was imagining that my friendship with Cristo wasn't far from his mind.

Cristo and I were buddies. Being a few years older than Cat and I, he was the first real man I flirted with. While our relationship was comfortable, sometimes even demonstrative because the Popescus were affectionate with one another, we were only friends. Of course, Nicu didn't know that, and I knew there was no love lost between them. If my newfound jealousy was anything to go by, I could only imagine what a man like Nicu felt, knowing I'd spent a lot of time in Cat's home.

But I wasn't about to open that can of worms when things were so easy between us, so I blabbered, "Yup, Cat's my best friend. More than that actually. She's like a sister to me. After all, she saved me." I swallowed hard, my gaze fixated on the slices of bread turning crispy in the toaster oven.

His eyes shot to me.

I turned away and returned to my seat at the kitchen table, behind him.

"She doesn't know that, of course, but I was seriously depressed when we met. My family had been destroyed, my father was in jail for what felt like forever, and Mother had abandoned me in a boarding school in the middle of winter, in rural Massachusetts, of all places. The school was prestigious, but the stillness and quiet of the countryside was enough to drive a New Yorker like me crazy."

I inspected my nails. "I was suicidal, actually." I paused there, waiting for his reaction. When I got none, I snuck a quick look at him. Face wiped of emotion, which couldn't be taken at face value, I watched as he plated the egg, tomato, and pepper concoction from the hot pan onto two dishes. His head was canted to the side, as if he was listening carefully and didn't want to interrupt.

I went on, "Suicidal thoughts, to be exact. I was in so much pain, but I couldn't do that to my dad. He'd been through enough already." I was too ashamed to tell him the entire story, a story that would've ended badly if it hadn't been for Cat. "He was a man full of hubris. He had everything. He was handsome, charming, and clever, but he didn't come from the kind of WASPy old-family money Mother came from. Although far from poor, his family hadn't hoarded their wealth for generations like my mother's family had. Not only did he strive to prove himself worthy, but he wanted to exceed her expectations. In the end, he found himself in a quicksand of financial disaster." I paused. "And when he was caught, she dumped him almost immediately."

I rarely spoke about my history. Only Cat knew the sordid details, and that happened over the course of several years, after she'd confided in me about her family. But that wintery day, in the middle of the semester, when Cat approached me at the cafeteria, boldly dropping her tray on the empty table in front of me, she'd thrown me a lifeline.

"He lost everything. Who would visit him on Christmas Day or his birthday? Everyone abandoned him. His wife, his colleagues, his friends, his family. He was a pariah," I whispered quietly. "He still is."

Suddenly, Nicu was down on his knees, my hands cupped tightly in his.

My eyes snapped to his.

Gaze fierce, he swore, "I will never abandon you. What happened to your father and you was wrong. *Wrong*. On so many levels, I don't even know where to begin. That's not family. Family sticks by you *no matter what*. What you do for your father proves you've learned that pivotal lesson. You could've easily turned your back on him, from humiliation, from wanting to escape the stigma of his tarnished name... but you didn't. It's a testament of who you are at the very core of your being. The fact that you sought solace in Cat's traditional family is another example of what you're unwilling to admit. Stop denying the obvious. You're exactly like me: loyal and family bound. *You are* mafie."

I twisted my head away.

"For whatever reason, you're unwilling to see it, but I do," he said, with a shake of his head. "There's more than one way to be part of my society. It's not only about being born into a clan, the way I was. What happened wasn't worthy of you, but I have a family worthy of you. Believe me, some families understand the true meaning of allegiance. They take it seriously. They'd never abandon you. But there's no need to go into that right now. I'm a patient man, and I can bide my time.

"Like baking bread," he gestured to the perfectly toasted

slices of bread on the table beside us. "It takes time to wait for the yeast to activate and the dough to rise. Bread must proof not once, but twice. I remember as a kid being amazed when *Bunică* would pull out the bread after a proofing and show me the risen dough. Your rise won't be any less impressive."

I was unwilling to see it because it was too scary to acknowledge. This moment in his kitchen, with a cup of coffee and a plate of food sitting on the table, steam rising and wafting a delicious fragrance my way, was perfect. He was perfect. His family seemed perfect. And yet, it was predicated on criminality. But it went even deeper than that. There was a frighteningly deep-rooted fear in me. *My* family had once seemed perfect as well, and look how it had imploded. I couldn't risk my heart again. I just couldn't.

Pursing my lips together briefly, I mocked, "You did not just compare me to a loaf of bread!"

"There is no greater compliment, baby girl. Bread may seem simple. It may be taken for granted by people today, but it is the staff of life. It's been eaten by human beings for 15,000 years, and it's essential. The French Revolution was triggered by the rising bread prices because the French couldn't afford their baguettes. Do not underestimate bread."

"Look at you, Mr. Philosopher," I quipped.

Another smile broke out on his face, lightening the mood between us.

Getting on his feet, he pointed at the food. "Now eat up. I didn't slave away at a hot stove for you to let it get cold. I may be patient, but I have yet to show you my surprise."

My brows hit my forehead. "There's more?"

"Oh, baby doll, there's so much more."

15

NICU

Once I made sure Jewel had eaten, I took a shower with her. Using the full extent of my self-control, I didn't fuck her. It was a close thing, though. We got dressed, and I gave her a pair of pants that were a holdover from when Tasa lived in the city. We were twins and had spent more than the average amount of time together before she ran off.

Jewel had to wear one of my plain black T-shirts. I reveled in the knowledge that she was in one of my shirts. She tied a knot at her abdomen, showing off a sliver of skin that made me want to eat her up. Fuck, no other woman tested me like she did. She was so goddamn sexy, I had to forcibly restrain myself from dragging her into bed.

As much as I wanted to take her again, I was on a mission. I wanted to share with her the part of my life, outside of my family, that kept me sane. Focused, I hustled her out of my apartment before we missed the main event.

She didn't know it yet, but I was taking her racing.

I didn't keep my racing vehicles in the basement parking lot of my building. As convenient as the building parking was, it wasn't conducive to tinkering with my cars. I drove her to the Sky Garage Penthouse in downtown Manhattan, where up on the fourteenth floor, my two beauties had a spectacular view of the Empire State Building.

Jewel skidded to a halt in front of my two identical Bugatti Chirons. I was a twin, so of course I had to honor that by having two of the same models, one electric blue and the other cherry red.

Her head whipped in my direction.

"What is this?" she asked incredulously.

"These are my girls. Meet Betty and Veronica," I replied with a grin.

"You're kidding me, right? You did not name your cars from an awful Archie comic book."

"Nah, just joking," I conceded. "I haven't named my cars after imaginary women."

Nodding, she looked at them, but then immediately turned back to me. "But you've named them, haven't you?" she declared.

She was quick on the uptake; I'd give her that.

"I have," I admitted.

"Well, what terrible names have you given your fancy metal death boxes."

I barked out a laugh. *This girl.*

"Blue and Cherry."

She gave a fake shudder. "Only marginally better."

"So what's the surprise?" she asked, cocking her hip out. She looked at me suspiciously. "I don't need a car."

"They're not for you," I retorted with a laugh. "Each of these babies is worth over two million dollars."

She gulped. "Oh, wow, I was not expecting that."

"Yeah. Wow is an understatement," I countered, opening one of them and waving her toward the passenger's side.

"We're going to race one of these so-called *metal death traps*, as you eloquently called them."

She stumbled midstep. "*Race* them?"

"Yup," I replied smugly, eyeing her from my position in the driver's seat as she hovered near the open door hesitantly.

"As in *we* will drive this thing in a race today?" she clarified.

"Yep," I repeated with an encouraging wave of my hand. "Hop in."

She took a step back. "Uh…I don't think so."

"Jewel," I warned. "Nothing is going to happen to you. It's a little amateur drag race. No biggie. You'll be perfectly safe with me."

"Why do you want me to do this?" she asked, her head tilted to the side.

"Because it's exciting and fun. I want you to feel the speed and the road underneath you when you're on a track. There's nothing like it."

With an exasperated sigh, she dropped into the low seat. Grabbing the seat belt, she muttered, "You better not get me killed. Otherwise, you're the one who will have to go to Otisville and tell my father. I promise, you do not want to get him mad, and killing his only daughter will do just that."

"Noted, baby doll," I crooned.

She was too fucking adorable when she was irritated. It was one of the reasons I liked to keep her on the edge of an orgasm until she was spitting at me like a wet kitten.

The instant she was buckled in, I revved the engine for her. She let out a little scream and gave me a vicious glare. It was too easy to get her riled up, yet I didn't bother restraining myself.

Eyeing the interior critically, she begrudgingly admitted, "It is pretty, I'll give you that."

I peered down at the ostentatious silver "3B" inscribed in the center of the steering wheel and snorted. "Pretty is not the word I'd use."

The interior was a symphony of crisp minimalism with organic lines that gave the space warmth. It was a cross between a spaceship and a womb. That didn't begin to include the bells and whistles that made this one of the most sought-after cars on the planet.

As I turned the steering wheel with the heel of my hand, I said, "It's nothing short of magnificent." *Much like you.* "Pure quality." *Again, you.* "But with monstrous horsepower beneath this exquisite shell." *Like your heart, no matter how much you try to hide it.*

I knew better than to verbally compare her to a car, but Blue wasn't just any car; she was a Bugatti, one of the most exquisite hypercars out there, and my lifesaver. Having Jewel in my car was a fantasy come true. Scratch that, fucking her in my car would be a wet dream come true, and I fully intended for it to happen at some point in the near future.

"You know, you're a man of contradictions," she said, her fingers lightly caressing the soft leather of her seat. Pride bloomed in my chest. My woman couldn't help but appreciate the seductive powers of my car. I tuned back to what she was saying.

"Considering how controlling you are, I mean. Upon meeting you, I wouldn't have guessed that you were into something that centers around risk and speed."

"That's what you get for judging a book by its cover," I teased, then I turned sober. "But seriously, the risk is minimal. It's not like I do this for a living. I'm a speed demon, but I race for fun. As a kid, I did crazy shit to get that dopamine hit. Don't know if it's ADHD or what, but my brain needs that natural high. It settles me. Helps me focus. If I go too long without it, I get antsy. It's like there's a buildup of pressure, and I need to let off steam. Once I get my fix, I'm good for a while."

That had to be the most I'd thought about, much less spoken about, my unusual hobbies. And she didn't even know about the small plane I had in White Plains, just north of the city. That was a revelation for another day. First and foremost, I had to get her hooked on racing. I would have loved to take her to a simple race so she could feel the energy of other cars whizzing by, but I thought it might be too much for her first time, so I reserved the track for the morning. It cost a bit to clear it out on a Sunday, since weekends were a big draw for racers and spectators alike, but it was worth the price to ease Jewel into the sport.

I turned onto the West Side Highway, going northbound out of the city, and activated the app to alert me to various police speed traps. Zooming in between cars, we jetted along the Hudson River with the Palisades to our left. I gave her a little taste of going fast when we drove through patches of light traffic. Her gasps and little squeals of delight as the vibration mounted with each tap of the throttle delighted me. My family would have nothing to do with racing. Only Tasa used to ride with me, but she always preferred my bike, so I raced on my own.

With one hand firmly on the steering wheel, my other unbuttoned her pants and slipped down to find her pussy. I whiled the time away by playing with her until she was begging me to come. Not able to wait, I turned off into a curve in the road. It was too much to maneuver my big body in the small space to get my tongue on her pussy. Since I wasn't going to bounce her on my dick on the side of a highway, I pulled up her T-shirt and exposed her breasts so I could feast on them while I thrust two fingers inside her cunt. My tongue flicked at her beaded nipple in tandem with the thrusts of my fingers. I'd prepped her long enough that she only needed a little toggling of her clit, and she shot off the seat with a throaty scream. Her body went limp, and I caressed her pussy until she was ready to resume our trip.

By the time we reached the racetrack, I was thrumming with the familiar expectation of letting loose on the tarmac. I loved the familiar odor of gasoline and burnt rubber that clung to every raceway. We were waved through to the pit stop, where one guy from my crew checked the car. There wasn't much need, since we were going on a cold track. When we were ready, I handed Jewel her helmet and put mine on.

Then we rolled to the starting line.

Her eyes darted to mine. I gave her thigh a comforting squeeze, returned my hands to nine and three on the wheel, and we were off. I started slow, for me, but like always, from the first moment I pulled away, reality was obliterated. The trivial worries and irritations of life evaporated.

The wheels spun, the engine purred, and—the whole world exploded. As usual, my stomach flipped. My insides were thrown about as Blue rocketed us forward. It felt like time and space were squeezed into a small capsule...and then tossed out the window. Sprinting across the asphalt, I turned around the first corner. It was sublime. The closest thing to reaching heaven.

Glancing to my right, I saw Jewel, hands clenched tight around the seat, mouth frozen in a permanent O. Her chocolate-brown tresses whipped to her right, the tips slapping against the metal window frame. Her faceted amber eyes were on fire. A harsh burn of fierce pride ripped through me. She *loved* it. Just like me. I knew a religious experience when I saw one, and this was as close to spiritual ecstasy as one got. I knew because I'd had the same conversion.

I had but a second, and then my sharp focus was back on my ride. Angling properly, I rolled on the throttle to zip around corners, and then we were back around for a second loop. I gave her a few more laps, reaching a comfortable speed of 190 mph—nothing too crazy, just enough to get through the S-shaped chicane turns.

After flashing by the start/finish line for the fifth time, I backed off the throttle. We finished the remaining loop, and I pulled into the pit stop lane. When I turned to Jewel, I found her shaking, adrenaline coursing through her veins.

My heart lurched. I grabbed her hands and called out to snap her back to reality, "Jewel, Jewel."

A thread of worry weaved its way into my heart. What if she didn't like it? What if she was in shock?

"How was it?"

Her glorious eyes, lit like two bonfires, turned on me, and she rattled out a breath. "Th-that was incredible."

I broke into a grin. There was not a shred of doubt in my mind. This woman was made for me.

"We were one," she rasped.

One with the car. I knew exactly what she meant.

"It was almost as good as having your mouth on me," she gushed.

The crew member opening the door choked out a strangled laugh. I ignored him, reveling in the compliment she'd given me.

"It was amazing!" she went on. My smile broadened even wider. "I can't believe I lived without experiencing this before." She grabbed my hand and squeezed. "Can you take me again? Can I drive?"

My smile fell off my face. My heart dropped. "Absolutely not."

Her brows slammed together. "Why not?"

"Uh-oh," came a mutter from my man. I gave him a searing look, and he melted away.

"It's dangerous."

"But you do it?" She crawled out of the car, swaying on her legs, and my crew member's hand shot out to steady her. I sent him another look, and he immediately stepped back. I had to give him credit because he didn't release her until he was certain she was steady. Slapping my hand on the roof of Blue, I ripped my helmet off my head.

"Is it because I'm a woman? That's it, isn't it, you big... boor! You race, and you love racing, so it can only be because I'm a woman."

That was partially true, but not the entire story. It was the protector inside me rearing his head.

"It's dangerous, Jewel. That's why. You racing this car will shave years off my life. More than racing has ever done."

Her lips pursed together tightly; hurt and disappointment clouded her vivid eyes. I scrubbed my face. Shit, I couldn't do it. I couldn't see the bright excitement die in her eyes. I might regret it, because the idea of her being in danger would likely kill me, but I couldn't introduce her to something that I absolutely loved and tear it away an instant later. I understood the thrill of racing only too well.

"Fuck, alright," I yielded. Jabbing a finger at her over the car, I warned, "But there will be rules. I will teach you, and you will listen to every damn instruction I give you, or swear to God, I will pull the car over and redden your ass in front of every worker and spectator in this place."

She just grinned at me, unrepentant and completely unfazed. "Sure," she answered saucily.

I scrubbed at my hair. "Christ, I can tell I'm going to regret this."

She spun around, struggling with her helmet until it was off. Rounding Blue, she strode over to me, so goddamn strong and purposeful, placed a soft hand on my heart, and said, "I promise to listen to you. Nothing will happen to me."

"And it's not because you're a woman," I chuffed. "Mostly. Racing is dangerous. I know what I'm doing, but many things can go wrong when you're going fast. The smallest misstep, and the car can flip over a half-dozen times. I've seen it happen."

Her inquisitive eyes bored into mine. "Has it happened to you?"

"No, but I've crashed multiple times." I gripped her hand securely against my chest. "I don't want to clip your wings, baby doll, but there isn't a world that exists where I will be the cause of you getting hurt. Understand?"

"I understand. And I won't let anything happen to me, okay?" she promised.

I was willing to give her a chance. For her, not for myself, even if I didn't think it was a promise she could keep.

My phone beeped, and I saw I had a series of text messages that must've come since we left the city. Half a dozen were from Tatum, venting his frustration with the Hagi clan again. What was an unusual emotional range was becoming his new normal. There was a message from Sebastian, complaining about the Hagi family *and* Tatum. The situation was devolving into chaos.

Then there was a text from an unknown number. I clicked on it. A video popped up. My hand curled around my phone, squeezing tightly as I watched a dark, shaky clip of me helping Jewel into my car last night. This was a message, and I had a strong suspicion of who it was from.

My head snapped up, scanning the horizon. There were only the employees and people milling around the racetrack. Anyone of them could be a spy.

"What's wrong?" Jewel asked. Head tilted to the side, her curious eyes zeroed in on me.

Cristo normally didn't set me off, but this...bringing Jewel into our rivalry...would bring my blood to a boil. Except, being with Jewel gave me the equilibrium to know how to handle the situation. I wiped the expression off my face and cracked an easy smile.

Turning back to Blue, I said, "Nothing, baby doll. I don't like business interrupting my time with you. Let's get back to the city. I'm taking you out for lunch."

My eyes surreptitiously searched the area one last time before dropping into the seat of my car. Again, nothing.

Fuck.

There was a threat underlying that video, whether he was sending me the simple message that I was being watched or whether he planned to use my relationship with Jewel as blackmail. If he thought I was afraid of being outed, he was about to be seriously disappointed. I didn't give a fuck who knew about us. It was an easy fix. I'd eliminate that threat by outing my own damn self. Taking hold of the narrative, I'd show Jewel off at the most public place possible.

16

JEWEL

Nicu took me to a café off Queens Boulevard. It was a hangout for Romanians, which told me he was boldly announcing to his world that we were a couple. The frat party last night had stripped him of any tolerance for keeping me in the shadows. No more, is what he was declaring. *No more.* Which meant I had to tell Cat right away, before she found out on her own. She deserved to hear from me. It had to be done, but I was anxious about it. Honestly, in the years we'd known each other, Cat and I had never had a fight. Not one. She was happy with Luca; I knew that. And as more time passed, the sting of what I'd done lessened. Yet my shame felt as fresh as ever, since I only seemed to be falling deeper into Nicu, and I couldn't stand the idea that Cat might think less of me.

I might be able to pass for Romanian in the looks department, but it quickly became evident to the patrons of the restaurant that I was a stranger. By the time we were seated at a table, facing the street no less, people were whispering. I had to stifle a groan when Nicu took my hand and dropped a kiss on my knuckles.

"Don't look so pained," he said, followed by one of his devilish laughs.

"You're enjoying this, aren't you?" I groaned. "You enjoy putting me on the spot."

"I enjoy treating you like you're my woman," he rejoined. Leaning forward, he pressed his lips to mine. "And you *are* my woman. So I will treat you accordingly."

"Ugh," I reproved.

He chuckled and took the menu from the waitress who had suddenly materialized, her big brown eyes wide as she blinked at me.

I snapped the menu open and ducked my head, pretending to focus intently on it, although the words were blurry. At heart, I was an introvert. I wasn't shy per se, but I'd learned the hard way that attention was rarely a good thing. After the media circus around my family when my father was arrested and put on trial, I instinctually shied away from the limelight. Last night was more proof that I was better off in the shadows.

"Wine," Nicu commanded, nodding to the waitress to give us time to look over our menus. Once alone, he murmured, "I can order for us, if you like."

I gave him a scathing look over the top of my menu. "I'm perfectly capable of ordering for myself. I've been at Cat's house more than enough times to know what's on this menu."

Nicu's lip twitched, but thankfully he stayed silent. Unfortunately, someone gasped behind me. I cringed. Someone had overheard me and now knew I was Cat's friend. Furtively glancing over my shoulder, I locked eyes with the girl Nicu had flirted with at Cat's wedding tasting. I was so screwed. There was no way a young girl like her would hold back on juicy gossip like this. Cat had complained more than once about how gossipy the *mafie* girls were.

The woman beside her, who looked closer to Nicu's age, slitted her eyes at me. Pure hatred poured out of them. *Uh-oh.* She looked like a woman scorned, and I knew the saying about that. Whipping my head back around, I scrunched down in my seat.

"Sit up," came an order from across the table.

I peeked around the side of my menu. Nicu gave me a stern, reprimanding look that made me squirm in my seat. God, he was so hot when he glowered.

I shrugged him off. "What?"

"Don't crouch down. Sit up in your chair. You have nothing to be ashamed about."

Our gazes clashed and warred.

"Sure about that? I could think of a few things that make me look bad. Like, really bad," I replied.

He shook out his cloth napkin and carefully placed it over his lap before returning his gaze to me. "Never shirk away from anyone here. Ever. It demonstrates weakness, and they will never let you forget it. God knows you have no problems acting strong with me, and I'm the only person who counts. Remember that."

Okay, he had a point. If I'd learned anything from my family's debacle, it was that the paparazzi would eat you alive if you showed weakness. If I was going to be with him, even for a limited time because, hello, he was a criminal, I didn't need my first impression to be that of a cowed, pathetic little girl.

Straightening my spine, I threw my shoulders back and resumed looking over the menu.

"Better," he praised me.

I picked out a few dishes I recognized and took my time

looking around the café as the waitress came over with a bottle of wine, which she uncorked and served. The place was dominated by a black and white color scheme, starting with the floor, which was a checkered design. The tasteful pale-green walls displayed vintage travel posters of Romania interspersed with framed photographs of what I assumed were Romanian cities and monasteries. The tables were large, and a long wooden bar dominated one side of the café. Overall, it was classy, but cozy.

Nicu ordered from the waitress in Romanian, who seemed more comfortable speaking in her native tongue. She said something that made him laugh. For once, my jealousy was not roused. She was businesslike and respectful, unlike the flirty cocktail waitress at his club.

"To us." He raised his wineglass. "*Noroc.*"

I knew that was the traditional toast, so I returned his with one of my own. We were sipping out of our glasses, eye-fucking each other over the rims, when we were interrupted by a woman who suddenly materialized out of nowhere.

Glancing up, I groaned inwardly. This was the woman who'd hate-stared at me earlier. I couldn't deny she was gorgeous, dressed in a slinky black dress with heels for Saturday brunch, while I wore his twin's cast-off pants and an enormous T-shirt that hung shapelessly on me.

Bending down so she could give Nicu a nice view of her cleavage, she took her time kissing him on both cheeks. Pulling back just slightly, she purred, "Nicu, baby. *Cum te descurci astăzi?*"

My blood pressure went from zero to sixty in a hot second. She said a bunch of other stuff in Romanian, but thankfully, Nicu cut her off. "Speak English, Ioana. I'm with a guest."

She turned to me slowly, as if she'd noticed me for the first time, and sniffed. "Oh my God, I thought she was Romanian. You mean she *isn't*?" Her eyes took me in with haughty perusal from head to toe. "How can that be?" she asked with a touch of disgust.

My gut churned, the fruity sweetness of the wine turning sour in my mouth.

"You've guessed it. She's not Romanian," he drawled, his lids dropping to half-mast as his eyes raked over me. His hot gaze turned the burning heat inside me to a smolder. Clearly, not being Romanian meant nothing to him. His hand found mine on the table and squeezed it. Ioana's eyes narrowed on our hands, the corners of her scarlet-colored lips turning downward in a deep frown.

"That's no good, Nicu. A prince like you should be with a Romanian girl. A good girl like my sister."

My jaw dropped open. The gall of this woman.

"Or a not-so-good girl like me," she added in a seductive voice. She slid a fingertip down Nicu's arm. "I'll divorce my husband if need be. Anything to save you from this."

Ewww. No subtlety in this woman.

I tugged my hand away, but Nicu's grip tightened.

"Says who?" Nicu asked in a deceptively quiet tone, although there was no missing the muscle flexing in his jaw.

Her own popped open, and she put her hand to her chest in feigned surprise. "Why, your *mamă*, your *bunică*, and most importantly, your *şef*."

She was a heavy hitter, this one; I'd give her that.

His eyes slid over to Ioana and held her gaze long enough that she shifted in discomfort before breaking their stare. "Who are you to tell me what my family expects of me? We may have fucked, but that gives you no authority over *me*. I'm a Lupu."

"You are," she hissed. "Not only a Lupu, but one known to follow the rules. I may not be a Lupu, but I'm ma—" Her eyes darted to me as she stopped herself from saying the word *mafie* aloud and finished with, "I'm Romanian, and as such, I'm looking out for you." She flung a hand in my direction and hissed, "You, of all people, to come around, flaunting this trash in our faces. You should know better."

Nicu released my hand and stood up, his chair screeching behind him. In a tone I'd never heard him use before, he said, "What did you say?"

She lifted her chin and said, "What?"

"Repeat it. Repeat what you said to me," he ordered in a deadly tone.

The café was so quiet you could hear a pin drop.

Suddenly, the other girl was at her sister's side, jerking her elbow to drag her away, but Ioana wasn't having it. In a way, I admired her. I might not like her, but she was ready to die on her cross, and for that, I had to give her credit.

"Please, Nicu, she doesn't mean what she says. You know her," the other girl pleaded. "She's bitter about her marriage."

Ioana yanked her elbow out of her sister's grip and sneered, "I did mean it. I meant every word of it. You're a Lupu, and you're the only one left unmarried. You owe it to your family to marry one of us. You shouldn't be with a whore like her."

"Oh, so I should be with a whore like you," he snapped.

I inhaled sharply, but no one noticed. This was a show-down between two factions of their society. Just as I had suspected, Nicu wasn't serious when he suggested he wanted to keep me. As much as I had an issue with him being a bad guy, his world had an issue with me. This was proof of it.

"Don't you dare tell me who I owe what to," Nicu went on. "I know my duty. I do my duty every fucking day of my life, taking care to protect your life." He pointed at someone at another table. "Yours." He pointed again. "And yours, and yours. I've dedicated my fucking life to all of you. To my family. To this clan. I'm a fucking man, not a lapdog, and I will decide." He smacked his palm to his chest. "*Me.* No one else but me."

Ioana threw her hands up. Her sister, frantic now, began speaking in rapid-fire Romanian. Chastising her. Begging her. Ioana wasn't having any of it. I felt bad for the younger girl, since she was distraught over her sister confronting Nicu. It hinted at the level of power Nicu wielded and how fearless Ioana was to challenge him.

Shaking off the younger woman, she stood tall and spat out, "Yes, you do a lot, but why should we women be the only ones who are forced into marriage whether we love the man or not? Whether the man is good or not? No!" She stamped her foot and shook a clenched fist at Nicu. "If you can be with this slut, then we can do whatever we want. And if that's the case, then I'll be the first to divorce my husband. If the rules go to hell, where will we be then, huh?"

Holy shit, what was going on here? There was more to this story for Ioana than Nicu violating the rules. This was personal. I stared up at the stark agony in her eyes. Very personal. It was about her husband, and she'd obviously been forced to marry him.

"Enough," bellowed Nicu.

Stepping to her, he pressed his chest to hers. Fury encompassed his face. Even I had sat back in my seat, and I wasn't afraid of Nicu.

"Was I unclear as to who she is to me? To the Lupu clan?

Because she is floors above you, Ioana, and you better damn well get on your knees in front of her and beg forgiveness."

Taking a step back, Ioana gasped.

"I'm fucking serious," he gritted out. "Unless you want me to get your husband to punish you for disrespecting me like this, you better get on your knees right now."

He was serious. Jesus, he was completely serious. His face was strained with fury. His fists were clenched at his sides. The tendons of his neck were taut, the muscle in his jaw ticking away. Shock overtook me. I shook my head vigorously. I didn't want this. I'd never condone punishing a woman for speaking her mind. This was about saving face after insulting a Lupu, but there were deeper currents of abuse. I didn't want to be part of this. I definitely didn't want Ioana on her *knees* in front of me. If anything, I wanted to help this woman.

Ioana's eyes ticked away from his, flew back, and found the same rageful expression on his face. Her chin dropped, her face was wiped of indignant rage and replaced with agony. My heart cracked for her. She realized she'd gone too far. With his reputation as the imposer of rules, she must have thought she could shame him into repudiating me.

To my horror, she turned to me and slowly got down on her knees. The sound of her patent leather heels scraping the tiles of the floor echoed throughout the café. The *swish-swish* of her dress was deafening as she settled in front of me. I shook my head in denial, but she stared up at me, hatred and pain swirling in her deep brown eyes. And all I wanted to do was hug her and take her pain away.

I put my hand on her shoulder, about to tell her to stand up, but she shrugged it off brusquely as if my pity only insulted her further, so I retracted my hand and just... waited. The tension in the restaurant was tangible. Everyone had their eyes on us. How could they not? This would ripple through the ranks of *mafie* circles, and there was nothing I could do about it. It had little to do with me, but unfortunately, that didn't make it any less painful to witness.

"I apologize for insulting you—" She fluttered her hand at me impatiently, requesting my name.

"Jewel," I supplied.

She was like an injured animal trying to gnaw its paw off to escape the clutches of a steel trap. I admired this woman, and if anything, I wanted to fix her. Whatever had happened to her, and I suspected it had to do with her husband, was unfair. She was without options. Her pain was real. Her intelligence palpable. Her rage beyond reproach.

Voice ringing loud and true, she declared, "Jewel. I apologize for calling you a whore and a slut."

My stomach churned. It was agonizing, watching her brave stubbornness in what was obviously a bad domestic situation. I nodded numbly.

"Do you accept her apology?" Nicu intoned.

My gaze flew up to his. He wanted to hear it. A little away from us, her poor sister wrung her hands together in distress. I couldn't allow this to go on.

Placing my hand on top of Ioana's clammy ones, I said, "There's nothing to forgive. You don't know me, so those words have no meaning to me. I wasn't insulted. You were only being loyal and taking care of your community, but I assure you, I will do whatever is necessary to follow your customs."

"You can't make yourself Romanian, but you shouldn't worry too much." A sad, wry smile drifted over her mouth. "Being Romanian is not all it's cracked up to be."

"No, I can't, but I'm willing to show my respect for what every other woman has to go through."

She inhaled sharply. "Be thankful that's not your fate," she murmured. "Give thanks every fucking day of your life. Nicu is a good man. You're lucky to have him."

Pushing my chair back, I stood up and put out a hand. After weighing her options, Ioana placed her hand gently in mine and allowed me to help her up to her feet. The instant we let go, her sister threw her arms around her and dragged her away, saying something quickly to Nicu, probably apologizing and begging him to not punish her further, as he had threatened.

Her sister propelled them out of the café. Staring after them, I watched as her sister shook her head, reprimanding Ioana, as they turned the corner. Then they were gone.

I turned my gaze on Nicu. "Don't hurt her."

"She apologized. I won't need to," he assured me.

Taking my hand, he brought me into his chest. "Jesus, sorry about that. Ioana has always been...spirited, and her life isn't easy. But there's no justification for what she did."

"Of course there is," I replied. "She's obviously suffering. Whatever happens, Nicu, you have to promise me you won't hurt her or allow her husband to hurt her."

He caressed my hair. "You're so fucking sweet it makes me ache."

I shook my head. "I'm not. Promise me."

"I promise," he answered immediately. "I won't allow her to come to harm. I'm sure her husband will hear of this, but I will speak to him. He won't go against a direct order from me."

I let out a sigh of relief. "Okay." Ioana's haunted eyes came back to me. "Okay," I repeated. If I ever became part of this society, even marginally, I was going to fight to save these women. Change was the only thing that would make this situation okay.

17

JEWEL

The time had come to tell my best friend that I was currently kind of with her ex-fiancé. I didn't know where we were going, but I decided to do the most mature thing possible when it came to falling for a guy who'd dedicated his life to criminal enterprises: stick my head in the sand. Between adjusting to Cat's absence and my father's recent parole denial, I was giving myself a mental break.

I couldn't tear myself away from him until late Sunday evening, and the past week had been a whirlwind of classes and cramming so I could spend every free moment with Nicu. Miracle of miracles, Cat hadn't heard about the incident in the café. I chalked that up to her and Luca living in a love bubble, her full load of classes, and being consumed with wedding preparations. I didn't often run into Cat on campus, but the fear and paranoia were getting to me.

My one condition to Nicu was that we couldn't go anywhere public, although he'd made it clear that he was anxious to show me off to his family. *God forbid.* After Ioana, the thought caused me to break out in hives. I forced a promise out of him *not* to breathe a whisper about us until I spoke to Cat. Considering his evident impatience, he was surprisingly accommodating. I never thought I'd say this of a *mafie* made man, but he had the patience of a saint.

After almost a week of living incognito, I couldn't take it anymore. The stress was building with each passing day. Guilt was eating me alive. Any more was too horrible to contemplate. Either the fever had to break or I would.

I sat nervously at our usual table, the surface worn and the edge chipped from decades of use at my favorite coffee shop. Staring across Amsterdam Avenue, I let my nerves settle as I gazed over at the façade of the Cathedral of St. John, which always struck me as lopsided with only one massive tower completed. What I loved most about the structure, besides its mix of different architectural elements, was that despite being unfinished, it maintained a regal presence that shouted, "And yet, I am still the largest cathedral in the world!"

The waitress deposited my iced cappuccino in front of me. I nodded my thanks and returned to staring at the cathedral as I waited for Cat. A part of me was still scrambling for a way to get out of this predicament. Perhaps there was still a chance to break it off with Nicu and avoid having to admit what I had done. *Nah.* I dismissed the idea almost instantly. I'd sooner cut off my right hand than miss out on anything Nicu. It was clear as day that I was falling for the guy, and I had no idea what to do about it. He filled a hole in my heart, even if he was stalkerish at times. Again, it surprised me how little that worried me. For years, I'd done everything alone—except when Cat brought me home with her, like a stray dog. The reminder only amped up my anxiety.

A little rap on the windowpane cut through my musings.

Cat was on the other side, waving excitingly with a wide smile on her face. Her eyes sparkled, and her cheeks were slightly flushed, probably from speed walking the five blocks it took to get here.

The little bell on the door tinkled to announce her presence. After giving me a warm hug, she dropped into the rickety wooden chair and chattered, "Oh my God, what a day I've had. You know how packed Thursdays are. Luca's coming to pick me up once we're done. We're heading over to my parents' house for more wedding stuff. I'd invite you, but you'd be sooo bored. Sheesh, can't wait until this wedding is over with, already."

Her parents had been momentarily furious at me when they found out about my involvement in helping Cat pursue Luca, but all was forgiven once everything was worked out between the families.

I nodded mutely, trying to focus on what she was saying, but Cat was too perceptive to not notice my mood and instantly asked, "What's wrong? You look stressed out."

The waitress brought over the coffee drink I'd already ordered for her as she carefully looped her laptop bag over the back of her chair.

Once we were alone, I squeezed my eyes shut and blurted out, "You have every reason to hate me, but I swear I never intended for any of it to happen."

My eyelids popped open, and I pleaded with my eyes for her mercy.

Cat stared at me, eyes wide and innocent. "You're scaring me. What's going on, Jewel?"

I shifted my gaze away from her, unable to look my best friend in the eyes.

Flinching, I declared, "I hooked up with Nicu the night you seduced Luca at the club." Taking a big breath, I launched into the explanation I'd prepared, "After you left with Luca that night, Nicu and I stayed a bit longer. We flirted quite a bit, and when he accompanied me home, it didn't stop at the door of my dorm room. He came in, and we"—I swallowed audibly—"We had sex."

I rambled on, "I threw him out and swore I'd never see him again, but suddenly, it was like he was everywhere I turned." I made a fist and thumped it on the surface of the table. "Even after your engagement with him ended, I rejected his overtures. But I saw him again at your engagement party and we ended up fooling around." *Since I'm in confession mode, might as well let it all out.* "After that, I continued to fight him, but in the end, I was too weak. I'm so weak."

I lifted my eyes up to her. "We spent last weekend together. I'm so sorry I didn't tell you earlier, Cat. We've never had any secrets between us, and I've been harboring this for months. At first, I was ashamed because it happened when you two were engaged. I should've told you once you and Luca were solid, but I thought I wouldn't have to face you if I cut it off with Nicu.

"For the past six years, it was just the two of us against the world, but now, everything's changed. You started a new relationship and were super busy preparing a massive wedding. I got a little lonely, and Nicu was persistent. I couldn't resist him anymore, but by then, the omission had grown and grown from the initial betrayal into this...this monster of a lie. I didn't want you to think less of me. It's always been sisters before misters with us, and I let a man come between us."

Cat blinked repeatedly. She licked her lips and looked away from me for a moment before seeking me out, and she said, "That was not what I expected to hear, but I'm more surprised than anything else. Luca is the only man I want, and I wanted him from the moment I met him. I don't harbor any hidden feelings for Nicu, if that's what you're worried about in the back of your mind. If any of this had to do with Luca, that's another story, but Nicu..."

She looked at the far wall as if doing a scan of her body and her feelings. Returning her gaze to me, she said, "Nope, nothing there."

I perked up, my shoulders going back as hope trickled into my chest. "Really? What about keeping it from you for so long?"

"You should know better," she chided gently. Grabbing my hand, she squeezed it and said, "It's partially my fault because I abandoned you by disappearing and putting all my focus on Luca and the wedding. I didn't do it on purpose, but I got caught up in the newness of falling in love. If I had been around, there's no way I would've missed that something was up. This is as much my fault as yours."

I expelled a whoosh of air.

"No," I replied with a determined shake of my head. "You're in love. You have a new life, and I don't want you to think I'm not happy for you." I swallowed around the tightening muscles of my throat. "I know what it's like to be hurt by someone you trust, even if they didn't do it on purpose. You're more than my closest friend. You're like a sister to me, Cat. The thought that what I did might have threatened that..." I sniffed back an unexpected cry, swiping at an errant tear that escaped.

Gripping my hands tightly, Cat brought them close to her chest and said, "Never! I love you, Jewel. I adore Luca, but you're my person. We've been through so much together. And it's because of you that Luca and I are even together. Nothing would've happened if you hadn't forced me to go after him."

My shoulders slouched forward as relief washed over me. Cat was still my bestie. Our friendship, our sisterhood, was still intact.

Forehead furrowing, her brows gathered. Worry flittered across her face.

My curiosity piqued, I said, "I see you thinking, Cat. Something's bothering you."

She pressed her lips together in a line. "It's just...well, I understand why you're attracted to Nicu. I mean, he's got that handsome rugged thing going. Tall and big, with piercing blue eyes and a square-cut jaw. He has the air of a mean-looking model. The only thing is he's always come off as somewhat...spoiled to me."

Okay, that was not what I'd expected to hear. Controlling, certainly. Brutal, most definitely. Reckless, perhaps.

"Spoiled?" I repeated, in the form of a question.

She released my hands, and her spine hit the back of the seat. Her fingers tapped restlessly on the top of the table, her expression thoughtful. "He's not like Alex, who's been carrying a heavy weight on his shoulders since a young age, or like Luca, who was his father's whipping boy. Tasa was downtrodden by her family's expectations, until she ran off. Compared to them, Nicu has had a charmed life. He's the golden boy, and while he acts like he's the bastion of the Lupu way of life, he's never suffered a day in his life."

A thread of indignation on his behalf filtered through me. She was being a little harsh.

"You make him sound like he's a playboy who's flittering his life away, doing nothing but wasting his family's money without doing a hard day's work."

She pursed her lips together. "I didn't say that, but I don't see him overextending himself. He does what's required of him, but not an ounce more, unless it benefits him. He went to college because it was expected of him, but only did the bare necessity. He convinced Alex to let him skip graduate school, even though it's practically a requirement for those boys. Then there's how he treated me. *He* hadn't been forced, and yet he punished me for it. Instead of making the barest attempt to know me, he spent his energy trying to bring me and Luca together so he could get me out of his hair. He *says* he follows the rules, and he does, until they're inconvenient for him. Then he gets around them. He just seems selfish to me," she concluded.

"You've never mentioned any of this before," I noted.

Her hand landed on mine. "It wasn't worth mentioning, because I didn't care about Nicu. But he's clearly set his sights on you, which means his character has become my business. Just watch, he's going to end up persuading his mother, his *bunică,* and most importantly, his *șef* to give him a pass and marry you against tradition. More importantly, though, I don't think he's worthy of you," she finished.

I fell back into my seat, reeling as if slapped in the face. Cat was one of the most perceptive people I knew, and I trusted her implicitly. Not only was she an expert on the intricacies of their society, but she'd also known of his reputation for years. She'd spent time analyzing him when she was slated to marry him. I knew, for her, Nicu going around tradition was particularly damaging. In her conservative community, following traditions wasn't only about keeping their world intact, like Ioana had suggested. It was a sign of integrity. Cat had sacrificed her desire to go to college to follow her family's wishes about marrying Nicu, but she'd done it. For the greater good of her family. While Luca had bucked the system like a rebel, he'd boldly defended his decisions, and Cat admired him for it. Nicu sneaking to get around them for his personal benefit was almost a moral failing in her eyes.

I didn't know what to say or how to counter her arguments because I didn't know half of what she knew about him. I couldn't speak of her accusation that he did just enough and not one iota more. If he got away with things, well, that I could believe. The man was persuasive as fuck. Hell, he'd persuaded me out of my panties on more than one occasion, and I'd been fighting him tooth and nail.

My bestie had yanked my proverbial head out of the sand and forced me to stare at what I'd been dodging for a week. Not only was Nicu a criminal bad boy, but, despite his image, he was tantamount to a spoiled brat.

She continued, and every word hit me like a punch to the gut. "Your mother's a self-absorbed narcissist and one of your father's major flaws is his selfishness. I don't want to see you with someone who shares the same qualities." She shook the hand she was holding. "Jewel, you deserve better."

That struck me in the solar plexus. I was stunned into silence. The thing was...I had a visceral reaction to her judgment. A gut rejection of her words. He was nothing like my family. *Nothing*. I'd heard him talk about his family. I saw his face soften every time he picked up his sister's call. Then there was the way he treated me. I'd never met a man as caring, patient, and passionate as Nicu. It didn't make sense that he'd cop out on his traditions when he showed such devotion to his family. Maybe there was more to the story than she knew.

Needing more clarification, I said, "When you first got engaged, you said he stepped up because Luca refused. He didn't have to like it, but he did it. Didn't you say he was the type of man who did what he was told?"

"That's what I thought at first, but I was mistaken," she mused. "I was comparing him to Luca, who's an outright contrarian. Nicu is more subtle, but he gets his way. Luca's refusals came out of pain. He rebelled because he'd suffered at the hand of his father. That's not the case for Nicu. Nicu doesn't have an excuse for not following orders. I mean, you've seen my life. You've seen what Cristo has to do. Being part of this society means abiding by rules and following commands. No exceptions. *None.*"

This was true for her family. Although I was an outsider, I'd sensed from Nicu that things worked a little differently in the Lupu family. There was more give than in Cat's family, but I didn't feel I had the clout to say that to Cat. Anyway, she'd admitted to having made a mistake already, so her judgment wasn't infallible. Yet, Cat was extremely watchful and intelligent. Her assessment couldn't be dismissed outright. Her comments about rules in her family and clan were an uncomfortable reminder of what I had put out of my head. I mean, how many times had I snottily criticized how archaic and backward her society was? Now it was coming to bite me in the behind.

"Yikes, I'm not great at following rules," I conceded.

"That's another thing. I grew up in this world, but you..." She looked at me askance. "Are you sure you want to get in deep with a guy like him? You've had a taste of my life. He's not just anyone; he's a Lupu prince. Assuming he gets his mother and Alex to play nice, you'll be attached at the hip to his family. I mean, look at Luca. As much as he hates the Popescus, because of me, he's been 'hanging out' with my dad lately. Spending quality time with Cristo is too much to ask, but when we visit my parents, he goes downstairs to my father's office."

The problems kept piling up, and I felt a sharp pain blossom behind my eyes.

"I hadn't thought of that," I replied.

More than once, I'd been touched by the way he talked about his family. Their loyalty and sense of coziness came through. It had touched me and made me yearn to be part of something greater than myself. Perhaps I had conflated it with the wonderful holidays I spent with Cat and her family, conveniently forgetting what they had put her through. They'd heartlessly pressured her into an engagement with Nicu and later blackmailed her to spy on Luca to further their own interests. Both times, they had tossed Cat's personal desires aside like yesterday's trash and used her for their own advancement. Nicu's family seemed different, but they were still *mafie*. The question was simple. How different were they? I had no answer, and after her judgment of Nicu, I didn't feel comfortable bringing it up.

My stomach churned. I didn't know what to think about the bombshell she'd dropped. Overwhelmed, I stared down at my iced cappuccino and admitted, "The more we talk, the more I need a drink, not a coffee."

"Hey," said Cat. "This is just one person's opinion."

"A pretty important person," I threw back. "I trust you, and I know you're only saying this because you're looking out for me. It's not a stretch of the imagination to know that getting involved with a man like Nicu is a complicated matter. I let myself get carried away this past week. He didn't seem to think his family was an insurmountable problem. Either way, that doesn't negate what you said about his character."

"I may be wrong," she insisted. "I'm not going to lie and say I haven't spent a lot of time thinking about him at one point, but I also never got to know him. I certainly don't know him as well as you do."

Do I know him better, though?

I was thinking so hard that my temples were throbbing. Clutching my forehead, I admitted, "Oh God, I'm getting a headache."

She placed a hand on my head and caressed my hair gently. "Listen, why don't you come with me and Luca to my parents' house? You can relax. Have a nice glass of wine. *Bunică* will have cooked up a storm, knowing that Luca is coming over. I swear she has a little crush on him. He turns those gray eyes on her, and she melts. Literally melts." She rolled her eyes. "It's ridiculous."

I should go back to the library and catch up on completing an English essay, but the idea of escaping from my problems and relaxing with good food and wine at her parents' place was more than appealing. I was always up to spending more time with Cat, and like she'd said, she and Luca would be busy planning the wedding with Cat's mom. I could stay in the background, hang out, and take a break from overthinking this thing with Nicu.

It was *Bunică's* cooking that cinched my decision. That lady could *cook*. I'd either brainstorm for my essay at her house, or I'd take it easy and make up for it tomorrow.

"Okay, I'll come," I agreed.

"Perfect," she said with a clap of her hands.

Little did I know that such a harmless decision would set off a cataclysmic chain of events.

18

NICU

What in the hell is she doing at the Popescus? I seethed to myself. Just when I thought I was getting somewhere with Jewel, she threw me another curveball.

Jewel was close to Cat, so it only stood to reason she'd visit, especially since Cat had taken Jewel in over the years. While I wasn't thrilled about her visiting the Popescus, I was pissed that she'd lied to me about it.

It was irrational, but I was doubly pissed that my own brother had driven her here. Another thorn in my side was how well Luca got along with Nelu, that cocksucking prick. As the șef of the Popescu clan and Cristo's father, I hated him on principle. Over the years, the man had tried to undermine my family like it was his one motive in life. He was a snake in the grass.

Alex had specifically told me to back off when I got on Luca's case about the time he spent with Cat's family. He told me it was part of the peace, that it was a good sign, and that he was getting from Nelu what he couldn't get from our own father. Yeah, good luck with that, I thought bitterly.

Maybe, just maybe, Nelu was getting a little soft in his old age and after the death of his beloved *consilier*, Simu, but there was no doubt Cristo remained the worst of the lot.

How did I know Jewel was at Cat's house?

Because of the tracker in her motherfucking phone. That's how. She already knew I'd messed with it, but I didn't think she knew everything I'd done. I was in a teleconference with Tatum and Sebastian, who were out in Cali, trying to wrangle the Hagi clan into submission, when I saw the tracker device moving downtown. I got alarmed when I saw it cross the East River into Queens. *Where the fuck is she going?*

When I saw the address, my head nearly exploded. It was the shock more than anything, but the energy in my body surged. Once my call was done, I drove like a madman to see what the hell was going on. I was currently outside their house, down the street some ways to stay out of range of their cameras. Thank fuck I had a pair of binoculars in my car.

And what the fuck did I see through the big bay window of the living room? Jewel and Cristo siting close to each other on a sofa, all chummy. *Fuck.* I was so going to redden her ass.

She raised a glass of red wine to her lips. Goddamn, she was drinking, too. If last time was any indication of what happened when she drank, this was setting up to be a clusterfuck of a night. My fists trembled with barely restrained violence. Regardless of her conduct, there was no way I'd allow my girl to get pawed at by that fucking little Popescu prick. My blood was boiling, and the tension in my neck, jaw, and fists told me I was swirling around the top of a spiraling maelstrom, but it was too late to step away. The time to stop was before I'd hopped in my car and jetted across the Queensboro Bridge. I was here now, and I wasn't budging. Unless it was to pull Jewel out of there.

Jewel tossed her head back with a laugh, baring her beautiful long neck to Cristo.

I ground down on my back teeth. This was unacceptable. She was supposed to tell Cat about us this afternoon. We were supposed to meet up later, go out to dinner at a restaurant of my choosing, where I was going to show her off. Then I was bringing her home. Fuck, I was supposed to be balls-deep inside her later tonight.

And I had every intention of making that happen.

But instead of being at my side at the French restaurant in Tribeca where every high-level *mafie* boss went to eat, she was sitting beside that little asswipe. Earlier, she'd sent me a text telling me she was eating out with Cat and that she'd catch me later.

Oh, yeah?

From my viewpoint, Cat and Luca were nowhere to be found. No supervision of Cristo and Jewel. If that had been a *mafie* girl, *Bunică* would've been forced to chaperone. The tension in my head increased tenfold. I could feel every cell in my body, hell, every atom, start rumbling and colliding into each other, building pressure and more pressure.

I felt a prick of betrayal that Luca wasn't there, at the very least. Of course, he probably didn't know about me and Jewel. Then again, perhaps he did. If Jewel had told Cat, then there was a strong possibility he knew as well. If that was the case, leaving Jewel alone with my nemesis was unforgivable.

Cristo leaned in a little closer to Jewel. I swear he was scenting her. I narrowed my eyes into the binoculars to get a better look, but to no avail. Oh, she had a truly painful lesson on the menu tonight.

My jaw clenched hard enough to snap in half, my grip around the binoculars so tight I was surprised they didn't bend. I could feel the savagery taking over.

It had taken over, in periodic episodes, until my father's death. After letting it run its course during that bloody summer of revenge, I'd learned to lock it away, only letting it out while riding or flying. There were a few slips, like when I'd fucked Cristo's girl, but otherwise, I'd learned to tame my impulses. The *mafie* life had taught me how, but that didn't meant it wasn't a struggle. A struggle I was getting perilously close to losing.

For the first time since my father's death, I was unraveling. It was coming on me in a wave of blood red, and it was bad.

Cristo placed his hand on Jewel's shoulder while simultaneously pushing her long hair back. Now he was touching her hair. *I'm going to fucking kill him.* My control was slipping by the second. All the mechanisms I'd developed over the years to restrain myself vanished. Counting numbers? *Fuck that.* Counting backward? *Hell, no.* Leave the area, take a walk, get out of the situation? *No, no, and no.* Do a body scan and release tense muscles? *Yeah, that one never worked for me, anyway.*

There was only one thing to do, one idea that kept battering at my overheated brain on repeat: go get her. Go. Get. Her. Fucking go and get her the hell away from him.

Before I knew it, the binoculars were tossed into the gutter and I was stalking toward the Popescu house. Purposefully striding up the stairs to their front door, I went through the various options. Ring the doorbell? Knock on the door? Kick the door in?

Hmm, tough choice.

Not.

Kick the door in, it is.

I reached the top, pulled my torso back and karate-chopped the front door. Wood splintered. Metal bent inward. The door flung open, slammed against the wall, and bounced back into my face. I halted its forward momentum with the palm of my hand and stomped into the foyer.

In a trance, I was in the living room.

I saw Jewel's shocked face, eyes wide, mouth open.

She was saying something, or screaming it, I wasn't sure.

Couldn't hear over the rush of sound in my ears.

One glance confirmed she was safe.

My focus zoomed in on Cristo.

Cristo.

Goddamn motherfucker. He was going down.

I leapt over the back of the sofa and landed on him, body-slamming him over the coffee table. Wood crashed under our weight. Porcelain, glass, plates of food flew everywhere.

My fingers wrapped around his thick neck, squeezing, squeezing. I choked the hell out of him. His face was red. He clocked me. My head whipped to the side.

Fuck, he got me good. Not surprising since we were almost equally matched. Almost, but not quite.

Cristo's nails raked and gouged my hands. He was a vindictive fucker. I may have the element of surprise on my side, but that was fading quickly.

I saw Cat at the edge of my vision. Both she and Jewel were screaming. Luca would skin her hide if she got hurt. And I'd skin Jewel's if she got involved. Cat yanked Jewel back a couple of times. Smart girl.

My head snapped back. Cristo's fist smashed into my nose.

Then Nelu and Luca showed up, Nelu wielding a gun

that he immediately lowered when he saw us rolling around on the floor.

"For Christ's sake, Nicu, what the hell are you doing here?" I heard Luca bellow out, penetrating the haze surrounding me. He grabbed Cat, who tugged Jewel along with her, and brought her to his side. Good, I preferred her a farther distance from us.

Placing a staying hand on Luca, Nelu ordered, "Give them a bit of time. This has been building for years."

My shirt was sticking to my back from when Cristo got on top of me and crushed me against the floor littered with food. I was back on top, my fist swinging out to connect with his jaw. Nelu was right about one thing. This had been building for years. Although he was letting it play out because he hoped Cristo would give me a beat down in retaliation for killing Simu. Fat chance of that happening. Cristo got a few good hits in, I'll admit. I felt a blooming pain in my left eye, and blood was coasting down the side of my face, pooling in the crease of my sealed lips before dripping down onto Cristo's pristine white shirt.

Between the red dots and the black smudges, it wasn't pristine anymore, I thought with glee. Splotches of discolored skin covered his face, likely matching mine.

"You little shit," Cristo griped. "I should end you for what you've done."

"What are you talking about?" I asked as I dodged one of his hits. "For Simu or busting into your home?"

"Both, motherfucker."

"Come on and try it, asshole. You can't hurt me."

"Tata, throw me the gun," he thundered.

"No can do, son. You'll have to use your fists," he singsonged with a laugh.

His fist hit straight up, catching me in the chin. Pain exploded, ripping my head back.

Jewel gave a little screech.

My fist slammed down again, but Cristo swerved in time, and my knuckles connected with the hard floor. *Fuck.*

"Alright, enough," warned Luca.

A moment later, both Luca and Nelu threw themselves into the melee, tearing us off each other. Luca got me in a choke hold and wrangled me out of the room, down the hall, and into a small bedroom. I allowed it, considering I got what I wanted, which was Jewel far away from Cristo.

Tossing me on the small twin bed, he slammed the door and locked it.

"What in the ever-loving fuck, Nicu?" he asked, staring at me incredulously. Crossing his arms over his broad chest, he continued, "Do you even know how much trouble you're in? You busted down the door of a *șef's* house, barged in, and attacked his eldest son."

He leaned in and sniffed me. "Not drunk. Are you high or something? Swear to God, Alex is going to skin you alive."

I sat up and wiped the blood still trickling down from an open wound near my temple with my sleeve. Besides the pain, I was pretty fucking pleased with myself. I always felt good after releasing the burgeoning pressure of fury that needed an escape. I'd achieved my goals. I'd gotten to burn off my rage with the fight, and I'd gotten Jewel away from Cristo.

"No, I'm not fucking high," I scoffed. "You don't have a clue as to what's happening here."

"Then fucking enlighten me, *frate*, because you're not leaving this room until I have some answers."

"Don't tell me you're sticking up for these assholes? Now that you're married to her, you're taking their side?" I yelled.

Luca did that thing he did with his eyebrow, raising it as if to mock me. "Are you fucking serious right now? Just because Nelu and I aren't at each other's throats doesn't mean I'm on their side. Don't go making this about me when you're the one who fucked up. I didn't go storming into a șef's home. For once, the tables are turned. The Golden Boy's screwed up, and I want to know why."

"Don't call me that," I grumbled, ashamed of the nickname from my childhood. It reminded me of my father, and I didn't want reminders of him. His favoritism sat heavily on my shoulders after the revelations of how he'd cheated on Mamă and abused Luca.

"This hasn't happened since we were kids," Luca powered on. "Don't think I've forgotten how things went down back then."

I groaned as memories of my past reared their ugly heads, killing my high. Fuck, I forgot how annoying Luca could be when he pulled his big-brother shit. Of course, he'd bring up the time before I found an outlet for my excessive, destructive energy. I was constantly getting into trouble for pulling pranks and other mischief-making or, alternatively, getting into fights in school with other *mafie* kids. I couldn't keep still, and school couldn't hold my attention. Despite being a menace, I never got punished, because I was the apple of my father's eye. I was grateful to him for not making a difficult time harder. I was torn after finding out my father was such a flawed creature. He was a great father to me, but one that I no longer knew how to love.

Unlike my brothers and Tatum, I wasn't a straight-A student. There was a good chance I had an undiagnosed learning problem, but my father had scoffed at any attempts by teachers to broach the subject. Not only was it considered shameful in our culture, but his infertility problems exacerbated his reluctance to admit there was a problem. Tasa and I were proof of his virility, and if I turned out to be a fuckup... Well, that was unacceptable.

Education was an integral part of our *mafie* society, of our survival in our criminal enterprises. We'd learned from the Bratva, the Russian mafia, where nuclear physicists were as pedestrian as pebbles on a mountain path. People looked down on me because I was the only son who hadn't gone to graduate school, even if I'd graduated college with a major in organic chemistry and a minor in chemical engineering. Everyone thought Alex had let me get away with something. It hadn't been that simple. Only after seeing how much I struggled did he let me off the hook.

Considering how adamant he was about education, people assumed he'd given me a break because I was the spoiled youngest prince. That was not how Alex operated. He'd conferred with Luca and Tatum, who'd been intimately aware of my behavior as a kid, having come to my rescue more than once. The three of them had made the final decision to put me out of my misery and direct my energy into work that played to my strengths.

I moved to stand, but Luca ordered, "Sit right where you are. You're not getting out of this until I get an answer to every one of my questions."

"Is that so?" I scowled up at him.

"You've hated Cristo for years and somehow managed not to kick in the door of his house and beat him to a bloody pulp."

"I did get him good, didn't I?" I said with a grin. The blood in my mouth had probably stained my teeth red, but I didn't care. Throwing him my cell, I grinned wide and said, "Take a pic of me like this."

"So you can post it on Insta and antagonize him even

more? I think not. Out with it, Nicu. You're sweet on Cat's friend, so I'm guessing she's the trigger of your Tasmanian-devil rage."

My smile dropped. I swiped a hand over my face. "Jewel and I are together."

Both his eyebrows rose at that one. Leaning against the locked door, he motioned with his hand for me to continue.

"We hooked up the night you took Cat home."

"Is that so?" he inquired politely, a deadly cold tone beneath his innocent question.

"Don't look at me like I've disrespected her, asshole. You're the one who blood bonded with *my* fiancée."

He scrubbed the five o'clock shadow on his chin. Every Lupu brother had that, but his scruff was blond, unlike the rest of us.

"Alright, alright," he conceded, but jabbed a finger at me. "Don't act like you weren't relieved about it."

"I was, but I didn't dishonor her by fucking her best friend. She was in *your* bed that night."

"Fine," he bit out. "Carry on."

I gave him a one-shouldered shrug. "She kicked me out because *she* felt like she was being disloyal. Kept me at a distance for what seemed like forever. I saw her again at your engagement party. We fucked there."

"Christ," he muttered.

"Please, motherfucker. You did the nasty with Cat during *my* engagement party."

His head snapped up. "You knew about that?"

"Wasn't confirmed until now, but I suspected something was going on between the two of you when she slipped downstairs to the basement where you worked out. Doesn't take a genius to put two and two together when she came back upstairs like she'd seen the devil. Apparently, she had," I teased. "Surprised your dick didn't scare her off."

His eyes narrowed as a thought crossed his mind. "Does Cat know about you and Jewel?"

"I seriously doubt it. We were careful. Jewel was paranoid, but she planned to tell Cat when they met for coffee earlier this afternoon."

Seemingly satisfied with my answer, he continued, "So let me guess, you followed her here because you're a possessive psycho and spied into Nelu's home, where you saw her talking with Cristo."

"Talking," I huffed. "That's what we're calling it now?"

"They've known each other for years, Nicu. Granted, they flirt a little, but if Cristo had wanted her, he would've put the moves on her long ago."

"That was before," I grumbled. "You know how he is with me. And he keeps tabs on me, so I'm sure he's found out about us."

"He does keep tabs on you," he conceded. "We may be at peace, which for Cat's sake I pray continues, but our families will always be rivals. It would be foolish not to be aware of what the other is doing. Didn't realize I should be keeping tabs on my own brother, though, 'cause it's a sad commentary if Cristo finds out my little brother's secrets before I do."

"Please. That's why they're called *secrets*, so you don't find out about them. You've been wrapped up in planning a wedding with your new wife. You don't have time to look after me. Anyway, I'm a grown man. I don't need a babysitter."

"Sure about that? For a grown man, you're about to be in a whole world of pain," he warned. "Seriously, Nicu, Cristo wasn't going to maul her in the middle of his family's home with his women in the kitchen and me downstairs with his father."

I ran my hand through my hair and ruffled it. "Fuck, you know what happens to me. You remember how I used to be. Impulsive. Full of energy that wasn't easy to control. When I saw him playing with her hair, I fucking lost it. He taunted me at your engagement party and the tasting, but I couldn't stand there and let him paw my woman."

He barked out a laugh. "Oh, she's your woman, now?"

"Yeah, she is," I ground out in a dead-serious tone. "I'll drag her to the altar if I have to."

Lips pressed down and eyebrows drawn close together, he shot me a grave look. "Does she agree? Does she know what marrying into this family entails?"

"We haven't had an explicit talk yet, but I've made my intentions perfectly clear."

"She's not a *mafie* princess like Cat or as close to a *mafie* girl as you can get, like Nina. Putting Alex's and Mamă's possible denial aside, this is a matter of life and death. It's not a laughing matter."

"Don't you think I know that, Luca? I haven't come to this decision lightly. I know exactly what this means, and I'm telling you I have no intention of letting her go. That's nonnegotiable."

"Even if it means losing the family?"

That pulled me back. Hell no, I wasn't going to lose my family or clan. Nor was I going to lose Jewel.

I cursed under my breath. "Is that what you're telling me is on the line?"

He pressed his shoulder into the door and shook his head with a long sigh. "No, I'm not saying that. You know we have your back no matter what, but I was testing how far you were willing to go."

"I can have both, and I intend to. I'm never turning my back on my family; you know that. But I can't let her go, either."

"Alex married an outsider, but he's șef. He also chose a girl who was best friends with his little sister and as close to our family as an outsider could be. Hell, she was even a virgin. That's not the situation you find yourself in," he pointed out.

I was well aware that I wasn't making it easy for myself, but she was worth it. I'd have them both, my family and Jewel. My stomach clenched. Anything worth having was worth fighting for, and I fought dirty on a good day. On a bad day, I fought like a savage.

"Alex opened the gate to the possibility of marrying an outsider when he married Nina," I argued. "He set the example, and I'm following it. As you so often joke, I'm Alex's lapdog, always there to do his bidding. I was willing to sacrifice myself by marrying Cat when it was necessary, but we are in a time of peace and expansion. If there's a time to get away with keeping Jewel, it's now, and I plan to take advantage of it."

My fists curled, nails biting into the flesh of my palms as I waited for Luca's reaction. He stood there, ruminating over what I had said. He opened his mouth to speak when there was a rap on the door.

I glared at it, frustrated by the interruption, but when Luca threw it open, damn if it wasn't a sight for sore eyes.

Jewel hesitated by the door, holding up a bowl of water and a first-aid kit. She gently asked, "May I come in?" but I didn't miss the fire in her eyes for an instant.

19

JEWEL

I waited in the living room with Cat long enough for Luca and Nicu to come out. We'd cleaned up the mess of food from the fight while Cristo went to patch himself up in the bathroom.

To say I was mad would be an understatement.

I was furious.

Cat shot me worried looks while I waited, my fingers clenching the arms of the armchair I was sitting in. She knew exactly how pissed off I was by my silence. My throat was scratchy from the desire to screech at the top of my lungs. *What the hell was he thinking?*

It took me a good, long moment after the men were separated to comprehend the extent of what Nicu had done. He'd followed me to Cat's house, which meant he had a tracking device on me, because I'd told him I was eating dinner out with Cat. Then he'd spied on me, which should not have surprised me. I was sure I knew the instant he lost his temper. It was when Cristo had played with my hair.

For a man like Nicu, that was like waving a red flag at a bull.

I could understand his distress. I would've been enraged if I'd caught a woman touching him, but there were a few crucial differences. First, I would've trusted him. He clearly did not trust me, which was outright insulting. It's like he didn't know me at all if he thought I was stupid enough to get seduced by another man. Cristo and I flirted, and granted, he'd never gone quite so far before, but I could've handled Cristo just fine on my own. Saving me from a frat party full of strange men when I was drunk was one thing. Barging into my friend's home during a relaxing dinner was an altogether different thing. I was sick to my stomach at his behavior. I glanced over at the busted-in front door, which still hung from its hinges. There were stubborn stains on the rug, despite all the scrubbing Cat and I had done. *Should I offer to get the rug cleaned?* Ugh. Violent, criminal men were a drag. Just, ugh.

Sick of waiting, I'd asked Cat for a bowl of warm water and a first-aid kit as a pretense to give Nicu a piece of my mind and marched over to the bedroom door. Taking a deep breath to calm myself before I gave in to the urge to kick in the door, I knocked firmly.

The door swung open, and there was Nicu, his face bruised and bloodied, sitting on the bed. *Oh my God.* My stomach twisted with worry. I thought he'd won the fight, but Cristo had gotten in a few good shots. Luca was standing sternly by, probably giving his little brother the lecture of his life. My anger was tempered by Nicu's bruises and imagining the things Luca had said to Nicu, things like how could he possibly consider being with someone like me. His family probably considered me a whore for having a sex life. I hadn't had a lot of partners, but I sure as hell wasn't a virgin, either.

I entered the bedroom cautiously.

Nicu's eyes zeroed in on me, his gaze blazing with a sense of ownership. That, at least, told me that whatever his brother told him hadn't chastened him in the least.

"Hey, baby doll," he murmured.

Luca's head snapped toward Nicu upon hearing the nickname. I groaned internally. As if fighting Cristo wasn't enough, he just had to keep claiming me in public.

"I brought something to help you clean up," I said, holding up the stuff I was carrying.

"Come here," he ordered, patting the narrow bed beside him.

As I approached him, I stumbled in my step as I got a better look at his face. Yikes, it was worse close up.

"I should get ice," I said, fear fluttering through my chest. "You need something for the swelling."

Nicu gave his brother a meaningful look. "Luca will get it."

With a beleaguered sigh, Luca stomped away wordlessly, although he made sure to push the door wide open on his way out.

"Close the door," he demanded.

I placed the bowl and the kit on the night table and did as he asked. He was going to need a closed door for the chewing out I was about to give him after I dealt with his wounds.

As I moved toward him, he snagged me around the waist and put me on his lap.

I shoved at his chest, torn between worry and anger. "Nicu, I'm angry with you. Let me take care of your face, and then I'm going to rip into you so hard you'll know better than to ever pull something like that again."

"Sorry, baby," he rumbled.

That caught me off guard. No one in my family ever

apologized. Not once. My father never apologized for the turmoil he threw our family into. He never admitted to guilt, preferring to go through a lengthy, drawn-out trial than to admit he'd done something wrong. Then he'd tampered with witnesses, which led to a hung jury. Again, he made a conscious choice *not* to spare us another trial.

Saying sorry was a good beginning, and I respected that, but I needed more.

"What are you sorry about, exactly?" I queried, as I opened the first-aid kit. Snagging an antiseptic wipe, I dabbed at the cut by his temple. He flinched, but he stayed painstakingly still for my ministrations.

He frowned. "For almost hurting you, of course. It couldn't be avoided, but I didn't want you to get caught in the middle of our fight. Thankfully, Cat kept you out of the way."

I let out an irritated huff. That was not nearly enough. He was going to have to do better. Much better. What about disrespecting Cat's space, ruining her living room, embarrassing me, or how about not trusting me in the first place?

I opened my mouth when Luca threw the door open and dumped a plastic bag full of ice and a kitchen dish towel on the bed. Without another word, he stalked out, leaving the door open once again.

"Asshole," Nicu muttered at Luca's back.

Without turning around, Luca gave him the middle finger over his shoulder before disappearing again.

Placing a butterfly strip over the cut, I stood up and shut the door again.

When I returned to Nicu, he swooped me into his embrace and settled me back on his lap. Resuming where we'd left off, I prodded, "Anything else you're sorry about?"

His ice-blue eyes narrowed as he reflected on my question. The fact that he had to think about it aggravated me, and my anger shot to the forefront.

"No, I don't think so," he replied.

Incredulous, I threw up my hands. "What about the fact that you knew where I was or that you followed me and broke the door of my best friend's house, violating her home? What about destroying property and beating up a guy simply for flirting with me?"

"Relax," he tried soothing me. "Cristo and I have been at it for years. Where do you think half the scars on my body came from?" He pointed to a little clip near the corner of this top lip that I'd noticed, assuming it was from a rowdy childhood. "This is from him during a bar fight when I was eighteen."

"I'm not a tool you can use in your epic feud with Cristo," I snapped. His lack of awareness was kicking my temper higher and higher.

"This isn't about Cristo," he instantly replied. "Well, it's mostly not about him. This is about another man touching you. It riled me up worse because it was him, but mostly because I'm certain he did it on purpose."

"That's impossible. Even Cat didn't know about us."

"We spy on each other constantly, Jewel," he said dismissively. "He's had someone on me ever since my engagement to his sister. I got a video sent to me of the two of us. He was taunting me with that, and then again tonight. Let me ask you this, has he ever been touchy like that with you before?"

"No, this was the first time," I replied tentatively.

Shit, I was so naïve when it came to their society. Cristo and I had flirted and teased each other in the past, but he'd never made a blatant move like he did tonight.

"Even if he didn't know I was outside his house watching him, hitting on you would've gotten back to me. He would've made sure of it, if only to antagonize me. He doesn't do anything without a purpose. Believe me, it's my business to know my enemy almost as well as I know myself," he proclaimed.

"Great, so I *was* a pawn," I griped.

"Yes, but not to me. Jewel, you know how I feel about you. This isn't a fucking game to me. I may have lost my temper, but I've always been straight with you about who you are to me."

I flashed him an irritated look. "Have you been completely honest with me, Nicu? Because you've messed with my phone. You tracked me down here, and that wasn't a coincidence—"

"Actually, it was."

I slitted my eyes at him, scrutinizing every inch of his face. The muscle of his jaw spasmed. Yeah, I didn't believe him. He was lying to me, and I didn't like that one bit.

"You're lying," I called him out.

He let out a growl of frustration. Unfortunately, the sound was also sexy, and my tummy fluttered in reaction.

He threw up one hand. "Fuck, okay, I was lying."

I slid off his lap and stood in front of him. Fists on my hips, I snapped, "Dammit, Nicu. How can I trust you if you lie to me?"

"There are lies, and then there are lies. Some are for your own good," he replied as he jerked at the collar of his shirt, clearly uncomfortable. As he should be. The arrogance, the sense of entitlement to make decisions on my behalf, stunned me.

"You're kidding me, right? If that's what you expect of me if I date you—"

"You *are* dating me," he replied instantly. "We *are* together. Period."

"Don't hold your breath on that one, buddy," I snapped. "Because I'm not about to allow a *man* make unilateral decisions for me, even if it is for my safety."

My father had made decisions that irrevocably altered my life, and not for the better. My mother dumped me at a boarding school without asking me or so much as getting my feedback. It was their way, no matter what the cost was to me. Regardless of how I felt about Nicu, now that I was finally an adult, I sure as hell wasn't going to turn my agency over to him, especially with the way he was acting.

"When it comes to safety, like a lockdown because of an imminent threat, you better believe you'll follow orders," he snarled.

"Even if that was something I would contemplate, which let me tell you is not a given, that isn't what happened here. You lied to me about keeping track of where I go, because you didn't want to own up to it. Besides, you acted like a madman out there." I jabbed at the door. "Disrupting my friend's home and embarrassing me in front of her."

"Don't worry about Cat. She knows *mafie* men. We're jealous and irrational," he said, dismissive of my complaint.

I ground down on my back teeth.

"You're impossible! You have an excuse for everything, but you're not *listening*. I don't like seeing you lose control. I don't like violence and chaos. I've already had my entire world collapse around me. I also don't like that you keep things from me or make decisions on my behalf without discussing it with me beforehand. At first, your possessiveness made me feel safe, but not anymore. You don't own me, Nicu. You can't do whatever you want without any consideration of how it might affect me."

My chest heaved with frustration.

And then it hit me like a bolt of lightning. *Oh my God,*

this is what Cat's talking about. Nicu *was* selfish. Immature and self-centered. He couldn't see my side of things. He couldn't see how his behavior impacted me. He couldn't see *me.*

The realization crushed me. My pulse started going double time. *No.* I could not abide this. I'd suffered enough with my parents. Mother didn't see me. She visited when it was convenient for her, when she already happened to be in the city for another reason. I was only and always an afterthought to her. It wasn't much better with my father, but at least, I could forgive him. He lived behind bars, surviving day by day.

They were my parents. My past. I could do nothing to change them or it. But I wasn't about to knowingly fall into a relationship that perpetuated the dysfunction in my family. I thought Nicu respected me. I'd seen his possessiveness as a form of caring. Now, I wasn't so sure. Maybe he primarily saw me as an object, like the nickname, baby doll.

Heart beating out of my chest, I put my palms out and backed away from him.

"I can't do this. The only thing you've authentically apologized for is for physically putting me in harm's way, but you can't see how your behavior embarrassed and hurt me. On top of that, you lied to me. You won't listen to me. You want me to turn my will over to you to make decisions for me. The truth is you don't want a true partnership, Nicu. You want ownership. A pretty doll you can dress up and fuck, but most importantly, who will do your bidding and sit quietly while you make all the proper decisions about her. That's not me. That will *never, ever* be me," I finished with a lungful of air.

His hand went to his nape and rubbed. Looking confused, he said, "What the hell are you talking about? Of course, I respect you. I lied because I was afraid of how you'd react to the tracking app on your phone. That's my bad, but I respect you."

Disappointment crackled over my skin like a hundred tiny blades. *Words.* They were just words. I didn't hear conviction in them. I didn't hear comprehension of what he'd done or acknowledgment of my concerns.

My shoulders stooped in defeat. "Did you not hear everything I just said?"

"I heard; I just don't agree with it. You're not a blow-up doll I want to cart around, biddable and without personality. If that were the case, I'd already be married to a *mafie* girl. You've been a pain in my ass since the beginning, fighting me every step of the way. We've only just gotten to a good place, and I didn't want to give you ammunition to pull away from me *yet again*." The level of frustration in his voice amped up. "Okay, so I fucked up. It wasn't my proudest moment. Yes, I lost my temper. Believe me, it's a source of shame for me. I haven't lost my temper in years. *Years.* But I lost it tonight. Over you."

His expression was stark with the shame he was describing. I appreciated that he was opening up to me, but it only added fuel to the fire, proving we weren't compatible.

"Listen, Nicu. I don't know if I can do this," I declared, my heart feeling like it was being ripped in two. Tears of exasperation and grief sprung from my eyes.

He pointed a finger at me. "Oh, no you don't! See, that's the reason I didn't tell you. I knew you couldn't handle it and would try to run away."

My eyes flashed; my nostrils flared. I breathed out heavily and opened my mouth to scream in frustration when there was a gentle knock on the door. I whipped around as Cat poked her head through the opening.

"The walls are thin," she disclosed cautiously. "We can hear everything. It's time you stopped, for now." Turning to Nicu, she disclosed, "Luca called Alex, and he's ordered you to meet him at the café. I suggest you don't keep him waiting, for both of your sakes. Nicu, you need to see your *şef*. Pick this up another time."

"Yes," I hurried to agree, desperate to get away from his presence. In my mind, there was nothing more to say.

Pointing at me, he said to Cat, "I'll leave, but I want her home."

My upper lip curled. I was about to shoot him a bitter comeback when Cat put a hand on my arm and answered, "I'll personally escort her home, Nicu. I give you my word."

"Right away," he insisted. "If you care for Cristo, you'll make sure to keep her away from your brother. It'll be on your conscience because nothing's off the table, Cat. I'm dead fucking serious."

Dipping her head with an acquiescence I wasn't used to seeing her display, she hushed out, "Of course, Nicu. I'll make sure of it."

Grr. I was so furious at him I could've throttled him. Getting me away from Cristo was all he cared about. And how did he turn Cat into a simpering miss? I wanted to slam a door or throw a punch or stomp on the ground. I wanted to throw a hissy fit, is what I wanted. Instead, I snapped my mouth shut and gritted my teeth as Nicu stood up and came to me.

I stiffened as he cupped my cheek. "We'll talk later. I'm in some serious shit right now. It may take a while, but I'm coming for you, Jewel. I'm warning you; this isn't over."

Holding myself rigidly, I tried not to be affected by his warm hold, his fingertips lovingly caressing my skin, sparking tingles that left me feeling both enraged and impotent.

I jerked my head away. He leaned in and placed a lingering kiss on my temple. For a long moment, we were suspended together, his spicy, sultry scent coiling around me like thick incense, and then—he was gone.

20

NICU

One mistake and my life had turned into a clusterfuck. Jewel was furious with me when I left Cat's house, escorted by Luca. Still buzzing from the fight, I only later realized how thick I'd laid it on during our argument. I hadn't meant to sound so barbaric. I was listening to her, or at least, I thought I was. In my defense, I was trying to emphasize that her safety was paramount, and for that reason, there would be no negotiations. At least, that's what I thought I was doing. Jewel was new to *mafie* life, and it hadn't been the best time to hammer that point home.

As for lying—that had been a bad miscalculation. I wasn't in the habit of lying. Nor was I afraid of her reaction, assuming it would be negative. The walls in these houses were paper thin, and I didn't want to have an in-depth argument with the entire Popescu family listening to every word we said. So I'd tried to cut it off before we got into it.

It blew up in my face.

In the end, I was grateful for Cat's interruption because I kept digging myself deeper with every word out of my mouth. Only now, with things left hanging between us unresolved, I was left agitated and restless.

When Luca deposited me at the threshold of Alex's office, I had another surprise waiting for me. I was to be banished to California.

For the time being.

I felt ashamed, frustrated, and borderline desperate to be going so far from Jewel, but I had no choice. Alex was pissed. Even if it was the first time, I could say with absolute certainty that I'd do everything in my power to avoid a repeated performance. Luca had called Alex in advance to take control of the narrative and save me some grief, but Nelu had beaten him to it. Whatever the bastard had told my eldest brother, he was in the kind of mood I hadn't seen since the time he and Nina broke up. And that was saying something.

Having my şef ream into me gave me a new level of respect for Luca. How many times had Luca gone toe-to-toe against Alex? Too many to count. It was more proof that my father must've really beat the shit out of him to engender such unyielding fearlessness.

Despite my arguments, there was no getting around my main offense of breaking into the home of a şef. It didn't help that we'd recently cemented a peace treaty with a clan that we'd struggled against for decades, a dream my father had worked toward but wasn't able to achieve in his lifetime.

I was currently on a late-night flight to L.A. to meet up with Tatum and Sebastian, who were in the middle of a budding fight with the Hagi clan. Since Jewel was still furious with me, the only silver lining of being shuffled onto a plane this late at night was that it gave her space to calm down and, if I was lucky, come to miss me a little. Luca escorted me to the airport, and I spent that time convincing him to help me and make sure Jewel remained safe. I didn't know what Cristo would do. He wouldn't hurt her, if only because she meant everything to Cat, but that still left a lot of leeway for inflicting damage.

Worry slithered in my gut.

Would she end up missing me? This was our first argument. People didn't break up after one bump in the road, did they? I wouldn't know since I'd never been in a real relationship. My only reference points were my parents' marriage, which turned out to be a farce, Alex and Nina, and finally, Luca and Cat. A helluva lot more went down the time Alex and Nina broke up or the time Luca ended things with Cat. I mean, those were major relationship-defining moments, not a fleeting scuffle with a rival followed by a verbal disagreement. *Couples didn't split up over that, did they?* Shame reared up as some of the things I'd said to Jewel came back to me. Heat pricked the back of my neck.

Fuck, I better be right because after the week we'd spent together, I couldn't let her go. Not that I had the slightest clue how I would win her back.

The other thing that stuck in my craw was how Cristo got involved in laying out the terms of compensation for my blunder... As if reading my mind, my phone lit up, and I saw that my twin was calling me. She was up with her baby again, and likely sensing I was available, she was trying me.

With a row to myself in first class, I figured I had enough privacy to take the call. Staring out through the small oval window into the dark night sky, I put the phone to my ear. Tasa launched right into a tirade without so much as a hello.

"Holy shit, Nicu. You attacked Cristo in his father's house? Are you out of your mind? No, don't answer that. You weren't thinking. I know you, and this has 'outburst' written all over it. It's a throwback to when you were a boy, except now, you're a full-grown adult and there are consequences when you pull this shit," she ended, finally stopping long enough to gulp down air.

I rolled my eyes. *Family.* How could I forget this busy-body aspect of being part of a tight-knit family? And especially of having a twin sister. Even far away, she knew me better than I knew myself sometimes. Tasa could home in on a problem with the precision of a surgical knife. Having a twin who was invested in my success could sometimes be a double-edged sword, like right now.

"Who told you?"

"Luca."

"Judas," I grumbled.

"Whatever, Nicu. This was of your own making, and I don't want you backsliding after so many years. So what happens now?"

"What happens now is that I'm on a flight to L.A. to provide backup for Tatum and Sebastian. I've been banished for a week, possibly two." I gritted my teeth, pounding the plastic arm of the seat with my clenched fist. "Gonna be the longest weeks of my life. The only upside is that it will give Jewel time to cool off. When I return, I have to make an official, public apology to Cristo. Him dictating terms to me via Alex pisses me off, but Alex thinks it's what I deserve, so he's backing the punishment."

My pride smarted at my brother taking my enemy's side, but he wanted to make the consequence painful enough that I didn't forget the lesson. It was working.

"You did go overboard," she muttered. "You know I'm no fan of Cristo, but this warrants a gesture of humility toward the entire Popescu family."

"What does Cristo want? For me to rent out ad space in Times Square?" I huffed out.

"Ha," she barked out. "I don't even think that would satisfy him, but you'll have to do something impressive to pacify him and his father. You said your girl is mad at you... Was it the fight alone or something more?"

I squeezed my eyes in pain. Worry about my future with Jewel, shame at disappointing her and Alex, and disgrace of having lost my shit kept me on edge. Bouncing my knee up and down, I confessed, "Oh, she was furious that I got into a fight with Cristo, no doubt. But I also put my foot in my mouth. More than once, I might add."

"Oh, no, you didn't," she replied with a laugh.

"Are you laughing at me?"

"Yes, yes, I am," she confided smugly.

"Don't you know better than to admit that? I'm your older brother. You should at least pretend not to gloat."

"Older brother, my ass. I could pretend...but then that would be a lie. I wouldn't want to wound your ego with such a false show of sympathy," she trilled. "Stop deflecting. Out with it, what did you do?"

I winced, not wanting to rehash what had happened, but I could only get her advice on how to fix it by revealing my stupidity. "She thinks I should've apologize for beating up Cristo, because I embarrassed her. Tasa, the fucker laid a hand on my woman. He knew about me and Jewel, laid a trap for me, and I fell for it. She said I humiliated her. Then I royally fucked up. I didn't listen to her, I ordered her around, and tried to lie to her. It was a clusterfuck, only made worse by the fact that it happened at the Popescus'. Cat is alright, but her brother's a fucking monster," I complained.

"I shouldn't have to remind you to be extra vigilant around him, little brother. He's a sneaky one, like all the Popescus. You need to be more like Alex. Think. Anticipate.

Pounce. Our families may technically be at peace, but they can't be trusted. Cat's different, but that's as close to a miracle as one can get. She makes Luca happy, so I have nothing against her, but the rest of them are snakes," she concluded, echoing my own sentiments.

Returning to the subject of Jewel, I admitted, "I fucked up, and my pride wouldn't allow me to admit my mistake during our argument. Now she thinks I'm a hothead who reacts on impulse, and she's not wrong. It took years to shed that image. One blip in my control, and now I'm back to being the reckless one again." A sigh rattled out of my chest. "She accused me of not taking her feelings into account. And she was right."

Panic sliced through me. What if I couldn't convince her that the man who'd raged and beaten-up Cristo wasn't the real me? That I wasn't that out-of-control kid I used to be. If I hated that part of myself, how could she love me despite it? I'd only made a bad situation worse by letting my mouth run off without thinking.

"Hey," Tasa chided me softly. "You're an incredible man, Nicu. And I'm not just saying that because you're my brother. Yes, you have your faults. You have a temper, and you can be stubborn at times, but I don't know a single person who loves as hard as you do. You give your entire heart, no holds barred. Do you know how rare that is? If she can't see what you have to offer, then screw her."

Tasa was right. When I loved, I loved unconditionally and wholeheartedly. Without reservations. I didn't just love Jewel. I was in love with her. The thought of not having her in my life set my pulse racing in a mad rush. I'd fucking lose it if she shut me out. I could barely handle it in the beginning. I could never tolerate it now.

Space to calm down, I was willing to give her. Space forever? No fucking way.

Dong.

The chime went off, followed by the seat belt sign lighting up. I finished my conversation with Tasa as the stewardess came down the aisle to prepare for landing. We flew over the crisscross grid of Los Angeles, with a blue mountain range in the background. A hazy sun rose into the sky, illuminating the smog over the city skyline.

It wasn't New York, I thought as the plane descended. Outside of flying and racing, I never left New York.

Any yet, here I was.

I didn't need a chaperone, but it was comforting to see Tatum's familiar face at the terminal. As soon as we settled into the smooth leather seats of his black Range Rover, he asked, "Damn, Nicu, what the hell happened?"

Tatum didn't like things out of sorts, which meant he was already stressed enough with the growing tensions he was experiencing with the Hagi. The man was charming, erudite, and clever. Like a snake charmer, he could usually manipulate people into doing whatever he wanted, which meant things were dire if he was incapable of settling flaring tempers.

His reaction didn't surprise me, considering Tatum was essentially an extension of Alex. He was also the most even-keeled, self-possessed man I knew, so he couldn't relate to what I was going through. He would never find himself in my situation, losing his shit over a woman.

"You know better than to let Cristo get to you," Tatum chided. He massaged his forehead. "Believe me, I feel your pain. I'm living through my own version of hell with a miniature Cristo, only this one is in the form of a female. I get it. For once, I get it."

I did a double take. "Say what?" I peered closer, inspecting him attentively.

"I've never had to deal with such an infuriating, irrational, and completely impossible woman before. So confrontational," he muttered under his breath.

The corner of my mouth popped in a smirk. "A woman, you say?"

"Did I say woman? Female, perhaps, but more like a she-devil. I highly suspect she only uses her fine-ass figure to lure men into her lair so she can devour them whole. Like a black widow. She's a monster."

"Who's the mystery woman who's put you, of all people, in a tizzy?"

"The Hagi princess. Clara." He did a fake shudder. "Oh, you may find her attractive, with her smooth dark hair and big eyes, but don't let her faux innocence fool you. She may look like a doll, but she hisses like a viper. And like Cristo, she has beef with us over Simu's death." He snorted. "As if that could've been helped. I've explained to her time and again that it was an unavoidable kill. He had his fingers around Luca's throat, choking him, when he was shot."

Tatum glanced over at me with a hard look on his face. "And for the love of all that's holy, do not mention you were the one to pull the trigger on Simu, or everything Sebastian and I have worked for over the past couple weeks will go to hell. I'm warning you; I have to get the fuck out of here before I lose my mind. I need to get back to the city. The sunlight here is killing me. *Killing* me," he emphasized.

I peered over at him curiously, never having witnessed him this...flustered before. "How does she have a say in anything? I mean, she's a *mafie* princess. Since when are they involved in the business end of things?"

"Dear God, you're going to quickly learn that things are different out here. They're so-called 'reformed,'" he air-quoted with his fingers. "Not traditional, like us, or so she revels in reminding me, time and again. The first time I questioned why she was at a meeting, she cut her father off midsentence to answer me. I've never seen anything like it. Did her father reprimand her or anything? Not at all. Turns out, it doesn't matter that she's a woman. Her younger brother can't become șef, so I don't know what the hell they plan on doing, but I can tell you that she's deeply involved in every decision of her clan. There's an added wrinkle because Clara and her father's *consilier* work in tandem, and you remember who that is, don't you?"

"Simu's uncle." I grunted out.

"Although the term 'uncle' is a bit of a misnomer. Technically, yes, he's Simu's uncle, but he was much younger than Simu's father. With only a five-year difference between them, he and Simu were raised like brothers."

"Oh, fuck no," I said.

"Oh, fuck yes," Tatum countered with a grimace. "And Clara hates us. Almost as much as the Popescus when we were feuding."

"So outside of the tussles between Cristo and me, we've basically subbed one feud for another," I declared.

"Couldn't put it better myself," he mumbled.

I looked out of the window onto the six-lane highway still filled with bumper-to-bumper traffic though it was long past peak morning rush hour. Staring out at the never-ending lanes, I mused aloud, "Is it worth the trouble to expand out here? This place looks like a cesspit."

"Pfft, you're telling me? I've been here for over two

weeks. You touched down an hour ago. Ultimately, it's not our decision to make. I understand Alex's motivation. Everything's settled with the Popescus. We can't sit on our laurels if we want to keep our position as the most powerful family in the United States. At this point, it's become a point of honor. If we back off now, we look weak, and reputation is half the battle. We should've pulled out earlier if we hoped to remain unscathed. There's no way we could live down being bullied out of L.A. by a little clan like theirs, no matter how ferocious they are," explained Tatum. "My suggestion to you is, settle in for the ride."

I flicked my gaze over to him once more. He met my eyes and held them.

I'd do my duty, but there was only so much time I could spend here. Sooner or later, I'd have to return to New York to settle the unfinished business between Jewel and me.

21

JEWEL

One fight.

One. Fight.

We had one itty-bitty argument, and the guy jumped ship like I was the Titanic. It was demoralizing on a level I hadn't experienced since my dad got arrested.

Cat and I were back at the Hungarian Pastry Shop, which was fitting since this is where the craziness of the past forty-eight hours had begun. It was the bookending to one of the worst episodes of my life. That's why love sucked. When my father was incarcerated and Mother disappeared like she'd only been a figment of my imagination, I swore to myself I wouldn't be emotionally vulnerable again. I'd made an oath and stayed the course, but being with Nicu was like slipping into a dream state where the rules no longer applied.

Well, this is what you get for forgetting how bad things can be. Because right now, my life was dreary and depressing. I glanced over my shoulder, peering out into the cold, rainy late-autumn day. Through the rain-smeared windowpane, I squinted down the street, hoping for a glimpse of that familiar figure.

Nothing.

There were only pedestrians clutching their rickety umbrellas as they rushed by. I went on to study the façade of the cathedral across the street. Again, nothing.

Just like my parents, Nicu had disappeared as if he'd never existed.

With a frustrated little shake of my head, I tore myself away and morosely stared down at my tall glass of iced cappuccino, the whipped cream with the dusting of cinnamon on top untouched.

Disappointment settled in my gut.

I'd waited for him to show up, but there was no doubt about it.

He was gone.

It was a shock, because everything I knew about Nicu dictated that he would've beaten down the door of my dorm room or blown up my phone by now. Threading my fingers through my hair, I allowed a bitter, knowing smile to coat my lips. I knew it wouldn't last. Nothing good ever did.

Cat fidgeted in her seat; eyebrows drawn together. Her lips pressed in a flat line as she kept her eyes on me.

"Stop it," she demanded in a soft tone.

"Stop what? You look like you have to say something, so out with it," I grumbled.

Taking a huge breath of air, she launched in, "Could it be you're pushing Nicu away because of what happened to your father? You know, because he abandoned you?"

She held up her hand as I opened my mouth to interrupt. "No, let me finish. Even if it wasn't on purpose, your father *did* abandon you, Jewel. He left you, and then your mother left you, so now you feel the need to push Nicu away before *he* has a chance to leave you."

"That's..." I sputtered. *So true.* Instead, I finished with, "...absurd."

"Is it, though?" she persisted. "At school, there were more than a few guys who were into you. You'd only let them get so close. When things got real, you'd feel threatened and ghost them. The thing is, you didn't really care about them, so it was okay not to lead them on. But you feel deeply for Nicu, and I would hate—I mean I would really, really *hate*—it if you tossed this away out of fear."

"You're the one who told me he was too selfish and wasn't worth my time," I argued.

"Hmm, I might've been wrong," she observed. "I was watching him carefully. The guy couldn't keep his eyes off you. He wore his emotions on his face, and he was torn up about what happened. I can honestly say I've never seen Nicu upset. Nothing fazes him, but he looked shell-shocked after you were done with him."

I dropped my head, staring down at my fingers, interwoven in a tight grip. I pursed my lips and scrunched my forehead, looking inward and thinking hard.

"Granted, he acted badly when he crashed into my house, but he did it because he's crazy about you. He knew the consequences, but he didn't care. That was an act of selflessness," she concluded. "Selfless because I can only imagine what Alex did to punish him."

She gave a little shudder. "Romanian *mafie* clans are loving, family-orientated people, but when you cross a line, they're quick to teach you a lesson. Whatever your worst nightmare is, they recreate it *without mercy*. Think about that."

"Is that statement supposed to entice me to join your world? Because if so, it really isn't succeeding," I snipped.

"No, it wasn't, but I assume you wouldn't hold our way of life against him. I assume you would join my world because you love him. I don't know...maybe you're willing to throw it away because you had it easy when it came to love," she pondered. "Instead of realizing how precious it is and knowing it's worth the fight."

Her words stung.

I sputtered, "Hey, that's not fair. My parents' love wasn't easy."

She gave a shrug. "I'm talking about romantic love. You can fall in love with whomever you want. You can choose to marry or not marry. You can choose to live with someone as a partner. Really, the world is your oyster when it comes to love. Perhaps something as inconvenient as the not-picture-perfect family is too much."

Ouch. That hit below the belt, and it struck its target, as I'm sure my normally sweet best friend had intended. I'd seen how circumscribed Cat's life was. She had a heavy burden to carry to uphold her family's expectations and further their ambitions. As for her little comment about family, it was a not-so-subtle reminder of the imperfection of my own family. While I had men interested in me, they were commoners, for lack of a better word. But to men who'd grown up in my world, I was toxic by association to my father. Something I'd only made worse by not turning my back on him. Unlike Mother.

Nicu's family might be mafia, but mine was no less criminal. A pang of guilt thrust a thorn in my heart. I'd judged him so harshly.

"Okay, okay, point taken. You know very well it's not what they do for a living that rubs me the wrong way. It's their archaic traditions. I don't like the way women are treated."

Cat sighed. "I know, and I don't have a magic bullet for you. Everyone has their role to play in a family, and everyone is stuck with a set of expectations that they must meet. It's true that we women are coddled and protected, in exchange for an arranged marriage. But don't tell me that in your society, there aren't women who marry men they're not so crazy about to secure an elevated social and financial status," she countered. "It's not that different."

That was true, of course. My own mother was a perfect example of someone who'd abandoned her husband when he was deemed unfit.

"True," I murmured. "I admit that, in the end, I wouldn't reject Nicu because of the parts of your society I don't like." I winked. "If anything, I'd try to infiltrate it to change it from the inside, like the rebel I am."

She squeezed my hand. "I'm sorry. I don't mean to sound resentful. You're lucky you have so much freedom when it comes to relationships. It's just that things aren't black and white. There are many subtleties that drive people to do what they do. Sometimes the motivation is family, sometimes it's money, security, fame. There are dozens of reasons why women and men marry, and they don't always have to do with love.

"But we're digressing from the real topic, which is that you're pushing Nicu away because you're afraid of loving him. I'm not going to try to defend his actions, but this issue would've come up eventually. How could it not, considering what you've been through? You've witnessed the lowest points of my life, Jewel, but I haven't forgotten..." she said pointedly.

I swiveled my head away, avoiding her penetrating gaze,

and the memories of her finding me on the bathroom floor when I didn't show up for class one afternoon, of her dragging me into the shower and administering small, sharp slaps to my face as cold water pelted down on me. I had secreted away pills from Mother's stash to end my life. Looking back, I didn't think there were enough to kill myself, but I'll never know how close a call it was. The shame of that time burned in my gut, but I pushed it away. There was no point in dwelling on it. I had survived, and that was all that mattered.

"I know you haven't," I murmured.

"Then you know you deserve happiness. If this man makes you happy, you should hold on to him for dear life, and if that includes forgiving his stupidity, then do it," she intoned. "Believe me when I tell you, you don't want to look back and wish you'd made different choices only to realize you were tripped up by your own issues."

I heard the pain in her voice even after everything had worked out between her and Luca. Cat knew me better than anyone. Was she right that I was afraid? There was no doubt that he'd acted like an idiot, but was I too hard on him? Had I pushed him away?

I thought back to Jack, the guy I lost my virginity to. He'd tried to get close afterward, but I wanted nothing to do with him. Then there was Daniel. I broke it off, citing his immaturity. I couldn't argue the same thing about Nicu. Nicu was nothing like either of them. He was all man. After Daniel, there was Connor. I nixed him, claiming that he was boring. I was only in high school, but plenty of kids had coupled up by senior year, and Cat had already been engaged to be married.

Thinking back, I pulled away when they wanted to cuddle in bed or when they blew up my phone, constantly texting me. Maybe it wasn't *constant*, but it sure felt like too much. Their attention was child's play compared to Nicu's, but his stalking never bothered me. In fact, I liked it. Letting my gaze drift to the street, I sighed. Turned out I craved it.

Eyes scanning the length of the block, my heart sank when he was nowhere to be found. I felt safe with him and his stupid, relentless attention. Damn him for changing me. Damn me for finding comfort in his constant presence. For missing him. There was no denying that I missed his incessant shadowing. I felt incomplete without it.

Was he teaching me a lesson, or had I been such a bitch that I had finally run him off?

I turned to my best friend and confessed, "I've pushed him away harder than this, and he didn't disappear."

"The other night was crazy. A lot of things were said in anger. He needs time to cool off," she suggested.

"Hmm, that doesn't sound like him," I reflected. "He's not the kind of man who backs off. He's the kind of man who comes at you harder, so his absence is a clear message."

"Don't jump to conclusions," she advised. "You don't know everything about him or how he'll react to every interaction."

"It's hard not to," I griped with a long, dejected sigh. "It's *really* hard not to."

Cat was right. I didn't know every single thing about him. Maybe he needed time. I could give him that. I could wait for him. I *would* wait for him, but I couldn't help but fear that he'd decide I was too high-maintenance. Until now, he seemed to like that about me, but I might have gone too far. Pushed him away one too many times. Another, darker, part of me would almost be relieved if he dumped me. It was cowardly, but Nicu pushed my boundaries and challenged me in ways that were downright uncomfortable. I was torn between aching for him, craving him, and being grateful that I could slip back into the safe shell of my life before him. I hoped I wouldn't choose fear over love, but I wouldn't know until he showed up.

If he ever showed up again.

22

NICU

S even. Fucking. Days.

Seven days since I left Jewel and my life in New York. Wearily, I sank deeper into the overstuffed armchair in the airless library of the Hagi house, brooding while my fingers impatiently tapped away. The space might be vast, but it was stuffed to the gills with furniture and tchotchkes. For a distinguished house in the hills, just above Sunset Boulevard with a sweeping view of the city, they crammed their house like it was the Grand Bazaar of Istanbul.

The urge to text Jewel drove me hard, but I pushed it down. Using the tracker on her phone, I kept tabs on her as she moved around the city. It came as a surprise that she hadn't disabled it, giving me a degree of hope. I wanted to reach out to her, but the truth was that, for the first time in my life, I was afraid. Unable to see her expression or pull her into my chest and hug her close if we got into an argument over text, it could quickly degenerate into something ugly. As desperate as I was to reach out, I couldn't risk her breaking up with me over text. She'd left me a voicemail, and I replayed it incessantly, but again, I was afraid to return her phone call for fear we'd get into it. The only way to do this was when we saw each other. So instead of reaching out, I hunkered down and waited out my punishment.

Stuck in this stifling library counted as punishment enough. I'd been forced to listen to Tatum and Princess Clara, as we'd dubbed her, go at it for hours. How did they have the stamina for this? As if I needed a reminder of how much I missed Jewel, watching Clara in action clinched it. She was like a rabid pit bull. Even at her most infuriating, my woman was nothing like this. She pushed my limits and tested me like no one else, but in the best of ways.

A week had already passed since I arrived, and we were getting nowhere fast. The Hagi şef, Boian, looked like an old grizzly warrior, which was fitting since it matched the meaning of his name. He seemed amenable to negotiation, but anytime we started getting somewhere, Clara inevitably derailed us.

Infuriated, Tatum would jump in, and the both of them would debate, haggle, and argue for hours until either Sebastian or I ended the meeting. It was like dealing with squabbling children. I'd never seen Tatum in such a state. In spite of their incessant bickering, I sensed an undercurrent between them. We'd be better off if they blew off some steam in the bedroom before returning to the bargaining table.

Interrupting Tatum in the middle of what oddly sounded like a rant, I put my hand up and ordered, "Stand down, Tatum. Go take a break."

His mouth was agape, but he snapped it shut midphrase, stood up, and stomped outside.

It wasn't particularly polite of me, but I needed a moment, and I wasn't going to get that with him rattling on.

The frustration wafted off him regardless of how much restraint he was exerting to suppress it in front of the Hagis.

Unfortunately, we were at an impasse because the Hagi family had a choke hold on the rest of the clans in and around Los Angeles. Tatum and Sebastian had spent the better part of two weeks finagling them into working with us, but the Hagi had something over on each of them. Either that, or the families remained loyal to the Hagi because they came from the same small city of Suceava, in the region of Bukovina, in northeastern Romania. It was the birthplace of an old medieval civilization, and the people were known to be proud to the extreme. It was as close to being blood related as one could get. I had to hand it to the Hagi. For a small clan, they were tenacious. Much like Clara.

Time was ticking. I had to get back to Jewel before I lost my shit. Meanwhile, Tatum was determined to win and was willing to stay here as long as necessary to succeed. He was determined to either outwit Clara or wear her down. Or both. After watching the dynamics within the Hagi family, I'd concluded that the problem whittled down to a seemingly passive, yet crucial player: Simu's uncle, Grigore. Whenever Clara was about to relent, Grigore swept in and bolstered her resolve.

If I had any hope of getting back to Jewel, I had to think outside the box. As Tasa had suggested during our telephone call, I had to think like Alex. Like a strategist. What would Alex do? He'd analyze the players and seek out their weaknesses. Grigore was behind Clara's obstinacy. Until they were separated, we'd never get anywhere. And worse still, if something didn't break soon, this could devolve into violence.

Even if the Grigore problem was eliminated, the crux of the issue was that Clara didn't trust us. We were a big, ostentatious, and powerful clan. We weren't from Suceava or the region of Bukovina, and we'd killed Simu. Even though she knew we were completely within our rights, she was emotionally conflicted. Whenever she had a moment of levelheadedness, Grigore came up from behind and egged her back into irrationality.

The solution popped into my head. First, we needed to separate them, no matter the cost. Second, we needed to give her a chance to get to know us and to give us a chance to woo her. Sure, we were an ambitious and bloodthirsty bunch, but no more than her or any other *mafie* family. On the other hand, we weren't that bad. Hell, we were the most powerful family in North America. We could be charming, when we wanted to.

"God, he's unbearable," Clara grumbled once the door swung shut. Jabbing a thumb at the door, she asked, "Is he always like that?"

"Never," Sebastian replied succinctly.

"You must bring it out of him," I quipped.

Her eyes narrowed on me.

Holding my hands up in a gesture of surrender, I said, "Relax, it was a joke."

Her tense shoulders sagged. She had bags under her round blue eyes. This was straining on her as well. She was attractive and would be more so if she gave herself a break from her standing bitch mode.

Focusing solely on her, I jerked my head toward Grigore, and said, "Let's make it even and have one less person here."

Grigore wheezed as if I'd just punched him in the gut, which wasn't far from what I wanted to do.

"What?" he spluttered.

Focusing solely on Clara, I held her gaze and said, "I have a proposition, but I'm not into exercises in futility. I need the two most toxic people out of the room before I introduce it to you." I raised an eyebrow in challenge. "Do you agree?"

Tatum was the farthest from toxic a person could get, but whatever. It was a small but necessary lie to make Clara kick Grigore out. Her gaze slid over to Grigore, who looked like he was about to have a stroke.

Before she had a chance to answer, the Hagi șef surprised us all by flicking his fingers at Grigore, an order for him to leave.

Huh, I might have an ally on my side.

For whatever reason, Boian allowed his daughter an incredible amount of power. It reminded me of a șef loosening the leash on his heir to gain experience before handing over the crown. But the notion that a șef would turn his empire over to a daughter was preposterous. Perhaps he was about as done with these failed negotiations as I was.

The corners of Clara's Cupid's bow lips drooped into a frown, but surprisingly, she did not contradict her father.

Grigore stood in a huff and made about as graceful an exit as Tatum had. I hoped they didn't kill each other if they crossed paths outside.

Once the door clacked shut, I allowed a moment to pass. It was like a window had opened in this oppressive library, stuffed full of Baroque furniture like an estate sale at an English country manor.

I rubbed my hands and started, "Blood bonds are the backbone of every family. Between clans, where those bonds of blood and birthplace do not exist, there is trust. You, Clara, clearly have little trust in us. And that's understandable. Our recent ambition seems to have come out of nowhere, having been in this country for decades, and yet we never bothered to venture west of the Hudson River. I might explain that we were busy solidifying our power base, and it took that long before we felt comfortable extending beyond our known territory. But we're here now, and we aren't going anywhere." I paused meaningfully. "I want you to be cognizant of that one pertinent fact. We are here to stay."

Her shoulders went back. "Is that a threat?" she spat out.

"No, no, it's not, but it *is* a reality, and one that you must accept."

I steepled my hands over the arms of the chair as I had seen Alex do, time and again. "To do that, I suggest you learn more about us. Come to New York for six months. You can live with my mother and grandmother. You can get to know us. Perhaps after some time spent in our world, seeing us as living, breathing human beings, and not monsters that indiscriminately kill rivals or intrude on other people's territory, you'll come to understand more of who we are. And who we are is not necessarily your enemy. We have lucrative treaties and contracts with other clans. We've built a network that crosses continents. We know how to play nice, and we can benefit you because, believe me, you'd rather deal with us than another clan. We aren't the only ones with an eye on California. Sooner or later, a foreign group *will* arrive at your doorstep."

I purposely avoided Simu's death. It would do no good bringing it up, even if it was the elephant in the room. We could work on that issue when she lived among us. His death was tied to Grigore's influence over her, but separation from him coupled with spending time with us might naturally resolve it.

"You sound so sure of yourself, but not everyone is greedy like the Lupu clan," she retorted.

"It's not only greed that motivates people to look

beyond their own territory. It's expansion and growth. You'll see. Once the Hagi clan matures, it will happen to you. Aligning your family with a powerful clan is the way of the world, and no clan is as powerful as ours," I replied calmly.

"I don't know..." she prevaricated.

"The truth is you have little trust in us. That is the root cause behind your reticence. I'm giving you the opportunity to see for yourself what we are like. I would not take my offer lightly. We've never extended one like this before," I added with a meaningful look.

It would be more than bad form to reject my proposal. It would be an insult, and if these negotiations devolved into violence, they could only blame themselves. Clara would come off as insane too. There was no rational explanation for outright disregarding my offer. Since we had made a clean kill with Simu, she couldn't use that as an excuse. I smirked inwardly. It would be suicide to refuse me. I had her right where I wanted her.

Clara's gaze darted to her father, who turned a hundred and eighty degrees to scrutinize me carefully. He broke into a laugh and said, "Well played, Nicu. For the youngest, you're not only good for your looks. Seems you have a brain on your shoulders."

"Not so fast," Clara cut in. "I can't be away from my family for that long. Six months is too much."

Ah, negotiations. She'd accepted the fundamental premise, and now we'd haggle over how long. Perfect.

Picking invisible fluff off my pressed slacks, I asked, "What would you suggest?"

"A month"

"Impossible. It will take you at least a month to meet everyone, much less remember their names. Forget about getting to know them. I'll shave off a month, if you'd like," I offered blithely.

She pursed her lips in displeasure. "Three months."

I tapped my knee, pretending to think on her suggestion. "Perhaps four months, but that's my final offer."

Going once.

She darted a look at her father. He inclined his head slightly.

Going twice.

"Fine," she bit out.

Sold.

"But don't think I'm going to make it easy on you Lupu people. Especially that one," she pointed a finger at the door, referring to Tatum. No problem, I'd make sure to have Alex put him on guard duty with her.

Fucking finally, I could get the hell out of here. Hopefully, it wasn't too late.

23

JEWEL

Seven days.

Seven days had passed since Nicu disappeared, and I was a hot mess. I laughed derisively at the thought of how composed I'd been during my conversation with Cat after the debacle at her house. After three days, I broke down and texted him. Nothing. I left a voicemail. Again, nothing. If this was payback for all the times I'd ignored his texts and calls, then he'd made his point.

I kept looking over my shoulder, expecting to see Nicu's recognizable broad set of shoulders, swathed in the fine wool of his fitted Italian suits. Seven days later, and I still checked out my surroundings, but now it was with a sinking heart because he never materialized.

Sitting on my bed, I hugged my knees to my chest as I morosely stared out my dorm room window. I curled my toes inside my fluffy socks. He'd vanished, and as if to taunt me, even the weather had turned. The stunning crimson, burnt orange, and vivid amber leaves had been stripped off their branches by the perpetual rain and gusts of wind that darkened the sidewalks and plunged the world in a dreary tint of gray and sepia.

At first, I prayed. Then I bargained. Finally, I reached the anger stage. And still, he didn't show. Not a telephone call or a text. Nothing. Dejected, I fell into a gloomy mood that nothing seemed to be able to pull me out of.

Cat had suggested that Nicu needed time to cool off.

Too much time without any communication had passed for that, which led me to one conclusion: he'd left me.

Like my father, like Mother. I didn't even get a chance to choose fear over love. He chose for me. I thought a part of me would be relieved if it were over, because I could go back to the security of my old life. I'd been dead wrong. Instead, it was living in hell. That's what being thrown from paradise was. It had happened to me with my family and now with Nicu.

I sniffed as I plucked at a loose thread on the sleeve of my midnight-blue angora sweater.

My focus was shot.

My studies languished.

My heart was shattered into pieces

I felt bereft. He'd abandoned me, and I couldn't blame him. I hadn't made it easy to love me, but there was one thing I did blame him for—he'd lead me on with his constant stalkerish presence. He'd set me up to believe he'd stick around. After everything I put him through, I hadn't anticipated he'd bail after one argument. Granted, it was an ugly one.

The point was that he'd left me. Now, if I could only get to acceptance...

Sofia broke into my thoughts. "Sheesh, I'm getting sad just looking at you," she confessed.

Shit, I'd forgotten she was there. I gave a little shrug, and then moaned. Even my shrug reminded me of him.

"What can I say? I'm depressed."

Lying on her belly, Sofia laid down the book she was reading on her bed and wagged a finger at me. "Come on, girl. Snap out of it."

I gazed out into the street; night was descending rapidly, as it tended to in late October.

"You're going to see him again. He's going to show up to his brother's wedding, and then you'll kiss and make up."

I groaned. "God, please don't remind me. It's only two weeks away."

I thought I caught sight of a tall shadow under an awning, kitty-corner from my building, and my spine straightened. The man stepped into the light of a lamppost, then dashed across the street in the pouring rain. My shoulders dipped in disappointment. It wasn't Nicu. Regret smacked me in the face.

Jerking my head away from the window, I scolded myself. I had to stop doing that. When was I going to get it through my thick head? The guy wasn't coming back. I ached for him. Ached. For. Him. There was an empty feeling in my gut, and my heart felt like it'd been carved out with a knife, left to bleed out. I thought nothing could replicate the pain I'd experienced when my family broke up. I was dead wrong. This was a strong contender. A tightness wrapped around my throat, and tears pricked my eyes.

"There won't be any making up or kissing. He ghosted me, Sofia. I can't forgive that," I sniffed. *Especially after what he knows of my past.*

Goddammit, I did not want to cry. I would *not* cry.

Sofia was at my side in an instant, wrapping her arm around my shoulder and cooing, "Everything will be okay,

Jewel. I promise. Maybe not today or tomorrow, but you'll get through this. And fuck him. Just fuck him, because if he was so quick to disappear over one little argument, then he doesn't deserve you. What kind of man does that anyway? I mean, I'm Dominican, and we argue like we breathe. It's an expression of love. You don't ghost someone after one silly fight."

I snuffled into my elbow. "I hate him. I hate him for giving me hope that someone would love me. I hate him for making me think he would always be there. I hate him for abandoning me, because that was the absolute worst thing he could've done. The one and only thing I could never forgive."

I barked out a laugh of disbelief, embarrassed at how over-the-top ridiculous and self-pitying I sounded, but I couldn't help myself. I'd fallen in love with the bastard, and he'd repaid me by betraying my love and repeating what my parents had done. He couldn't have hurt me more if he'd tried.

Tears spilled out of the corners of my eyes, skating down my cheeks. I hadn't cried when my father was handcuffed in front of me and pushed into the back of a police car. I hadn't cried when I first saw him, haggard, on the other side of a glass partition at Rikers. I hadn't cried when Mother dropped me off at school with a peck on the cheek and an awkward goodbye. I only cried after visiting my father alone.

And now, again.

This is the low that Nicu had brought me to, and once it started, I couldn't stop. I wept for the dissolution of my family nine years ago. For the years of dashed hopes, broken relationships, and all-around heartbreak. I cried for my father, who fought to survive in that cramped, hostile place.

I even cried for Mother, who fled to escape our family shame. She'd suffered in her own way, never expecting her charmed life to go off the rails like it did. And finally, I cried for myself and for my broken heart because that's what Nicu had done. He'd broken me.

THE FOLLOWING DAY, I had to go up to Otisville to visit my father. I woke up with puffy, red eyes and a headache that rivaled the hangover I had when Nicu rescued me. There was no way I was in any shape to meet my father, but I'd never missed a visit when I wasn't away at boarding school. If I didn't show up, he'd worry, and he didn't deserve any added stress simply because my heart was in the equivalent of a dumpster. So I sucked it up, pulled on some clothes, got a bagel and coffee at the corner deli, and drove upstate for visiting hours.

After waiting in a long line and going through the ritual of security, I slumped over at one of the bolted-down metal tables and waited for my father.

The instant he saw me, he stalled for an instant before coming over to me. His mouth tightened, deepening the grooves at the corners. My heart sank at the new lines of strain on his face. Being incarcerated took a toll on him, and here I was, showing up miserable. I always made sure to put on a brave face, to smile and joke and keep things upbeat, no matter what.

But not today.

Today, I couldn't gather up the strength to do anything more than the bare minimum, which was to show up.

Sliding onto the bench across from me, he launched in with the million-dollar question. "What's wrong?"

I shrugged and gazed down at my hands. How to answer that question? I'd never had a sex talk with either of my parents, much less talked about dating a man or getting my heart broken by a two-bit *mafie* player.

In a hard tone, he asked, "It's that Romanian you're with, isn't it? What did he do?"

My head snapped up. "H-how do you know about him?"

"Nicu Cornelius Lupu, youngest son of the Lupu mafia family. Twenty-three years of age. Graduated Columbia University with a major in organic chemistry. And a rap sheet almost as long as mine, although no felonies stuck," he rattled off effortlessly.

My jaw dropped. "Uh..."

"You think I don't keep tabs on you, Jewel? You're my one and only *daughter*. I'm a criminal with a network of past and present associates at my disposal who can get me any information I want. I know the names of your teachers and every single girl who lives on your floor. I know your grades. I know *every*thing there is to know."

He reached out and patted my hand self-consciously. "I may not be affectionate. That was not the kind of family I came from, but never underestimate how much I care for you. Why do you think I named you Jewel? You are my jewel. Both you and your mother, no matter how far she's run away. We Westons may not be much anymore, but we love only once, and we love unconditionally."

My eyes widened at that statement. "You mean, you still love Mother?"

"Of course, I do. I will always love her, and once I get out of this hellhole, I'll find a way to restore my name. Then, and only then, will I go after her," he revealed. He leaned over and murmured low but determinedly, "And I will win her back."

What the hell...?!

I cleared my throat. "How long have you known?"

He tipped his head back a bit and looked me over. "Since your last visit. You let something slip, and I instantly knew there was a boy. I had to find out more, so I set a friend out to investigate. He came back with surprising information. Didn't I tell you not to get involved with a man like him?" he chided.

"Yes, you did, but it doesn't matter now. We argued and he left. He's," I swallowed hard, "gone. For good."

Releasing my hand, he crossed his arms over his chest and chuckled. I frowned at him. What was so funny? What was left of my heart was in shreds. I was not equally amused.

"Oh, that guy?" he said with a snort. "I wish I were so lucky. He's not gone for good, I can assure you of that much. Don't you worry, he'll be back."

"You don't know him, Dad. Don't say things just to try to make me feel better," I scolded him.

"I'm not," he replied succinctly. "His oldest brother sent him to L.A. He's been there, working on his family's business. I guarantee the moment he's back in the city, he'll come to you."

Shock waves ran through me. My father, locked up far away from the city, knew more than I did about my own life. I blinked up at him. It was like I didn't know the person in front of me. Who was this man? How far did his reach go? And why did he seem so easily reconciled with the fact that Nicu was part of the mafia?

"I thought you'd put a contract out on him before you'd let me be with someone like Nicu," I joked.

"I considered it, of course. But then I thought, who am I to cast stones? Although I tried to guide you, actions speak louder than words. How can I fault you for falling for a man like him when I'm in prison? That would be hypocritical to the extreme. And it would be unfair. You love him. I know what it's like, and after not being there for you in so many ways, I wasn't about to take that away from you."

"I'm not happy now," I protested miserably. "He left me. After one argument, he left. Not even a text to let me know he was in L.A." I threw out my hand. "I mean, I had to learn it from you of all people. Even Cat didn't bring it up with Luca since she hesitates to dig into Lupu business. But I shouldn't have to rely on Cat or you for information. I should have been the first to know. A person can't just up and leave without a word, without any contact."

My head cast down, I picked at my nails. "I can't forgive him for that. If he was so in love with me, how could he pick up and leave without a word? He didn't reply to my texts or call me back. Before your arrest, you and Mother were inseparable. Even now, you want to be with her, after she turned her back on you like a coward."

"Hey," he snapped. "Don't speak about your mother like that. She did what she had to do to survive. She's not perfect, but neither am I. It may seem to everyone that she's forgotten me, but you don't know what's between a man and his wife, Jewel. Has she remarried? Has she even had a boyfriend? No, she hasn't, and as beautiful as she is, she could have anyone. She's waiting for me as much as I'm waiting to get the hell out of here."

I wouldn't say she could have *any*one. I mean, the woman was in her fifties, and while she was a refined, handsome woman, no amount of Botox or cosmetic surgery could change that. But I'd grudgingly admit that I clearly didn't know a lot about their life as a couple.

"Don't judge people too harshly, including your beau," he suggested softly.

I snorted. "*Beau?* Seriously, Dad?"

"You've been hurt in your life. I get that, but don't let it color everything that comes after it. I'm certain he's less than perfect. You don't have to convince me. I'm your father, so of course, he'll never be worthy of you. That goes without saying. But your face lit up in a way I hadn't seen in a long time when you mentioned him."

He paused and then went for the kill. "He makes you happy. All I'm saying is give him a chance to explain himself. Even if he doesn't deserve it. Do I deserve to be forgiven? The simple answer is no. I threw my life down the toilet and destroyed my family, and yet, you've found it in your heart to stay by me. I pray your mother gives me that same bit of mercy. If I didn't think I had a chance, I'd die an old, broken-hearted man."

I sniffled. "I don't know if I can do that, Dad. I don't know if I can."

He wrapped his fingers around my arm and pulled me into a bear hug over the table. The guard rumbled out an order, and my father pulled away.

He had one more word on the matter. "Try, Jewel. Try."

24

NICU

I was back, thank fuck.

Couldn't get out of Los Angeles fast enough once the contract with the Hagi clan was set in stone. I headed out for Jewel as soon as I dumped my stuff at my apartment. With the tracking device, I knew she was back on campus after having gone upstate to visit her father.

The weather was beautiful. The sky was a brilliant blue above my head. I drew in a long breath of crisp, cool air, the kind that held the scent of autumn in the city. My heart pounded against my breastbone. Luca had given me a heads-up that Jewel was still pissed off at me. That, I had not expected. Since I had no idea how she would receive me, I did the next best thing to get her acclimated to my return. I staked out a spot across the street from her dorm room. If she happened to look outside, she'd spot me.

God, I fucking missed her. Being so close to her, yet unable to touch her, to bring her in for a hug, to pound my cock into her... It was wreaking havoc on my nerves.

Luca suggested I back off until I met her at the wedding. Perhaps that was the best route to take. To be patient and hang off seeing her until we met in a public setting where she wouldn't have the opportunity to rage at me. It had worked once before, at Luca's engagement party, but who was I kidding? I'd never last that long. It'd be a miracle if I lasted the night.

Dusk fell around me as I stood in my spot. The streets teemed with students, laughing and joking around, getting ready for a Saturday night, and Halloween to boot. The light in Jewel's room turned on. She'd been somewhere in the dorm, maybe hanging out in another girl's room, maybe fixing herself something to eat. The gossamer curtain swished open, and her head popped out, turning as she scanned the street quickly. Her gaze halted, eyes burning into me.

I stood still, holding my breath for her next move.

She disappeared, and the lights went out a second later.

Yup, she'd spotted me.

Her response: she was playing dead.

I smirked. Did she really think I'd let her get away with that?

I jaywalked across the street, halting vehicles with my palm straight out. Slipping in between honking cars, I made it over to the other side unscathed. A few minutes later, I waved to the guard on my payroll, bypassed the slow elevator, and took the stairs two at a time up to her floor. Passing a few of her floormates fluttering in and out of various rooms, I skidded to a stop in front of her door and rapped on it loudly.

Nothing.

I smirked and warned, "Open up, Jewel. I know you're in there."

"Go away," she shouted.

I chuckled. No one did it for me like she did.

"I'm not fucking leaving. Either you let me in, or I make a scene," I threatened.

There was a crash and then stomping toward the door. It swung open. She stood there like an avenging angel, holding a lamp in her raised hand.

"*You*," she spat out. "What the hell are you doing here?" With a curl of her lip, she jeered, "I didn't think I'd see you again, or at least not until you were forced to be in my presence at Cat's wedding. You coward."

I huffed out a laugh. I hadn't expected a homecoming, but did she just call me a *coward*?

Ridiculous.

Gripping her wrist in case she tried to bean me with the lamp, I pushed my way inside. Throwing the door closed, I twisted the lock behind me and took her in.

She was a sight for sore eyes. Waves of long crimped hair flowed down as if she'd kept them in braids for too long and had only undone them moments ago. God, she was stunning. Her amber eyes flashed fire, and her cheeks were rosy with fury. Her chest rose and fell, pressing her lush tits against the tight shirt she was wearing.

My gaze flickered over the room. I already knew Sofia left to visit her family on Friday and Saturday nights, but I was pleased to see Jewel didn't have any costumes or sexy clothes laying around. If my guess was correct, she had no intention of going out tonight. There was my good girl.

Taking the lamp out of her hand, I placed it on her desk. Getting into her space, I stepped her back until her knees hit her bed, right where I wanted her. The luscious sweet rose fragrance that spoke of home and a hard fuck drifted toward me.

Her palm smacked my chest, halting my momentum. Her scent might be sweet, but she wasn't. Not yet, anyway.

"Listen up, asshole. You left me. Right after an argument, you left, and now you think you can just waltz back into my life like nothing happened? Like you didn't *walk out on me*?"

My head canted to the side, and my forehead crinkled. Her full bottom lip tremble slightly. Fuck. She was upset. Holding it together, but definitely upset.

I pulled off my cashmere coat and jacket, laid them over the back of her chair, and explained, "Alex forced me to go to L.A. as punishment. It was fucking hell, baby doll...being away from you every day. But I figured you were so pissed off at me that I should step back and give you space." I unhooked one cuff link and dropped it on her night table with a clinking sound. "I'd hounded you for weeks, and you did so good, but I thought I'd do right by you for once. Especially after my fuckup." The other freed cuff link joined its mate.

Her brows knitted together, and her lips pursed in the most adorable little pout as she stared at me. "W-what are you doing?"

"Undressing, of course," I replied matter-of-factly as I loosened my tie.

She shook her head. "For the love of God, why?"

I tugged at my tie and twisted my lips into a smirk. "Why do you think?"

My tie slipped out of my hand, and I unfastened the top button of my shirt.

"We are *not* fucking right now. We are arguing," she stammered out, although I didn't miss how her eyes fixated on my chest as I exposed more skin, her pupils expanding.

"We are not," she insisted.

"Oh, but we are," I countered. "And I'm going to tell you why. I've been without you for over ten days. Ten fucking days. I'm tired of fucking my hand with no relief. It's like I've broken out of jail, babe. We can resume this fight afterward, but I need you." I gave her a serious look. "And you need me, too. I can see it." I dropped my gaze meaningfully to the beaded nipples poking against her T-shirt. She wasn't even wearing a bra, another indication that she was in for the night.

Her hand slipped onto my skin as I pulled my shirt open. Her nails dug into me, but she shook her head. "No, Nicu, this isn't right."

I towered over her and bluntly stated, "Baby doll, we need this. I need it. You need it. Don't deny us." I dragged a finger between her breasts. "Don't. Do. It. We can argue for as long as you want afterward, but I'm fucking dying here." I swallowed hard. It wasn't easy baring my soul, but I was fucking *hangry*, hungry and angry, for her. I'd do anything to get close to her. I'd been denied for too long. It was almost too much, and I was at the end of my tether.

Hand trembling with need, I grabbed her nape and pressed my hard-as-fuck cock into her soft belly. "Please, baby. I never beg, but I'm begging you." Her eyes fluttered shut for a moment, and then snapped wide open again. She stared into my eyes, flickering right to left and back to right. My blood was boiling, my muscles coiling, ready to pounce. Whatever she saw there—most likely the depth of my desperation—must have convinced her.

"Oh, fuck it," she acquiesced.

A whoosh of relief swept through me. My chest released a long breath I hadn't realized I was holding. Thank Christ.

She caught the flesh of her bottom lip between her teeth, and it was game over. I'd been teetering on the edge for too damn long, and that little gesture tipped me over. With a hand planted on her chest, I shoved her gently onto her bed. She let out a squeal of surprise. I stripped off the remainder of my clothes with little grace. She followed me, yanking her shirt over her head and freeing her tits. I dropped to my knees. The way they bounced and jiggled in my face had me half crazed with lust.

Her jeans were barely halfway down her legs when we collided in a frenzied kiss. Gutted by the passion she reciprocated, I devoured her. My hand found her throat, and I brushed over the fine tendons as she strained to reach my mouth when I shifted away from her.

Taking her jaw, I wolfed her down. Did she think I was happy being away from her? Did she have any idea the restraint I had to draw on to stay away? How often I'd cursed myself for not having installed a hidden camera in this very room so I could spy on her and consume every moment I could.

I more than missed her. I felt like my guts had been carved out of my belly with a hunting knife. It had eviscerated me from the inside out.

I dragged the jeans down her legs. "You don't know how many times I had to fuck my hand this week. Not since I started having sex have I rubbed my cock raw like this. And it did nothing to temper the crazy. I was going fucking *crazy* without you."

My hands splayed over her buttocks, cupping them as I nuzzled against her smooth belly. Prostrate, on my knees, I gazed up at her heavy-lidded stare as I gave her belly button a long lick.

I shimmied down farther and spread her thighs until I was face-to-face with her shaved pussy. *Fuck.* If we were over, why did she shave? Was she taunting me? Closing my eyes, I inhaled deeply, taking her wicked scent inside me. For some reason, her scent settled my raw nerves.

"Oh, please," she growled. "That's nothing compared to what I've been through."

My tongue was out, and I was just about to taste her when I paused and asked, "What do you mean?"

I had Luca keep tabs on Jewel, and I hadn't heard anything out of the ordinary.

"You'd know if you'd have returned my texts or called me for once," she rebuked, hurt washing over her face before she quickly masked it.

"Woman, if I so much as called you, I would've broken my sentence and jumped on the first plane back to the city. Then I would've really been fucked. Alex would've exiled me to Romania, and that's before he imposed a more creative punishment. He has the power to forbid me from keeping you, and that wasn't a chance I was willing to take."

I took my first lick of her pussy and hummed. She jerked in my hold.

"And I feared you'd take the first opportunity to break up with me," I admitted.

She moaned as I sucked on her clit. "You're not wrong there, because I did break up with you," she replied as she arched her back, pushing her thick breasts up in the air. Unable to stop myself, I grabbed hold of each lush mound and flicked her nipples in time with my tongue.

She might think she broke up with me, but there was no way I was letting her go. Already, our conversation was going far better than expected because I had my nose and tongue buried inside her sweet honey. Hunger reared up as I smothered my face in her juices, smearing them over me. I curled and twisted my tongue around her clit, determined to make her come, knowing that I wasn't going to last. Her thighs fell open wider, and I rammed my shoulders to pin them to the mattress for better access. Nice and fast, I swiped from side to side with gusto, putting the perfect amount of pressure on her clit until she seized up on me.

Her moans rang in my ears like the finest melody as she flew over the edge. Her fingers gripped my hair, nails scoring my scalp, egging me on. She didn't have to worry about me going anywhere. I stayed with her, suckling her clit until she twitched with sensitivity.

I reared up, shrugging off her clasp. With a shaking grip, I guided myself home. Fucking finally. My crown pushed between her glistening pussy lips. They wrapped around me, and I swear to fuck, they sucked me in like a vacuum. Goddamn, but her hole was a snug little thing made just for me. Only halfway in, and my cock got fatter, expanding against the pressure of her muscles clamping down around it. Her inner walls undulated around it, massaging me from all sides.

Losing control, I thrust in hard. Once balls-deep, I had to move and move fast. Pistoning in and out, I drove into her, shoving her up the bed with the force of my thrusts. Ten days of deprivation, and I was rutting her like a wild beast.

I glanced at her face, relieved to see it twisting with pleasure once more.

"Mine," I roared as my hips flexed. I buried myself inside her, only to pull out half a second later and plunge inside again. "This is my cunt. It's only slutty for me. Isn't that right? *Say it*," I commanded.

"Yes, it's only yours," she screeched as her muscles stiffened, her tiny heels digging against the small of my back. Eyes wild, she clawed down the Lupu wolf tat across my left pec, leaving four red stripes behind.

Like a crop to the flank of a racehorse, seeing those marks spurred me on. I pounded into her, the squelching of her slickness combining with mine, wet smacks echoing through the room.

"You're mine," I howled. "Mine, mine, mine."

Her claws came out again. Eyes brilliant and hard, she swiped at my face and hissed out, "You left me. I may be a slut for you, but you don't deserve me."

I pulled out and flipped her over, settling her on her hands and knees before pushing back inside her clenching pussy. Fuck, I loved how she gave me the control to move her as the spirit moved me.

In her ear, I growled, "I never left. I pulled back, but don't worry, I won't ever make that mistake again. I'm not your father, Jewel. I'm not going to fuck up and disappear on you."

"How can you promise that?" she challenged. "You're in constant danger. Your father was gunned down in the street. Even if you live, who's to say you won't end up in prison like mine. If I was stupid enough to be with you, it'd be a disaster waiting to happen."

I rammed my cock inside her, nice and hard, making her moan from the angle. As hard as it was to concentrate, I was glad we were having it out while we were fucking. "None of those things will happen," I intoned as I sped up.

"You can't promise me that."

I was determined to prove her wrong, to fuck her into submission, into believing me. Taking her hair, I wrapped it around my fist and used it to steady her as I rode her harder.

"You were alone when your father got caught, but I have family. Family means everything. When my father got killed, Alex stepped up. My brothers and I hunted down the killers. We have enemies, but we're careful. Vigilant. We have each other's back. Nothing will happen to me."

"If you're gone, I'll have no one," she shouted.

"Not true. You'll have Cat. You'd have my family, who will love you like their own."

"But I'd lose *you*. I can't go through that pain again," she pleaded, a catch in her voice.

That was the essence of her pain, of her fear. Abandonment. She wasn't really scared about losing me to my lifestyle; she was afraid of losing me, period. I had to make her understand that I was never going to desert her.

"You were made for me, and I'm not letting you go, Jewel," I roared. "So you'll fucking deal with it. No, life is not perfect. None of us are guaranteed a happy fucking ending, but that doesn't mean I'll let you throw away what we have because you're afraid. You'll just have to be strong, like every other fucking *mafie* girl. I will not die. I will be here to fuck you like this every single day."

I didn't know if it was my words, but her pussy clamped down on me as if she was making a claim that my cock was hers. Before I could slow down or pull out, come erupted out of me like a geyser. The room bobbed and weaved. My vision faded out, my world narrowing down to Jewel's wet, warm pussy milking my seed. Even once I was completely drained, I couldn't stop fucking her. I needed to mark her, from the inside out. It wasn't until the stitch in my side became too sharp that I stopped.

I dropped my chest, slick with sweat, onto her back. She slid down, flattened to the mattress, and I laid on top of her, unable to move for long moments as I caught my breath.

I knew our fight wasn't over, but I had no intention of coming out as anything other than the victor.

25

JEWEL

Nicu raised himself off me. Lying down and stretching out on my narrow twin bed, he maneuvered me until I was draped over him. Considering his size, it was the only way we could both fit.

Stroking my back with light brushes of his fingertips, he murmured, "Nothing's going to happen to me, Jewel. I swear I will never abandon you. And you will become part of my family. You will be one of us, and they will take care of you."

I lifted my eyes up to him and saw the hard determination swimming in his crystalline blue eyes. If anyone could force the world to do his bidding, it was Nicu. I loved how his brittle cold irises burned for me. I loved his passion and his untamed nature, his loyalty, and his unrelenting devotion to anyone he loved. His intensity never flagged. Unlike me, he'd never entertain the idea of giving up. Ever. The concept didn't exist for him. If he wanted me, he'd have me, regardless of my fears or anything else that might come up. He had the unwavering courage to strip himself bare for me. He never faltered when it came to expressing how he felt about me, how much he wanted me, or how far he was willing to go to keep me.

His voice hardened. "Do you understand?"

I melted when his tone got rough and demanding. He peered down at me with a severe expression on his face. My father's and Cat's words came back to me, reminding me of what was at stake here. It also didn't help that the man played me like a maestro, leaving me limp with pleasure. Between his words and his actions, I didn't have the energy to fight him.

But that didn't mean I no longer had misgivings.

One thing confused me. "How do you know your family will accept me, much less bring me into the fold?"

"Because I know them, and if I love you, that will be enough for them. There's no way they wouldn't love you on their own, anyway," he said, as if it was a done deal.

My brows drew together. I wasn't so sure. The Popescus were certainly not this easygoing. I couldn't believe the Lupu family would be that different. *Mafie* was *mafie*.

"Hmm, don't they want you to marry someone of their choosing and from their world? I can't forget the grief Cat went through with her family. She would've never been able to choose just anyone, regardless of whether she fell for them or not. It just so happened to work out because Luca is a Lupu."

"That's the Popescus for you. Not only are they strict, but she's their only princess. My situation is different," he replied.

My eyes narrowed on him. "It's not fair that because Cat's a woman, her burden is heavier than yours."

"It's a double standard, if that's what you're suggesting, but it's not solely about her gender. She happens to be the Popescus' one and only daughter. It would've been different if she had a couple more siblings to share the burden with. The pressure wouldn't have been so intense. There's no denying that there are discrepancies between men and women. Men must be inducted and women must get married. The system is exploitative of everyone, but in different ways."

He huffed out a laugh. "Try dismantling it, and you'll get pushback from young women who see marriage as a way of solidifying their futures or pulling their families up the ranks."

"It didn't seem that way with Ioana," I noted.

"Ioana's case is complicated. I won't deny that the tradition of arranged marriages is a thorny issue. Once you have your Lupu tat, have at it. Let your inner feminist out and bring on change. I'm not attached to this practice. God knows it's created a lot of stress for us lately."

My eyes fell on his tattoo, the Lupu wolf head with bared teeth. Every member of the Lupu clan had this tat, whether it was after an induction or a marriage. Cat was due for hers any time now. Technically, she could've already gotten hers since she and Luca were secretly married, but she was waiting after the ceremony to get it. Part of the rite of passage was a party held by the women of the bride's new family. It was only attended by women, much like a bridal shower, but the gifts were replaced with lots of drinking. As I glanced at the wolf head on his chest, with red marks from my nails slashed over it, a part of me wanted a matching image on my skin.

"Would they really be open to it?" I pondered out loud.

"Romanians are resilient and adaptable," he relied confidently, as if that accounted for everything. I, on the other hand, wasn't so sure. I couldn't get the suffering Cat had undergone with her family out of my head. And I'd never forget the stark misery I'd witnessed in Ioana's eyes.

"Seriously, though, doesn't Alex expect to pick out who you'll marry?"

He gave me his signature little shrug. "Not necessarily."

"He picked Cat for you," I reminded him.

"Yes, but there was a pressing need at the time. I'm not a figurehead, like he is, and I can argue that he opened the floodgates with his own choice in a wife."

"And he can counterargue that he's şef and can do whatever the hell he wants," I pointed out.

"He can, but he won't. It was one thing when he needed me to buttress the flagging contract with the Popescus and I didn't care who I married. Right now, I'm in a sweet spot, and it's imperative we take advantage of it." He cupped my pussy and growled near the shell of my ear, "Not only that, but I have no intention of being starved of this luscious treat ever again. That's another crucial difference."

My lips twitched. I arched a brow at him. "This is just about sex for you. I see...so that's how it is, huh?"

He snorted. "Baby doll, if you had any idea how deep this goes for me, you'd leap out of bed and run down the hall, screaming at the top of your lungs. You think I'm letting you go? Think again. That's *never* going to happen. If you thought I was obsessed before, our brief separation taught me that I didn't go hard enough. Otherwise, you'd never have questioned my commitment for an instant. I regret not putting a hidden cam in this room, for instance," he mused.

A spike of jealousy shot through me. I inhaled sharply. "Then you'd see Sofia naked, not only me."

He scoffed, "Sofia who? I've only got eyes for you, baby girl."

I harrumphed in protest. "There's no way you're going to see another woman undressing. Anyway, that's creepy."

"Not a problem because I have the perfect solution," he replied with a suspiciously wide smile on his face. "You'll move next door to Cat."

Something niggled at the back of my mind, triggered by something he'd mentioned about Alex. Pushing off him so that I could look him in the eye, I asked, "What did you mean by a sweet spot you have to take advantage of?"

Stroking my arm, he said, "Things can change in the blink of an eye. We're at peace now, but Cristo and I have an ongoing feud that can flare up at any time." He met my gaze with an arched brow. "As you've already witnessed. We also have threats on the horizon from other clans. We're expanding out west, which was why I was sent to Cali. Then there's the continual skirmishes with the Bratva, our nemesis since before they murdered my father. Right now, we're in a lull. It's the moment to press my advantage and persuade Alex to allow us to get married."

Staring down at him, I blinked. "Say what now?"

"Marriage," he clarified. "You and me."

"Are you serious?"

"Fuck yeah, I'm serious. If you don't want me installing a camera in here, that's your only other option." He took a huge breath and declared, "My mother's too traditional for us to shack up, and if we wait, who the hell knows what will come up. It will be perfect timing to announce our engagement at Luca's marriage. That will make Alex look good, too."

His normally light eyes turned a stormy dark hue.

I hadn't considered marriage. I loved the way he displayed his feelings toward me, but what I didn't love so much was the drive behind his proposal. His concerns were so practical and centered around his mother and Alex.

I didn't harbor girlhood dreams of a Disney-style proposal with him down on one knee and a big diamond ring in a little black box, but getting married because it was good timing for his *brother* was the least of my concerns. And it should've been the least of his concerns. *I* should be his primary concern, considering he'd just proposed to *me*. Nicu didn't seem personally invested, much less excited, about getting married. No, none of that. His main consideration was how it would affect his family.

A red cloud of accelerating rage edged my vision as I rasped out, "Do you want to marry me, or do you simply feel pressured into it?"

"I was going to have to marry eventually," he declared with an irritated, one-shouldered shrug. "Now. Later. Never. It doesn't really matter to me."

I felt pressure around my head squeezing it tight, tight, and tighter. I tore myself away him and scrambled off the bed, feeling like my heart was being ripped out of my body.

"Oh my God," I breathed out. "You're unbelievable. You're suggesting we get married simply because it's *convenient*. Your brother isn't demanding anything from you at this moment so let's get married because this is a good time for him? What about us? What about me?"

"We'll be together. That's what matters. Like I said, if we wait, who knows what could happen. I could get snagged into another engagement," he replied, frustration lacing his tone.

My heart rate was going *rat-tat-tat* like rapid gunfire.

"Are you saying you would consider an engagement with another woman if your brother insisted upon it?"

He paused for a moment.

A moment too long.

I broke the silence. "That's what you're saying, isn't it?"

"No," he replied carefully, although I could see him almost twitching under my scrutiny. "I'm saying why risk complicating things when we know we want to be together. Let's face facts, it would get complicated, unnecessarily complicated, if I was called to marry another woman to alleviate a volatile situation or solidify an allegiance."

Ka-pow. And there it went. The sound of my head blowing up.

"Oh my God, get out!" I shrieked, my finger jabbing toward the door.

He glared at me and sneered, "You can't throw me out whenever we have an argument, Jewel."

"You better believe I can. Do you not realize how insane you sound? Usually, when a man proposes to a woman, it's because he can't live another day without her, because he loves her, because he wants to share his life with her. None of those reasons have popped out of your mouth. You've only cited concerns about your mother, your brother, and your family. You don't care about marrying *me*. The only reason you're considering marriage is because your mother wouldn't want us living together and you have to marry eventually. What's best for us as a couple doesn't even make the cut. Your only priority is your family."

"What's so wrong with that?" he spat out as he jumped out of bed and started yanking up his pants.

Fury-laced adrenaline pumped through my blood, and there was no holding me back. "Nothing's wrong with that, but I'd be your wife. When would I become a priority? I suspect the answer is never. Announcing my engagement or setting my wedding date would be dictated by what works for Alex. Not me. Not us."

"You're being ridiculous," he accused as he threw on his shirt. Buttoning it with short, rough moves, he continued, "You know I love you. I was fucking miserable without you, although now I'm beginning to wonder if I was out of my goddamn mind because anytime I don't say or do exactly the right thing, you lose your temper. I've never hidden who I was or what I do. My life is my family and clan."

"Sure, that can be true, but that doesn't give me confidence that you want to marry me." I threw up my hands. "What you're basically telling me is that you have to get married at some point and you want to be with me, so hell, let's just combine the two and go with that."

Stopping midway through buttoning his shirt, he stared at me incredulously. "What's wrong with that? That's logical."

"It might be logical, but that's not how you propose to someone, you idiot! No woman wants to know that the reason the man she loves has asked her to marry him is specifically *not* related to her."

He wagged a finger at me angrily. "And you can't keep kicking me out every time you get mad at me, Jewel. At some point, you're going to have to make a choice. Do you want to be with me or not? And when I say 'me,' that includes my family," he snapped. "Our traditions, our customs, and our needs. I know you're an only child, but it's not just about you."

That hit me in the gut like a two-by-four, but I rallied and answered, "I'm ready for that, but I'm not going to discount my own needs on something as big as this, and you shouldn't ask me to. How can you not see that? I'm not telling you to be selfish and willful, but what about having your own brain and making your own decisions instead of following them blindly?"

Nicu stalked to me, stepping me back until my spine hit the wall. Slapping a hand on the plaster, he replied in a low, hard tone. Rage like I'd never seen directed toward me rolled off him. Suddenly, fear slithered inside me that I'd gone too far, that he was ready to end things. "Luca accuses me of being Alex's lapdog often enough. I'm not going to take the same shit from you. If you can't take me as I am, then forget it."

He pushed off the wall, stomped away, and threw the door open. Poking a finger at me, he threatened, "One day, Jewel, you're going to have to decide if you want me. I have my faults, but I've never made any bones about how I feel about you. Either that's enough or it isn't."

Stunned, I watched him storm away. I'd never seen him this angry before. Not even at Cristo. I was touched when he first brought up marriage, even if I hadn't expected it. How did things devolve so quickly? Again, he didn't seem to understand where I was coming from. The reality was that Nicu was hardheaded, and he wasn't going to change. I had to decide whether his love was enough, because I'd have to take him as he was. I wasn't sure I could do that.

26

NICU

"Let me kill him," I pleaded with Luca. "Come on, let me slit his throat and gut him like a goat. You hate him. I *loathe* him. Alex will say good riddance. Just give me the fucking permission I need, Luca. Let me do it. I *need* to do it."

Sitting with his arm spread over the top of the white leather couch in his living room, he gave me a pitying look and said, "You know I'd love to give you permission, but Cat loves him, and I can't do anything that would hurt her. His death would undoubtedly do that. He's made some mistakes with her, but he's also been good to her. Protected her before I was in the picture. Always made sure she was taken care of. I can't forget that."

I twisted away from him and threw up my hands.

"Fuck!" I howled to the ceiling.

"I know how you feel, *frate*, and my heart goes out to you."

My head dropped forward, and my shoulders sloped inward.

"Fuck," I muttered. "Is Cat the only thing standing

between him and death? I'm your *brother*, dammit. Don't I come first?"

His eyes turned a hard slate-gray, a color that gave nothing. There would be no compromising on this.

"What kind of idiotic question is that? Of course you don't come first. How can you ask me such a thing? Cat's well-being comes first. It will always come first. Before you, before family, clan, and nation. Before me, even. Whose job is it to protect her?" He fisted his hand and beat his chest. "Mine. It's my fucking job. That and my love are the only things that allow me to claim her heart, marriage be damned. So, no, asshole, I will not do anything to compromise her happiness."

My head snapped back at his words. My fight with Jewel came roaring back to me along with her accusation that I didn't put her first. And here, the brother I loved unapologetically put his woman first.

He softened his tone. "We'll find a way to make him pay. Without killing him. We'll find a way, without touching a hair on his head."

Staring down at my hands, I blew out a harsh breath.

"What's wrong, Nicu. You've wanted to kill him for years, but you've never pressed this hard before."

I didn't have so much bottled-up frustration inside me before. There was no way to release the gnawing regret that ate at my very heart. Nothing could take it away. Nothing could ease it. Not racing, not flying, not riding my bike. I had zero interest in fucking another woman. I had nothing to preoccupy me from the fact that I may have fucked up the best thing that ever happened to me. I was coming to realize that, along with our explosive attraction, Jewel and I easily lost our tempers. I controlled myself around others, but with her? Not so much.

And now, Luca's blunt response put Jewel's claims that I put my family's interests over hers in stark relief. My brother, who I knew loved me and would lay his life down for me, had no issue shooting me down in favor of his wife.

Ignoring his question, I mumbled, "Jewel called me out as being nothing more than Alex's lackey."

I had given him the opening of a lifetime to start ribbing me, but he stayed remarkably silent.

Turning my head, I glared at him. "Go on, tell me she's right. Fuck knows I snapped at her when she said it."

He looked at me with pity, yet again. I gritted my teeth, about to bare them at him like a raging beast. My nerves were snapping like live wires. Although I was still fuming, I was also desperate for Jewel. I knew she was right, but my pride was bruised and holding me back from running to her, when that was what I ached to do. God, I was fucked in the head.

He clamped a hand over my forearm and said, "That's a sore spot for you. Your loyalty is one of your best qualities. I gave you such a hard time about it over the years. I was lashing out at you for other reasons. It wasn't fair of me. I'm sorry it caused a rift between you and your woman."

I shrugged in acceptance of his apology. Luca never apologized.

"What triggered her to say that?" he asked.

I shut my eyes and let out a long sigh of frustration. "I asked her to marry me, but I focused on how it was good because Alex wasn't looking to arrange a marriage for me. I might've mentioned how I didn't care about marriage, but that Mamă wouldn't let it go if I lived with her. I might've taken her answer for granted and also mentioned how we should announce our engagement at your wedding because it would make Alex look good."

A deep chuckle emanated from him, making me clamp my jaw in irritation. Grinding my back teeth, I only continued because I was in desperate need of his advice. "And if you think I fucked that up, I did it without mentioning how announcing my engagement to Cat's best friend at your wedding would add to the general spirit of the festivities. How it would make it easier for the traditionalists to swallow my marriage to an outsider, being drunk on the high of a good wedding and, well...basically being straight-up drunk. She accused me of being more concerned about Alex and our clan than of being truly interested in marrying her."

I let him laugh until it tapered off, while I clenched my fists, desperate to punch a hole in the wall. Any wall.

"Oh, little brother, you were never the smoothest one of the lot," he chided softly.

I refused to look at him, because if I couldn't stand to see the pity on his face, I'd have to clock him. "What do you mean?" I grumbled, although I had a fair guess of what he was talking about.

"When you propose to a woman, especially an outsider, you should at least attempt to be romantic. You're not totally to blame, though. Listen, we were never taught how to deal with American women. If she were a *mafie* girl, it wouldn't be an issue because you wouldn't even be proposing to her. Her parents would approach Alex, and you'd meet her after the arrangements were finalized, and not a day before. None of it would be in your control. Not your engagement. Not your wedding. In a way, you're lucky to experience this level of freedom with her."

He paused and gave me a meaningful look. "More freedom is a good thing for you. In fact, this girl is good for you. She tests you, pushes you in ways that make you a stronger man. More independent. After your father's death, your job was to do what you were told to do so that Alex and I could handle clan business and take care of Tasa. You've done those jobs well. The problem is, we didn't delegate more responsibilities to you, and that left you a little immature."

"Hey—" I cut in.

He held up his hand. "It's not an insult. It's how it was. You were our younger brother, and your father was murdered when you were still a kid. You can't blame Alex and I for wanting to protect you. Look how you blossomed in Cali, taking the reins and creating a solution when none presented itself. In the beginning, when we were deciding who to send out there, none of us considered you. You didn't even think of it. We've underestimated you all this time because we coddled you."

I pulled back, shock inscribed on my face. "Coddled? I was inducted right after Papa's death. After killing a man. As a thirteen-year-old," I replied, dripping with sarcasm. "That's not exactly what I would call 'coddled.'"

He waved my declaration away. "Sure, you grew up fast in some ways, but in other ways, we took care of every decision so you wouldn't have to. It was me and Alex duking it out on every subject under the sun, with Tatum weighing in with the deciding vote when there was an impasse. California with the Hagis was the first time you were given the opportunity to handle a problem, and you came through with flying colors."

He stood up and moved toward the kitchen. "You want coffee?" he asked.

With a nod, I rose and followed him into the next room. I slid onto the bench against the window looking out onto Columbus Circle.

He clanged about as he pulled out the coffee grounds and began preparing the ibric to make Turkish coffee.

"What I'm saying is that we made you who you are today, including your focus on your *şef* and what he wants. Alex is more of a father to you, anyway. But you're a man now, and it's time you focused your energy on *your* life. Not the family. Not the job you're tasked with. Not just your cars and bikes. This is an opportunity to build your own life, your own family. Jewel tests you the way a *mafie* girl never could. With a *mafie* girl, you wouldn't be compelled to change. And change is good, Nicu. Don't doubt that."

"I fucked up bad," I moaned. "I came off flippant about marrying her. I acted as if I didn't care. She accused me of only wanting to marry her because it was expected of me, and she's right. I want her, but I don't care if I'm married."

My heart plummeted as I thought back on our conversation. "She sensed my weakness and asked what I would do if Alex arranged someone for me to marry. I didn't answer quickly, and that was answer enough for her," I confessed.

Placing the ibric on the hot flame of the stove top, he chuckled. "I blame myself for your situation. If I hadn't been so unhappy, if I hadn't acted out and argued with Alex every chance I got, you would've had more space to explore dissension and contradiction. Since I was always the one to battle him, you had no way to stretch your wings. It's normal for you to respond the way you did. It's how you were brought up to behave. Now that you've had time to think about it, how would you react?"

"Differently," I replied. "Maybe not as quickly as you responded about Cat earlier, but if Alex asked me to marry someone else, I'd fight to keep her. I was twisted up inside and didn't know how to answer, but the truth is I can never let her go."

"You love her," he declared.

The words settled in my chest as truth.

I *did* love her. I would do anything for her. What was I thinking, answering the way I did? Luca was right. It was a knee-jerk reaction because I was so used to being at the beck and call of my family, but there was no way she'd get away from me that easily.

"Let me give you some advice, little brother. Jewel's a keeper. If you have any sense, you'll lock her down," Luca advised as he poured the coffee into two cups. His head swiveled around his shoulder, and he pinned me with a stare. "I'd get on that, if I were you, because you're not wrong. In our world, shit can turn manic in the blink of an eye. I've fought Alex for years; I'm used to it, but you aren't. I'd try to avoid a confrontation if I were you."

Fucking hell. For some reason, the moment of peace between Luca and me was broken, and now he was back to being my annoying, know-it-all older brother. I couldn't fuck, I got no relief from racing, but I knew one way to relieve the incessant, unshakable pressure I felt building around my cranium. I couldn't kill Cristo outright, but I sure as hell could fight him.

I found Cristo at a club, where he often hung out, not far from his home in Queens. He had his usual entourage of sycophant Popescu yes-men around him, soldiers, and the new *consilier*, a man straight off the boat, probably from their old neighborhood in Bucharest.

I'd convinced Tatum to come with me, telling him he was the only one who could stop me from killing the bastard. We sauntered into the chintzy club, so unlike The

Lounge. Every wall was a mirror, as if that would trick people into thinking the place was larger and more crowded than it really was. Through the smoky red-and-violet lighting, punctuated by a tacky strobe light that did nothing to build any kind of allure, I spotted him at one of the back tables.

"Remind me why I'm here again?" Tatum grumbled beside me as we crossed the dance floor.

"So I don't kill him," I said.

"You shouldn't do this," he counseled.

"What I shouldn't do is kill him, which I won't. Anything outside of that is open to interpretation, and I'm interpreting that the man needs a beat down," I explained.

I stalked toward him and stopped right in front of Cristo, ignoring the crowd around him. We had entered Popescu territory, and Alex was going to be pissed off, but no one would kill us. We were the most high-ranking made men of the Lupu family.

"Barging in again, I see?" drawled Cristo, looking me up and down with derision. "What brings you to my part of the neighborhood?"

"What do you think?" I spat out. "We have unfinished business to attend to."

"Back from exile, and your first stop is me? I should be flattered," he mocked. "Your big brother shipped you out to California, but it wasn't more than a smack on the hand, because you haven't learned a thing. You're still as stupid as ever."

I shoved him on the shoulder. "You touched what's mine."

"Funny, I didn't hear her say she was yours. I didn't see her pulling away from me when I kicked it to her. I sure as hell didn't see a ring on her finger. She's a free agent. She can do whatever the hell she wants," he challenged.

"Fuck that, you knew I was out there, watching. I don't know how you knew, but you did. We were interrupted, but there's no one to stop us right now."

I put up my hands and wiggled my fingers at him. "You want me? Here I am. So come on," I taunted.

"I fucking hate you. I hate every fucking Lupu, but I especially hate you," he spat out as he stood from the tall stool, thrusting it back and letting it crash to the floor. "The minute she stepped through the door of my father's house, I knew you'd come running after her. Of course, I goddamn knew you were out there, and I took pleasure in torturing you. Payback for the shit you did to me and my family because you know what this is ultimately about."

Oh, I knew. With a Popescu, it was always about revenge.

"Simu. This is about Simu."

"Damn right, it's about my *consilier*. Did you actually think I would let it go? You somehow convinced everyone, including my father, that it was a clean kill, but I know better. Simu was too smart and ambitious to get caught in your trap. He had big dreams. Sometimes, he was bigger than his britches, but if he had to be handled, it was for me to do it." He slammed his fist in his chest. "*Me.* Not a pussy outsider like you. Most certainly not a bastard Lupu," he spat out.

Rolling up the sleeves of his button-down shirt, he circled me and said, "It'd be my goddamn pleasure to beat your ass."

"Fuck, when will you ever learn, you Popescu pig?" I asked in exasperation. "Why is it so difficult to believe that he went after my brother over Cat? He was jealous. He attacked Luca. That couldn't be tolerated."

He swung at me, but I ducked him easily.

"Why, you ask? You say he was jealous, but I don't believe you. He wasn't in love with my sister. He found her useful, but he didn't love her." He took another swipe, but I deflected it with my palm and moved off.

"And that's the kind of man you chose for Cat? You knew he didn't love her, but you were willing to marry her off to him?"

Following me, he hissed, "Please, motherfucker, don't act high and holy. She was going to marry you and you didn't love her. At least, he'd have respected her more than you ever could. At least, I'd have controlled him and made sure he treated her right. *Unlike you.*"

Another hit came my way. This one, I blocked and threw a light punch of my own, giving him a little taste of what was to come.

"And when he killed you and took over, as he planned to do? What then?"

Taking the hit on his chin, he retorted, "That was never going to happen. What kind of idiot do you take me for? Don't you know to keep your enemies close? Oh, wait. No, you don't. Because you're an idiot of a Lupu."

Done playing around, I charged him, shoulder hitting his abdomen. I rammed him backward into the wall with a hard thump, a fine dust of plaster bursting around the outline of his body. With him wedged between the wall and my shoulder, I slammed into his solar plexus. He wheezed out and hissed.

Stepping back, I threw an uppercut, catching him in the chin again. His skull bounced back against the wall. Probably seeing stars, he shook his head. I could practically see the steam coming out of his ears.

His eyes narrowed on me, and he attacked, swinging

right, then left, like a machine. He beat me back, clipping me here and there despite me shielding my head with my arms. Pain sliced through me as his fist connected with my ribs. The punches kept coming, pushing me back until my spine hit a column. But this wasn't like the time at his house. There was no one to stop us. We were going to do this until one of us was unconscious, so I was taking my punches, letting him wear himself out.

Cristo's eyes were aflame with unadulterated hatred, likely matching the hatred in mine. I welcomed his hate. I reveled in it.

He threw another jab at the same spot on my ribs, and I swore I heard them crack. Fuck, that shit hurt. I grunted and eyed him through my arms, swinging until I bashed him in the temple. My fist skimmed past his brow, busting it open.

"Fuck!" he bellowed. Blood gushed from the cut, spilling on both of us.

Got him. Fucker.

He stumbled back a few steps, and I pressed my advantage. He was heaving out harsh breaths, tired from the wasted punches he threw at me. I drove him back, whipping him with punch after punch. I brought my knee up a couple of times, getting him in the gut. Cristo wasn't one to go down easily, though.

We took turns, attacking and retreating. At one point, we were hugging each other as we caught our breaths. Sweat poured down the center of my back. Blood in my eye clouded my vision. I swiped at it, attempting to remove it, red streaking the white of my sleeve. Wheezing and grunting, we twirled each other around, struggling to unbalance the other and gain leverage in our twisted dance.

Finally, after what felt like hours, but was probably less than half of one, he tired. We broke apart and circled each other again. Getting into position, I pivoted my back foot and made sure I had the right amount of weight on it, giving me power to launch my fist forward. Relaxing my whole body, I exhaled tightly. Lifting and extending my right elbow, I swung just as Cristo turned his head slightly. I clipped him behind the ear, a vulnerable area of vital nerves. He stumbled back, swaying on his feet, dizzy. I finished him off with one more kill shot, and he went down like a lead balloon.

I staggered back, my head swimming after the hits I'd sustained. The sycophants rushed around Cristo, pulling him up and smacking him lightly on the cheek while Tatum looped my arm around his neck and dragged me out of there. Blood dripping from my mouth, I grinned like a loon and let him haul me out of the club.

27

JEWEL

Two weeks had passed since my argument with Nicu. I'd caught him stalking me a few times, which only irritated me because of the huge wave of relief I felt whenever I spotted him. I hated that a part of me, one that I failed to stifle, that feared he'd give up on me. But no, he was around. What he was thinking, I had no idea, since he hadn't tried to approach me.

He'd given me long, lingering looks at the rehearsal dinner, which I returned with angry glares. Other than that, he kept his distance. Seeing him, even while throwing daggers at him with my eyes, made me ache for him. We were in limbo, but we were nowhere near done with each other.

I'd noticed bruises around one of his eyes and found similar marks on Cristo, so I figured they'd had another clash. I rolled my eyes. Those two couldn't help themselves. And yet, as stupid as Nicu could act, I missed him. Which only further convinced me that I was in love with him. He was such an idiot that, really, it was the only explanation for wanting him after that ridiculous proposal.

I sensed he was waiting for me to make the first move. To stand before him, stripped of my defenses as he had so often done for me, and publicly claim him. After kicking him out yet again, it made sense he'd want me to fight for him. He'd straight out told me I had to choose, and he was waiting for my answer.

Which left me facing the proverbial fork in the road. Either I accepted him as he was, with his family and his faults, or I walked away.

I'd thought long and hard about this, about him, his family, his lifestyle. There were risks involved in being with a man like Nicu, but that no longer bothered me too much. I'd already seen the havoc that could be wrecked on a family that supposedly had everything one could dream of in terms of wealth, status, security. Nothing was guaranteed, and I had come to accept that.

I was ready to throw myself into the crazy whirlwind of being with him, but the only thing holding me back was his total disinterest in marrying me, and if we stayed together, marry we must. Yes, he wanted me, but he'd been so lackadaisical about marrying me that I couldn't help but hang back. He was waiting for me to act, but I didn't want to put my heart on the line only for him to marry me for his family. I might not be the most romantic woman in the world, but that would kill me.

It put me in an untenable situation. My parents may have broken up, but they had been devoted to each other while they were together. They'd doted on each other. Even now, they hadn't divorced, which I was convinced was one of the reasons that kept my father sane.

The day of Cat's wedding finally arrived with all the fanfare associated with such an important joining. The bridesmaids congregated at Cat's house, where we helped her get ready. Luca and the Lupu men came to take her to the church. Luca was newly clean-shaven, having gone through the wedding tradition of the "shaving of the groom," signifying that he'd passed from boyhood to manhood. The bridesmaids, along with Cristo's help, put Luca through his paces, making him answer silly questions and other challenges that included prodigious amounts of *țuică* before we allowed him to whisk Cat away to the church.

At the Orthodox church, everyone stood in their designated spots around the altar in the sanctuary, waiting for Cat to come up the aisle. The church was sumptuous, with an elaborate chandelier above the altar illuminating Luca and the priest. Behind us stood the iconostasis, a screen with multiple layers of painted gold-leafed icons that separated the nave from the altar. I was holding Cat's crown, elegantly shaped of gold leaves, like Caesar's laurel wreath. I was to hand it over to the priest during a part in the ceremony called the *Pirostrii* or Crowning. He would then place it upon her head. Witnessing all the trappings of this special wedding right on the heels of Nicu's botched proposal stirred longing in me.

Accompanied by her father, Cat was a vision in her gorgeous Vera Wang wedding gown made of Chantilly lace, organza, and tulle. Her hair was braided elaborately, intertwined with flowers and ribbons. After the rings were exchanged and the Crowning, the couple shared wine from the same cup while their hands were bound together with a ribbon. The ceremony touched me, leaving me discreetly wiping the sniffles from my nose. As Cat and Luca walked around the altar, my eyes drifted toward Nicu, and the last remnants of my anger fell away. He was so heart-stoppingly gorgeous, in a tuxedo that fit him like a glove, his hair styled with a rogue lock curling toward his forehead.

I wanted this experience for us. The love, the commitment, the give and take, the communication that Cat and Luca shared...it could be ours. Okay, the last item on that list still needed work, but the others were already there.

Nicu snagged my gaze across the platform and locked on me. My heart cracked open at the pining in his eyes. His gaze scored down my fitted dress to my shoes and then back up, bursting with raw hunger and ownership.

If nothing else, he still wanted me.

Too soon, the ceremony was over, and we exited the church, throwing rice and confetti on Cat and Luca as they walked under a bridge of flowers held up by several guests. In the crush of people on the narrow street outside the church, luxury cars were lining up to take us to the restaurant for the wedding party, which would last till the break of dawn.

I found myself being pushed toward a waiting car. Excited to get to the celebration, especially for the fake kidnapping of the bride from the wedding party, I ducked into the backseat. The men were normally in charge of this wedding custom, but Emma and I decided to hijack it from them and spirit Cat away before they had a chance. Luca would have to find her and pay a "ransom" before he could have her back.

The car door was slammed shut behind me, and I found myself with the last two people I ever expected to spend time with: Nicu's mom and twin sister. The car lurched as the fleet of sleek black vehicles started moving. My spine hit the leather back of the seat. *Shit, shit, shit.* Nerves fluttered in my tummy. Of all the people in the world, I was not prepared for this. But prepped or not, I was going to have to fake my way through this encounter. Plastering a smile on my face, I nodded to them both.

An elegant woman, Nicu's mother was dressed in a gorgeous champagne-colored, scooped-neck dress made of chiffon and lace. Tasa was wearing a matching dress, her long brown hair swept down in luxurious waves, her large melted-chocolate eyes curiously inspecting me.

Nicu's mother nodded to me with a bright smile on her face. "Ah, you must be Jewel, Cat's maid of honor."

Tasa's eyes expanded slightly, confirming that she knew who I was to her brother. I groaned inside, spreading my lips into a smile so wide it was almost painful. Although Tasa had moved out of the city, she and Nicu were still close, so I suspected she knew far more than her mother, who viewed me as nothing more than her newly minted daughter-in-law's outsider best friend and maid of honor.

"Yep," I replied brightly. "That's me."

Really? That's it. That's all you've got? I thought to myself. Cringing, I shrank deep into the back seat, wishing I could disappear. Of course, we'd been introduced and attended the same parties for the past several months, but we'd never spoken to one another. The sudden shock of being stuck in a car with Nicu's closest female relatives had turned me shy. Here I was, having an ongoing love affair with her youngest son, her baby boy, for the past several months, and she hadn't the slightest clue he'd proposed to me, no matter how badly he'd done it. I couldn't even consider the more salacious activities we'd engaged in. It was so awkward. I was the farthest thing from a potential daughter-in-law this woman would ever conjure up for her last son.

She chuckled knowingly.

I raised my eyebrows in surprise, uncomfortable and bracing myself for... I didn't know what exactly.

Tasa turned to her and asked softly, "What is it? What's so funny?"

Nicu's mother turned her gaze on me, and I was hit with a mixture of shock and yearning. She was giving me the same penetrating blue-eyed stare her youngest son often did. Now I knew where he got it from.

"Oh, you know. I find it amusing that Luca is already married," she confided in a faux whisper, leaning in close to me as if she was about to impart a great secret. "They think I don't know they had a civil marriage months ago. They think they've gotten one over on me, kept me in the dark, but I know almost everything that happens in their lives."

"Mamă!" Tasa gasped.

My own eyes widened. That was not what I had expected. Before I could stop myself, I stammered out, "H-how do you know that?"

"I know my son. My sons," she emphasized with a shrug that reminded me of Nicu. "Just like I know Nicu is in love with you. I'm not sure why he hasn't already taken care of things and made it official, since he knows what is expected of him. I adore my son, but despite the difficulties he's had, he sometimes acts no better than a spoiled little boy." She nodded meaningfully. "I know, I know. He needs a bit more aging, like a good red wine."

"He's also the least eloquent," piped up Tasa. "I'm pretty sure he's fumbled something somewhere down the line. I love my brother more than you can imagine, but there's no denying he can act like an idiot."

Nicu's mother shook her head. "If only they came to me more often...their lives would go much more smoothly, but they insist on learning on their own. Like this one," she jutted her thumb toward her daughter.

"How much do you know exactly?" I inquired warily. This was essential to how I approached speaking with her, although I doubted she'd reveal everything. This woman was wily, there was no doubt on that count, and I was a near-stranger to her. She had no reason to trust me.

Folding her arms over her ample chest, Tasa parroted my question. "Yes, Mamă, how much do you know exactly?"

"I know more than you think, whatever that is. But I'll humor you and tell you some of what I know. I know he met you when he was engaged to Cat. I know he fought Cristo not once, but twice, over you. I know that he loves you," she rattled off casually.

She didn't know everything, such as the proposal, which came as a relief. Yet she knew a hell of a lot more than I'd expected. Surprisingly, she didn't seem fazed by any of it. Of course, considering the world she lived in, I'm sure it would take quite a bit to surprise her.

She wasn't hostile toward me after admitting what she knew about Nicu and me. I figured I had nothing to lose by being straightforward with her. Who knew? She might even be able to give me some advice on how to deal with her knuckleheaded son.

"He actually proposed...well, kind of. He technically asked me to marry him, but he seemed more concerned about how the timing would work out for Alex than about actually marrying *me*," I disclosed. "It wasn't only the way he went about it." I gestured out to the procession of cars in front and back of us. "It's all of this. This...this world of yours."

"Our world is not easy; I won't lie to you. After leaving my home and starting anew here, I lost my husband in a brutal manner. He was the love of my life, despite his many faults. With him gone, my children had no father. One lesson I've learned is that something worthwhile is rarely easy. If it starts out easy, it's usually an illusion, because life always throws you a curveball. No one is spared."

She laid her hand gently over mine. "Above all else, we Romanians are pragmatic, so I'm not surprised to hear he was less than romantic when he proposed to you." My eyes cut to hers. "Losing his father so young, Nicu learned early on that the foundation can be torn from under you in an instant. At that time especially, we only had one another to depend on. It magnified a lesson pivotal to our way of life: that family is everything. If you're looking for a picture-perfect love or an ideal family, then we are not for you. But if you are willing to open your heart to people who will do anything, including die for you, then you've hit the jackpot."

I thought back to the last conversation I'd had with my father, of his belief that my mother was waiting for him to be freed from prison and be reunited with her. I didn't know if it was true, since Mother never spoke of him to me, but I knew the dream sustained him. The conversation where he'd divulged that nugget of information was the first time we'd spoken of Mother in years. We tended to keep things secreted away and bottled up until it exploded in our faces.

In contrast to our reserved family, I had no doubt where I stood with Nicu. There was something unbelievably grati-fying about that. Nicu had a few glaring faults, but he never hid how he felt about me. He was always completely honest, and his love was constant and dependable.

Yes, the way he'd asked me to marry him was truly awful, and yes, some of the *mafie* traditions drove me batshit crazy, but his mother was right. There was no denying the love and commitment they had for one another. And not just when they came together like they had for this wedding. It was a daily thing. When I visited the Popescus, people were constantly in and out of each other's homes. In the *mafie* world, their lives were interconnected.

It was only five blocks to the reception, and as the car turned the corner, I saw the awning of the restaurant. The driver pulled up to the entrance and a suited man opened the door. Before stepping out, Nicu's mother turned to me and laid a soothing hand on mine. "All you have to do is ask, you know. If you want something from him, let him know. He'll do everything in his power to make it happen."

Her words lingered with me as she was whisked away into the restaurant.

Tasa turned to me before following her mother and said, "She's right, you know. Normally, women get a tattoo of the family they marry into, but when Nicu was inducted and came back with the Lupu tat, I threw a fit. He was my twin, and I wanted that tat as well. I was grieving, but I was also acting like a brat.

"He might've only been thirteen, but he marched into Alex's office and convinced him to let me get the tat. I remember the determination on his face when he'd faced his newly crowned *șef*. He said, 'She's my sister and my twin. She's lost her father, just like me, and I'll do whatever it takes to make her whole.'"

My heart cracked at the love in those seemingly simple words. I could totally see a young, gangly Nicu standing up to his older brother for his sister's sake. He'd do anything to make her stop crying.

Her fingers pulled open the neckline of her dress, and she showed me the wolf head baring its teeth.

"I'm the only person who wears this tat without being inducted or married. If you give him a chance, he'll do anything for you," she promised, and then she stepped out of the car.

Slowly, I dragged myself across the banquette of the leather back seat. A gloved hand reached in to help me out. I took it as I gathered the skirt of my gown and exited the car. I think I had my answer.

28

JEWEL

I marched into the venue, knowing what I had to do. The question was whether I could pull it off in front of his entire family and clan. The reception wouldn't end until after dawn, so I had time to approach Cat with my plan. I hoped to talk to her before she was carried off for her mock kidnapping to The Lounge, where we'd ply her with drinks until Luca came to win her back.

I immediately got waylaid by Cat's mother, who ushered me into a room to have photos taken with the wedding party. Once that was done, she hustled everyone into the main hall, where we awaited the grand entrance of the couple. They were announced by Alex and Nina, who were the *Nasi* of Cat and Luca's wedding, a strong couple who acted like godparents to a just-married couple. After a series of toasts by them, Cat and Luca threw their glass flutes, shattering them on the marble floor for good luck. Then everyone sat down and the procession of food began.

Cat had cautioned me that there would be several rounds of food since the reception would stretch late into the night. I finally managed to catch her as she left the dance floor and sidelined her into an alcove for a quick talk, where I revealed my plan. Not only did she give me her enthusiastic agreement, but she urged me to do it straightaway before I lost my nerve.

Anxious, I made my way through the throng of people toward the dais where the entire wedding party was sitting around tables arranged in a semicircle. Fidgeting with my hands, I stepped up to the platform and stopped directly in front of Nicu, where he was seated between Alex and Tasa. Jacket unbuttoned, he reclined back in his seat, one arm looped over Tasa's chair. He resembled royalty, lounging on his throne, commanding and dominant. He must have run his fingers through his hair because it was a bit mussed in the front, giving him that slightly disheveled look I loved so much. Even with my nerves amped up, I ached for him.

He stared at me as I approached, eyes narrowing in focus, the aquamarine blue turning darker by the second.

Suddenly, the DJ silenced the music, probably at Cat's signal. There was still a trickle of chatter, laughter, and clinking silverware, but the sound level fell off when I dropped to one knee in front of him.

Nicu's eyes flared wide. The fork he was holding fell from his grip, clanging loudly in the near-silent hall, which suddenly felt unnaturally huge.

I swallowed hard and gazed up at him.

He leaned forward, his eyes penetrating deep into mine, like they always did. He was sifting through my soul, trying to figure out why I was on my knees in front of him.

In a voice that quavered slightly, I said, "When I close my eyes at night, I see only you. When I look into my heart, I see only you. When I think of my future, I see only you. And when I wake up every morning, I want to see only you. I know no one will ever hold my heart the way you do, Nicu."

Taking a deep breath, I gave him a wobbly smile. "I ask you, Nicu Cornelius Lupu, would you be my love, my other half? Would you be my husband?"

Eyes ablaze, he stood up, pushing his chair back with a deafening screech that echoed in the complete silence of the crowded room. My heart lurched, pounding so hard I was sure it would beat its way out of my chest. I gulped down over the tightness in my throat. I was still an introvert and baring my soul in front of his family and clan was nerve-racking. Sweat trickled down my spine as I maintained my focus on him.

He skirted the long table and prowled toward me, moving like a sleek panther, in control of every muscle of his body. When he reached me, I had to crane my neck to meet his gaze.

He stared down on me with smoldering eyes, and declared, "If I say yes, you know what that means, right?"

He fell to his knees before me. His delicious scent wound around me like waves of incense curling out of an incense burner in church. I leaned in toward him, getting wet from the nearness of him, the heat of him radiating onto me.

"What?" I croaked out.

He let out a low growl. "It means I own every goddamn inch of this." In front of everyone, he smacked my buttock. "It means I put a ring on it. It means you get fat in the middle from carrying my babies."

He leaned in close, so close that I could see the indigo circle outlining the multi-faceted blue of his eyes. They bled regret. "I'm so fucking sorry, baby. I'm sorry I fumbled my proposal so badly that you had to step up to do it right." He slid a hand around my throat and cupped it firmly. "But now that you have, you better be ready for everything, because I'm locking this *down*."

His eyes inspected mine, moving right to left and back to center. His jaw tightened, a muscle popping like a heartbeat.

"Fuck, you're wet for me," he rasped out in a low tone only for my ears.

I bit my lower lip to prevent a needy moan from slipping out. Eyes glistening with budding tears, I nodded my head. I already knew I loved him, but like a stake to the heart, the realization struck me of just how much I was in love with him. I was bursting with an intense desire to consume him whole, to make him as much mine as I was his.

I asserted boldly, "I want it all, Nicu." A loud rush roared in my eardrums. "A ring. A baby. Every morning, every day and night. I can't take another day without you." I took a deep breath and admitted, "I tried, you know. God knows how hard I tried, but I can't take it anymore. I'm miserable without you, even more than when we're arguing, and that's saying something. It's like the world is bleached of all its color without you. You did this to me, so you need to fix it."

He curled his hand around the back of my head and brought me into him. "From now on, you're mine, baby doll." His mouth crashed down on mine possessively, and I felt like I was going to melt right into the floorboards.

Scooting closer to him, I wedged my body into the cove of his embrace. My nipples tightened to hard diamonds, begging for friction as I rubbed against his chest. He slanted his head, and his tongue, dirty and obscene, took everything I had to give.

I couldn't see them, but I heard them. There was an eruption of sound as the room got to their feet, like in a standing ovation, clapping and whooping with cries of joy.

Without breaking our kiss, Nicu rose and pulled me to

standing. When we finally stopped, he stepped back. Eyes on me, he took a knee and whipped out a black velvet box.

He has a ring for me. How could that be when he didn't want to get married?

"I was a fool for letting you think for one second that you weren't the center of my world. For so long, I didn't care whether I got married or not. You've changed that. You're everything for me. When I thought I lost my chance with you—" He shook his head, speechless. Swallowing hard, he continued, "I fucked up, and I knew if I ever got a redo, I'd be ready. I've been carrying this with me everywhere I go, waiting for a sign that you'll forgive me, that you're down with giving me another try. I know I don't deserve it, but I'm so fucking grateful that you love me despite my stupidity."

He snapped open the box, revealing an enormous yellow-diamond ring. The thin, delicate band lined with tiny white diamonds made the citrine-colored solitaire pop.

"I chose it to match your eyes," he professed.

His declaration made my heart flutter. He'd thought it through. He'd gone to a jewelry store and, thinking about my eyes, sifted through the different options until he found the perfect—and ginormous—one especially for me. A warm wave of love suffused me.

Taking the ring out of the box, he grasped my hand and slid it over my ring finger.

Rising tall, he towered above me. To my surprise, he bent down and tipped me over his shoulder in front of the entire crowd of two hundred guests. I yelped as he stood up and strode out of the room, to the deafening applause of his family and clan members.

I smacked his back but knew it wouldn't make much of an impact. We reached a door, and he kicked it open and dropped me to my feet. Holding me until I stopped swaying and the fuzz in my brain dissipated, he locked the door and rounded on me, backing me up into the sink of a bathroom.

Stripping off his jacket, he laid it over the hand towel rack. No paper towels or hand drying machines for this establishment. I rubbed my thighs together in anticipation of what he was going to do. From the glint in his eyes, there was no doubt where this was going.

Slapping his hands on either side of me on the sink, he braced himself as he said, "There's no going back. No more. No more kicking me out when we argue. You want to smack me, hit me, go ahead and try, but we duke it out together." He ducked his head until we were eye to eye. "Understand?"

I nodded briskly, my nipples so stiff they hurt from needing his mouth on them. When he got demanding like this, it made me achy with need.

"I'm going to keep following you and tracking you with your phone." He undid his belt and slowly unzipped his pants as he promised, "There's no holding back, baby doll. Like I said out there, every single inch of you is mine."

Without asking permission, he spun me around. My palms smacked against the porcelain sink. I pushed out my ass and ground it into his lap. His head dropped into the crook of my neck, and he groaned low, scenting me at the same time. Yanking up my gown, he tossed it up and slapped the exposed cheeks of my ass since I wasn't wearing a thong. He must have pulled out his cock because I felt the crown nudging my entrance.

"Fuuuck, you're soaked for me, baby," he murmured, palming one buttock as he guided his shaft deeper. Pushing through the tightness, he kept going until he was buried to the hilt. I flexed my inner muscles, testing his girth as he stretched me. My hips couldn't keep still as the pressure of his cock speared me.

Clutching the sides of the sink, he pulled out, only to sink in again. "I'm going to be in your cunt every day. Two, three times a day. My cock. My tongue. I'm gonna stuff a dildo inside while I fuck your ass. Every inch, every hole is mine. Why, Jewel? Why will I do that? *Tell me,*" he demanded.

"Because I'm yours. I'm your slut, your toy," I breathed out with relief.

"Damn fucking straight," he shouted. "I'm going to breed you. You're getting off the pill so I can put a baby inside you."

The yellow facets of my new ring glittered in the bright light of the bathroom, momentarily distracting me with its novel presence on my hand. Until Nicu stormed into my life, I didn't think I'd ever fall in love or be in a relationship, and I certainly never imagined I'd be engaged. I blinked up at him, locking eyes with him in the mirror.

"You think I put my family first, but what you continually fail to see is how obsessed I am with you. You dominate my thoughts. I walk around half the day with a stiff dick. For the first time in my life, I can't wait to be done with business so I can get back to you." His hand came around and clasped the base of my throat. "During the ceremony of my brother's wedding, all I could think about was wrapping you in my arms, dragging you to bed, and burying my cock inside you."

Arching my spine, I pushed back into one of his hard thrusts. "Fuck, you're tight. It's been too long since I fucked you. See how cruel you are, keeping this pretty pussy from me. It's my job to stretch this tight hole again."

He gripped my chin, twisting my head to reach my lips. His attack left me spinning at the heady scent of him enveloping me, his domineering tongue devouring me, and his determined cock pounding into me. He struck the perfect spot. I opened my mouth on a scream as he hit it on repeat. He wrapped his hand over my lips to smother my shriek at the last moment. His big body curved over mine as I circled around the rabbit hole of an oncoming climax.

"No more panties," he commanded. "I want access to this wet, needy pussy whenever the fuck I want." He gave a rough thrust, and I could feel his shaft expanding, could feel him getting close. He was fighting it, determined to stay for as long as possible.

"I'm gonna pick you up from school every single day. Probably end up drilling this cunt in the car before we make it home. Do you hear me, girl?"

Oh God, he was so *bad*, but it felt so *good*. He knew how much I loved his dirty talk.

"Yes," came out muffled through his fingers.

I was seconds from coming when he pulled out. He chuckled above my head, circling his cock around my entrance, teasing me. I shrieked my frustration into his hand. Mean, heartless bastard.

Leaning over me, he intoned, "Maybe I won't fuck you. I'll put you on the passenger seat without any panties. I'll play with your clit while I drive home. Watch your juices leak all over my car seat, filthy girl. When we get home, I'll put you on your knees. You'd like that, wouldn't you? Make me come in your mouth or spray your face and tits. Which is it, Jewel? How do you want me to finish off?"

"Face," I mumbled. "Tits."

He nodded sagely, breaching me with the tip of his dick. "That's what I thought. You like to drive me to the brink of sanity. Nasty girl, you like to control me with your dirty little mouth."

I nodded vigorously. Hell yeah, I did. I loved to watch

him lose control with my lips moving up and down his cock. Giving him access to my throat. Loved to watch him lose his mind and know I did that.

"You want Luca and Cat to hear me lose my fucking mind over my slut of a fiancée."

His hand slunk around and thumbed my clit. I jerked into him, and he entered me fully again, fucking me with deep languid strokes. His hand released my mouth and slammed down on the counter to stabilize him, freeing me up to talk.

"I've been your slut since day one. I love when you dirty my mouth with your come, when you spray my face. Down my neck. On my tits. I like to watch it drip from my nipples," I taunted him.

His finger played with my back entrance. My hips twitched right and left, but I couldn't move away from him.

"Take over in the front," he ordered, and I instantly strummed my clit in his place.

"Oh, this virgin ass is going to be mine tonight," he intoned, pressing in until he popped through the ring of muscles. My thighs quivered from the intensity of sensations rolling over me.

"I'm gonna prep it. Then I'm gonna take it. Use it for *my* pleasure."

I shuddered at the way he pronounced *my*. His thrusts increased in speed and force. Along with the unusual experience of his finger or thumb in my ass, his cock was rougher and more demanding. The pressure on both ends had me whirling like a pinwheel.

I came as he gnashed his teeth above me. Pounding into me like a punishment fuck, I collapsed over the sink, my head barely missing the metal faucet as I went down. Pleasure short-circuited my brain, and I was spinning, spinning down into the drain of a hard orgasm. So hard, I feared I might've blacked out.

I found myself panting, my cheek plastered to the porcelain surface of the counter. Nicu fell on top of me. He must've come as well because I felt the flood inside me and my inner thighs were coated.

Nicu buried his face in my neck, his silky breath gusting over my shoulder. I wasn't the only one affected by the intensity of what had happened.

"Fuck, baby, I'm heavy," he mumbled as he pulled himself off me. I was boneless and weightless at the same time. Either way, I couldn't move. He leaned down and gave me a gentle, chaste kiss on my bare shoulder before peeling me off the counter. Dragging me into him, his strong arms banded around my waist.

"God, I missed you," he murmured with his chin on the crown of my head. I loved the way he was so much bigger than me, the way he could wrap himself around me, a fragile little doll to his tall, large body.

I'd barely gotten myself together when there was a discreet knock on the bathroom door. Nicu's fingers tightened around me, bringing me even closer, as if he dreaded letting me go.

Nina's soft voice came through, "I'm sorry to disturb you guys, but we need Jewel for the kidnapping."

"Coming," he replied gruffly. A deep frown etched across his forehead, clearly unhappy that we'd be separated again.

"I can't wait to take you home and be alone with you," he griped in my ear.

29

NICU

"Where's my bride?" came a bellow from below.

"Cat! Quick, hurry and hide near the bathroom," Jewel ordered with a pointed finger toward the spot down the hall of the VIP section of The Lounge, where she and Luca had apparently hooked up the night I met Jewel. It was an extra little touch to the mock abduction of Luca's bride. We'd caught Emma and Jewel escaping with Cat outside the reception hall and convinced them to let us guys into their plan. Which was a good thing because I wasn't about to let Jewel out of my sight.

There was a great *stomp, stomp, stomp* on the stairs. The curtain swung open, and Luca stood there like an avenging berserker, eyes wild, as if we really had stolen his bride from under him. Alex and Tatum followed close behind, with Cristo right behind them. Struck with possessiveness, I instinctually moved toward Jewel.

She glanced up at me, and the muscles of her throat moved in a hard swallow. She hated seeing the remnants of my fear in the way I drew close to her as if she'd disappear, but if I knew anything about my little warrior, I knew she'd do everything in her power to show me how much I meant to her. Fighter that she was, I also knew the custom of arranged marriages was on its last leg in my clan. I was so damn proud of her. She had free rein in my book; I'd be her biggest champion. Wrapping an arm around her, I was gratified to see her curl into me, rubbing her cheek against my sleeve and purring with pleasure.

"Where is she?" Luca growled in a low and dangerous tone.

Emma giggled at his show of possessiveness. "Oh, stop, Luca. She's fine. But you have to get through this before you can have her," she warned, waving her hand over the room.

The bridesmaids in charge of this kidnapping had placed a shot glass of țuică beside every lit votive candle on every table of the lounge, and there were a dozen.

Glaring at her, he muttered, "You're kidding me."

"No, dear brother, I am so not kidding you. You must drink your weight in țuică to retrieve her. The shots are numbered. Once you drink it, flip the glass over. The last one has the final clue that will lead you to your bride," she explained.

Emma was a sweet, reserved, nerdy girl, but I'd quickly learned she had a diabolical sense of humor. And very little mercy when it came to her brothers, or men in general. Cristo's eyes were locked on her, a dumbstruck look on his idiotic face like I'd never seen before. I knew that look all too well. Well, fuck. On one hand, I'd have him off Jewel's back if he was as smitten with Emma as he looked. On the other hand, fuck no. He wasn't about to touch a hair on my half sister's head.

My thoughts were interrupted by Luca, who turned to Emma with, "This is your doing, isn't it?" He followed his accusation with a look that would've had me taking a step back, but she simply returned his stare unfazed. "I can tell," he accused. "It has your name written all over it. I'm going to get you back for this."

She chuckled. "Easier said than done since I have no intention of ever marrying, brother," she tossed back at him. My eyes shot to Cristo, who broke into an arrogant smirk that made me want to smack him. Aww, fuck. That statement was like throwing down a challenge to a man like him.

Urging Luca on with her hand, she said, "Go on, then. Get to it. Your bride is waiting to be rescued."

With one last threatening scowl, Luca moved to the first table, scooped up the shot glass, threw it back, and slammed it down with a bang. I nuzzled Jewel's hair as we watched him make his way through the room. I was enjoying this, knowing that soon, it would be my turn with Jewel. I couldn't wait. I wanted the biggest wedding in existence to show off my bride. I'd already told Mamǎ that everything would be over-the-top. It was going to be stupid big and flashy. Fireworks and anything else I could think of. No one would doubt how I felt about this woman after our wedding, especially not her.

Finally, Luca reached the last shot glass. Lifting it up, he found the paper underneath with a little rhyme we'd made up to clue him in to where Cat was hidden. Once he downed it, he pivoted on his heels and rushed down to the hallway where she was waiting.

They emerged moments later, with Cat in his arms. Stalking past us, he let out a triumphant shout, and they were gone.

By the look of determination on his face, I guessed we wouldn't be seeing them at the party for a while, if they came back at all. Tucking Jewel closer, I murmured, "I need you again."

She gazed up at me with such edgy neediness, it rasped and crackled over my skin like a caress.

"What about the rest of the party? It's only past midnight..." she said.

"They'll be too drunk to miss us," I assured her, tightening my hold on her, worried she'd fight me. "I doubt Luca will return either. I want you in my bed, baby doll. Brace yourself. It's going to be days before I let you out again."

Addressing my anxiety, she vowed, "I won't kick you out ever again. I won't run ever again. This is it, Nicu."

"You're right about that because we're moving in together, so you can't throw me out, and if you ever try to leave me, I will hunt you down and fuck you into submission. That is my promise to you," I swore as I turned us toward the stairs. "Come on, let's go, baby doll."

She trustingly placed her hand in mine, took a step forward, and tugged me along as she clarified, "*Home*, Nicu. Let's go home."

EPILOGUE

TATUM

"I loathe you," Clara snapped, her hands fisted by her sides.

I was at the wedding of a man who was like a brother to me. I should be joyous. At the very least, I should be drunk.

Instead, I was fuming.

I'd taken a breather in the terrace outside the venue of Luca's wedding reception and came upon Clara. As usual, she'd goaded me with snide comments. This woman was impossible. Haughty and arrogant, she'd been needling me throughout the evening.

That didn't include the weeks in California where she took every chance to make my life a living hell. What had Nicu been thinking, suggesting she spend a few months with the Lupu clan in the city?

I knew she detested me, and the feeling was more than mutual. In fact, I'd guess I had an edge on hating her more. But when she hissed at me like a wet cat, the drive to bring her down a peg surged through me. It was petty of me. But for once, I didn't care how it made me or the Lupu family look. I didn't care if I had to get close up and personal to make her feel uncomfortable. Payback was in order.

I slapped a hand on the wall beside her head, penning her in.

Thrusting my face into hers, I growled, "You hate me, you say? Sure about that?"

Her eyes flared wide, the bright blue splintered into shards of green and turquoise. She shuddered out a soft breath that coasted over my skin. I stepped closer, until my lips were inches from hers, and before she had a chance to do or say anything to piss me off more, I coasted my lips over hers.

Gripping her delicate jaw, I flicked my tongue against the seam of her lips. She opened her mouth on a gasp so I licked my way inside, and fuck if the taste of her didn't hit me hard.

She jolted in surprise.

It was obvious. At twenty-one years old, she had never been kissed before.

The realization that I was the first took me aback, but not enough to let me pull any punches. On the contrary, I pressed my advantage.

Tilting her head for better access, I took her wickedly sarcastic mouth harder. A mouth that had spewed comebacks and snippy insults for months, goading me to smother her. But I found myself getting lost in her taste. It was delicate and sweet, the antithesis of everything she was. I couldn't stop myself from delving in harder, maybe a tad too hard for a pampered virgin like her.

Not only did she yield to me, because by now I'd expected her to scream bloody murder, but she'd timidly placed her hands on my chest. It expanded with pride.

Her fingers spread open, exploring me haltingly. She

leaned in, pressing her full tits against me, and tentatively licked into my mouth.

I groaned at the innocence of it.

Fuck, I wanted more.

But I wasn't the type of man to do this to a sheltered *mafie* princess. That was for the Lupu brothers. They could do whatever the hell they wanted because they were heirs, each and every one of them. Their father, may his soul rest in peace, was a hard man with demanding expectations. My father was also a hard man, but without any of the accolades. He instilled in me that I could never step out of line. Perfection was the rule of thumb and mistakes were not to be tolerated.

Of course, I hadn't expected perfection in tasting this sassy little bitch, and that's exactly what I'd gotten. Which was why I should stop. I'd made my point. It was time to pull back.

Only...I found myself in a struggle between the good son, who prided himself on his reserve, and the bad man, who craved to devour this woman.

I forced myself to pull away, but she moved with me, not allowing for an inch of space. Clara was like a Lupu, taking what she wanted when she wanted, and for once, I wanted to do the same. I was tired of being good and perfect. I wanted to indulge. For once, I was greedy.

My hand smoothed up her side, cupping her plump breast. Talk about luscious. I'd already found myself staring at her tits on more than one occasion, dragging my eyes away an instant before she caught me. Although, I'm almost certain she sensed my gaze on her.

I thumbed her nipple peaking under my ministrations. She moaned into my mouth, the vibration shuddering down my body to my cock. Fuck, my balls grew heavy at the sweet, needy little sounds she made.

It dawned on me that she was wet, and abruptly, I needed to feel her silky, moist flesh on my fingertips. I needed the knowledge of how much she wanted me.

Sliding a hand down, I caught the hem of the short, flirty dress she'd worn, little tease that she was, and yanked it up. Then my fingers were over her panties.

The heat coming off her scorched me. My pinky finger wiggled between her pussy lips, and fuck, but I felt her juices through the silk.

She was drenched. Soaked.

For me? It was a heady thought.

"Spread your legs," I commanded in a voice I barely recognized.

She shifted on her feet, tilting her pelvis to give me better access. Fuck, I liked her following my order. I pushed a thick finger in deeper, but the gusset of her panties prevented me, and like a heat-seeking missile, my finger needed more. It demanded that tight, wet flesh to be parted by my digit.

Prodding her panties to the side, I pushed inside.

Motherfucker. Slippery *and* tight. The perfect combination. Too bad she had such a nasty little mouth, but the thought of putting her on her knees and making use of that mouth for good instead of evil crossed my mind. My cock jerked in my pants. Damn, did I want that.

The dirty girl writhed on my hand, her hips twitching as she worked herself on my fingers. It was just how I imagined it, because yeah, I'd fantasized about her in my bed. This was even better. Her tight muscles sucked me in. She was a sensual creature, I'd give her that. I may not like the woman, but feeling her walls clamp around my fingers was close to divine.

I moved my mouth to her ear. "You say you hate me, but your tight pussy is greedy for my touch. Tell me what you want, little girl. Tell me, and I'll give it to you," I promised darkly.

With a decade between us, it seemed right to call her "little girl," although I'd never felt the drive to do so before. But here, I undoubtedly had the upper hand. Finally. Because Clara challenged me every chance she got.

Not now, though.

Now I had something she wanted, something only I could give her.

My brow furrowed. She could get it from her idiot of a *consilier*, Grigore. The thought of that bastard touching her goaded me to start stroking.

I let out a low, deep growl. "You want something, you come to me. Only me. I'm the only one who will satisfy you, you hear? You will never go to any man but me." The vow fell from my lips unrestrained as I cupped her pussy. "I'll be the one to take this, to fuck this tight channel and burst through your cherry. You'll bleed on *my* cock."

What the fuck?

I didn't talk like this.

I didn't act like this.

Yet the words had spilled from my mouth, like an oath. Like a curse.

I stumbled back, pulling my fingers out of heaven. My cock strained against the zipper of my tuxedo pants, my nuts feeling like they were about to burst, wanting to spray come all over her face and inside her womb. To mark her. To breed her.

Where in the ever-loving fuck was this crazy shit coming from?

I couldn't have this woman.

I shouldn't even *want* this woman.

She was toxic.

We hated each other.

I scrubbed a hand down my face, scenting her delicate fragrance. I wanted to thrust my fingers into my mouth and *suck, suck, suck* until there wasn't a drop left. Until I'd absorbed her juices into my very cells. I dragged them down my face, tugging at my chin to stop myself.

My lungs heaved. What the hell was happening to me?

Face distorted with horror, I rasped, "Fuck, that was a mistake."

She inhaled sharply. The glaze over her eyes vanished as she recoiled in disgust.

"A-A mistake? The first kiss of my life, and such an—" I strained to hear what she was about to say, but she cut herself off, pressing her full lips together. Shame flushed her supple skin a shade of pink right to the tips of her ears. Covering her chest with her arms, she turned on me with fury

"A mistake, you say?" she spat out, pulling her hand back and letting it fly across my face with a resounding *crack* that echoed off the walls of the buildings surrounding the terrace.

My head snapped back, skin aflame from the impact of her hand meeting my cheek.

"You arrogant bastard," she hissed.

I rubbed the imprint of her palm on my skin. Just as I'd suspected, it'd been her first kiss. A fissure cracked around my chest. A vicious, vindictive sort of pride spurted through me like lava from a volcano. She was right to call me a bastard for pilfering her first. Not only was I the first man to ever kiss this woman, but I was the first to ever fondle her untouched pussy. I was fucking *proud* of that, and I realized with a ruthlessness that startled me that if the opportunity ever came again, I'd repeat it in a heartbeat.

She was made of pure fire. I'd insulted her with my comment, but a kiss like the one we shared, a break in my control like the one I'd allowed, was dangerous.

If anyone happened to come upon us and witnessed what I'd done to her, we'd be at the altar with our wrists bound together and crowns placed on our heads by the end of the week. She couldn't want that, could she?

I shook my head. No, definitely not. Every single moment she was in my presence, she used it to undermine me, to establish how much she despised me.

Or did she?

Clearly, she didn't hate me quite as much as she pretended because there was no way a woman like Clara, even with our age difference, would allow a man to touch her if she didn't want it. I may have started it, as a challenge and simply to shut her up, but she'd kept it rolling.

Shoulders back, chin up, eyes flashing, she said, "Oh, it was a mistake, alright. You should be so lucky to ever touch or kiss me again. Don't for an instant think this changes *any*thing between us."

Her voice was a mixture of injury and rage, and yet neither of us believed a word of it. Even so, she was a proud woman, and I didn't like the distress on her face. Superiority, smugness, disdain. Those I was used to. But hurt? That, I could not stand.

I lifted my hand, about to reach for her, to comfort her, but she faltered, stepping back as if my touch would burn. Before I could say or do anything to try to make things right, she spun on her heels and stormed inside the restaurant, positively enraged.

Unhinged.

She was fucking glorious.

Not only did I have the incredible taste of her still on the tip of my tongue, but I'd turned her against me even more.

Discomfort pricked at my heart.

For the first time in my life, I wanted more from a woman.

A woman I'd lost any chance of ever having.

THANK you for reading THE SAVAGE HEIR! I hope you loved meeting Nicu and Jewel. As you might have already guessed, the next book in the Lupu Chronicles dark mafia series is The Perfect Heir.

CLARA

I am Clara Hagi, the Virgin Queen. I may not be allowed to marry but I will be the first woman to rule a *mafie* clan. The Lupu clan is encroaching on my world, but they won't get far.

I ache Tatum, their *consilier*. I love his piercing black eyes, his tall, muscles-bound frame, his touch, his commands, his beguiling strain of vulnerability—I love it all.

The one time and only time he kissed me—my first kiss —was a mistake.

That's what he called it.

A mistake.

I'll make him regret those words, if it's the last thing I do.

. . .

TATUM

Nothing good came from kissing that girl, Clara. A girl whose clan hates mine. A girl off-limits. A girl I should loathe.

As *consilier*, I live and breathe the Lupu clan, and I do it perfectly. Perfection is the only way to make up for my father's betrayal, a betrayal I'll take to the grave with me.

I'm charged with getting the Virgin Queen under control. Once I do, my clan will rule LA, just as it rules NYC. Every time I see her, I remember. Every time we spar, I want to kiss her. Every time we accidentally touch—and I hate to touch—I ache for her.

One kiss would never be enough. Maybe bedding her will get her out of my system, virginity bedamned. Make her pay for twisting me inside out. Make her hurt a little. Purge her from my body and mind.

She deserves better than a tainted man like me, but what if I've already fallen for the Virgin Queen?

NYC vs. LA. East Coast vs. West Coast. You've never read an enemies-to-lovers romance of warring clans like this one.

GET THE PERFECT HEIR ON AMAZON, APPLE, KOBO, NOOK and GOOGLEPLAY

START with Book One of The Lupu Chronicles, THE CHOSEN HEIR!

. . .

A WAR IS BREWING **between love and duty...which shall triumph?**

"SEXY MAFIA READ! Monique Moreau knocks this one out the park. Alex is what dreams are made of. He command's the room and doesn't back down from anyone but her." – 5 Star Review

HERE'S A TASTE...

"FUCKING HELL," I gritted out as I read the text over my grandmother's shoulder. Tasa was safe and she begged us not to look for her. *Really, Tasa?* As if I'd leave my baby sister to hang out to dry, regardless of whether she'd run away. Oh, and had she conveniently forgotten about her fiancé, Cristo? And what part of the term "dangerous enemies" had not penetrated her thick skull, despite my relentless repetition of that threat?

Bunică gave a nonchalant shrug of her skinny shoulders and a grin that showed off her gold tooth. That woman could get her teeth fixed a thousand times over, but she wasn't one to put on airs. As she always said, "I was born a peasant girl, and I'll die a peasant girl."

Peasant girl, my ass. She was as sharp as they came, and while she loved to ham it up with her country ways, she'd graduated from Romania's finest medical school. No lie, she could dig out a bullet and sew up the wound in under half an hour. It had come in handy on more than one occasion, when the doctor on our payroll didn't arrive quickly enough.

"What is she thinking?" I spat out. "She's roaming the country doing God knows what. No protection, no bodyguard, no—"

"Oh, hush, you act as if Tasa's an invalid instead of a smart young woman who can take on the world with one hand tied behind her back. She'll be fine. And you best leave her alone," she warned, poking at my chest with her bony finger.

I stared down at her, incredulous. Leave my sister to roam the country unprotected? *Is she insane?*

"Christ, *Bunică*, she's a female. Alone."

My eyes rolled up to the kitchen ceiling, seeking patience, as I took a seat on one of the stools scattered around the island in the kitchen of our family home. This was where *Bunică* practically lived so this was where family members came to talk to her. Was I the only rational one in this conversation? It wasn't like she didn't know who we were. It's not like she wasn't acutely aware that our enemies would start crawling out of the woodwork to kidnap Tasa.

"A *lone* female," I reiterated, emphasizing the word "lone" in hopes of getting through to my grandmother. "Of the *Lupu* clan." My gaze passed over the midnight-blue double oven range my father had imported directly from Italy when he busted out the back wall and extended the kitchen to please his mother and wife. The chrome from the state-of-the-art appliances gleamed under the bronze farmhouse lights.

We are the Lupus, the Romanian upstarts who quickly rose to the top of the New York City mafias. The speed of our rise was a point of embarrassment for the Bratva, the Russian mafia, and the main reason why they're so intent on destroying us. As for the Italians, they were a shadow of what they were before the takedowns and trials of the '90s.

Which had left a vacuum for my father to fill when he arrived in New York, solidifying our foothold in Sunnyside, Queens. Better known now as "Little Bucharest."

Returning my attention to *Bunică*, I reminded her, "Enemies? Remember them? Why do I need to mention this? It's not like you don't know what I'm talking about. She's in real danger."

She let out a cackle as she whipped out a bottle of *palincă*, a traditional Romanian spirit from the region she came from. Plunking down two small glasses, she poured two shots and pushed one over the kitchen island to me. The other, she threw back like a pro.

"What's obvious to everyone but you and your mother is that Tasa is her own woman. She's smart, and she's not going to get caught by some two-bit *mafie* idiot. She'll be fine."

I narrowed my eyes at her. She was too relaxed by far, considering her youngest grandchild had just run off to god-knows-where.

"What do you know?" I demanded.

Fluttering her wrinkled hand weakly in front of her chest, she lied without a shred of remorse, "Who? Little old me? Why, nothing!"

"You're as deceitful as the day is long," I snapped, my patience finally fraying.

"Back off," she warned, her innocent features turning dark. *Ah, there's the real* Bunică. "I don't happen to know anything, but if I did, you bet your last dollar I wouldn't tell you. I won't help you drag her back here and keep her prisoner until she marries that worthless *tâmpit*, Cristo. *Uck.* He's barely a man. And he has a little two-bit hussy of a side piece. Each of you must marry in the *familie*, but why him? *Bah!*"

"You're unbelievable, you know that, right? Come on, out with it," I insisted, flicking the fingers of my open hand at her.

"Like I said, my lips are sealed." She made a gesture as if locking her lips together and flinging away an imaginary key.

My jaw clenched. Women. The bane of my existence. And those two stuck together like super glue. It was hopeless on my part to try to sever the unbreakable.

"Fine, then," I replied, releasing a long, exhausted breath. "You're not the only person I can press for information."

Her hand nabbed the sleeve of my jacket, crushing the fine wool between her bony fingers. "Leave that poor girl alone. You know she's in love with you. Don't you dare take advantage of her."

My grandmother was talking about Tasa's little best friend, the beautiful, supple Nina, of course.

Nina.

Damn, that girl. Smelled like jasmine and a hard fuck waiting to happen. Just the thought of her brought crackling heat to my skin and a stiffness to my cock. That woman was my Achilles' heel, if ever there was one. Sweet as could be, with large brown eyes and a chest I could face-plant in and suck on for days on end. Annnd...

And she's also like a sister to you, asshole.

Not.

There wasn't a shred of brotherly feelings toward that little minx. Unless one included the taboo kind.

Laying my forearms heavily on the smooth wood of the kitchen island, I warned, "*Bunică*, it's Tasa we're talking about here. My little *sister*. For some insane reason, you don't think she's in jeopardy, but I happen to know exactly what our enemies are capable of. I know exactly what they do during a torture session. Once it's out that she's gone, finding her and using her to get to us will be at the top of their list. This is like a nuclear arms race, during the Cold War." I tapped the watch around my wrist. "Time is ticking, and I can assure you that this won't finish well. Least of all for Tasa. Who's going to want to marry her if she's tarnished? Think about that and come talk to me when you've regained your common sense."

"*Băiețel*, don't speak to your *Bunică* like that. I wiped your bottom when you couldn't even feed yourself. Any man should be grateful for the chance to marry my little girl."

I snorted out an exasperated sigh. I hated it when she called me *little boy*. Deciding it was in my best interest to pretend I didn't hear her last comment, I bent down low and dropped a kiss on the crown of her head. "Do you think I enjoy this? Do you think I enjoy having to lay down the law and act like an enforcer with the people I love?"

"You *do* enjoy it," she shot back. "You always think you're right. In that way, you take after your father. Regardless of what everyone in this family thinks, he wasn't a saint, you know. He was human, and he made his fair share of mistakes."

Yeah, right. She always said that, but it was never quite believable. The man was a brilliant businessman and strategist. He loved his family and was the paradigm of how to behave in our twisted world. He was honorable to his core. If I could live up to half of the man he'd been, I'd die content. Which brought me back to the issue at hand: Tasa's marriage.

"I've been negotiating with Nelu on this marriage contract between Tasa and Cristo for *years*. It's more than a simple wedding, as you well know. What's going to happen when he finds out his future daughter-in-law ran away? It will be perceived as a stain on his honor. It could legitimately lead to war when we've only just begun our truce. Not only is business booming, but Tata would be disappointed in me. I gave him my oath that I would do everything in my power to make this happen. There's too much on the line," I finished with a frown.

The responsibility of taking care of my family fell heavily on my shoulders, but on days like today, the weight was crushing. Although *Bunică* was whip smart, the truth was she couldn't relate. She'd always been taken care of. First by my grandfather, then my father, and now me. She could afford to focus solely on the personal, not the big picture. No, that fell on me.

"Pfft. And so you had to sell Tasa to do this? Of all people, you chose to sacrifice your little sister?" Reproval shimmered in her eyes at me.

"*Tata* would've commended me for it. *He* would've thought it was a brilliant move. With the Popescus, Tasa will be taken care of. She'll be protected. And it would solidify a peace that's eluded our families for decades."

Bunică stared at me like she was about to spit on the ground. "Don't make it seem like you're doing this for Tasa, Alex. It's beneath you to lie."

"I *am* doing it for her," I ground out, fists balling at my sides. Christ, this old woman was never satisfied. She was spoiling the girl with notions of love. Our life was based on duty and, for women, that included the duty to marry a man chosen by her family. As the boss or *șef* of this family, I might be given a leeway regarding this rule. But for a princess of marriageable age like Tasa, it was unthinkable.

"She's the baby of the family. The Popescus, curse their name, are worthless mongrels. Animals. Unlike the Lupu clan, they didn't gain power until the fall of Communism. That's a blink of an eye in the span of history, and you sold your precious sister to those heathens?"

I snorted. "They're powerful enough now; I can tell you that much. We can look down on the Popescu clan all we want, but only a fool would underestimate their potential to do damage. They're *vicious*. Ruthless. You know this as well as anyone." It was also common knowledge that their tempers were like hair triggers. One wrong move and *kapow*. I made a dismissive wave. "In any case, it's done. My hands are tied. There's nothing I can do but retrieve her and make sure her marriage goes off without a hitch."

She stalked up to me. Barely five feet tall, she went toe to toe with me and spat out, "Then, you will get no help from me. I will do everything in my power to thwart you. The marriage be damned."

"You're impossible," I heaved out, throwing up my hands. "You know the situation."

When Tata was bleeding out in the ambulance roaring through the quiet streets, his dying wish had been for me to take care of the family. I'd already failed on that promise, with Tasa stranded somewhere out there, alone and vulnerable. Possibly hurt. My back teeth ground together at that last possibility.

The second oath had been to reconcile our family with the lowbred Popescus. I didn't disagree with *Bunică* that every one of them was a bottom-feeder. No education, no class, no nothing. Violence was their greatest attribute. The two families had been at each other's throats for generations, clawing their way to the top by throat-punching the other. We may be at the pinnacle, but they came in at a close second.

Nelu, their *şef*, and Tata were always vying to be the top

dog. Tata often said that it was too late for their generation, that there was too much bad blood. But at his death bed, he declared, "There needs to be a marriage. It's the only way." Those last words were the proverbial nails in my coffin.

"Go back to your fancy apartment in Columbus Circle, Alex. I don't want you under my roof until you come to your senses."

Goddamn, this woman was impossible. She refused to acknowledge the possibility of a looming war. Instead, she was banishing me to the penthouse floors of the two towers of the Time Warner Center building in Manhattan, where my brothers and I lived.

Tasa had moved in with Nina a few avenues over, in a nice high-rise building overlooking the Hudson. Of course, Tasa, always with the rebellious streak, couldn't share an apartment with her twin, Nicu. Oh no, our building was too snooty and fancy for her. And Tasa was as opinionated as the day was long. Thank Christ, she had her little best friend living with her.

My back teeth ground down harder, my fists flexing by my sides, but there was nothing I could say when *Bunică* got into one of her fits. Turning on my heel, I marched out of the kitchen, grabbed my coat from the hallway closet, and stalked out of the house. What in the ever-loving fuck?

Tasa gone.

Contract in ruins.

Potential war on the horizon.

Everything I'd worked for gone.

Gone.

I was an abject failure. No, I refused to let that stand. I didn't care what it took to make this right. I'd fulfill Tata's oath. I'd drag Tasa back by her hair to marry the Popescu if need be. I'd make my father proud if it fucking killed me.

. . .

IF YOU LOVED THE SAVAGE HEIR, you'll love my steamy, bad boy biker series, the Demon Squad MC. Start this new series now with Kingdom's Reign.

OR READ about Alex's little sister, Tasa, in Whistle's War, a biker-mafia romance novel.

A MAFIA PRINCESS on the run. A Bratva prince turned biker. Will their love start a war?

HERE'S a glimpse of Tasa and Whistle's story...

TASA CHECKED the cell phone in her clenched hand for the hundredth time. Her excruciating audience with Alex in his upstairs office was over. *Finally.* Once again, her eldest brother had overreacted. Simply because he was the head of the family, he assumed he could rule over every single aspect of her life. *The nerve of him, giving me an order like I'm a child.*

Tasa fidgeted as she once again glanced out of the bay window of the Dacia Café, the center of her family's world. She couldn't wait for Nikki to pull up to the curb so she could get out of there before she stomped back up the stairs and wrung Alex's neck. Leaning forward, she spotted the ubiquitous black Mercedes pulling up on the quiet 43rd Street. Quiet in comparison to Queens Boulevard, the bustling commercial center of Sunnyside, Queens.

From behind, she heard a scuffling sound. Her mother moved forward, giving her a quick last hug from behind. Twisting around in her seat, Tasa returned her embrace and lifted her left cheek for a quick peck. "See you later, Mama."

A stern frown descended on her face as she gently chided her mother, "I'm not happy that you didn't stick up for me once with Alex. He's such a brute."

Her mother caressed her hair. "Darling, you have to settle down. You're too energetic, and you'll be graduating in the spring. It'd be one thing if you wanted to pursue a career in opera, but we know that's not your desire. What better way to move on to the next phase of your life but with a husband? Because with a husband, soon comes children."

That last part was the crux of her mother's never-ending argument.

Tasa rolled her eyes. "Always with the children."

"Children give meaning to a woman's life," her mother crooned.

"Not every woman," she grumbled under her breath, but the Mercedes was pulling up to the curb, and really, she had zero energy to continue this endless discussion. It's not as if her mother ever budged an inch from her notions of femininity and womanhood, all of which circled around being a wife and mother. Rather, she cudgeled her only daughter with them. Sure, that had worked out fine for her mother. She'd married the love of her life. Growing up in a small village in the valley of the Carpathian Mountains, she'd been utterly fulfilled by her role, but that wasn't Tasa. Not that anyone in her family seemed to care. She could've escaped those expectations with the opera. While she was a decent alto, she wasn't any more interested in pursuing an intensive career in the opera than she was in shackling herself to a man at the age of twenty.

Hitching her Dolce & Gabbana handbag over her shoulder, Tasa slipped out of the café, leaving behind the clinking of porcelain coffee cups on small saucers, and took in a deep breath of brisk, cold winter air.

Yanking the Mercedes passenger door open, she slid onto the leather seat with a sigh of relief.

"Tasa, are you trying to get me in trouble?" griped Nikki, giving her a side-glance with a small scowl.

"Oh, hush, and just drive if you don't want him catching you," she replied. Her control freak of a brother believed a princess like her shouldn't be seen in the front seat, beside her chauffeur-slash-bodyguard. There was a certain level of decorum to maintain. For Nikki's sake, she usually took the back seat when she came home to visit, but she was holding on to her temper by the thinnest of threads as it was.

"*Dragă mea*—"

Oh, sweetheart. Nikki always resorted to his mother tongue when he was upset.

"Don't *dragă mea*," she snapped as she dragged the seat belt over her chest and clipped it in. She didn't need his pity, the primary sentiment coming off his endearment. "Hit the accelerator already so we can get out of this godforsaken neighborhood. Then he won't see you."

He squeezed her knee briefly. His hand didn't linger, but Tasa was well aware of Nikki's feelings. It was only natural he should crush on her. After all, they spent so much time together, and she'd finally grown into her figure.

But he'd never cross *the* line. He might be family, but she was a princess. A princess was supposed to marry a prince. *Gag.* The thought of Cristo made her stomach turn. He was a good enough guy, if you were into the clean-cut bro type. Well, as close a version to that as a *mafie* prince could get. She'd known him since they were in diapers. Being only a few years older than her, they hung out in the same scene. The idea of kissing him was about as appealing as kissing her twin brother, Nicu. And Cristo was half in love with his little side piece, a cute girl named Una. There was no way she was marrying a guy who was already in love with another woman. She didn't expect him to give up on Una, and Tasa wasn't the sharing type. Of course, she couldn't divulge any of this to Alex. If he found out, Cristo would be in trouble with his old man. More importantly, she was afraid of her own reaction if her brother responded the way she predicted. *What, Tasa? You think men are loyal. You think Tata never cheated on Mama?*

Grrr.

Seriously, the less she knew about the way *mafie* men lived their lives, the better. A second family was probably out there somewhere, with kids who sported the same deep-brown eyes as she and her beloved father. She shook her head. Again, not something she wanted to know. With three overbearing brothers, she didn't need additional stepsiblings creeping out of the woodwork. She could barely breathe as it was, with the ones surrounding her.

Nicu was her other half in many ways, but he was far from perfect. And he got to live a normal life because he was a male and he was Alex's good little soldier boy. Luca, her middle brother, might be the black sheep, but he had all the liberties he could possibly want. Pressing her lips together, she focused her gaze outside the window at the passing brick townhouses. Her eyes began to burn. Luca. She sighed, as she often did when she thought of him. Such a tortured soul, with everything so bottled up inside.

That one, she was going to miss.

"What's wrong, babe?" Nikki asked. "What happened in there?"

She let out a weary sigh.

"What do you think happened?"

She'd gotten her marching orders.

"Be a good little girl and fall in line like everyone else. The Lupu family are a bunch of empty-headed dunces, all walking to the tune of their pied piper, Alexandru Lupu," she grumbled.

The *Lupul*, or the Wolf, as people called him, was the puppet master, pulling the strings of the mafia family from America to Paris, Milan, Bucharest, and beyond.

Blood was blood.

Duty was duty.

Orders were orders.

Blah, blah, blah. She felt like gagging after the number of times she'd heard that litany throughout her life.

"Sorry, babe. When he gets an idea into his head, he won't let it go."

"You can say that again," she conceded as she swiped at a rogue tear. "I'm impressed you even went that far." It was unusual for Nikki to say *any*thing against Alex. Suggesting stubbornness, while completely accurate, was borderline betrayal in a secret society where loyalty was the be-all and end-all. Another reason Nikki had never so much as tried to kiss her. It wasn't even the idea that he might be murdered for such an infraction. He'd simply never cross that line. Lupu allegiance was implacable.

He may not have been born a Lupu, but she knew there was some sort of ancient, secret blood ceremony that made him as good as blood. Fucking her would be the equivalent of incest, regardless of what the tenting in his pants told her. Considering she wasn't in love with Nikki any more than she was with Cristo, she didn't push it.

That, and she didn't want to get Nikki killed.

"He catches me at one club and comes down like a dictator," she grumbled.

"Babe ... it was the kind of club. And the fact that you escaped from me. You could've gotten killed ... or worse. What were you thinking?"

Nikki was talking about the sex club she's gone to with her best friend, Nina. So sue them; they were curious little virgins. Unfortunately, Alex had found the selfie Nina posted, sitting at the iconic bar. A selfie that included part of Tasa's shoulder, which bared her Lupu tat of a wolf. In the darkness and the strobe lights, Nina hadn't noticed and posted the pic. A pic Alex happened to view on her Instagram feed.

Oh, boy, did all hell break loose that night. And so began the lockdown. Other than attending her classes at Juilliard, she could go to the apartment she shared with Nina and home in Sunnyside. That was it. Now, she couldn't even shake Nikki off her tale.

But if everything went according to plan, things would be irrevocably changed in a few short days. She wasn't a Lupu for nothing, and as her *tata* had always said, "You have to fight for what you want in this life."

Damn straight.

He wasn't the only relentless person in her family. For instance, it took her for-ev-er to get any action between the sheets, but she'd managed in the end. It had taken seducing one of her vocal instructors to finally learn her way around the male body.

At the end of the day, she'd kept her virginity intact, something she was coming to regret. Her verdict, after her little adventure, was that sex was *way* overrated.

Which is why she'd ended up in Tribeca at the infamous sex club NSFW with Nina. Her curiosity had been piqued by the idea of something beyond vanilla. She'd already done every vanilla thing on her non-intercourse sex bucket list during her brief affair and had walked away with little enthusiasm. A few hours at the sex club, on the other hand, and she'd seen things that made her toes curl.

Nikki dropped her off at the lobby of the high-rise on 68th Street overlooking the Hudson and went to park the car in the underground parking. Entering the apartment she shared with Nina, she dropped her keys in the little crystal-cut bowl on the small Louis XVI wooden table in the vestibule. Part of the deal of getting the apartment near Juilliard, instead of commuting from Queens every day, was to have Nina come live with her and to have her mother decorate their apartment. Of course, she'd decorated it like a Prussian aristocrat from the mid-nineteenth century. Hence the old-people's furniture scattered around their apartment like at an auction house instead of posters of Degas dancers or Callas like in the Juilliard student dorms.

The apartment's best feature was the wall of windows overlooking an unimpeded view of the Hudson and the Jersey coast beyond. Throwing her coat over another atrociously overwrought sofa, Tasa kicked off her high heels and threw herself down beside Nina.

"How was it?" asked Nina without bothering with a greeting. A little furrow dug between her dark, fine winged brows.

"Jellie, are you?"

"Over Alex? Hardly," she scoffed. "I'd never be jealous of you."

"Mm-hmm," replied Tasa noncommittedly, tossing waves of her long brown hair over her shoulder. Nina was head-over-heels in love with Alex, although she felt the need to deny it in deference to their friendship. They'd been best friends since the day Nina tottered across the broken sidewalk from her house to Tasa as a toddler. While Tasa had the ability to get Nina out of her shell and Nina was her number-one partner in crime, her friend was really a gentle soul inside.

"He's like a brother to me," muttered Nina.

Double lie.

"Just because we joke that we must've been switched at birth in no way means there's a shred of sibling-like feelings between the two of you," Tasa fired back.

God knows both of them would've had easier childhoods if they'd been brought up by the other's household. Nina's mother was a badass who prodded Nina to take life by the balls, while Tasa's mother continually bemoaned her daughter's lack of ladylike manners. At least Tasa had *Bunica*, her grandmother, to serve as a buffer between her and her mother and Alex.

"It was disastrous. I swear the man thinks he's my father, and he acts worse than a tyrant. Besides the boring lecture about my reputation, which I truly think he actually believed, he gave me an ultimatum. Either the opera or marriage ... to Cristo."

While this was no huge surprise, Nina's eyes squeezed together in commiseration.

"No," she breathed out. Nina's loyalty was solidly behind Tasa, but she always believed the best in Alex, no matter how irrational he acted. Which was why Tasa had to keep every detail of her upcoming jailbreak from Nina. It hurt to lie, but realistically, the woman would crumble in under five minutes in Alex's presence.

The theoretical scene played out in her mind. Alex would wrap his arm around Nina's shoulder, bringing her in tight to his side to woo her into feeling safe with him. Nina, a softie to her core, would instantly melt against him. She'd look up at him, batting those absurdly long lashes of hers. He'd grace her with one of his beatific angel-slash-devilish smiles, and she'd turn into a puddle of goo. Game over. She'd gush like a bad oil spill in the Gulf of Mexico.

Tasa clenched her fists. *Pathetic.* Her oldest brother got everything he wanted, anytime he wanted.

But not this time.

If she had any hope of escaping her predicament, she had to play it smart. And Tasa could pride herself on that much at least. She may not be respectful or obedient, but she was nothing if not conniving. She'd been fantasizing about this for years and plotting its execution for months.

"You always expect him to act decently," she reprimanded Nina, laying her arm over the intricately carved, gilded wood curling up from the top of the couch. Her eyes drifted toward the windows, sunlight splashing through the panes and highlighting the jewel-like colors of the Persian rug across the floor. That was another thing about Romanians. Rugs everywhere. Almost every inch of their apartment was covered in intricate silk rugs.

"He's a decent guy inside. Granted, you have to dig *deep* sometimes, but he disappoints me when he acts like this. I expect better from him."

Tasa let out a little snort. "Good luck with that. He's such a hypocrite. The bedroom in his apartment is a revolving door of women, but he expects me to remain chaste and turn my virginity and life over to my husband at his command. As if."

"Well, there's the other option."

"Yes, be part of the bastion of high culture. What about giving me a chance to figure out what *I* want to do? I'm only twenty years old. You'd think I'd be given a few years to *live.*

To travel the world and explore. Who knows, maybe I want to be a fashion designer."

Nina tipped her head to the side, her lips pressed together to suppress a laugh. Nina wouldn't dare laugh in her face. She was too polite and kind for that. "Do you?"

"No." Tasa huffed. "What about an organic-apple farmer in Upstate New York? Does it matter? The point is that because he has the imagination of a flea, he's only come up with two options, and I'm forced to follow one of those. It's arbitrary and absurd and ... and ... insane! Like him!"

Another thing she'd never told Nina. That she'd changed her major to experimental dance. Her family would have conniptions if she turned away from a refined career singing opera to experimental performance art, or what they'd mockingly describe as twisting and flopping around like a dying fish on the floor.

"It's because he was so young when he was thrust into his position as head of your family and of that business empire," defended Nina. "It doesn't help that your brothers immediately knew they wanted to follow in his footsteps."

"It's not like we don't live in the twenty-first century," she threw out.

"You know he doesn't think that way. Your parents instilled in him the same idea every immigrant has. Come here and make something of yourself. You can't just have a random job. No, you have to be a doctor, a lawyer, or something crazy impressive like alto for the Metropolitan Opera."

Fiddling with the two tassels dangling from her silk blouse, Tasa muttered, "Whatever."

Nina peered into her face, watching her with a concerned expression. "So, what are you going to do?"

"I have no idea. I have one more semester at Juilliard. That gives me a little more time of freedom."

Liar.

Tasa knew exactly what she was going to do. She'd checked with the bursar's office, and after three weeks of school, she could get fifty percent of her $30,000 tuition refunded to her bank account if she withdrew. And that was exactly what she was going to do. Then she'd disappear and make her way to the source of cutting-edge experimental dance, Madame Pierrette's dance company in Montreal, Canada. Everyone who knew anything knew of the notoriously exclusive workshop she hosted every spring. A workshop Tasa got accepted to. It was close to a miracle and she wasn't going to pass up the opportunity of a lifetime. Alex be damned.

MORE BY MONIQUE MOREAU

The Lupu Chronicles

Welcome to *Little Bucharest*, the heart of the Romanian Mafia in New York City.

The lives of these powerful men revolves around three core elements: family, duty, and sacrifice. There's little for women and no time for love.

Each one of them will be cut off at the knees, humbled by a woman. Oh, how far these mighty men will fall before they learn the age-old lesson that the only way out is through...

Fans of sizzling hot alpha bikers and the sassy, strong women who tame them will love Monique Moreau's steamy MC series.

Kingdom's Reign (Books 1)
Cutter's Claim (Book 2)
Loki's Luck (Book 3)
Stanton's Sins (Book 4)
Puck's Property (Book 5)
Whistle's War (Book 6)
Her Hidden Valentine, A Squad Novella (Book 7)

ACKNOWLEDGMENTS

Thank you to my family for your support and patience each time I say, "Hold that thought!" while I pound out one more sentence. Thank you Alison Aimes for your encouragement, for being a fantastic and supportive friend, a mentor, and an all-around incredible person. A shout out to Monica Bogza of the Trusted Accomplice for editing and Lisa for spectacular proof-reading. To my special readers in my FB Reader Group, Possessive Alpha Reads, thanks for picking up an Advanced Reader Copy and getting excited about this book. To all the bloggers and booklovers who help spread the word and finally, but not least, to every single one of you who've picked up this book and given it a chance. Thank you!

Join Monique's Mailing list to receive goodies and release information
https://bit.ly/SteamyReadNewsletter
I have a Facebook group just for readers: Possessive Alpha Reads
Follow me on TikTok: https://bit.ly/MoniqueTikTok
Like my Facebook Page: https://bit.ly/MoniqueMoreaufb
Follow me on Instagram: https://bit.ly/MoniqueMoreauIG
Follow me on BookBub: http://bit.ly/MoniqueBookBub
Learn all about my books: moniquemoreau.com